# THE MOCKINGBIRD'S SONG

# THE MOCKINGBIRD'S SONG

# WANDA E. BRUNSTETTER

**THORNDIKE PRESS**
A part of Gale, a Cengage Company

Copyright © 2020 by Wanda E. Brunstetter.
All scripture quotations, unless otherwise noted, are taken from the King James Version of the Bible.
Scripture quotations marked NIV are taken from the Holy Bible, New International Version®. NIV®. Copyright © 1973, 1978, 1984, 2011 by Biblica, Inc.™ Used by permission. All rights reserved worldwide.
All German-Dutch words are taken from the *Revised Pennsylvania German Dictionary* found in Lancaster County, Pennsylvania.
Thorndike Press, a part of Gale, a Cengage Company.

Thorndike Press® Large Print Christian Fiction.
The text of this Large Print edition is unabridged.
Other aspects of the book may vary from the original edition.
Set in 16 pt. Plantin.

LIBRARY OF CONGRESS CIP DATA ON FILE.
CATALOGUING IN PUBLICATION FOR THIS BOOK
IS AVAILABLE FROM THE LIBRARY OF CONGRESS.

ISBN-13: 978-1-4328-8169-6 (hardcover alk. paper)

Published in 2020 by arrangement with Barbour Publishing, Inc.

Printed in Mexico
Print Number: 01     Print Year: 2020

**DEDICATION**

To prayer warriors and encouragers
Andy and Linda Barthol.
Many thanks for all that you do!


Weeping may endure for a night, but joy
cometh in the morning.

PSALM 30:5

# CHAPTER 1

*Strasburg, Pennsylvania*

With her nose pressed against the cold glass, Sylvia Beiler gazed out the window at the fresh-fallen snow in her mother's backyard. The back of her eyes stung as they followed the outline of objects the light of day cast into the yard.

Sylvia's breathing deepened, and she began to relax as she remembered a previous holiday. She smiled for a moment, thinking about her deceased husband on a night such as this. How wonderful it had been to be with him and the children, sharing the joy the holiday brought them.

*And such special times I had here growing up, before starting my new life with the man I loved. How would things be right now if nothing had happened to our precious loved ones?*

Sylvia shifted her weight when she heard a familiar sound that echoed of bygone days. Laughter and excited conversation

7

drifted from the living room into the kitchen where she stood, but she felt no merriment on this holiday. This was Sylvia's first Christmas without the three men who'd been so special in her life — her beloved husband, devoted father, and caring brother.

It was hard to understand how the rest of her family could be so cheerful today. Didn't they miss Dad, Toby, and Abe? Didn't they care how much Sylvia still grieved? Why weren't they grieving too?

With a weary sigh, Sylvia turned away from the window and sank into a chair at the table. She had offered to get the coffee going and cut the pies for dessert, but all she really wanted to do was go to her bedroom and have a good cry.

Closing her eyes, Sylvia let her mind drift back to that horrible day eight months ago when Dad, Toby, and Abe had decided to go after ice cream to have with Mom's birthday cake. Dad's horse and buggy had barely left the driveway to pull onto the main road when a truck hit them from behind. All occupants in the buggy, along with the horse, had died, leaving Sylvia without a husband and the job of raising two small children on her own.

She'd been depressed for so long she hardly remembered what it felt like to feel normal and happy. Unable to live in the home she and Toby had shared, Sylvia had moved in with her mother, where her sister, Amy, and brother, Henry, also lived. Each of them had faced challenges since that fateful day, but Amy seemed to be coping better than any of them.

*Probably because she and Jared are back together,* Sylvia told herself. *She's excited about her wedding next year and seems to enjoy helping Mom in the greenhouse. I can't blame her for that, but today, of all days, my sister should be missing our departed love ones.*

Sylvia's youngest brother still had a chip on his shoulder and had done some rebellious things since the accident. He'd been doing a little better lately, but Henry's rebellious nature and negative attitude had not fully dissipated.

Another thing that bothered Sylvia was Mom's old boyfriend Monroe, and how he'd made a habit of coming by to check on them and asking if there was anything he could do to help out. Monroe had reminded Mom several times that it wasn't good for her and the family to be alone without a man to watch out for them. Monroe always seemed to know when to drop by and would often stay, at Mom's invitation, to eat a meal with the family.

Those times when he waited for Mom to come in from the greenhouse were awkward too. Sylvia always tried to come up with topics of conversation, which had made her feel more uneasy as she wasn't comfortable around people she didn't know well. Each time Mom would come in from work, Monroe seemed eager to please. In Sylvia's opinion, the man was trying to worm his way into their lives. Something about the fellow wasn't right, but she couldn't put her finger on it. As far as she could tell, Monroe seemed to avoid the greenhouse. If anything was to be fixed, it usually pertained to the house or barn. It was obvious to her that Henry wasn't thrilled with the fellow either. He seemed even more irritable and standoffish whenever Monroe came calling. With more time on her hands during the winter months, Mom's routine was random, and she could come and go freely. Sylvia felt sure that was why they'd seen less of Mom's male friend lately. For now, things were nicer around the Kings' place.

Sylvia felt thankful her mother's greenhouse was closed for the winter and wouldn't reopen until early spring. She'd only worked there for the two weeks Mom had been in Clymer, New York, helping their brother, Ezekiel, and his wife, Michelle, when she'd given birth to a son in July. Those days had been difficult for Sylvia, and it was all she could do to conduct business or talk to customers who'd visited the greenhouse. Leaving her children to be cared for by their friend Mary Ruth had also been hard, even though Sylvia felt they were in capable hands. For now, she'd be able to breathe easy and forget about the greenhouse until spring.

Keeping her eyes closed, Sylvia massaged her forehead and then her cheekbones. *My place is here with Allen and Rachel.* Rachel had turned one last week, and Allen would be three in January. They needed a fulltime mother, not a babysitter.

Sylvia's mother seemed okay with the arrangement, but things might be different once Amy and Jared were married. After the newlyweds moved into a place of their own, Amy might not work in the greenhouse anymore — especially when children came along.

Henry also helped in the greenhouse, but not in the same capacity as Amy, who waited on customers, kept things well-stocked, and did the books to make sure they remained in the black. Between their place being vandalized, as well as a new

11

greenhouse springing up in the area, there had been some concern about whether they could survive financially. So far, they were making it, but if more destruction to the greenhouse or other areas on their property occurred, it might set them back too far to recover their losses. Since the greenhouse had closed for the winter, there had been no attacks of vandalism. Sylvia could only hope it would stay that way once the business reopened in early spring.

*I've got to stop thinking about all of this,* she reprimanded herself. *Worrying has never gotten me anywhere.*

"Sylvia, are you all right?"

The soft touch on her shoulder and Mom's gentle voice drew Sylvia's thoughts aside. "*Jah,* I'm fine. Just thinking is all."

"About Toby?"

Sylvia's head moved slowly up and down. "This is our first Christmas without him, Dad, and Abe. I miss them all so much."

Mom pulled out the chair beside Sylvia and sat. "I miss them too, and the rest of our family does as well."

"With all the merriment going on out there in the other room, it doesn't sound like anyone else is missing our loved ones as much as I am today."

Mom gave Sylvia's shoulder a light pat.

"That is certainly not true. Everyone deals with their grief in different ways. Also, with this being Christmas, which should be a most joyous occasion, it's a day to be thankful and celebrate."

Sylvia's throat felt so swollen, it nearly closed up. She couldn't say the words out loud, but truth was she was still angry that God had taken her husband, father, and brother. If their heavenly Father loved the world so much that He sent His only Son to earth to die for everyone's sins, couldn't He have prevented the accident that took their loved ones' lives?

"Don't you think your *kinner,* as well as Ezekiel and Michelle's children, deserve a happy Christmas?" Mom spoke quietly, with her mouth close to Sylvia's ear.

All Sylvia could manage was another slow nod.

"All right then, let's get out the pies and try to be happy for the rest of the day. Everyone has moved into the dining room, and they're waiting for dessert."

Mom rose from her chair, and Sylvia followed suit. For her children's sake, she would put a smile on her face and try to enjoy the rest of the day, even if her heart was not in it.

"Who made the pumpkin pies?" Amy's boyfriend, Jared, asked as they all sat around the dining-room table.

"She did." Amy pointed at Mom, and then she gestured to Sylvia. "My sister and I are responsible for the apple and chocolate cream pies."

Jared smacked his lips. "Since I had a small slice of each one, I can honestly say they're all delicious. Truthfully, though, pumpkin's my favorite."

Amy looked over at him and smiled. "Guess after we're married I'll be making lots of pumpkin pies."

"I look forward to that." Jared grinned back at her, before lifting his coffee mug to his lips.

A stab of envy pierced Sylvia's heart, seeing the happiness on her sister's glowing face. She remembered the joy bubbling in her soul when she'd first realized she had fallen in love with Toby. Their courting days were such happy ones, and being married to him made Sylvia feel complete in every way. She'd been convinced that they were meant to be together and felt sure they would have many years of marital bliss. Sylvia had looked forward to raising a family with Toby and growing old together. How could God have taken her hopes and dreams away?

She looked down at the napkin in her lap and blinked against the tears threatening to spill over. *I've got to quit feeling sorry for myself. It's not doing me or the rest of my family any good. For the sake of everyone at this table, I will try to act cheerful during the remainder of this day.*

Sylvia lifted her head, put a slice of apple pie on her plate, and then passed the chocolate cream pie to Ezekiel. "Here you go, Brother. I know this is one of your favorites."

He gave her a wide grin and nodded. "You bet. Whenever my *fraa* asks what kind of pie I would like, I always pick chocolate cream." Ezekiel's smile grew wider as he looked at his wife.

A tinge of pink spread across Michelle's cheeks. "I do try to keep my husband happy." She poked Ezekiel's stomach. "Especially when it comes to his requests for certain foods."

Ezekiel chuckled. "I'll admit it — I'm spoiled."

Sylvia forced herself to laugh along with most of the people at the table. Her children, as well as Ezekiel and Michelle's daughter, Angela Mary, were focused on eating their pie and wouldn't have understood what was so funny anyhow.

Sylvia glanced at her nephew, Vernon, asleep in the playpen that had been set up across the room. It was hard to believe he was five months old already. The little guy was such a good baby — hardly fussed at all unless his diapers were wet or he'd become hungry.

*I wonder if Michelle knows how lucky she is to be married to my brother and able to have more children.* Sylvia blotted her lips with the napkin. *Guess I should be grateful for the two kinner I have, because they will never have any more siblings.* The idea of getting married again was so foreign to her that she couldn't wrap her mind around it. No man could ever replace Toby.

Needing to focus on something else, Sylvia's ears perked up when Ezekiel began a conversation with her brother who had recently turned sixteen.

"Say, Henry, I haven't had a chance to ask — how are things going with you these days?"

"Okay, I guess," Henry mumbled around a slice of pumpkin pie.

"Is that crow you showed me when we

16

visited this fall still hanging around the place?"

Henry shook his head. "Haven't seen Charlie since the weather turned cold. Guess he left the area for someplace warmer — probably flew off with a flock of other crows." He tapped his chin. "I have heard of some crows that don't migrate in the winter. Guess my crow wasn't one of 'em though."

*Maybe the bird is dead. Someone could have shot him, or he might have died of old age.* Sylvia didn't voice her thoughts. No point in upsetting her temperamental brother. Although Henry seemed a bit more subdued now that the greenhouse was closed for the winter, leaving him with fewer chores to do, the chip on his shoulder had not fallen off.

"That's too bad," Ezekiel said. "I was hoping for another look at that noisy bird."

Henry shrugged his shoulders. "It don't matter; I've been watchin' other *veggel* that come into our yard, and I look for them whenever I go for long walks."

"Are you birding?" The question came from Michelle.

"Jah. Watching for different birds and writing down what I notice about them has become a new hobby for me."

Mom's brows lifted high. "Really, Son? Why haven't you mentioned this before?"

"I did. Guess you weren't listening."

"Bird-watching is a great hobby," Jared interjected. "I'd do it myself if I wasn't so busy with my roofing business and some other projects I've been helping my daed with."

Henry didn't respond as he poured himself another glass of milk. Sylvia figured he was probably upset because Mom hadn't listened when he'd talked to her about bird-watching before. Sylvia did recall him having mentioned it, and it really was no surprise, what with the interest he'd taken in the crow.

*It's good that my brother has found something positive to keep him occupied and out of trouble,* she thought. *Being on the lookout for certain birds, and jotting down information about them is a lot better than Henry hanging out with his friend Seth. From what I can tell, that young man has been a bad influence on my impressionable brother. Henry was not like that when Dad and Abe were alive.*

A knock on the front door pulled Sylvia's thoughts aside once more.

"Would you like me to see who it is?" Ezekiel looked at Mom.

She gave a quick nod.

18

Ezekiel rose from his seat and left the room. When he returned a few minutes later, blinking rapidly, he looked at Mom and said, "There's a clean-shaven Amish man in the living room who says he came to see you. He even has a gift."

Sylvia clutched her napkin with such force that it tore. *I bet it's Monroe Esh. I wonder what he's doing here. I hope Mom doesn't invite him to join us at the table.*

# CHAPTER 2

Sylvia watched as Mom left the table and headed for the living room. In an effort to be positive, she thought that maybe their visitor wasn't Monroe.

Michelle gave Sylvia's arm a light bump. "When you get the chance, I'd like to have your chocolate cream pie recipe. I believe it might be better than the one I've made before."

"No problem. I'll make sure to do that before you and your family head back to Clymer in a few days."

A few minutes went by, and then Mom returned to the dining room with her old boyfriend at her side.

All smiles, Monroe held a basket of fruit in his hands. "Merry Christmas everyone. I brought a gift that the whole family could enjoy."

Sylvia forced herself to smile and say, "*Danki,* that was kind of you." While the

20

fruit basket was nice, she'd hoped they could slide by this holiday without him coming by.

Amy also greeted him, but Henry merely sat there, fiddling with his fork. He clearly did not care for Monroe and had told Sylvia so several times. She couldn't blame her brother; Mr. Esh had some rather strange ways and was quite opinionated. He was also overbearing and obviously pursuing their mother.

Mom gestured to Ezekiel and Michelle. "Monroe, I'd like you to meet my son Ezekiel and his wife, Michelle. They live in Clymer, New York, but came down to celebrate the holiday with us."

Monroe set the basket of fruit on the floor and extended his hand. "I should have introduced myself when you answered the door, instead of just asking to speak to your *mudder.*"

"It's nice to meet you." Ezekiel rose from his seat and clasped Monroe's hand. Michelle did the same.

"Your *mamm* and I were friends during our youth. In fact, I courted her before your daed came into the picture and stole her away." He took a few steps closer to Mom. "Isn't that right, Belinda?"

Her cheeks turned crimson as she nodded. "That was a long time ago, Monroe."

"Seems like yesterday to me." He cleared his throat a couple of times. " 'Course, that might be because I never got married or raised a *familye* of my own, the way you did." His gaze traveled around the table. "And what a fine family I see here right now."

*I wonder if Monroe's trying to impress us or Mom by his compliment.* Sylvia clutched both halves of her napkin. *Well, I, for one, am not impressed. Monroe owns his own furniture store, but maybe he's trying to acquire Mom's business too. He could be what some folks call "an Amish entrepreneur." Who knows? Since Monroe has no wife or family, he might be quite wealthy and could be looking to make even more money. Surely his interest in Mom goes deeper than just reminiscing about how they'd once courted. Monroe knows how much Mom loved Dad, so I wouldn't be surprised if he wasn't looking to marry our mother so he could get his hands on the greenhouse.*

Mom pulled out an empty chair and said, "Monroe, would you like to join us for *pei* and *kaffi*?"

His sappy grin stretched wide. "Why, jah, I surely would. Danki, Belinda."

Sylvia rubbed her forehead. *Oh great. This man's presence at our table is not what we need today — or any other time, for that matter.* She looked over at Amy, who had set her cup down and crossed her arms. *No doubt my sister isn't happy about Monroe being here either.*

Sylvia's gaze went to Ezekiel and then Henry. Neither of them looked the least bit pleased when Monroe took a seat.

"Looks like you have a variety of pies on the table," the man said. "But I don't see any *minsfleesch.* Weren't those included in your Christmas desserts?"

Mom shook her head as she poured coffee into a clean mug and handed it to Monroe. "To be honest, none of my family cares much for mincemeat."

His mouth opened slightly. "Not even you, Belinda?"

"I don't mind it, myself, but it's not one of my favorites." She pointed to the pies on the table. "As you can see, we have apple, pumpkin, and chocolate-cream. Would you care for one of those?"

Monroe hesitated a moment, before pointing at the pumpkin pie sitting closest to him. "Guess I'll have a slice of that."

Mom cut a piece, placed it on a clean plate, and handed it to him. "Enjoy."

Sylvia watched in disgust as he dug into it with an eager expression. She hoped he

23

would leave as soon as he was done eating. The family had plans to play a few games after dessert, and it wouldn't be nearly as much fun if Monroe hung around.

She got up and went over to check on Rachel, who had begun to fuss. After changing the baby's diaper, she went to the bathroom to wash her hands, before returning to the table.

"What do you do for a living, young man?" Monroe's question was directed at Ezekiel.

"I have my own business in New York, making and selling various products for people who raise bees for their honey," Ezekiel replied. "I also have hives and sell my local honey to many people who live in our area. I used to raise bees and sell honey here before my wife and I left Strasburg." He gestured to Henry. "My young brother has taken over that business now."

Henry offered Ezekiel a smile that was obviously forced. "Oh, jah, and it's my favorite thing to do."

Sylvia felt the tension between her brothers as they stared across the table at each other. No doubt Ezekiel heard the sarcasm in Henry's voice. The last thing they needed were harsh words being spoken, especially with Monroe here taking it all in.

24

In an effort to put a lid on things, Sylvia stood. "How about if those of us who have finished eating take our dishes into the kitchen to be washed?"

"Well, I'm definitely not done eating," Monroe announced. "If no one has any objection, I'd like to try some of that apple pie now."

"We've all had seconds, so I'm sure there would be no objections." Mom reached for the pie pan right away and cut him another piece.

Sylvia groaned inwardly. Was her mother trying to be a polite hostess, or did she fancy Monroe's company? Sylvia hoped that wasn't the case. She couldn't even imagine having Monroe as her stepfather.

"Now don't look so worried." Amy patted Sylvia's arm as they stood in the kitchen getting ready to wash their dessert dishes. She kept her voice lowered and turned to check the doorway. "Mom was only being polite when she invited Monroe to join us for pie and coffee. She has no interest in him whatsoever."

"How can you be so sure?" Sylvia filled the sink with warm soapy water.

"Because she's told me so."

"She has said that to me too, yet whenever

the man comes around, she always welcomes him."

"Our mamm welcomes everyone who comes to our door. She's kind and polite, even to people like the homeless woman, Maude, who last summer took things without asking from our garden and helped herself to cookies that had been set out in the greenhouse." Amy nodded. "I've let poor Maude get away with a few things too."

"I wonder how that elderly woman is faring inside that old rundown shack during this cold, snowy weather." Sylvia reached for a sponge and began washing the dessert plates.

"I don't think she's there anymore. Jared and I stopped by the shack last week with some groceries Mom wanted to give Maude, but there was no sign of her — just an empty cot and old table in the middle of the otherwise barren room."

"Maybe she moved out of the area. Or perhaps, if she has any family, she went to spend the winter with them."

Amy picked up the first plate to dry. "I asked her once if she had any family, and she said no."

"I can't imagine how it would be not to have any family at all."

"Me neither," agreed Amy.

"Do you two need some help with the dishes?" Michelle asked, joining them in the kitchen.

"If you don't mind, you can put the dishes away once they've been dried," Amy responded.

"I don't mind at all." Michelle moved closer to the counter near the sink. "Your mamm is keeping an eye on the kinner in the other room, while Monroe plies Ezekiel with more questions about his bee-supply business."

"What are Jared and Henry doing?" Sylvia asked.

"Jared made a few comments here and there, but Henry left the room. Said he was going upstairs to read a magazine."

Amy chuckled. "Leave it up to our teenage brother to make a quick escape. He probably would have done that anyway, even if Monroe hadn't showed up."

"I have a hunch Mr. Esh has taken an interest in your mamm." Michelle put a stack of dry plates into the cupboard.

"Jah," Amy said with regret in her tone. "But I am certain that Mom doesn't want anything but a casual friendship with him. Besides, Dad hasn't even been gone a year, so in my opinion, Monroe shouldn't be trying to worm his way into our mother's life."

Sylvia gave a decisive nod. "Agreed."

When the last dish was done, Sylvia felt the need for some fresh air. "Think I'll slip into my boots and outer apparel and take a little walk outside in the snow. Do either of you care to join me?"

"I'll pass on that idea. I'd like to spend some time with Jared, and by now Mom may have set some games out for us all to play," Amy replied.

"It's too cold outside for me." Michelle rubbed her arms briskly. "Just thinking about going out in the snow makes me feel chilly."

"Okay then, I'll join you in the dining room after I come back inside."

Sylvia went out to the utility room, where everyone in the family kept their boots, along with jackets, sweaters, and shawls. After taking a seat on a folding chair to slip into her boots, she wrapped a heavy shawl around her shoulders, put on a pair of woolen gloves, and went out the back door.

Although it wasn't snowing at the moment, the air was colder than Sylvia expected. Unfazed by it, however, she tromped through the snow, reliving the days when she and her siblings had been children. They'd spent many happy days in this yard, frolicking in the winter snow; jumping through piles of leaves in the fall; flying kites in the field behind their house on windy spring days; and chasing after fireflies on hot, humid summer evenings. Oh, how Sylvia missed those carefree days, when her biggest worry was who would be the first one up to bat whenever they got a game of baseball going.

*Will my children have fond childhood memories when they grow up?* Sylvia wondered. *When Rachel and Allen are both old enough to be given the freedom to roam around the yard by themselves, will they find things to do that'll leave them with good memories?*

Sylvia worried that not having a father around to help in their upbringing and take them on fun outings might hamper what she'd hoped would be a normal childhood for them. Even if she didn't feel like doing anything just for fun, Sylvia promised herself that she would make every effort to spend quality time with Allen and Rachel in hopes of giving them some joyful memories.

Sylvia continued her trek through the backyard and made her way around to the front of the house. She looked in the window and saw Monroe sitting in Dad's old chair as he chatted with Ezekiel. It was difficult seeing this fellow trying to move in on her family.

*I wish Monroe would leave soon. Doesn't he realize he's cutting into our family time?* Sylvia tightened her scarf with her gloved hands. *Ezekiel seems to be conducting himself in a pleasant manner with Monroe. But he's a minister now, so I guess he has to be nice and do the right thing with everyone he meets. I hope my sister is right about Mom only wanting to be friends with Monroe and nothing more. I couldn't stand the idea of him moving in and trying to take Dad's place.*

Not quite ready to go back inside yet, she walked down the driveway to check for any messages they may have waiting in the phone shed.

After stepping into the small, cold wooden building, she saw the green light flashing on their answering machine. She took a seat on the icy metal chair and clicked the button.

"Hello, Sylvia, it's Selma. I'm calling to see how you and the children are doing and to wish you a Merry Christmas."

Tears sprang to Sylvia's eyes at the sound of Toby's mother's voice. She hadn't heard from her in-laws in nearly a month and had wondered how they were doing. She'd been meaning to call them, but the busyness of getting ready for Ezekiel and his family's arrival and helping Mom and Amy with

30

holiday baking had taken up much of Sylvia's time. Of course, that was no excuse. Wayne and Selma were Allen and Rachel's paternal grandparents, and they had a right to know how their grandchildren were doing.

After Sylvia listened to the rest of her mother-in-law's message, she dialed the number and left a response, suggesting that they come down from their home in Mifflin County sometime this spring to see the children. Sylvia also mentioned how much Rachel and Allen had grown.

When Sylvia left the phone shed, she glanced across the road and stood staring at the twinkling colored lights draped around their neighbors' front window. They also had a colorful wreath on the front door.

*I wonder why so many English folks feel the need to decorate their homes at Christmas. Is it their way of celebrating the birth of Christ, or do they do it because they enjoy looking at the colored lights?*

Sylvia hadn't seen much of Virginia and Earl Martin since the weather had turned cold. During the summer, and into the fall, she'd seen Virginia out on her front porch many times. Earl's truck sat parked in the driveway out front, but no other vehicles were in sight. Apparently, the Martins had no company today, or perhaps they had gone somewhere to celebrate Christmas. Since their detached garage was around back, Sylvia had no way of knowing if Virginia's car was there or not.

Sylvia turned back toward the house. *I would have been happier if Mom had asked the Martins to join us for dessert, or even Christmas dinner, then inviting Monroe to sit at our table. If he doesn't leave soon, I may do like Henry and retreat to my room with Allen and Rachel.*

# CHAPTER 3

Virginia's gaze went from her husband, sleeping in his recliner, to the small Christmas tree Earl had bought from a local tree farm three days ago. They'd decided to go smaller than the past years when they had picked out a much larger tree together. For some reason, Earl didn't want a big tree this year. Except for the lights he'd put in the front window at her suggestion, he didn't seem to be in a festive mood.

She flipped her fingers through the ends of her bangs. *But that's okay, since I'm not excited about the holiday this year either. In fact, I feel kinda empty inside.*

A loud snore from Earl brought Virginia out of her thoughts. From where she sat on the couch, her eyes began to water and burn from allergies. She'd dealt with this sometimes when they'd brought a live tree into the house.

She leaned forward and yanked a tissue

from the box sitting on the coffee table. *I'm pretty sure that silly little fir is the problem.* It sat on a small table across the room with pretty red-and-green fabric draped around its base. She had decorated the tree with colored lights and hung a few small ornaments from the boughs.

Virginia yawned and massaged her leg where it had started to throb. She shifted on the couch, trying to find a more comfortable position, while Earl continued to sleep like a baby.

In truth, for Virginia, Christmas was nothing special — just another boring holiday, since it was just her and Earl. She bit her bottom lip to keep from crying. *Family. I wish we had some family to share the holiday with and buy gifts for.* She pressed her palms against her cheeks. *Maybe I deserve the empty feeling I have inside. Could be that a woman like me isn't worthy of being happy and fulfilled. No man but Earl has ever really cared about me, and sometimes I'm not even sure how he really feels.*

Virginia closed her eyes, trying to remember if there had been any good Christmases when she was a girl. Maybe a few when her dad was sober. She'd had some fairly decent holidays when her first husband was alive too, but they'd been few and far between.

For the most part, Virginia's life had been full of challenges and lots of mistakes.

Pushing her negative thoughts away, Virginia glanced out the front window at her Amish neighbors' house. No colored lights there, that was for sure. It hadn't taken her long to learn that the Plain people didn't celebrate Christmas with flashy decorations on the outside of their homes.

She poked her tongue against the inside of her cheek. *Probably no trees or ornaments of any kind inside the house either.*

Two days ago, Virginia had seen a van pull into the Kings' yard. She'd been curious to see how many people had come to visit, but with the snow blowing she couldn't see well enough to make out much at all. The van had left a short time later, and Virginia didn't know if the people it had brought to the Kings' were still at the house. For all she knew, they'd come and gone already. It wasn't snowing at the moment, though, so she left her seat on the couch and went to peer out the front window.

*Earl would call me snoopy if he caught me doing this,* Virginia thought as she picked up the pair of binoculars she'd bought him for Christmas. Truth was, the gift was more for her than Earl, since she was home most of the time while he was in Lancaster selling cars at the dealership where he'd been hired earlier this year.

Moving closer to the window, and holding the binoculars up to her face, she saw two Amish buggies parked near the house. *They have company, of course. I think those people get more company than I've had in my entire forty-seven years.*

Virginia spotted an Amish woman step out of the phone shed and walk up to the house. *No doubt one of those King women, either making a phone call or checking for messages.*

She set the field glasses down and went out on the front porch for a breath of fresh air and a better look at the weather. Winter was not her favorite time of the year, but the one good thing about it was that the greenhouse across the road was closed, bringing less traffic noise and smelly horse manure. The sign out by the Kings' driveway even said: Closed for the Winter.

*Of course,* she reminded herself, *it'll open up again in the spring, and everything that irritates me about living here will start all over.* One thing for sure — Virginia wasn't about to go over there in the spring and buy anymore plants. The tomato plants she'd put in last year had both died; although that wasn't the Kings' fault. If she did decide to

36

grow a garden next year, however, she would get everything she needed from the new greenhouse on the other side of town. At least she could relate to those folks a little better, since they weren't Amish. Virginia had absolutely nothing in common with their neighbors across the road.

A frigid breeze blew under the porch roof, causing Virginia to shiver and rub her arms. *I was stupid for comin' out here without a coat. I need to get back inside where it's warm.*

When Virginia entered the house, she found Earl still asleep, only now his snoring had increased. In fact, the whole room seemed to vibrate with the aggravating rumble.

Irritated, Virginia marched across the room and picked up the remote. When a channel came on to a game show, she cranked up the volume.

A split second later, Earl came awake. "Hey, what's going on? Why's the TV blaring like that, Virginia?"

"Nothing's going on. I figured it was time for you to wake up. Thought I'd slice that pumpkin pie I bought at the local bakery the other day. Would you like a piece, Earl?"

He yawned and stretched his arms over his head. "Yeah, I guess so." He got up and snatched the remote from her hands. "I'll find us something decent to watch while you get the dessert ready."

"Okay, sure . . . since you asked so nice." Virginia limped out of the room. That cold air she'd subjected herself to had not done her bum leg any good. No doubt some arthritis had set in to the area where her old injury had been.

Virginia entered the kitchen and took out the pie, when she heard some Christmas music coming from the living room. She figured Earl must have found some sentimental holiday movie to watch on TV, where everything would come out perfectly in the end. *If only real life was like that.*

"Earl might be satisfied with watching some make-believe story, but not me," she mumbled. *I'm lonely and bored out of my mind living here in the middle of Amish country. Sure wish there was some way I could talk Earl into moving back to Chicago. At least there I had a few friends who seemed to actually care about me.*

Virginia cut the pie and placed two pieces on plates. *Maybe one of these days I'll get a bus ticket and go back to Chicago for a visit with my friend Stella. It would sure beat stickin' around here all the time.*

By eight o'clock, both babies had been fed

38

and put in their cribs, and even Allen and Angela Mary were winding down.

Henry hadn't come down from his room to join the board games being played in the dining room, and Sylvia couldn't blame him. Regrettably, Monroe was still here, sitting beside Mom at the table as they played a game of Uno with Jared, Amy, Ezekiel, and Michelle. Sylvia had played a few hands with them, but as fatigue set in, she'd moved into the living room to read to her son and niece, choosing a storybook written for young children. The pictures with the story helped to hold the youngsters' interest.

By the time she'd reached the last page of the book, Allen had dozed off and Angela Mary's eyes appeared droopy. Sylvia was tempted to let Michelle know that her daughter looked ready for bed, but she didn't want to interrupt the game everyone else seemed to be enjoying. Apparently, they had all accepted Monroe's presence and perhaps even appreciated his company. Either that or they were too caught up in the game to be irritated with the sappy expression on his face whenever he looked at Mom.

*I need to quit fretting about this,* Sylvia told herself as she picked Allen up and rose from the couch. She would put him to bed and then come back down to say goodnight to the others and let Michelle know that Angela Mary was now lying on the couch.

After Sylvia got Allen tucked into bed, and she'd checked on Rachel, she went across the hall and tapped on Henry's door. Since she saw a shadow of light coming from under the door, she figured her brother probably wasn't asleep.

"Who's there?" Henry called.

"It's me, Sylvia. Is it okay if I come in?"

"Jah, sure."

Sylvia opened the door. When she stepped inside, she found Henry on the bed, propped up with two pillows behind his back. "What are you up to?" she questioned.

"Just doin' some reading." He lifted the magazine in his hands.

"What's it about?" Sylvia hoped it wasn't the car magazine Amy had told her she'd caught him reading a few months ago.

"It's a bird magazine, and there's an article about our area, with a list of interesting facts concernin' the birds we could likely find here."

Even though Henry's room was dimly lit, Sylvia saw excitement on his face. "You're pretty enthused about bird-watching, huh?"

"For sure, and not just the ones that come into our yard. I plan to go into some of the areas mentioned in the magazine and look for certain birds." He set the magazine down and moved over to the side of the bed. "You should come with me sometime, Sylvia. Ya might wanna take up birding too."

Sylvia tugged on one of her apron straps. "It sounds like it could be interesting, and maybe even fun, but not in this cold weather. Just the short walk I took outside a few hours ago nearly chilled me to the bones."

"You could either bundle up with extra clothes or wait till the weather warms up. In the spring there'll be lots more birds to look at anyway."

"I might consider that, but it'll have to be when I can get someone to watch the kinner. Tromping through the woods or some meadow is no place for two little ones, who would no doubt get fussy and scare away the birds."

Henry nodded. "Well, let me know when you're ready to try it, and then we can plan which day we want to go out."

"All right, I will." Sylvia started for the door, but turned back to face him. "You coming back down to join the others?"

He shook his head vigorously. "Nope. Not

unless Monroe is gone."

"Sorry, but he's still here, playing Uno with the rest of our family."

"Figures!" Henry crossed his arms and gave a huff. "That man irritates me more than the bees I'm stuck takin' care of."

Sylvia waited to see if Henry would say more, but he only sat with a grim expression, staring straight ahead.

"Monroe's not one of my favorite people, either, but he is a friend of Mom's, so I think we should at least be *manierlich*."

"I was as polite as I could be while we ate our dessert, but watchin' the puppy-dog looks he kept giving our mamm made me feel like I was gonna *kotze*."

Sylvia lifted her gaze to the ceiling. "I think you're exaggerating a bit, Brother. I doubt that you felt like you were going to vomit."

"Did so. My stomach started to curdle, the minute that man came into the dining room. He's after our mamm. Can't ya see that, Sister?"

Sylvia gave a slow nod.

"So what are we gonna do about it?"

"I'm not sure there's anything we can do other than hope Mom doesn't get sucked in by all the compliments and offers of help Monroe shoots her way."

"How about this — I'll ask Ezekiel to put the man in his place, and you can have a little talk with Mom. In case she's not seeing it, she needs to be made aware that Mr. Esh is trying to worm his way into her life."

"I suppose I could bring up the topic to her, but I'll have to do it with care. I don't want Mom to think I'm meddling or trying to control her life."

"Makes sense." Henry rubbed his chin. "Maybe if Ezekiel sets the man straight, that'll be the end of it, and we can go back to the way it was before Monroe started hangin' around."

Sylvia hoped Henry was right, but she had a feeling it might take more than Ezekiel talking to Monroe to get him to back off. What really needed to happen was for Mom to tell the man she wasn't interested in a relationship with him. She'd done it once before, during their youth, and he'd accepted it and left Strasburg. Perhaps if she told him that again, he'd leave the area for good and move on with his life.

# CHAPTER 4

The following morning while Ezekiel helped Henry do chores in the barn, he decided to pose a question that had been on his mind since yesterday. "So Henry, I've been wondering . . . what do you think of Monroe Esh?"

Henry's brows furrowed. "Let's see now . . . Where do I begin? Mr. Esh started comin' by during the latter part of summer, and then it became more often and he stayed longer. He'd wait around to see our mother after she closed up the greenhouse, and poor Sylvia would have to make conversation with him till Mom came up to the house. Sylvia mentioned once that Monroe often commented how there should be a man around here to keep an eye on things." Henry's forehead wrinkled. "He'd chat with Mom and bring up about doin' some work in the barn or around the house."

"Did she let him do either?"

"Nope." Henry leaned forward with one hand on his knee. "I've always thought the fellow seemed pushy, and I don't like the way he looks at Mom with this phony lookin' grin." He paused a few seconds. "I personally think Monroe's a bit odd, not to mention that I'm almost sure he's waitin' for the right opportunity to ask our mamm to marry him." Henry reached down to pet one of the cats that had been rubbing his leg. "I'm glad you brought up the topic, because I was plannin' to talk to you about Monroe this morning."

Ezekiel forked some hay into Mom's horse's stall and leaned on the handle of the pitchfork. "And so you have. Is there anything else you wanted to say?"

"Yeah. I was hopin' you might have a talk with Monroe and let him know that Mom has no interest in getting married again, so he should quit comin' around."

Ezekiel chuckled. "That'd be pretty direct, wouldn't you say?"

Henry's head moved up and down. "That's what Monroe needs, 'cause I don't think he's good at takin' hints."

"Have you talked to Mom about this — asked if she has any feelings for Mr. Esh?"

Henry shook his head. "Sylvia's gonna talk to her though. She doesn't care much for

Monroe either, and from what Amy has said to me in the past, she also doesn't appreciate him coming around all the time."

"Neither do I." Ezekiel tossed another clump of hay into the stall. "But I don't feel right about *neimische* either."

"You have every right to meddle. You're the oldest brother, and it's your responsibility to look out for our mamm. It's the least you can do since you're not here anymore to help out with other things."

*Oh boy . . . Henry's still upset with me for not moving back here.* Ezekiel was taken aback by his brother's harsh tone and pointed stare. He'd thought by now that Henry would have accepted how Mom had said many times that she wanted Ezekiel and his family to remain in New York. In fact, she'd insisted upon it, stating that she could manage the greenhouse with the help of Amy, Henry, and Sylvia — although from what Ezekiel understood, Sylvia helped more with household chores than anything related to the greenhouse.

Ezekiel didn't want to return home without trying to do something helpful, though. He thought it would be good to mention the things Henry had told him about Monroe and get Mom's input as to how he might bridge the gap between him and

46

Henry. *If only my brother would try to understand why my family and I have remained in New York.*

"Listen, Henry, if I thought it was the right thing to do, I'd borrow your horse and buggy right now and head over to Monroe's furniture store for a little chat." Ezekiel paused to sort out his thoughts. "And I'm not saying I won't talk to Monroe, but I think I should speak to Mom about it first, and see how she's feeling in regards to Monroe hanging around. If she's not happy about it, and wants me to intercede, then I'll seek the man out. Otherwise . . ."

Henry shook his head. "Our mamm's too nice to say anything negative about Monroe. Even if she felt the way I do, I doubt she'd ever say it to his face. Someone in our family needs to take the horse by the reins and put Mr. Esh in his place. And if you're not gonna do it, then I will."

*Oh boy, I hope Henry isn't serious about confronting Mom's friend. It would only make matters worse and add more stress to the situation.*

Ezekiel held up his hand. "Whoa now, Brother, just calm down. Let me have a talk with Mom, and then I'll decide what to do. In the meantime, you need to focus on the chores you're supposed to do out here."

Henry stomped off to the other side of the barn in a huff.

*I'd like to approach this situation with wisdom and understanding.* Ezekiel closed his eyes and paused to offer up a prayer. *Heavenly Father, please give me the right words when I talk to Mom about Monroe. I don't want to say anything that might upset her.*

Sylvia had gotten the children up and seen to their needs, although things had been a bit hectic this morning with her littlest one being so fussy. Another tooth was trying to come in, and Sylvia massaged the area, hoping to help it break through. When she'd finally gotten Rachel settled down, she headed for the kitchen but paused outside the door. Taking in some deep calming breaths, she did her best to collect herself. *I hope I don't lose my nerve.*

Sylvia opened the door and stepped into the room. "Mom, if you have a minute, can I talk to you about something?" She wiped her sweaty hands on her apron before crossing the room to her mother, who stood at the counter, cracking eggs into a bowl.

"As you can see, I've already started fixing breakfast, but we can talk while I mix up the *oier.*"

"Okay. I'll help with whatever else needs

to be done as soon as we have our talk." Sylvia moved closer to her mother and made sure to keep her voice down so no one else in the house would hear. "What I have to say is about Monroe."

"What about him?" Mom began beating the eggs.

"It was a little disconcerting to have him join us yesterday."

"How so?" She kept whisking. "It's not like it's the first time Monroe's dropped by."

"You're right, but he's not part of our family, and in my opinion, he should have spent Christmas Day with his parents and siblings, not with us till way after dark."

When Mom offered no reply, Sylvia continued. "I, along with Henry and Amy, think Monroe is trying to worm his way into your life."

"That makes four of us," Ezekiel announced as he entered the kitchen.

Mom turned with a frown to face him. "Well, you and the rest of your siblings can quit worrying, because there is nothing going on between me and Monroe. He's just an old friend, not a single thing more."

"So you have no interest in him at all?" Ezekiel tipped his head.

"Not romantically." Mom placed her hand against her heart. "The only man I'll ever love is your daed. Plain and simple."

"I'm glad to hear it." Ezekiel flopped into a chair at the table.

"But Monroe is interested in you in a way that goes beyond friendship, Mom," Sylvia interjected. "We all know it. I'm sure you must realize it too."

Her mother nodded. "Jah, it's obvious to me as well."

"Want me to talk to him about it?" Ezekiel asked. "I can do it today or tomorrow, before we head back to New York."

Mom shook her head. "No, I'll take care of the situation. It's my place to let Monroe know that I am still in mourning and have no interest in a personal relationship with him or any other man at this time. If he doesn't back away, I'll let you know, and then you can have a talk with him, via a phone call if necessary."

"Okay." Ezekiel gave a nod. "I won't step in unless you say so."

"Danki." Mom turned back to her job of stirring the eggs.

Sylvia figured it wouldn't be long before her mother had the chance to speak to Monroe. After the warm welcome he'd received yesterday, he would no doubt be dropping by regularly again. She hoped the next time would be the last time he would come by to pay a social call. The fact that he didn't seem to understand, or even care, that Mom was still in mourning, was enough to turn Sylvia off toward Monroe, not to mention his strange behavior at times.

*I can't worry about this right now. I need to help Mom get food on the table before the rest of the family comes in for breakfast.*

Amy nearly jumped out of bed when she looked at the clock on her nightstand and realized she'd overslept.

*And no wonder,* she thought as she pulled the covers aside. *I was dreaming about Jared, and it was our wedding day. We looked so happy, as we stood before the bishop, answering his questions. If only it had been real and not a dream.* Amy wasn't good at waiting for things — especially something she wanted so badly.

Amy stood and plodded across the room. The fall of next year seemed like such a long ways off. She wished she could marry Jared tomorrow, but they needed enough time to plan all of the details that would need to be done for the wedding.

Amy had already chosen the material for her wedding dress. It was a dark burgundy fabric. She hadn't cut out the pattern yet but planned to do so after Ezekiel and his family returned to their home. Since the greenhouse would be closed until sometime in March, Amy had all winter to make the dress. Her excitement about the wedding would probably drive her to get it done as soon as possible, though. Just looking at it hanging inside her closet would give Amy a sense of joy. She loved Jared so much and couldn't wait to become his wife.

Amy reflected on the day she'd broken up with Jared, soon after her father, brother, and brother-in-law had been killed. She'd convinced herself that due to her added responsibilities, there would be no time for courting. Amy had always been one to make sacrifices for others, and this unexpected, tragic situation had been no exception. She'd firmly believed that her responsibility was to help Mom run the greenhouse, which meant giving up her desire to continue a courtship with Jared and eventually agreeing to marry him. It had taken Amy some time to realize she could make the time to spend with Jared, despite her busy work schedule.

Amy hurried to get dressed and put her hair up in a bun. She needed to get downstairs to help with breakfast. She was surprised someone hadn't already rapped on her door to remind her what time it was.

She opened her door a crack and looked up and down the hallway. Although no one was in sight, the wonderful odor of coffee brewing on the stove, mingled with the mouth-watering aroma of sweet sticky buns indicated that their morning meal was in the works. One more reason to hurry downstairs to the kitchen.

Belinda kept her thoughts to herself, but she was a bit miffed that Ezekiel felt the need to intervene on her behalf where Monroe was concerned.

*Doesn't my son realize I can speak for myself?* Belinda fretted as she heated up the frying pan to cook the scrambled eggs. *Did my oldest son and daughter really think I would be flattered enough to even consider a relationship that went beyond friendship with Monroe or any other man?*

Belinda and her husband Vernon had enjoyed a strong and sure marriage. She'd never loved anyone the way she had him. Her beloved husband was not a man who could easily be replaced, and truthfully, Belinda didn't see herself ever getting married again. Even though Vernon had died, her love for him would always remain strong.

*Monroe needs to know that,* she told herself. *The next time he comes over here, or if I should see him someplace in town, I'm going to let Monroe know how I feel, so he can clearly comprehend exactly where he stands. I'm sure once he realizes there is no chance for a romantic relationship with me, he will stop coming around. Then my life will go on as it was before he moved back to Strasburg.*

Belinda glanced at Amy and Sylvia, who were now working together to set the table. *My concentration needs to be on my children — helping Amy plan for her wedding; supporting Sylvia in every way I can; and guiding and directing Henry's life so he grows up to be a responsible, Christian man. I also have an obligation to be a good grandmother to my four precious grandchildren.*

Belinda prayed daily for her children and the little ones. Although she fell short at times, she always tried to set a good example. Even Ezekiel, who'd become a minister in his church district, needed her prayers. Last night before going to bed, Ezekiel had spoken to Belinda about Henry, and the fact that he still harbored bitterness because Ezekiel hadn't moved back to Strasburg.

She closed her eyes briefly and offered a quick prayer. *Lord, help me to keep my focus on You first and then on my dear family. Please guide and direct my life in the days ahead, and give me the wisdom to provide for my children and grandchildren whatever they require — whether it be physical, emotional, or spiritual needs.*

# CHAPTER 5

It had been two days since Ezekiel and his family left Strasburg, and Belinda felt the emptiness in her house, all the way to her bones. When there weren't chores to do, Henry had his nose in some book or magazine about birds. Amy spent every free moment working on her wedding dress and making lists that pertained to her and Jared's special day. Belinda helped with some of those lists, but when it came to her wedding dress, Amy wanted to do it by herself. Allen had come down with a bad cold yesterday, so Sylvia kept busy taking care of him and trying to keep her active little girl out of things.

Belinda felt at loose ends and found herself wishing she could move time forward to spring. She needed to be busy and missed working in the greenhouse. It had kept her mind from dwelling on the huge void in her life since Vernon and Abe had died. Work also helped Belinda not to dwell on the fact that Ezekiel and his family lived so far away and she didn't get to see them often enough.

"I have myself to blame for that, because I insisted that he remain in Clymer, even when he offered to move back here to help out," Belinda whispered as she finished putting their clean dishes from lunch in the cupboard.

She closed the cabinet door, and was about to leave the kitchen, when she heard a horse's whinny outside.

Belinda went to the window and looked out. A horse and buggy she recognized as belonging to Monroe pulled up to the hitching rail. She saw the horse's breath as it stomped at the rail, sending a few hunks of snow into the air.

Henry wandered into the kitchen and opened up one of the cupboard doors. "I heard a horse and carriage come up the driveway. Who's here?"

"Monroe pulled in, and he's getting out of his buggy." Belinda turned away from the window and glanced at her son.

Henry grimaced, while he got out a box of crackers. "Oh great. Not my favorite person," he mumbled. "Why is he here?"

"Probably came to visit." *Or try to sway me into letting him do some work, and then I'll feel obligated to feed Monroe and let him stay around the rest of the evening.*

Henry stepped up next to her and looked out the window. "He's tromping the snow down by his rig, and now he's moving gingerly in this direction. If you need me, I'll be in my room — so you and Mr. Esh can chat with each other without me here to listen and get sickened."

"Henry, I can't believe you said that. I do appreciate you letting me speak to Monroe alone, however." She gave his shoulder a tap. "What I have to say to Mr. Esh is a private matter."

He nodded and hurried from the room.

She moved away from the window and waited for Monroe by the back door. It would be weird for her to tell this man twice in his lifetime that she didn't share the same feelings for him as he did her. Belinda almost felt sorry for putting Monroe through it again, now, years later. But the fact of the matter was she wasn't ready to move on, especially under a timetable of less than a year. *And my children are not ready for that either.*

Having Monroe show up now was the opportunity Belinda had been waiting for, so she would gather up her courage and deal with the uncomfortable situation. Even though she'd been in black dresses since the accident, apparently it hadn't seemed to affect Monroe's way of thinking, because he seemed not to waver at coming by and visiting as usual.

Belinda stood off to one side of the door and listened as heavy footsteps clomped up the stairs and onto the porch. She waited for the knock before opening the door.

"Good afternoon, Belinda. How's your day been going so far?" Monroe greeted her with a cheerful smile and a slight tip of his head.

"So far so good." Belinda opened the door wider and stepped aside. "Won't you come in out of the cold?"

"Of course." He glanced toward the kitchen doorway. "I hope I'm not interrupting your *middaagesse.*"

She shook her head. "We ate lunch an hour ago, and I just put away the last of our clean dishes."

Monroe's shoulder drooped a bit, and he made a strange noise in his throat. "Oh, I see."

Belinda figured he'd probably hoped for an invitation to join them for the noon meal. "I'm surprised you're not at work." She pulled out a chair at the table and gestured for him to take a seat.

59

He removed his hat and jacket before responding. Once seated, Monroe looked up at Belinda and said, "I checked in at the shop to make sure things were running smoothly this morning, and everything was going fine."

"So what brings you by here this afternoon?" she asked.

"Came to see you and make sure you and your family are doing all right." He glanced at the kitchen door, as though expecting someone to walk through it. "Did your oldest son and his family go home?"

"Jah, they left two days ago."

"That's good. I — I meant to say it's good that they could spend *Grischdaag* with you."

She gave a nod. "Our Christmas wouldn't have been the same without them."

"Makes sense. If I had a family like yours, I'd want to spend time with them too." Monroe blinked rapidly as he stared at Belinda. "You're still just as pretty as the day we first met."

She flapped her hand in his direction. "Need I remind you that we knew each other when we were children attending school together?"

"I know very well when we met and need no reminder." His brown eyes seemed to grow even darker as he continued to gaze at her. "You were a pretty girl then, and grew more beautiful when you became a young woman. I envied Vernon when you chose him over me."

Belinda felt the heat of a flush creep across her cheeks and radiate down to her neck. She was not used to receiving such compliments and didn't know quite how to respond.

"Sorry for making you blush. I just wanted you to know how I felt back then . . . and even now. I'd like to think I might have a chance for a future with you, Belinda, and —"

Belinda held up her trembling hand. "Please don't say anything more, Monroe. You must realize that I'm still in mourning." She pointed to her black dress.

"I am well aware, but in four more months, it'll be a year since Vernon's death, and —"

Belinda shook her head determinedly. "While that is true, it won't change the way I feel about my late husband, or about you."

Laying a hand against his chest, Monroe drew a noisy breath. "I understand, and if my coming around so often is a problem, then I'll back off." A slight smile formed on his lips. "I'm a patient man, so I will wait till you're not wearing mourning clothes

61

and feel ready to begin a new relationship."

Belinda pressed her lips together tightly. *Doesn't this man understand? Why is he not getting it?*

She cleared her throat and looked directly at him. "I may never be ready to begin a new relationship, Monroe."

"Then again, after some time's passed, you might change your mind."

*This man is relentless. I hope I don't weaken and give in to his influence.* "Although anything is possible, it's doubtful that I will ever change my mind, Monroe. I loved my husband very much and still do." She paused to collect her thoughts and make sure her words were spoken correctly. "I hope you understand, but it would be in everyone's best interest if you didn't come around asking about us."

He winced, as though he'd been slapped. "I've only asked about you because I care and am worried about your welfare. And I thought maybe now that Vernon is gone, I might have a chance with you."

"I appreciate your concern, but as I said before —"

"There's no need to say another word. I understand completely." Monroe pushed back his chair and stood. "I won't come around anymore unless I need to buy something from the greenhouse." He hurried from the room so quickly Belinda didn't have a chance to say anything else.

When she heard the back door open and click shut, she lowered her head and closed her eyes. She'd hurt Monroe's feelings and felt bad about that, but it was necessary to let him know where he stood. Unless sometime in the future Belinda changed her mind, she would never have a relationship with Monroe Esh. From some of the things he had said, it almost seemed as if he'd been waiting for Vernon to die.

She pulled her fingers into her palms. *Oh, surely that couldn't be possible. No decent man would wait for a woman in hopes that her husband would pass away.*

"Did we have company?" Sylvia asked when she entered the kitchen a few minutes later. "I heard a horse and buggy pull into the yard, and then you speaking to Henry briefly. After that, I thought I heard you talking to someone else in here."

Belinda turned to face her daughter. "It was Monroe."

Sylvia frowned. "What did he want this time?"

"Said he came by to see how we were doing, and he seemed disappointed that we'd already eaten lunch."

63

Sylvia's gaze lifted upward. "That's not such a surprise. Whenever he comes around it's usually close to mealtime."

"Well, he won't be coming here again unless it's to buy something from the greenhouse."

"Oh?"

Belinda pointed to a chair at the table. "Have a seat and I'll tell you about it."

Sylvia did as asked, and Belinda sat in the chair beside her. She quickly went over everything that had transpired while Monroe was there. "I think I hurt his feelings, though."

Sylvia leaned close and gave Belinda a hug. "You did the right thing, Mom. I'm glad he took it so well and agreed to back off."

"I'm not really sure that he did take it well, but at least I finally got up the courage to speak my mind. By inviting Monroe to join us for meals and such, it probably seemed to him that I was interested in a personal relationship that could eventually lead to marriage." Belinda sighed. "There's a fine line between being courteous to people, and showing them so much kindness that they take advantage or expect something of you in return. I think that's what happened where Monroe was concerned. My being friendly and nice made him believe that he might have a future with me. And the fact that he'd mentioned that in four more months it'll be a year since your daed's death made me even more eager to put a stop to his pursuing me."

"I can't imagine you being married to someone other than Dad. It wouldn't seem right for another man to move in here and take over the role of your husband."

Belinda gave a nod. "I love your daed very much, and always will."

"I understand, because that's the way I feel about Toby. No one could ever take his place in my heart."

"I understand, Daughter. I wholeheartedly understand."

"What a lousy day I've had," Virginia mumbled. She'd decided to make something new for supper, and it was taking longer than she'd anticipated. *Earl won't be happy if he comes home and there's nothing ready to eat.*

The lamb roast she'd bought yesterday wasn't a tender cut, so she'd chopped it into smaller chunks to hurry it up. The microwave had been acting funny, so Virginia had put the baking potatoes in the oven, but they still weren't ready to serve.

Virginia walked from the kitchen out to

the living room. Looking at the front door, she stepped out onto the porch for some fresh air. She saw Amy come out of the house and get into an Amish buggy. The man with her looked familiar. *Hey, isn't that the fellow who reroofed our garage?* Virginia stared intently. *Yep, I think it is him.*

Virginia had met Jared when he'd come over to give them an estimate and had spoken to him again during the roofing process. He seemed like a nice young man, although she still wasn't too sure about the Amish people in general. In fact, when she had first seen Jared's horse and buggy parked in her and Earl's driveway, she'd nearly freaked, hoping the beast didn't do his business right there on the concrete. Virginia had felt sorry for the horse in a way. The poor animal having to work like it did, hauling people and work supplies around every day, seemed like animal abuse.

*But then what do I really know about horses?* she mused. Virginia had heard it said that horses, like mules, were beasts of burden and didn't mind the hard work of pulling a wagon or carriage.

*I just don't get the whole Plain life those Amish people live. Yet they seem content with it.* Shaking her head, Virginia moved away from the porch railing and went back into the house. After checking the potatoes and seeing that they still weren't done, she picked up her cell phone and called Earl. She wanted to catch him before he headed home from work.

Virginia punched in her husband's number and a few seconds later, he answered. "What's up, Virginia?"

"Well, the meal I thought would be good tonight isn't cooking so well, and it's taking longer than I expected."

"Don't worry about it. I'll pick up some take-out when I'm done here, which should be soon."

"Oh, that would be nice, because the oven isn't heating up well, and I'm sure that our microwave is completely shot."

"That's a bummer. Appliances don't last like they used to, and it may mean we'll have to buy a new microwave, or even another oven. I'll take a look at both when I get home. Gotta go for now, though. See you soon, Virginia."

"Okay, bye." She clicked off the phone and took a seat at the table. It didn't seem like Earl was upset, and for that, she was relieved. It never ceased to amaze Virginia how calm and understanding her husband could be.

Since Earl would be bringing take-out

home, there was no point in having the oven on. She turned it off, took the still-undercooked potatoes out of the oven and threw them in the garbage. By tomorrow evening, she'd hopefully have a new micro-wave, and then she could at least heat up something for them to eat.

# CHAPTER 6

Sylvia stood in the barn beside her horse, Sugar, wondering if she would ever work up the courage to take the mare out by herself. After Toby's death, Sylvia had sold his horse to her neighbors, Enos and Sharon Zook, who also kept an eye on her place. Henry had brought her horse over to Mom's place, where she'd been put in the barn. In the nine months Toby had been gone, Sylvia hadn't taken the horse out even once. Henry kept Sugar exercised and often took her on the road to run errands or make deliveries. Since he had no horse of his own and complained about Mom's horse being too slow, the arrangement for him to use Sylvia's mare had worked out well so far.

The thought of taking her horse and buggy out on the road by herself sent shivers of apprehension up Sylvia's spine. Although their family members' deaths hadn't been the fault of her father's horse,

69

the reality was that a horse and buggy couldn't compete with the power of a truck or any other motorized vehicle. One never knew what a vehicle on the road might do. Sylvia's sister could attest to that. While riding in Jared's carriage this past fall, a car driven by a teenage boy had spooked the horse, which could have ended in disaster. Fortunately, Jared had managed to get his horse under control before an accident occurred.

Sylvia gave Sugar's flanks a gentle pat. "I'm sorry if it seems like I've abandoned you."

The horse's ears flicked as if she was listening.

"Maybe someday, if I ever get over my fear of a potential accident, I'll take you for a ride somewhere."

"Let's do it now."

Sylvia whirled around at the sound of her sister's voice. "*Ach,* you startled me."

"Sorry, I wasn't trying to sneak up on you. I figured you would hear the barn door open and close."

Sylvia shook her head. "I didn't hear you come in at all."

Amy put her hand against the small of Sylvia's back. "If you want to go somewhere with the horse and buggy, I'll ride along to

70

help bolster your confidence."

Sylvia clutched her woolen shawl tightly around her neck. "I'd like to go over to my house and check on things, but I don't have the nerve to be the one in control of my *gaul*. When I first came out here to the barn, I thought maybe I could do it, but I didn't get Sugar any farther than taking her out of the stall and putting on her bridles before I realized that I'm definitely not ready." She paused to draw in a quick breath. "Even though Mom said she would watch the kinner while I was gone, I think I'll wait till Henry gets back from Seth's and see if he's willing to go over to the house with me. Of course, he will have to drive my horse."

"I can be in the driver's seat, and I'm more than willing to go over to the house with you."

"But I thought you were working on wedding plans this morning."

"I was, but I didn't plan to work on my lists all day." Amy glanced toward the front windows of the barn. "Since the snow we had at Christmas is almost gone, now's the perfect time to make the two-mile trip to your place. With this being the third week in January, you never know what kind of weather awaits us, so we need to take advantage of the nice day we're having."

"You're right, and we're likely to get a lot more snow before winter is over."

"That's true, so I'll hitch Sugar to your buggy, and you can go up to the house and let Mom know we'll be gone for a couple of hours."

"Okay, I'll grab some cardboard boxes from the utility room, in case there are some things I want to bring back with me."

"Sounds good. See you in a bit."

As Sylvia headed back to the house, a sense of thankfulness filled her soul. Amy had been supportive of her since Toby, Dad, and Abe had died. She was definitely a lot stronger emotionally than Sylvia. Her sister hadn't lost faith in God either.

*What will I do without my dear sister after she gets married?* Sylvia's throat constricted. *Amy might not have much time for me once she and Jared are married, and she may not even be able to work in the greenhouse anymore.*

*Clymer, New York*
"Have you talked to your mamm or any of your siblings lately?" Michelle asked when Ezekiel came into the house to get the lunchbox he'd left on the counter after heading out to his shop earlier that morning.

72

"Just a short message from Mom, which I found on the answering machine last evening. Sorry, I forget to mention it."

"That's okay. You were busy with paperwork for your business, and that was important."

"I was kinda busy, but I should have thought to tell you about her message."

"Did she say how things have been going for them lately?"

"Just said everyone was fine, and that most of their snow had melted." Ezekiel poured himself a cup of coffee, blew on it, and took a cautious drink. "She also mentioned that a group of young people would be coming to their house this Friday evening to roast hot dogs and marshmallows around the fire-pit."

"That sounds like fun. I wish we could join them."

Ezekiel couldn't miss the wistful expression on his wife's face as she stood near the kitchen sink, with her back facing the window. Was it the idea of sitting around a bonfire she longed for, or the pleasure of spending time with his family in Strasburg? He was about to ask, when Michelle posed another question.

"Did your mamm say anything about Monroe? Has he been back to see her after she made it clear that she has no interest in him romantically?"

Ezekiel shook his head. "She didn't mention Monroe at all, but if he had been coming around, I'm sure she would have mentioned it. I was pleased when Mom called us the day after she'd let him know where he stood." Ezekiel took another drink from his mug. "That gave me one less thing to worry about."

"Jah, me too. I hate to say this, but I have to wonder if Mr. Esh has more on his mind than a romantic interest in your mother."

Ezekiel tipped his head to one side. "What other kind of interest?"

"A financial one. He might want the greenhouse for himself."

"You could be right, I suppose, but if I have anything to say about it, that's never going to happen."

Michelle pushed a wisp of auburn hair back under her heart-shaped head covering. "Since your mother put Monroe in his place, I don't think we have to worry about him anymore."

"I hope not." Ezekiel pursed his lips. "From the moment I met that man, I had an uneasy feeling about him."

Michelle came over and kissed his cheek. "You're such a *schmaert* man."

74

He pulled Michelle into his arms and held her close. "I don't know how smart I am about other things, but I was schmaert enough to talk you into marrying me."

She tipped her head back and looked up at him. "You didn't have to talk me into anything. Besides, I was the schmaert one for saying yes to becoming your fraa."

*Strasburg*

When Sylvia opened the front door to her house and stepped inside, she dropped the cardboard boxes on the floor in the hallway. As she entered the living room, memories overwhelmed her like water from a broken dam. In spite of her efforts to stay calm, tears started flowing. "Oh Sister . . ." She gulped on a sob. "It's so hard for me to be here anymore."

"It's okay. Let the cleansing tears fall." Amy led Sylvia over to the couch, and they both took a seat.

"I . . . I'm sorry for being such a big bawling baby." Sylvia took a tissue from the end table beside the couch and wiped her nose. "It's just so hard being here in the home I shared with Toby and knowing I'll never have that kind of happiness again."

Amy clasped Sylvia's hand. "I understand how coming here must make you feel sad.

Have you considered selling the place and staying with Mom permanently?"

Sylvia scooted back against the couch and rested her head. "I have given it some consideration, but the idea of letting the house go to strangers doesn't sit well with me."

"Maybe you could find a suitable renter. Have you thought of that as an option?"

"No, not really, but it might be a possibility." Sylvia blotted the tears from her cheeks with another tissue. "My biggest concern with renting the house would be who might want to rent it. I've heard terrible stories about people renting homes and leaving the owner with a big mess when they moved out. Some folks don't pay their rent on time or at all. So it might be a bigger challenge to become a landlord than to just sell the house and be done with it."

"I understand. My advice is to pray about the situation and ask God to help you decide what the best course of action would be."

Sylvia gave no response as she massaged the bridge of her nose. The truth was, she saw little help in praying. Even after so many months had passed since the accident that took their loved ones, her faith in God had not been restored, and she doubted it ever would be strong again. There was a time when she did have faith, and believed in miracles, but it seemed so long ago.

She glanced around the room at all the familiar furniture. "What would I do with all these things if I did sell the house?"

"You might be able to take a few things over to Mom's, and maybe Jared and I could buy some pieces of your furniture and other items to put in our new home."

Sylvia blinked rapidly. "Now there's a thought."

"You mean about us buying some of your things?"

"No, I mean what if you and Jared bought my house, or even rented it from me? Nothing's been decided about where you will live yet, right?"

"Well, no, but . . ." Amy's voice trailed off, and then she picked up her sentence again. "Wouldn't it be difficult for you to come over here and visit? You said a few minutes ago that it was hard for you to be here anymore. I would feel bad if you didn't want to come over to my place to see me, and if we had a family function here you would not be left out."

Sylvia leaned forward with her arms against her knees. "I — I hadn't considered any of that. You're right, Amy, it would be most difficult for me to come to the home that had been mine and Toby's and see you and Jared living here happily together. It would be a reminder of how much I have lost." Sylvia rubbed her forehead. "Am I being *eegesinnisch* to think this way?"

Amy gave Sylvia's back several light pats and made slow circles with her fingers in a gentle rub. "You're not being selfish at all. Only you know what you can and cannot deal with. Besides, since Jared and I will be just starting out, we can't really afford to buy a home yet. We'll most likely look for something inexpensive to rent."

"Which could be my place, if I wasn't so emotional about being in this house."

"Don't worry about it, Sister. Even if you were willing to rent your home to us, our wedding's over seven months from now, and you'd have to continue to leave the house unattended all that time." Amy continued to rub Sylvia's back until she sat up.

"I'll give this some more thought. Maybe I'll end up selling the place and be free of all the memories that haunt me. Right now, let's get busy and gather up all of the things I want to take back with me today. I don't want to be here any longer than necessary."

"Let's go outside and get some fresh air."

Belinda bundled her grandkids, as well as herself, in warm attire. Allen and Rachel seemed eager to head out with Grandma as their voices raised a couple of octaves.

Once outdoors, the sun provided some warmth. They walked around the yard where snow had concentrated in more of the shaded areas. Allen's boots crunched in the snow as he made his way over to the frozen birdbath. He touched the solid water and slid his gloved fingers across the surface. "Look, *Grossmammi* — I'm skating."

"You sure are." Belinda smiled as she pulled Rachel across the yard on the wooden sled Sylvia had used as a child. *I wonder how my daughter is doing right now. She gets so emotional whenever she returns to the home she and Toby shared.*

Belinda was well aware that Sylvia still struggled with the past, but she tried her best to raise the children with love and tender care.

She stopped pulling the sled and bowed her head. *Lord, please keep mending Sylvia's heart and allow her to find peace and joy in her life again.*

Belinda's eyes opened and she looked at her precious grandchildren, so innocent, and with no knowledge of the inner struggles their mother faced on a daily basis. *I must keep hoping and praying that each member of my family will heal a little, day by day. The Lord has provided for our needs, despite each one of the setbacks and the vandalism on our property. Even so, I will continue to trust Him in the days ahead and not give in to despair.*

# CHAPTER 7

"Being here this evening and sitting around the bonfire talking and singing is so much fun. Danki for inviting me and Rudy to join you." Amy's friend Lydia spoke with excitement as the two of them carried hot dogs and buns from the house to the area where the fire had been started by Jared and the other young men present.

Amy smiled. "I'm glad you could both come. It wouldn't have been the same without you." She leaned closer to Lydia. "I'm real happy that you agreed to be one of my witnesses at Jared's and my wedding."

"I'm looking forward to it. Now I have a question. Will you be one of my witnesses?"

Amy's fingers touched her parted lips. "Are you and Rudy planning to be married?"

"Jah, but not till November."

Amy clasped her friend's hand. "That's *wunderbaar,* Lydia. Congratulations, and

81

jah, I would be honored to be one of your witnesses."

"Thank you. We're very excited about it, and even more so since both sets of our parents have given us their blessing."

"When your folks approve of the man you want to marry, that does make it much easier for everyone."

"For sure." Lydia placed the packages of buns on the picnic table near the fire. "I bet your mamm approved of Jared from the beginning of your courtship."

"Jah and so did my daed." Amy drew a breath and released it slowly. "It makes me sad when I think about not having him at our wedding."

"It is a shame, but if he was here, I'm sure he'd approve and be happy for you."

"I agree." Amy placed the hot dogs next to the ketchup and mustard that had already been brought out. "I invited Sylvia to join us this evening, but she seemed hesitant and made up some excuse about not wanting to leave the kinner."

"Wouldn't your mamm watch Allen and Rachel?"

"Of course she would, and Sylvia knows it, but I believe she's unwilling to allow herself the freedom to have a little fun."

"How come?"

"Because she hasn't let go of the anger and emotional pain she's felt since Toby, Dad, and Abe died. Sometimes I think my sister wallows in her self-pity, hoping to somehow drown out the pain."

"That's too bad. I'll remember to pray more often for her."

"Danki. Sylvia, like the rest of us, needs a lot of prayer."

Sylvia had set up a tray of marshmallows, chocolate bars, and graham crackers for Amy to take out when her guests were ready for dessert. Now bored, she walked from the kitchen into the dining room. Her mother hadn't come down downstairs yet. *She's probably enjoying her time with the children while I'm down here moping. Guess I should have been the one to be put to bed this evening.*

Muffled sounds of conversation and laughter could be heard from the goings-on outside, while Sylvia remained alone with her thoughts. *It seems like only days ago when that was me outside with all my friends. Toby and I were courting and so happy together. I remember the bonfire and how the glow from it made my beloved's eyes sparkle.*

Sylvia placed both hands against her chest. *Toby captured my heart from the first moment we met, and the more time I spent with him, the more I knew he was the only one for me.* She expelled a lingering sigh. *We made so many good memories at gatherings like the one going on outside. Those were precious times of bonding with our friends and each other.*

Sylvia's eyes watered, obscuring her vision for a moment. Knowing what she did now, Sylvia wouldn't have changed a thing. She felt blessed to have had those special times with Toby during their courting days and after they were married. The sweet children upstairs were also a blessing to her. Sylvia had no regrets about becoming a mother. Her only regret was that Allen and Rachel had no father to help nurture and guide them into adulthood.

She continued to wander around the room barefooted, until boisterous laughter caught her attention. Sylvia paused at the dining-room window, watching the glow of the bonfire outside. Amy and her friends seemed to be having so much fun. She felt a stab of envy. Her carefree, fun-loving days were behind her. Other than spending time with her children and sometimes laughing at their cute antics, Sylvia had little to feel joyous about. In a few months, it would be time to put her black mourning clothes aside, but her heart would still long for what she had lost.

Sylvia's mother came into the room and joined her at the window. "Looks like they're having a good time out there."

"Jah. It would seem so."

"The kinner are in bed, sleeping soundly now, so why don't you join your sister and her friends?"

Sylvia shook her head. "Henry was invited and he declined."

"That's only because he was invited to spend the night at his friend Seth's place tonight."

"Well, I'm not going out there. I wouldn't fit in."

"Of course you would. You're not that much older than those who have come here tonight."

"I'm a widow, and those four couples are all courting, Mom. Surely you must understand how displaced I would feel, sitting among them and trying to join their conversation."

"No more than I would, but Amy invited me to join their gathering also."

"Then by all means, you should put on some warm clothes and go outside. I need to stay here where I can hear Allen and Rachel if they should wake up and need me."

85

Sylvia turned away from the window. "Think I'll go back to the living room and look at the book Henry loaned me on bird-watching. I might learn something new about the birds found in this area."

Mom's eyes widened. "I didn't realize you were interested in birding."

"I'm not really, but Henry's so fascinated with it, and he seemed to want to share his interest with me, so I thought I'd at least look at the book. Maybe when the weather warms up a bit, I might sit outside more and study the birds that come into our yard. Henry sure enjoys doing that. I've seen him sitting in the loft of the barn, looking out the open doors, usually with a pair of binoculars in his hands."

Mom shook her head. "I don't like him sitting up there. If he gets too close to the edge, it could be dangerous for him."

Sylvia figured it was time for a change of topic. Lately Mom had been a bit overprotective, and not just of Henry. She worried more and voiced her opinion about things Amy, Sylvia, and the children did too. Hopefully when Mom got busy in the greenhouse again, things would go back to the way they were and her concentration would revert to other things.

■ ■ ■ ■

Virginia hurried to get the wonderful cut of meat she'd cooked on the table. She'd followed the instructions to the letter and felt sure it would be nice and tender. She placed their dishes on the table and poured brewed tea over ice in the glasses.

When Virginia carried the carved meat to the table and brought out the vegetables cooked in beef broth, her mouth watered. The rolls came last, steaming underneath the foil covering them.

Once everything was on the table, she stepped into the hallway and stopped at the mirror to fluff up her hair. Then she checked the new lipstick she'd put on earlier. "Earl, it's time eat."

"I'm coming, dear. The meal smells tasty, and you look nice too." He chuckled. "I saw you primping in the mirror."

Virginia grinned as she followed her husband to the table. As soon as they took their seats, she passed him the roast. Her mouth watered once again as she dished up her food.

Earl smiled as he loaded his plate and took a first bite. "This is a pretty good pot roast you fixed this evening." He smiled at Virginia from across the table. "You did a good job with supper."

She grinned right back at him. "I'm glad you like it, but I can't take all the credit. If you hadn't bought a new oven and microwave, nothing but the stovetop would cook well in this kitchen."

"I really had no choice, since I didn't want to get take-out every night." He wiggled his dark brows at her.

She rolled her eyes. "It figures all you'd be thinkin' about is satisfying your stomach."

"I think of lots of other things too."

"Like what?"

"My job and making my quota of cars sold every month."

"That's important all right; or else we wouldn't have money to buy food and pay the bills." She ate some of her microwave-baked potatoes and blotted her lips with a napkin. "Do you want me to look for a job so there's not so much pressure on you to provide for us? I could see if one of the stores in the area might be hiring."

Earl shook his head. "With the trouble you have with your leg, you'd never last eight, six, or even four hours of having to stand on your feet."

"I could look for a sit-down job, although

I don't know what it could be."

"There's no need for that. I've been providing for us since we got married, and I will continue to do so."

"You're such a nice man — always thinking of me."

"That's 'cause I love you, Ginny."

"I love you too, but please don't call me Ginny. My first husband used to call me that, but I've always preferred to be called Virginia."

"Okay, got it."

Virginia didn't want any reminders of her past or the man she had come to despise. She'd never admitted it to anyone or even said it out loud, but she'd been relieved when her first husband died.

"Sure is a nice evening for a bonfire." Earl's comment pulled Virginia's thoughts aside.

"Huh? What does a bonfire have to do with anything?"

"When I arrived home from work and got out of my truck, I noticed there was a bonfire going across the street. Figured it must be some kind of a young people's gathering at the Kings' place."

She wrinkled her nose. "More horse droppings in the road, no doubt."

"That could be a good thing. If I go out

there and shovel it up, we'll have more manure for our compost pile."

She pressed her hands against her ears. "This is not good table talk."

"You brought it up, not me."

Virginia shrugged and let her hands fall into her lap. "Guess I did. From now on, I'll have to be more careful how I choose my words."

*Gratz, Pennsylvania*

Dennis Weaver sat in the barn, with a gas lantern above him, staring at his father's empty horse stall. It was unbelievable to think that the horse had died the same day as his dad.

Dennis, now thirty-one, had loved being around horses since he was a young boy. He had a special way with them too. With a little patience and time well spent, he could get most horses to do pretty much anything he wanted. While Dennis wasn't what some would call a "horse whisperer," he had an understanding of them, which led to respect and obedience on the horses' part.

In time, when many of the Plain people in his community saw what he could do with his own family's horses, they began to offer him payment to train their horses to pull their buggies. By the age of sixteen, after

Dennis finished his eighth-grade education, he trained horses part-time when he wasn't helping his dad on the farm. As more people moved into the area, his business picked up. Unfortunately, there weren't enough Amish in the area to provide Dennis with a full-time income. Even after his dad passed away and his brother, Gerald, took over the farm, Dennis helped out.

His greatest wish was to not only train horses fulltime, but raise them as well. Dennis was convinced, however, that he'd have to move to an area where there were more people in need of his type of services if he wanted his business to succeed. So he'd asked around and decided that Lancaster County would be a good place to move. There was really nothing keeping him here. He had no wife or children — just his mother and four siblings, who were all married and had families of their own.

Dennis felt secure in the knowledge that if he moved away, Mom would be cared for. She'd have his brother and three sisters, as well as ten grandchildren to fuss over and spend time with. Soon after Dad died, Gerald had built a *daadihaus* for Mom, and then he and his family moved into the larger home that used to be their parents'.

Dennis moved from the empty stall over

to where his own horse was kept. "How's it goin' today, Midnight? Are ya ready for me to extinguish the lantern?"

Midnight whinnied as if in response, and then the gentle gelding nuzzled Dennis's hand with his nose.

He grinned and rubbed the horse behind his ears.

Dennis stood by the stall door for a few minutes, contemplating his future. He'd grown up in Dauphin County but was more than ready for a change. *Maybe the Lancaster area would be a good place for me to relocate.*

Dennis knew only a few people in Lancaster County. He had a friend he'd gone to school with who lived in Ronks now.

*Maybe I'll contact James and see if I can stay with him for a few weeks, until I find a place of my own or a house I can rent. It would need to have enough property where I could train horses and hopefully raise a few of my own.*

Although Dennis had saved up some money over the years, he didn't have enough to pay cash for a home and didn't want to go into debt. Renting a place would be a better choice for now.

*Think I'll give James a call in the morning and see what he says about my idea to relocate to Lancaster County. If he thinks it would be a good move for me and offers to let me stay there for a while, I'll pack up my things and make the move by early spring.*

Dennis turned off the lamp overhead and strolled out of the barn, letting the flashlight he now held be his guide back to the house. He paused and stared up at the twinkling stars overhead. *I have no idea what the future holds for me, but anything would be better than staying here with all the haunting memories from the past that are never far from my mind.*

# CHAPTER 8

*Strasburg*

*This is one of my favorite recipes.* Sylvia spread the crust batter for Cherry Melt Away Bars into a 9" x 13" inch pan. Picking up a quart of cherry pie filling Mom had bought at the store recently, she poured it on top. Normally, when the pie cherries in Mom's yard ripened, Sylvia and Amy helped to make the filling and processed it all in canning jars. But due to losing their loved ones in the spring and the busyness that followed, they hadn't done anything with the fruit. So the whole tree had been a happy place for the robins that came into their yard. Hopefully, this year things would go better in that regard and they'd have plenty of home-canned cherry pie filling to use in special desserts.

As Sylvia beat the eggs whites with cream of tartar, she glanced at her children sitting on a throw rug across the room playing with some pots and pans as though they were drums. In times past, this kind of noise would have given Sylvia a headache, but today she wasn't bothered by the pounding. It was nice to see Allen and Rachel, who were only two and a half years apart, getting along well with each other.

Once the egg whites were stiff enough, she gradually beat in some sugar and vanilla, then spread it over the filling she'd previously put on top of the crust. Before sprinkling chopped walnuts over the top, Sylvia paused to look out the kitchen window. One of her guilty pleasures was walnuts, of which she grabbed a handful to munch on. While pausing to enjoy the crunchy texture and hearty flavor, she saw Mom heading in the direction of the greenhouse and Amy going down the driveway toward the phone shed. They both walked with a spring in their step, with arms swinging at their sides. No doubt they felt the exhilaration of the lovely weather that had greeted them on this twenty-first day of March. From the way Mom and Amy had talked during breakfast, they looked forward to opening the greenhouse today.

*Better them than me,* Sylvia thought as she sprinkled the nuts and opened the oven door. *If I had to work in the greenhouse today,*

*I'd be on edge and thinking the whole time about how my precious little ones were getting along with whomever I had hired to watch them.*

Sylvia closed up the bag of walnuts and put it away. Then she tossed the empty cherry pie can in the garbage and began cleaning up the mess she'd made on the counter. When she glanced out the window again, she saw what looked like a mockingbird sitting on a branch in the maple tree. Its feathers appeared to be gray.

Curious, she left the kitchen and found the bird book on the coffee table in the living room. Sylvia thumbed through the index for mockingbirds, eager to know whether the bird she'd seen was what she believed it to be.

She found the correct page and noticed some different colored pictures of mockingbirds. One in particular caught her attention. It looked similar to what she'd seen in the tree, although she couldn't be sure and would wait to talk to Henry about it.

*When Mom and Amy get done for the day, maybe I'll ask one of them if they'd be willing to keep an eye on the kinner while I take a walk to look for birds.* Sylvia placed the book back on the coffee table. *If Henry's not busy this afternoon, maybe he'll want to get out his binoculars and join me. That would be better, especially since he knows more about birding than I do right now.*

Excitement bubbled in Belinda's soul as she placed the Open sign on the front door of the greenhouse. *I hope we have another good year.*

She hardly got much sleep last night, with her mind busy thinking about everything that needed to be done. She always had a nervous stomach on opening day. It reminded her in some ways of the first day of school. Belinda knew the feeling would wear off soon enough, and she'd be as good as rain again. What a relief to have winter behind them and be able to do the work she enjoyed so much.

Of course, she had spent some time out here during the colder months, tending to seedlings in pots and making sure the heat in the building remained at an even temperature. Plants and trees also needed watering, but not as often as they did during the warmer months.

Belinda looked forward to their first customers of the day, and she hoped they would stay busy until closing time.

She glanced at the small clock sitting on a shelf under the checkout counter, wondering what was taking Amy so long. She'd gone to the phone shed to check for messages and said she'd come to the greenhouse as soon as she was done. Either there had been a lot of messages that needed to be responded to, or Amy had taken the time to see if their mail might have come early.

It didn't really matter if Amy wasn't here at the moment, since there weren't any customers yet. Henry was still in the barn feeding the animals, but he should be here soon too, and then Belinda would have plenty of help.

While she waited, Belinda walked up and down the aisles, making sure everything was placed appropriately so customers would have no problem finding whatever they'd come in to buy. The shelves full of seed packets had been fully stocked; jars of honey and jam sat ready for purchase; bulbs that needed to be planted in the spring had a place of their own; and all the solar lights, fountains, and outdoor items were positioned so people would see them as soon as they walked through the door. When the weather got warmer, they would move the outdoor items, now in the greenhouse, to a special area outside.

When Jared had no roofing jobs to do this winter, he'd made a small shed with double doors that housed many gift items Sylvia and Amy had made. Even Henry had gotten into the act by painting some horseshoes for people to hang up as decorations. It amazed Belinda what things the tourists would buy because they'd been made by the Amish. At least, that's what she'd heard many people say.

An image of Monroe popped into her head. She wondered if he would come by to purchase something and ask how they were doing. Belinda wasn't ready to deal with him. Monroe could be so pushy, and he didn't take hints too well. Regardless, she'd have to walk that path when and if it happened. For now, she needed to concentrate on running the greenhouse in an orderly fashion.

Once Belinda was certain that everything was ready for customers, she returned to the checkout counter and took a seat on the wooden stool. While she waited for Henry and Amy to show up, she would make a list of some things she hoped to get done in the greenhouse this week, in addition to getting caught up on some chores in her home.

*Ronks, Pennsylvania*
Dennis grinned at his friend James from across the table. "Your fraa sure makes some

tasty *pannekuche.*"

James nodded as he forked a piece into his mouth. "You're right about that. Alice's pancakes are the best. You can tell her how much you liked them when she comes back to the kitchen after feeding the *boppli.*"

"I will." Dennis gestured to the newspaper beside his plate. He'd been looking through the ad section to see if there were any homes in the Strasburg area that he could rent. He'd found a few, but none of them had the large property he needed. He could probably move into a smaller house for now and then offer horse training to people in the area, but he'd have to go to their property to do it. If he went that route, the idea of raising his own horses would have to be put on hold.

"Would it be okay if I used one of your horse and buggies for a while today, since mine haven't arrived yet?"

"Sure, no problem. I'll be working in my shop all day. I have lots of orders for windows and doors, so I won't need my gaul or the *waegli.*"

"Danki, I appreciate that." Dennis picked up the newspaper. "Think I'll take this with me today so I can drive by some of the places listed. Afterward, I may do a bit of bird-watching. It'll be interesting to see which birds are common here compared to what I've seen up in Dauphin County."

"Maybe they're pretty much the same," James responded. "Strasburg is only a few hours from Gratz, you know."

"True, but the lay of the land is different. Some of the birds I saw up there may be scarce down here, and vice-versa."

"Well, you know more than I do about it." James pushed his chair away from the table. "I'd best be getting out to work in my shop. If I don't see you till suppertime, I hope you have a successful day."

"I hope your day goes well too." Dennis smiled up at his friend. "Once again, I appreciate you letting me stay here temporarily. With any luck, it won't be much longer and I'll be out on my own."

*Strasburg*

After checking for mail, and finding none, Amy went to the phone shed and took a seat. *What was that I saw moving there in the shadow near my feet? I hope it isn't a* maus.

Amy froze inside the small cubical, until her eyes honed in on what she'd seen. *It's not a mouse — only a toad. I can deal with that.* She chuckled and shooed the little fellow out the door.

The green button on the answering machine blinked rapidly, letting her know there were messages. The first one was from Brad Fuller, sharing good news. Sara had given birth to a nine pound baby boy yesterday morning. The infant had been over a week late, and mother and son were both doing well. They'd named their child, Herschel Clarence, after Sara and Brad's fathers.

Amy smiled. She was happy for the Fullers and looked forward to having children of her own someday. She would call and leave a message of congratulations, and maybe some evening in the next week or so, they could hire a driver to take them to Lancaster so they could see the new baby.

Amy listened to a few more messages from people checking to see what day and time the greenhouse would be opening. She was pleased that folks seemed eager to have the greenhouse up and running for business again.

The last message, although a bit garbled, caused Amy to take a sharp intake of breath. "You need to sell out and move, before it's too late."

Amy replayed it several more times to be sure she'd heard the words correctly. Each time she listened, it became clearer that someone wanted them gone.

She sat several moments, feeling rooted to

her chair. *Who is this person who wants to shut our business down, even to the point of saying we should move?*

Once Amy gained control of her emotions well enough to stand on her shaky legs, she flung the door open and ran all the way to the greenhouse. She found Mom inside, sitting behind the counter, but there was no sign of Henry.

"Daughter, your face is whiter than snow." Mom's brows drew together. "Is something wrong?"

Amy hesitated. *I don't want to add more worry to Mom's already full plate. There's been enough to deal with so far, but she has a right to know.*

Making no mention of the message from Brad, Amy told her mother about the threatening call.

Mom gasped and covered her mouth with both hands.

"Don't you think we ought to let the sheriff know about this?" Up to this point, Mom had refused to divulge the previous incidents to anyone but their immediate family — excluding Ezekiel. She'd remained insistent that he should know nothing about the vandalism, for if he knew, he'd insist on moving back to Strasburg.

Mom removed her hands and spoke to

Amy in a strained voice. "Tell them what? We have no idea who left that message, so there's no evidence for anyone at the sheriff's office to go on."

Amy shifted her weight from one foot to the other. "Even so . . ."

Mom leaned forward, lowered her head into the palms of her hands, and massaged her forehead. "When the vandalism stopped last fall, I thought it was all behind us. Now with the phone threat we received, I fear more destruction to our property will follow, and I — I don't know what we should do."

"Pray. We need to do a lot of praying," Amy responded.

"Jah, for sure." Mom clasped Amy's arm. "Let's not say anything to Henry or Sylvia about the threatening message you discovered."

"How come?"

"You know your *bruder* — he tends to blab things when he should keep quiet." Mom shifted on her stool. "And Sylvia would be troubled if she knew about the message. There's no point in telling either of them because they — especially Sylvia — would only worry." She rubbed her arms briskly, as though she'd been hit by a sudden chill. "And for sure, we don't want Ezekiel to

104

know about the phone call we received. You know how he'd respond to that."

"He'd be ready to sell out and move back to Strasburg."

"Exactly. So, unless I change my mind about telling anyone, mum's the word. Understood?"

Amy gave a slow nod. "I understand."

# CHAPTER 9

Tossing another old T-shirt into the bag she
held, Virginia scratched her head. Ever since
she and Earl had moved here, she'd wanted
to go through the closet and discard some
of her older clothes but hadn't taken the
time.

She slid a few tops off their hangers. *I'd
like to go out and do some shopping. Even
living in this small community, a gal needs to
look presentable.*

Virginia continued to fill the sack and
stopped when a dress from the past came
into view. "Oh, now, this needs to go. I can't
believe it's even still in the mix." She held
up the dowdy, navy-blue dress. She'd worn
it during her first marriage, and seeing it
now was a negative reminder of the past.

"Goodbye." She stuffed the dress deeply
into the bag. "Think I'll quit with this one."
All the clothes needed to go to the local
thrift shop, but Virginia would wait until

she'd gone through everything first.

Growing hungry, she stowed the bag in a corner of the closet, closed the door, and made her way to the kitchen. She'd been on her feet too long and should have sat on the bed to do her sorting.

In the kitchen, Virginia opened the refrigerator to see what she might fix for supper this evening, when her cell phone rang. She closed the door and limped across the room to pick up the phone.

Virginia recognized the number and quickly answered. "Hey, Stella. How's it going?"

"Everything's fine here. How about you?"

"Same as usual. Nothing exciting, that's for sure." Virginia reached down to rub her throbbing knee. "Unless you call listening to the steady *clippity-clop* of horses' hooves exciting."

"Still getting lots of horse-and-buggy traffic on your road, huh?"

"Yeah, and now that the greenhouse across the road is open for business again, the noise will only increase. There have been cars, trucks, and of course, smelly horses pulling Amish buggies going past our house today."

"Guess there's never a dull moment."

"Yeah, and sometimes I think I'm goin'

out of my mind."

"Say, I've been thinking it's about time that I come to Pennsylvania and pay you a visit. Would it work out for you, or are you too busy with other things?"

Virginia snorted. "Not hardly. Most of my days are spent watching game shows on TV and working crossword puzzles, although yesterday I washed all the windows, inside and out. And today I started sorting through old clothes." She groaned "Big mistake, and I'm paying for it now."

"Your bum leg?"

"Yep." Virginia pulled out a chair at the table and sat. "Most evenings are just as boring. After supper, it's watching television or working crossword puzzles again, while I listen to Earl snoring up a storm from his easy chair. So feel free to come anytime. It'll be a welcome change for me."

"How about a week from next Monday? Since your hubby will be at work during the days, maybe he won't mind an extra person in the house."

Virginia perked right up. "Sounds great, Stella. How long can you stay?"

"Maybe three days, if that's okay. Sure don't want to wear out my welcome."

"Not a chance. I'll look forward to seeing you."

"As you know, there's a meadow on the other side of our neighbor's property, and it's a good place to spot birds," Henry said as he and Sylvia walked along the shoulder of the road. "So let's head over that way first."

"Okay, but I don't want to go too far or be gone too long, because I need to be back in time to help fix supper," Sylvia replied.

"Didn't ya hear what Mom said before we left? She and Amy are gonna take care of fixin' supper this evening, and we'll eat a little later than usual."

"I did hear that, but I would feel guilty if I wasn't there to help."

"You oughta get over that, Sister, because you have the right to have a little fun once in a while."

Sylvia wasn't sure how much fun this little trek would be, but she offered no response to her brother's comment.

As they neared the clearing, Henry pointed to an Amish man holding a pair of binoculars up to his face. "Looks like someone else had the same idea as us, and I'm pretty sure he must've spotted some kind of interesting bird on the branch of that bush over there." He lifted his own binoculars and took a look. "Yep, I was right. There's an eastern kingbird." He handed the field glasses to Sylvia and pointed. "Here, take a look. It's a gray-black bird with a white belly and chin."

She looked in the direction he'd pointed, but all she saw in her vision was the Amish man's straw hat, sitting atop a full head of dark hair.

Sylvia lowered her hands and handed the binoculars back to Henry. "I didn't see any sign of the bird." She made no mention of the Amish man's head.

"It's right there." Henry stood next to her and held the lenses in front of her eyes. "Do ya see it now?"

She shook her head.

"Oh, for goodness' sakes. Are ya lookin' where I pointed?"

"I thought I was."

"Then ya must be completely blind." He puffed out his cheeks and groaned.

"Don't speak to me like that," she snapped. "I am not blind, and I'm not stupid."

"Never said you were."

"The way you spoke to me, in that disgusted tone of voice, made it seem like you thought I was *dumm*."

"Well, I don't think you're dumb. I just can't understand why you're not able to see the kingbird."

"I'll try again." Sylvia held the binoculars close to her face.

"Don't bother. The bird's gone now anyways. Let's walk into the meadow a ways farther and see what other birds we can find."

"Okay." Sylvia was glad she'd worn a pair of sturdy shoes and her long black stockings.

As they approached the middle of the open field, the Amish man turned in their direction. "I thought I was alone till I heard voices." He glanced at Henry's binoculars. "Are you two bird-watchers, like me?"

Henry bobbed his head. "Don't recall seeing you around here before. Are you new to the area?"

"Jah. I've only been here a few days." He held out his hand. "My name's Dennis Weaver. I moved down a few days ago from Gratz." The man glanced at Sylvia, then back at Henry.

Henry clasped the man's hand. "Nice to meet you. My name is Henry King, and this is my sister Sylvia."

Dennis shook Sylvia's hand too. "Do you two come here often?"

Sylvia was about to respond, but Henry cut her off. "I've been here looking for birds, but this is my sister's first time. She's new to birding."

"I see." Dennis looked at Sylvia again, and this time he smiled.

Her cheeks warmed as she lowered her head a bit.

"So where are you staying?" Henry asked. "Do you own a place here in Strasburg? Did you bring your family here?"

"Henry, don't be so nosey." Sylvia bumped her brother's arm.

"It's okay. I don't mind." Dennis kept his attention on Henry now. "My mother and siblings live in Dauphin County, and I'm single, so I moved down here by myself. I'm currently staying with a friend in Ronks, but I have been looking for a place to rent that has some acreage with it."

"I own a home you might be interested in," Sylvia blurted out. "Maybe you'd like to look at it sometime." Her face grew warm. *Now what made me say that?*

With an eager expression, Dennis nodded. "That'd be great. How about tomorrow morning? Would that be too soon?"

"Umm . . . well . . ." Sylvia realized that she'd have to drive her horse and buggy over to her house if she agreed to meet him there

112

in the morning, and she'd need someone to watch the children while she was gone or bring them along, which would make it difficult to show the house.

"If it's going to be a problem, I understand."

"No, it's not a problem. Tomorrow morning won't work for me, but I could meet you at the house around five-thirty tomorrow evening."

"That'll be fine."

"If you have a pen and something for me to write on, I'll give you the address and also the phone number where I can be reached, in case you have to cancel for some reason."

"I have something to write with, but no paper." Dennis pulled a pen from the pocket of his dark-colored trousers. "I'll just write it here on my arm."

Sylvia bit back a chuckle. She'd never seen anyone use their arm instead of paper. When she could speak without laughing, she gave him the information, and he wrote it down on the inside of his left arm.

"We really should get going now." Sylvia looked at Henry.

"Jah, okay. Guess we'll have to do more bird-watching another day." He looked at Dennis. "It was nice meeting you, Mr.

113

Weaver."

"Nice meeting you too." Dennis returned his gaze to Sylvia. "I'll look forward to seeing you tomorrow."

All Sylvia could manage was a quick nod. She had no idea why she'd offered to let a total stranger look at her house with the idea of possibly renting it. *I don't know what came over me. I must be daft in the head.*

On the way home, Henry remained quiet for a while, before slowing his pace and clasping Sylvia's arm. "What were you thinking, agreeing to show that man your house? He's a complete stranger, and we know nothin' about him except where he's from."

"He seemed nice enough. I saw a kindness in his eyes. If he likes the place, I'm going to rent it to him."

"Why?"

"Because I can't keep expecting my neighbors to watch the place, and I'm never moving back there, so it doesn't make sense to let it sit empty any longer. Next month it'll be a year since the accident, Henry."

"I don't need that reminder."

"Sorry, but it's a fact, and I need to find some closure."

Henry kicked at a stone with his boot.

"Don't see how rentin' your house is gonna give you any closure."

"For one thing, I won't have to go over there anymore or worry about whether someone might break in and take things."

"I get that part, but havin' someone living in your house is not gonna bring an end to your grief."

"I realize that, but having someone living in the house will give me a sense of peace."

"So you're set on doin' this, assuming Mr. Weaver likes the place and wants to rent it?"

"Jah."

Henry shook his head. "Oh boy. Our mamm's not gonna like it when she hears what your plans are."

"Please don't say anything to her, Henry. I'm the one who should tell her, since I'll need to ask if she or Amy can watch the kinner for me tomorrow." She stopped walking and reached over to touch his arm. "I do have one favor to ask."

"What's that?"

"Would you mind taking me over to my house tomorrow to meet Mr. Weaver? I wouldn't feel right about meeting him there alone. Besides, as you know I'm not comfortable taking the horse and buggy out by myself."

He lifted his shoulders in a brief shrug. "Sure, why not? If Mom knows I'll be goin' along, she's less likely to make a big deal of it."

"My thoughts exactly." Sylvia tapped his shoulder. "Oh, and Henry, before I forget . . . danki for going with me today to look for birds. It was an interesting adventure."

"Well, we only found one specific bird, but sure, no problem. Besides, the other day you told me about the gray bird you'd seen. I'd hoped we'd both get to see it today, and I could be sure it was a mockingbird. So anytime you wanna go birding again, just let me know."

She gave a nod. "I definitely will, and hopefully there's another pair of field glasses around the house for me to use when we do go out again."

As Dennis traveled back to his friend's place in Ronks, he tried to figure out if the young woman he'd met was married or single. There'd been no mention of a husband, but it seemed odd that she would own a place to rent out. Maybe some relative, like a grandparent, had died and left Sylvia their home and land, and rather than selling it or moving there herself, she'd chosen to rent it out.

There were so many questions Dennis wished he had asked, and maybe he would when he met up with Sylvia at her house tomorrow.

While Henry ran out to the barn to make sure his dog was fed, Sylvia hurried into the house. She found her mother and sister in the kitchen scurrying about, and the table had already been set.

"You're back sooner than we expected," Mom said. "Didn't you and Henry find any interesting birds?"

"Just one that's worth mentioning. Although I never actually saw it. Henry spotted the bird through the binoculars, but for some reason, I could not locate it. All I saw through the field glasses was an Amish man's straw hat."

Amy stopped what she was doing and turned to look at Sylvia. "Was the hat on the ground?"

"No, the man was wearing it." Sylvia glanced around the room, and when she didn't see Rachel or Allen, she said, "Where are the kinner? I figured with supper being made, they'd both be in the kitchen wanting to play with pots and pans."

"They're in the living room, playing quite nicely," Mom replied. "Now what were you saying about an Amish man's hat?"

Sylvia explained about meeting Dennis Weaver, and how she'd offered to let him look at her house as a possible renter.

Mom's eyes widened as she folded her arms across her chest. "You did what?"

"I said he could look at the house, and I was hoping to do it tomorrow after the greenhouse closes for the day, because I need one of you, if you're willing, to watch the kinner for me again."

"I'm always willing to spend time with my grandchildren, but don't you think you're rushing things a bit? I mean, what do you really know about this man?"

"Well, nothing, but he had kind eyes and was very polite, so . . ."

"It's not like you to be so trusting of a stranger," Amy cut in. "And how are you planning to get over to your house? Are you going to walk, or ride your scooter?"

Sylvia shook her head. "Henry said he'd take me with the horse and carriage, so since he'll be there when I show Mr. Weaver the house, that should give you both one less thing to worry about."

# CHAPTER 10

*I wonder what's up with Sylvia. Why would she jump right into something without giving it a good amount of thought?* Belinda fidgeted with her apron straps. *Her father and I didn't raise our children to make such rash decisions. Oh Vernon, if only you were here to offer your opinion on this.*

She rested a hand on her waist as she studied Sylvia's body language. "Are you certain you're doing the right thing by showing your home to the stranger you met yesterday?" Belinda asked when Sylvia got ready to head out with Henry that evening.

"I am quite certain, Mom. I have to rent out the house, and Mr. Weaver needs a place to stay."

*I'll do a little more pressing to make sure she's thinking this through.* "But you don't know much about him," Belinda argued. "And you haven't even run an ad or notified others that your place is available to rent."

"I don't need to now, since I've already found someone." Sylvia grabbed her handbag and opened the back door. "Henry's waiting outside with the horse and buggy, so I'd better go. I hope the kinner are good for you and Amy while I'm gone."

"I'm sure they will be fine. Oh, and don't forget . . ." Belinda's words were cut off when her daughter went out the door. "Well, thanks for listening," she mumbled with a huff. "I think my daughter is acting headstrong and foolish."

Belinda moved to the kitchen window and watched as Sylvia got into the buggy. A few seconds later, she heard footsteps coming up the porch steps and figured it must be Amy.

"I don't know what's come over your sister lately," Belinda said when Amy entered the room. "She seems to have lost all sense of good reason."

"Because she's thinking of renting her house to a man none of us knows?"

"Jah. I definitely dislike the way that sounds. It's not like Sylvia to speak to strangers, much less make such an unexpected offer." Belinda released a heavy sigh. "I wish your sister hadn't run into that fellow when she and Henry were out bird-watching."

"Perhaps we are worrying too much about nothing." Amy spoke in a soft tone. "Maybe when she meets the man at her house, he will have changed his mind. Or he might not show up at all."

"Guess I can hope for that." Belinda tapped her chin. "Having a renter you don't know at all could mean nothing but *druwwel.* And believe me, we've got enough troubles already to keep us busy and on our toes."

Amy nodded. "Speaking of trouble . . . Have you told Sylvia or Henry about the threatening message I heard on our answering machine yesterday?"

"No, and I'm not planning to." Belinda looked directly at Amy. "I hope you erased that horrible message."

"I did, Mom, but by erasing it, the evidence that it happened is now gone."

Belinda tapped her foot. "And that's how it should be — gone and forgotten."

"Forgotten? How can we forget something like that? It was the creepiest message ever left on our machine. Gives me the shivers just thinking about it."

"I have to agree with you, Amy. Whoever it was needs help." Belinda paused. "You and I need to get past this though, and we can if we try not to think about it."

"What if it happens again?"

"Then we'll pray a little harder and ask God to convict the person responsible for the call." Belinda slipped her arm around Amy's shoulders. "That's all we really can do, Daughter."

*I hope Mom can understand me better and see how much this means, even if I have acted spontaneously. I'm trying to heal, and so far, the decision I made is making me feel like I've taken control of something that needs to be done.* Sylvia watched her brother, who seemed so comfortable driving the horse and buggy. *At least he appears to be in my corner, and that'll help me be able to see this through.*

When Henry guided Sylvia's horse and buggy into her yard a short time later, she saw another horse and carriage waiting at the hitching rail. Dennis Weaver sat on a wooden bench on her front porch.

She grabbed her purse. Mr. Weaver being here already waiting for them was a good sign that he truly was interested in seeing the place.

As soon as Henry pulled up to the rail, Sylvia got out of the buggy and headed for the house. "Have you been waiting long,

Mr. Weaver — I mean, Dennis?"

"Nope. Got here about five minutes ago." He stood and gave her hand a warm, firm handshake. "From what I've seen outside so far, it looks like you have a nice place here."

"Danki." Sylvia put her key in the door and opened it. "Let's go inside, and I'll show you around."

Shortly after Sylvia and Dennis entered the living room, Henry came into the house. "What do you think so far, Dennis?" he asked. "It's a nice place, jah?"

Sylvia wished she could give her brother's arm a poke, but he wasn't standing close enough to do so. "Let's allow him to make his own decision, okay, Brother?"

"Jah, sure." Henry pulled off his straw hat and tossed it by the door.

"I'm liking what I see so far." Dennis lifted his own hat, revealing a good amount of thick brown hair. "This room has a comfortable appeal. Looks like a nice place for relaxing at the end of the day."

Sylvia's mind flashed back to some of the evenings she and Toby had spent in their living room. She'd always felt comfortable when they relaxed here together, but now, being anywhere in this house made her scalp prickle.

"It's an older home, with creaky floorboards and drafty rooms, but it could be quite nice if some of the rooms, like the kitchen, were updated a bit."

"Looks okay to me just the way it is." Dennis leaned against the back of the sofa. "Will any of the *hausrod* be left in the home, or would I need to provide my own furniture?"

"I'm planning to remove all my personal items, but most of the furniture will stay here."

"I see."

"Would you like to look at the rest of the house now?"

"Sure thing."

"All right then, please follow me." Sylvia looked at Henry to see if he wanted to join them, but he waved her on and flopped onto the couch.

After Sylvia gave Dennis the complete tour, including the four bedrooms, attic, and basement, they went outside to look at the barn and all the property that went with the house.

"The *scheier* is plenty adequate for horses," Dennis commented.

"Jah, there are four stalls in the barn, which was more than I needed."

When they left the building Sylvia showed

him the pasture. "Ten acres comes with this house."

"Sounds good. Have you decided how much you'll be asking for the rent?"

She stated the amount, and he nodded. "Sounds reasonable."

"When my husband was alive, he fenced in the pasture, but we only had two horses, so they had all the room they needed to roam around."

Dennis's head jerked back slightly. "Oh, I didn't realize you were a widow, but then I should have guessed, since you're wearing all black. I'm sorry for your loss, Sylvia."

Before she could form a response, Henry spoke up. "Sylvia's husband, along with our dad and brother, were killed in an accident last spring." He dropped his gaze to the ground. "It was a tragedy that none of us was prepared for."

Dennis's brows pulled down. "That's sad. I extend my condolences to both of you."

Sylvia swallowed hard, hoping she wouldn't break down in front of this near stranger. "I've been living with my mother and two siblings since the accident, and it's been a difficult transition."

"I can imagine how it must have affected your whole family, because . . ." Dennis paused and pulled his fingers down the sides of his cheeks. "Umm . . . This is not something I normally talk about — especially with people I barely know, but I think I should share it with you."

Sylvia tipped her head. Dennis looked so serious. "What is it you wish to say?"

"I lost my daed in a hunting accident. We'd gone deer hunting with my uncle, and it ended in tragedy when Uncle Ben accidently shot Dad. I saw the whole thing happen, and I couldn't do a thing about it."

Sylvia gasped, and Henry stood with his mouth gaping open.

"I'm so sorry for your loss." Those were the only words she could think to offer.

"Life is hard, and there are usually no explanations that make us feel better about the hardships we must face on this earth. We just have to figure out the best way to get through them." Dennis looked at Henry, then back at Sylvia. "Were your family members riding in a carriage when their accident happened?"

Sylvia nodded.

Henry explained the details of the accident, while Sylvia tried to keep her composure. It was always hard to talk about the sorrowful event, and the look of sympathy on Dennis's face didn't make it any easier. One thing was certain: he understood the way she felt.

*Will the pain of losing our precious family members ever end?* Sylvia asked herself. *Will I always carry a deep ache in my heart?*

Dennis leaned on a fence post as he stared out at the pasture. "Yep, the more I look at this area the more I feel that it would work out well for training horses."

"That's good to hear."

"How soon would it be before I could move in?"

"Probably by the beginning of next week. I'll need some time to clear out all my personal items, along with any furnishings I don't want to part with that will fit in my mamm's house. Would that be soon enough, Mr. Weaver?"

"That should work out fine. And please, call me Dennis."

"Right. I'll try to remember." Sylvia reached up to make sure her head covering had not become crooked from the wind that recently picked up. "One more thing. How many beds will you need?"

"Three would be nice. One would be for me, of course, and the others for any of my family who might come down from Dauphin County to visit."

"That should work out fine then, since I'm staying at my mamm's place, where there are enough beds."

Henry interrupted their conversation when he pointed to a tree on the right side of the pasture. "Look . . . there's a male cowbird! See its glossy black feathers and chocolate-brown head? If there were feeders out in your yard, Sylvia, I bet he'd come right to them."

Sylvia and Dennis both looked in the direction Henry pointed. At least she was able to see the bird without the aid of binoculars.

"It's a member of the blackbird family," Dennis commented. "It reminds me of a female red-winged blackbird." He looked at Henry. "Did you know at one time cowbirds followed bison to feed on insects that were attracted to those immense animals?"

"Didn't know that. How interesting." Henry leaned forward with one hand on his knee. "I like finding out new information about the veggel here in this state."

Dennis gave him a thumbs-up.

Sylvia couldn't help but notice the enthusiasm in her brother's voice. Bird-watching, which began for Henry last year when he started feeding the crow in their yard, was definitely a good hobby for him.

When the bird flew out of the tree and across the road, Dennis turned to face Sylvia. "May I go ahead and write a check for the first month's rent now?"

"It would be better if you wait until I get everything out of the house that I want, and I will also need to clean the place real good."

He flapped his hand. "Don't worry about that. I can clean it myself before I move in."

Sylvia shook her head vigorously. No way would she allow him to move into the house without her cleaning it first. "If you will give me a phone number where you can be reached, I'll call as soon as the place is ready. Then I'll schedule a time to meet you over here with a key and you can pay for the first month's rent at that time."

Dennis smiled and held out his hand to shake hers. "Agreed."

When Sylvia and Henry arrived home, Mom met them at the door. "I'm glad you're back. Supper's ready and we need to hurry and eat, because our driver will be here at seven-thirty."

Sylvia touched the base of her neck. "Why do we have a driver coming? Did something happen that I should know about? Has someone been hurt?"

"Yeah, Mom," Henry questioned. "What's going on?"

"We're going over to the Fullers to see

their new boppli. Don't you remember that I mentioned it this morning?"

Sylvia shook her head. "I was aware that Sara had had her baby, but I didn't realize any plans had been made for us to go visit them this evening."

Mom looked at Henry. "Do you remember me mentioning it, Son?"

"Yeah, but I thought it was tomorrow night that we'd be going."

Their mother sighed. "I'm beginning to think no one listens to me anymore. I got better response from my kinner when they were growing up than I do now."

Sylvia looked at Henry and shrugged her shoulders, then followed Mom into the kitchen where Amy waited near the stove. Allen was seated at the table on his booster seat, and Rachel sat in her wooden high chair.

"Mammi," Allen said.

"Mammi," Rachel repeated, clapping her chubby hands.

Sylvia bent to kiss the tops of their heads. "I hope you were both good for Grossmammi and *Aendi* Amy while I was gone."

"They were sweet as cotton candy." Amy smiled and came over to tweak Allen's nose.

He giggled. Rachel did too, even though her nose hadn't been tweaked.

130

"How did it go over at your house with Mr. Weaver?" Mom asked after she put a loaf of bread on the table.

Sylvia figured they were having sandwiches for supper, because a tray had been piled high with lunch meat and three kinds of cheeses. "It went fine," she replied. "He liked the house, barn, and the amount of land that comes with it. As soon as I get the rest of my personal things out and have cleaned the house from top to bottom, he'll move in."

Mom pursed her lips, but she didn't say a word. Sylvia hoped she'd thought it over and had come around to accept her hasty decision. But even if her mother didn't approve of the idea, Sylvia wouldn't change her mind. She'd made an agreement with Dennis, and she would not go back on her word. Despite what Mom, or anyone else thought, in Sylvia's heart, she felt that she'd made the right decision.

# CHAPTER 11

*Ronks*

"I have some *gut nei-ichkeede* to share with you," Dennis said when he arrived back at his friend's house and found James in the barn, cleaning his horse's hooves.

"What's the good news?" James looked up at Dennis with a curious expression.

"I'm gonna be renting the place I told you about."

"From the woman you met when you were out birding?"

"Jah." Dennis leaned against the horse's stall. "I should be out of your hair in about a week."

"No problem. Is the place furnished?"

"Yeah, but Sylvia said she might take a few pieces of furniture. There will still be enough stuff for me to use without having to buy anything, though."

"That's good. How about the property? Is there enough land for you to train horses?"

"Yep. Ten acres comes with the place. I could raise horses there if I decide to go in that direction."

"Sounds like things are working out for you then."

"It would seem so, but only time will tell." Dennis lifted his shoulders briefly, and then let them fall. "Also found out she's a widow, and she doesn't want to sell the house."

James set the tool he'd been using aside and straightened. "Is she planning to move back there sometime in the future?"

"Not from the sound of it, but then, one never knows. Hopefully if she does, she'll give me plenty of advance notice. Sure wouldn't want to buy any horses and then find out I was gonna have to find someplace else to relocate them."

"Well, you know the old saying: Take one day at a time."

Dennis gave a nod. He knew that saying all too well, because ever since his dad passed away, the only way he could survive emotionally was to take one day at a time.

*Lancaster, Pennsylvania*
Sylvia was surprised to see their driver Polly pull up in a smaller van than she usually drove. She got out, went around, and opened up the sliding door in the back.

"Hello, Sylvia," Polly said in her usual robust voice. "It's nice to see you and the children, but where's the rest of your family?"

Sylvia smiled as she walked to the van with Rachel and Allen. "They should be out soon. How's it going?"

"Pretty well. My mother is at one of her bingo games, and Dad's out fishing." Polly gestured to the van. "My larger rig is in the shop getting work done, but this one is big enough to haul your family this evening."

"You're right. There should be plenty of room."

"Your children are sure cute. Seems like they've grown since the last time I saw them."

"Yes, and the proof is that I had to let the hem down on two pairs of Allen's trousers the other day."

Mom, Amy, and Henry came out of the house, while Sylvia put the children in the back of the van and fastened them into their safety seats.

"Hello, Polly." Mom and Amy greeted her with a smile, but Henry said nothing. It appeared that he wasn't too thrilled about going on this trip to Lancaster. No doubt he'd rather spend the evening with Seth or one of his other friends.

Mom chose to sit in the back with Allen and Rachel, while Amy sat in the seat in front of them, next to Sylvia.

"Now where are we headed?" Polly asked as she climbed into the driver's seat.

"Hang on a minute. This doesn't want to clip in." Mom struggled with her seatbelt until it finally fastened. "We'll be heading over to Brad and Sara Fuller's place. Sylvia has the address."

Sylvia reached into her purse and handed the slip of paper to Polly, as Henry, still quiet, got in and took the passenger's seat up front.

"Thanks," Polly said. "I have to take care of a few errands for myself and my mom. How long do you think you'll be there visiting?"

"I'm not sure," Mom replied, "but I'll call your cell number when we're ready to be picked up."

"Okay, sounds good."

As they headed in the direction of Lancaster, Sylvia eyed the farms along the way while listening to Mom chatting to the children. The closer they got to their destination, the farther away Sylvia wanted to be. It would be difficult seeing how happy Sara and Brad were with their new baby. *Just one more reminder that my husband is*

135

*gone and we'll have no more children to-gether.*

Rachel began to kick the back of Sylvia's seat as she fussed and carried on. Sylvia reached into her tote bag and pulled out a toy, which she handed back to Mom. She hoped it would suffice and felt relieved when her daughter quieted.

Sylvia fidgeted with her purse straps, wishing she had come up with a good reason to stay home this evening. She'd been taught from an early age that it was wrong to allow jealousy to take over when someone had something you wanted. While she had no logical reason to be jealous of Sara, Sylvia's envy came from the fact that the Fullers' child would have two parents to love and nurture him, while her children only had a mother. *I'm not sure how good of a parent I am,* she thought. Without Toby's assistance, raising Allen and Rachel was proving to be a challenge.

In the last week or so, Allen had begun throwing temper tantrums whenever he didn't get his way. Sylvia struggled to deal with them and often felt like giving in and allowing him to have his own way. But that would not be good parenting. It probably wouldn't be long before Rachel began to imitate her brother's actions, and then Sylvia would have more trouble on her hands.

Maybe Sylvia wouldn't have such a difficult time making decisions on how to handle her children if she felt content and her soul was at peace. But even the few moments when she did feel a bit of happiness, like when she went birding with Henry, something usually happened to snatch it away. Sylvia wondered if she would ever really know what true contentment and tranquility felt like.

"We're here." Their driver's announcement halted Sylvia's introspections. It was time to put on a pleasant face.

When they entered the parsonage, which had been built on the lot next to the church where Sara's husband preached every Sunday, Brad greeted them at the door.

"Come in. Come in. It's so good to see all of you." He shook everyone's hand and gave Sylvia's children a pat on the head. "Sara and I have been looking forward to your visit and introducing you to the newest member of our family."

Brad led the way to the living room, where Sara sat in a rocking chair, holding the infant. Everyone gathered around — even Henry — to get a look at the bundle of joy.

"He's a beautiful baby." A sense of joy

mixed with anticipation filled Amy's soul. Oh, how she looked forward to marrying Jared and hopefully becoming a mother someday.

After everyone pummeled Sara and Brad with questions about how she and the baby were doing and how much the child weighed, Sara asked if anyone would like to hold the baby.

"I would." Amy was the first to speak up.

Sara stood and let Amy take her seat, then handed the precious bundle over to her. Following that, she took a seat on the couch between Mom and Sylvia.

"We have a little something for the baby." Mom reached into her tote bag and removed a package wrapped in blue tissue paper. She handed it to Sara.

While Sara opened the gift, Amy watched Sylvia's expression. Her pinched expression and flushed cheeks made Amy believe that her sister struggled with envy.

*Does Sylvia wish she could have another boppli, or is my sister thinking about Toby right now and feeling envious because Sara has a husband and she doesn't?* Amy put the baby against her shoulder and gently patted his back. *How will Sylvia deal with it when Jared and I get married? Will it pull us apart when I move out of Mom's house and set up house-*

138

*keeping in the home Jared and I choose to live in?*

Amy glanced in the direction of her sister again. *Perhaps my being gone will strengthen Sylvia and Mom's relationship. It has seemed a bit strained lately, especially since Sylvia announced her intentions to rent her house to a man she barely knows.*

Like their mother, Amy didn't approve of her sister's decision, but it was Sylvia's life, and she had a right to do as she pleased. Amy hoped everything would work out okay, and that Mr. Weaver would prove to be a good renter and not take advantage of Sylvia's willingness to offer him a place to stay.

Refocusing, Amy watched as Sara held up the pair of light-weight blankets Mom had taken the time to make. In addition to those, they'd all chipped in and put seventy-five dollars in the card that went with the gift.

"We thought you could use some money to buy whatever you still need for the baby," Mom explained when Sara removed the bills from the envelope.

"Thank you all so much. This money will surely be put to good use."

Amy looked over at Henry. He and Brad sat in chairs next to each other, but she couldn't tell if they were actually talking to one another, because their heads were turned away from her.

Sara got up and went over to stand beside Brad. "Look at the nice blankets Belinda made for the baby." She handed the card to him. "And the Kings gave us money to get the baby something he needs."

"That was a thoughtful gift. Thank you." Brad smiled up at Mom and thanked Amy, Sylvia, and Henry as well.

"Have you had many visitors since you brought your little one home from the hospital?" Amy asked.

Sara nodded. "A lot of the church people have come by with gifts and food, so I wouldn't have to worry about cooking."

"Mary Ruth along with Lenore and her family were here last night," Brad interjected. "We enjoyed having them, and it was good to see how Lenore and Jesse's children are growing." He looked at Rachel and Allen, playing on the floor with some toys Sylvia had brought along. "It's also nice to see your little ones, Sylvia. They've both grown since the last time we saw them."

"They don't stay little long enough to suit me," Sylvia commented. There was that wistful expression again. Amy hoped her sister could hold it together and wouldn't start crying, like she often did at home.

"How does it feel to be a daddy?" Mom asked. "Have you gotten used to the idea yet, Brad?"

He shook his head. "It's sort of surreal. The first night Sara and the baby came home from the hospital, I hardly slept a wink."

Sara chuckled. "It was the baby's crying that kept us both awake."

Everyone laughed, including Sylvia, but her expression continued to appear strained. Amy was almost positive her sister was merely going through the motions of being polite and trying to do the right thing. It had probably taken all of Sylvia's willpower to come here tonight.

*Poor Sylvia,* she thought. *I hope someday she finds the kind of happiness I've found with Jared.*

*Strasburg*

"How'd your day go at work?" Virginia asked as she took a seat on the couch beside her husband.

"Okay." Earl's gaze remained fixed on the newspaper he held.

Virginia grimaced. *Sometimes I wonder how he can be so engrossed in that stupid paper.* She looked down at her clenched

141

fingers. *It's either the dumb news blaring on the television, or him staring at the newspaper in front of his nose.*

"Did you sell many cars?" she asked.

No response.

Virginia waited a few seconds then she bumped his arm. "Did ya hear what I said?"

"Uh-huh."

Virginia grew weary of her husband's lack of attention. *I'd like to wad up that newspaper and toss it in the trash.*

"Then why didn't you answer my question?" she asked through clenched teeth.

He looked away from the newspaper and blinked. "What question was that?"

She lifted her gaze to the ceiling. "I asked if you sold many cars today."

"A few."

"Guess a few is better than none."

"Right."

"Don't you wanna know how my day went?"

"Sure."

"It wasn't the best. I started to clean and organize the guest room but discovered the sheets for that bed are worn out and need to be replaced. The curtains also need to go, because they're faded."

"Okay, sure. Do whatever you think needs to be done."

"Something else bothered me too."

"What was that?"

"There was more traffic than usual going down the road."

"Is that so?"

"Yes, and as I have pointed out before, it's because of that stupid greenhouse." Virginia groaned. "I didn't have a moment's peace."

Earl dropped the paper into his lap and turned to look at her with furrowed brows. "Will you please keep your mouth shut long enough for me to read the paper? All you ever do is flap your gums about things you can't control." His eyes narrowed as he breathed audibly through his nose. "It's no wonder your first husband left you."

Virginia pounded a fist against her right thigh. "He did not leave me. I've told ya before — he died. Did ya hear me, Earl? My first husband died!" *Wow, how hard can it be for my man to remember something like that? Furthermore, doesn't he realize how much it hurts for me to talk about my first husband?*

Earl let the paper fall to the floor as he held up his hands. "For heaven's sake, woman, calm down. You're makin' a big deal out of this."

Virginia sucked in some air and tried to relax. Just talking about her first husband made her edgy. Why did Earl have to bring up this topic, anyhow?

He reached over and clasped her hand. "Sorry, if I upset you. I just wanted a little peace and quiet tonight and a chance to read the paper without interruption."

"No problem, Earl. You can have the rest of the evening to yourself. I'm going to bed." Virginia stood up and limped out of the room. She still hadn't told Earl about Stella coming, but tonight was not the time to do it. Hopefully, tomorrow he'd be in a better mood and then she would let him in on the plans. In the meantime, Virginia needed to spruce up the guest room a bit, to make sure it was ready for her friend.

As she entered their bedroom, a horrible thought came over Virginia. *Earl got really upset when I tried to talk to him about how I feel. His angry expression made me think he might want to hit me.*

She flopped down on the bed and let her head fall into her hands. *Would he ever go that far? If so, what would I do about it?*

# CHAPTER 12

"I didn't realize this house was so dirty," Sylvia said as she swept the area in her bedroom closet where all her and Toby's clothes had once been. His, she'd donated to a local thrift shop, and hers had been taken to Mom's and hung in the closet of the bedroom where she'd been sleeping since Toby's death.

"Places we don't see have a way of accumulating dust bunnies." Amy laughed. "Like under a bed. When no one is in a home for a while, the dust can truly settle on things."

"Jah." Sylvia stepped into the middle of the room and looked around. "Everything in here looks pretty good now, don't you think?"

Amy nodded.

"We have more to do upstairs, in the other rooms — also the closets and bathroom need to be cleaned."

145

"I have a feeling we'll be here for a while, Sister."

"Probably so."

"Too bad Mom didn't have the energy to come with us. You could have let the kinner fall asleep here while we all pitched in and cleaned."

"If they would have cooperated, that is. More than likely we'd have spent most of the time getting my two active little ones out of things."

Amy chuckled. "You could be right about that."

"I know I am."

"So which room do you want to tackle next?"

"Let's head upstairs and work on the bathroom." Sylvia held onto the mop and bucket.

Amy carried the broom with the dustpan and headed for the stairs.

"I'll be right up," Sylvia called. "I'd better grab some disinfectant wipes from the downstairs bathroom."

"Okay. I'll see you upstairs."

After entering the bathroom at the end of the downstairs hall, Sylvia picked up the box of wipes. *My sister looks tired this evening. I hope I'm not pushing too hard to get this work done. She should have said no*

146

*if she wasn't up to helping.*

Sylvia left the bathroom and started down the hall. *I'm looking forward to renting this house out and earning some money. Now I'll be able to help Mom with some bills, or at least pay for groceries so I won't feel like I'm taking advantage of her hospitality.*

At the bottom of the stairs, Sylvia paused, recalling how sounds of her own little family used to be heard in this home. She wasn't ready to let go of this house permanently, but maybe someday she would feel strong enough emotionally to make that big decision.

She climbed up to the second floor and entered the bathroom, where her sister stood in front of the counter, cleaning the mirror.

"Mind if I ask you something?" Amy questioned.

Sylvia set the wipes on the counter. "Of course not. Ask me whatever you want."

"Is there a specific reason you decided to rent this place, rather than sell?"

Sylvia winced. This topic was difficult to talk about without crying, and she'd done way too much of that since Toby, Dad, and Abe died.

"I'm trying to understand your reasons," Amy persisted, "but if it was my house, and

I had no plans to move back, then I'd sell and use the money to buy something else."

"You and I handle things differently. Also you're not married yet and don't have children. The bond between Toby and me was strong. We enjoyed our life together until the accident." Sylvia stared toward the window. "Why would I need to buy another home? The kinner seem content to live at our folks' place. They like being close to their grossmammi, and she enjoys them."

"What about you, Sylvia? Are you content to live there indefinitely?"

Sylvia lifted her shoulders in a brief shrug. "I'm okay with it, at least for now."

"If you're content to stay with Mom, then why not sell your house?" Amy slipped an arm around Sylvia's waist.

She swallowed hard, trying to push down the lump that had formed in her throat. "If I sell my house, it'll be like parting with the last shred of evidence that I was married to Toby."

"That's not true. You have Rachel and Allen. There's a part of their *daadi* in each of them, just like there's a part of you."

Sylvia dabbed at the tears that had escaped her lashes and rolled onto her cheeks. "This is the place where Toby and I set up house-keeping together. We made so many wonderful memories."

"Being here makes you sad, though, right?"

"Jah." Sylvia could barely get the word out.

Amy's hand went from Sylvia's waist to the middle of her back, and she gave it a few gentle pats. "I'm sorry that I don't fully understand the way you feel, because I've never lost a husband. Even so, if it were me, I'd sell the house."

"Maybe someday I will. Just not now." Sylvia picked up the box of wipes and pulled a few out. "We'd better get this room done so we can work on the others and make sure they look presentable. Now that the furniture I decided to keep has been taken to Mom's, I plan to let Dennis Weaver know he can move in. Who knows — maybe someday I'll sell the house and property to him."

Belinda leaned back in her easy chair and closed her eyes. *This feels good, and the smell of the lavender lotion I rubbed on my hands is soothing. If I could, I'd take a warm bath and soak for a while. But since my daughters are still gone, that wouldn't be a good idea in case one of the children needed me.*

Today had been busy at the greenhouse from the moment they'd opened until Henry put the Closed sign in the window on the front door. It had been nice to see so many regular customers as well as a few tourists come in. Two women who'd come together bought some of Belinda's canned goods and several potholders Sylvia had made to sell. Belinda remembered the comments they'd made while she rang up their purchases at the checkout. The first woman mentioned stopping by the bigger greenhouse on the other side of town, but said she enjoyed the Kings' greenhouse more. The second woman added, "My sister and I traveled all the way from California because we wanted to see Amish country and learn more about Plain living. We've enjoyed chatting with you because there are no Amish people where we are from."

Belinda had to admit she felt better hearing those women talk positively about her business. She needed to let go of the worry she'd been carrying about the future of the greenhouse.

She stretched out more fully and wiggled her bare toes. *I need to pray more and keep trusting God to provide for our needs.*

Belinda didn't know how Amy had found the strength to go with Sylvia to her house for cleaning after such a long day of waiting on customers. But the two of them had headed out as soon as they'd finished supper, after Belinda offered to wash and dry the dishes.

Although tired herself, Belinda would have gone with them if they'd had someone to watch the children. Taking them along would have been a mistake. Henry had gone over to see his friend Seth again, but even if he'd been here, he wasn't responsible enough to keep an eye on Rachel and Allen. It seemed like he always had his nose in a magazine or some book about birds these days. She'd hoped he would take more interest in the honey bees, but that didn't seem to be the case. At least he complained about the job less, so that was a good thing.

Since the children were tuckered out from playing so hard, Belinda had been able to put them to bed sooner than their normal bedtime. It wasn't that she didn't want to spend time with her grandchildren. She just felt too exhausted tonight.

The house seemed peaceful as evening crept along. Belinda hoped her son and daughters would arrive home soon. Another day of work was around the corner, and she needed to get her rest. *Even if I went to bed, the fact is, I'd just lay there worrying until they all arrived home.*

Belinda yawned. *Think I'm going to check on Allen and Rachel.* She rose from her chair, then headed upstairs. When she peeked in on the children and heard their soft, steady breathing, she smiled. Since all was well, she headed back to the main floor and went to her room.

After slipping into her nightgown, robe, and slippers, she couldn't help but smile. Vernon had given them to her for Christmas two years ago. He'd been such a thoughtful husband. Oh, how she missed him.

Back in the living room, she took a seat in the recliner again. She sat with her eyes closed, thinking about Vernon and how, when their children were young, they used to enjoy spending a few hours alone each evening after their sons and daughters went to bed.

Switching her train of thought back to the greenhouse, lest she give in to depression, Belinda reflected on how Maude, the near-homeless woman, had come by looking for a handout today. Belinda had never said no to someone in need and ended up giving Maude a jar of honey, a loaf of bread, and several other food items that didn't need refrigeration. Even though the bedraggled woman hadn't said thank you, Belinda felt good about helping her.

Thankfully Monroe hadn't come by since their conversation after Christmas. Apparently he respected her wishes and realized she was not ready for a relationship that went deeper than friendship. She was certain there was no way she could ever get married again. She'd done the right thing by letting Monroe know where he stood.

She glanced at the clock across the room and frowned. It was almost ten-thirty. *Henry should have been home by now. I told him no later than ten.*

As worry took over, Belinda got up and went to the window, looking out into the darkened yard. A chill of apprehension shot through her as she thought about Amy, Sylvia, and Henry, who could all be out on the road at this very moment, heading for home. She knew all too well how suddenly an accident could occur, and hoped no one in her family would ever experience such a tragedy again.

Leaning against the windowsill, Belinda closed her eyes. *Dear Lord, Please keep my children safe and bring them home soon.*

A horse whinnied, and when Belinda opened her eyes, she saw the lights on the open buggy Henry had used this evening. She sighed with relief. At least one of her children had made it home safely. Now if Amy and Sylvia would only get here.

Belinda moved away from the window and went back to her chair. A short time later, Henry came in.

Belinda got up and went over to give him a hug.

"What was that for, Mom?" He looked at her with a curious expression.

"I missed you, and I'm glad you're home, even if you are late."

"Sorry, there was more traffic on the road than usual."

Belinda tilted her head toward him and sniffed. "Is that cigarette smoke I smell on your *hemm*?"

Henry's posture went rigid as he took a whiff of his shirt. "Umm . . . yeah . . . guess so."

"Henry King, have you been smoking?" Her body tensed as she waited for his response.

"No, Mom."

"Then why do your clothes smell like *schmoke*?"

He blinked rapidly while rubbing the back of his neck.

She tapped her foot. "I expect an honest answer, Son."

"Seth's the one who smokes cigarettes."

154

Henry shifted from one foot to the other. "I'll admit, I did give smoking a try once, but I hated the way it smelled and tasted."

"So the smoke your sisters and I have smelled in the barn a few times was from Seth?"

Henry shrugged. "I've never seen him light up a cigarette in our barn, but I suppose he could have come in there sometime when I wasn't looking."

Belinda's fingers clenched into her palms. "Seth is a bad influence on you, Henry. I don't think you should hang around with him so much anymore."

The door opened and Belinda's daughters stepped in.

"I'm so glad you're home." She gave them both the same kind of hug she'd given her son. "It's late, and I was getting worried."

"We had more cleaning to do than I realized," Sylvia explained. "Were the kinner good for you? I assume they're in bed?"

Belinda nodded. "They were tuckered out, so I put them to bed a little earlier than they usually go down."

"That's good. A little extra sleep won't hurt them." Sylvia yawned noisily. "And speaking of sleep . . . I'm really tired, so I'm going up to bed." She kissed Belinda's cheek. "Night, Mom."

"Good night."

"Think I'll head for bed too." Amy gave Belinda another hug. "See you in the morning."

When her daughters left the room, Belinda turned to speak more with Henry, but he was gone. No doubt he'd quietly left the room while she'd been talking to his sisters. *He was probably trying to avoid more lecturing from me.* Belinda sighed. She hoped Henry was telling the truth when he'd said he had only tried smoking but quit. The last thing she needed was one more thing to stress about.

# CHAPTER 13

*Ronks*

"Alice wrote down a message for you, Dennis," James said, stepping out onto the porch. "It's from that Amish woman you told me about who wants to rent you her house."

Dennis got up from the rocking chair, where he'd been reading the latest edition of *The Connection* magazine, and took the piece of paper his friend handed him. The corners of his lips twitched as he read Sylvia's message. "Her house is ready for me now." He grinned at James. "She wants me to meet her there at seven o'clock this evening to give me the keys. That's when I'll pay her for the first month's rent."

James thumped Dennis's back. "I can tell you're pretty excited about this."

"Jah. I needed this change in my life, and Sylvia's house and property is the perfect place for me to live at this time."

"I wonder why she wants to meet you so late in the day." James leaned against the porch railing.

Dennis pulled his fingers through the back of his hair as his shoulders lifted. "Maybe she's not quite finished clearing things out of the house. Or it could be because she's working in the greenhouse."

James's brows lifted on his forehead. "What greenhouse?"

"The one her mamm owns. She mentioned it the other day while she was showing me through her house. Sylvia said it's on the same property as her mother's house."

"What about her daed and other family members. Do any of them work at the greenhouse?"

"I'm not sure about other family members, but Sylvia's husband, father, and brother were all killed in a tragic accident when a truck hit their buggy. Remember, I told you she was a widow."

"Yeah, that's right. Just didn't know the cause of her husband's death or that others from her family had also died." James shook his head slowly. "Sounds like she's been through a lot."

"Jah. I could see the sadness in her eyes. It's the same look my mamm has whenever she talks about my daed."

"Certain circumstances in our lives can sure be hard."

Dennis gave a nod. "Unfortunately, some are more difficult than others." *And some people, like me, experience tragedies that are too difficult to talk about, so we try to hide them from others who wouldn't understand.*

## Strasburg

"While I open the greenhouse, would you mind going out to check the mail and see if we have any phone messages?" Mom asked Amy after the breakfast dishes were taken care of.

"Sure, I can do that. I'll head out there right now and meet you in the greenhouse shortly."

"Sounds good. See you there."

Amy went out the back door and headed down the driveway. Her first stop was the mailbox, which she found empty. Apparently it hadn't come yet.

She glanced across the road and saw Virginia's husband come out of the house and head for his truck. Before she had a chance to wave, he cupped his hands around his mouth and hollered, "Morning. How are ya?"

"I'm well. How about you and your wife?"

159

"We're doin' good." He gave another wave, got into his vehicle, and drove off.

Amy smiled. Earl was a lot friendlier than his wife. Whenever Virginia saw Amy, she either looked the other way or sometimes mumbled a brief *hello*. Amy didn't understand what the problem could be, but then she guessed some folks just weren't the friendly type. Earl's wife might be one of those people who preferred to keep to herself.

Amy turned and headed back up the driveway. When she reached the small wooden shed where their phone was housed, she opened the door and stepped inside. There was no blinking light on the answering machine, and when she picked up the phone to make a call, there was no dial tone either.

*I wonder what's going on.* Amy stepped out of the phone shed and looked up at the place where the wire was connected. A cold chill ran through her body when she realized it had been cut. *Oh, no . . . not another act of vandalism.*

Belinda had barely taken a seat behind the checkout counter when Amy rushed in, wide-eyed and face ashen.

Belinda felt immediate concern. "What's

160

wrong, Daughter? You look *umgerrent*."

"I am very upset." Amy's hand shook as she brushed at a piece of lint on her dress.

"The line going into the phone shed has been cut. There's no electric power in the building at all."

"Are you sure it was cut and didn't blow down from the wind or something?"

Amy shook her head. "No, Mom, the line was definitely cut."

Holding onto the edge of the counter, Belinda sucked in her breath. "Oh my. I bet whoever left that muffled message on our answering machine was the one responsible for cutting the wire." She clasped Amy's arm. "What are we going to do about this?"

"The first thing we should do is call the sheriff. Then we need to let the phone company know our line needs to be replaced."

Belinda shook her head determinedly. "No one's been hurt, and I am not going to bring the law into this. We will, however, need to ask the neighbors across the road if we can use their phone to call the phone company."

"I'll walk over there and see about it right now." Amy leaned down and gave Belinda a hug. "If Henry's still in the barn, I'll ask him to come here so you're not in the greenhouse by yourself. I don't think any of

161

us should be alone anymore."

"Now how did I forget to buy dishwashing detergent? I'm sure I wrote it down on my list when I went grocery shopping." Grumbling with each step, Virginia went to her purse and drew out the paper. Tracing her finger along each crossed off word, she found there were a couple of unmarked places.

She thumped her head. "I can't believe this. Besides the detergent, I forgot to pick up the deodorant Earl asked me to get."

Virginia put the list aside and walked down the hall toward the bathroom. Entering the room, she opened Earl's drawer and rummaged through his toiletries. "There's his deodorant." When she lifted the container, it felt light. A feeling of regret came over her as she pulled off the lid to reveal an empty cartridge. Although he hadn't mentioned it, her husband had been a little out-of-sorts and short with her this morning. Discovering that she hadn't bought the deodorant he'd asked for, in addition to her burning his toast could have been the reason for his sullen mood.

Virginia replaced the lid and tossed the empty deodorant in the garbage can. She would go to the store before he got home and get him a new one.

Standing in front of their bathroom mirror, she fiddled with her short hair. Virginia pursed her lips. *It needs something fresh done to it. My friend will be visiting from Chicago soon, and I don't want to look like a drab country bumpkin.*

She grabbed a tube of styling gel, squeezed some into the palm of her hand, and rubbed it into her hair. Virginia smiled as the gel began to give her hair some lift. *I do believe that style looks kind of good on me.*

Leaving the bathroom, Virginia stopped to look in at the guest room. She felt happy with the new curtains she'd purchased for a reasonable price. She'd also found a set of sheets with a nice thread count for the bed.

Leaning against the dresser, Virginia thought about how good it would be to see Stella again. *I wonder what we can do for fun while she's here. Guess I could get some ideas from the internet.*

She stepped out of the room and closed the door behind her, then headed for the kitchen. *Sure hope my friend doesn't want to check out the Amish while she's here. As far as I know, Stella hasn't shown any interest in them or mentioned to me that she might want to meet any of the Plain people who live in*

*Lancaster County.*

Virginia was about to start up the dishwasher, using what was left of the detergent, when a knock sounded on the front door. "Now who in the world could that be? I hope it's not someone selling something I don't need."

She dried her hands and made her way to the front door. When Virginia opened it, she was surprised to see Amy King standing on the porch. *Well, wouldn't you know . . . speaking of the Plain people, here's one now.*

"I'm sorry to bother you, Virginia, but could I borrow your phone?"

"I thought you Amish folks had a phone in that little wooden building near the end of your driveway." Virginia leaned against the door frame, trying not to stare at the young woman's plain but pretty face and her quaint-styled dress. *I don't understand why they don't see the need to wear makeup, nail polish, or stylish clothes.*

"Yes, we do keep our phone in a shed, but someone cut the wire that leads to the shed, so the phone is not working." Amy's statement pulled Virginia's musings aside.

"Is that so?" Virginia gave her earlobe a tug. "I wonder who would do such a thing."

"We don't know, but I need to call the phone company to let them know what happened and see how soon they can come out and replace the line."

"Oh, okay. I'll go get my cell phone and look up the number for you."

"Thanks so much. I really appreciate it, Virginia."

"No problem." Virginia limped her way to the kitchen and got out the phone book. Even though she didn't care much for her Amish neighbors, she couldn't very well refuse to let Amy use the phone. How would that make her look?

After Virginia brought her phone and the number out to Amy, she went to the kitchen for a cup of coffee. As she stood sipping the enticing beverage, while giving the young woman some needed time to make the call, Virginia tried not to listen in on the conversation.

When Virginia returned to the living room a few minutes later, Amy was off the phone.

"Did you get a hold of someone to fix your phone line?" Virginia asked.

Amy nodded. "I was told they would be out sometime today to take care of it for us." She handed Virginia the cell phone. "Thank you for letting me use this."

"Sure, no problem." Virginia opened the door to let her neighbor out, in time to see a horse and buggy turn up the driveway to the greenhouse. She was tempted to make some comment about it, but what was the use? Short of lighting a fire to the place, Virginia figured there wasn't much she could do about the greenhouse.

*Clymer, New York*
Ezekiel yawned and drank the rest of his coffee. He'd had some difficulty sleeping lately, because his family in Pennsylvania had been on his mind. Were they doing all right? Mom said so the last time they'd talked, but he could never be sure without going there himself to check on things.

He closed his eyes. *I need to give my worries to You, Lord. I can't add one more minute to my life by fretting about things that are out of my control.*

Ezekiel set his empty mug aside. It was hard not to worry about his family back home and the burdens they'd carried since the accident. Even though he no longer lived there, Ezekiel knew how much effort it was to keep the greenhouse running.

Scratching his head, Ezekiel's focus changed. Recently, he'd gone with Samuel Stoltzfus, another Amish minister in his church district, to talk with someone getting ready for surgery to remove a cancerous tumor. At first, Ezekiel felt overwhelmed, but as he listened to the church leader give needed comfort to the ill person, he got a better understanding of the importance of this part of his ministry. Samuel had spoken calmly, as he gave reassurance and hope, which made the tension in the room ease. Ezekiel was inspired by the other minister's way of handling this person's situation. He knew it would be good to read his Bible daily. Following the good advice from the bishop, as well as the other minister and a deacon who'd been called to this type of work several years ago, Ezekiel would do his best and try to keep his focus on the Lord.

As Ezekiel took a seat at the workbench in his shop, he glanced at the calendar hanging on the nearest wall. In a few weeks it would be his mother's birthday, as well as the one year anniversary of his father, brother, and brother-in-law's deaths. It would be a difficult day for him, as well as the rest of his family. He wished he could simply blot the day off the calendar and out of his mind, but it was not possible.

Ezekiel still missed the special men in his life, and could only imagine how difficult it would be for his mother, sisters, and younger brother to celebrate her birthday this year and not think about the accident that had occurred the evening of her party last year.

He left his chair and paced the room as an idea began to form. *Think I'll take my fraa and kinner there for a visit that day. It might help Mom to have her whole family around on her birthday. I won't tell her we're coming. We'll just show up and give her a birthday surprise.*

# CHAPTER 14

*Strasburg*

"Morning, Belinda. How are things going here?" Monroe asked when he entered the greenhouse at two o'clock that afternoon. He smelled of men's aftershave, as he often did, and his pale blue shirt looked new. This was Monroe's first visit since Belinda talked with him after Christmas. She hoped he wasn't here to pester her about seeing him socially again. She'd set him straight once and didn't want to have to do it again.

Belinda felt her stress level rising as Monroe stood with a wide grin, looking at her and no one else. *Why do I feel like a weak kitten when I'm in his presence? I have to give Monroe credit, though — he's sure insistent.*

Belinda shifted uneasily on the stool she sat upon behind the counter. "We're doing all right. How are you, Monroe?"

"My business is going well, but I miss seeing you."

Looking away from his gaze, she bit the inside of her cheek. "May I help you with something, Monroe?"

He placed his hands on the surface of the counter and leaned forward, until she felt his warm, minty breath on her face. "Just dropped by to see how you're doing now that you're open for business again."

She pulled back slightly. "We're all fine."

"As I was coming down the driveway I saw a man from the phone company outside your phone shed. Looked like they were putting up a new line."

Belinda nodded. "Amy discovered that the old line had been cut this morning."

His brows furrowed. "That's not good, Belinda. Sounds to me like someone is trying to antagonize you and your family. Has there been any other vandalism done besides the phone line?"

She shook her head, choosing not to mention the garbled phone message they'd received. It wasn't actually vandalism anyway, and there was no need to tell him about it.

Monroe glanced around and pulled off his straw hat, revealing his thick head of hair. He fanned himself with the brim a few times, which filled the air with more of that heavy aftershave. "Where's the rest of your

170

family? You're not out here alone, I hope."

"Henry and Amy are helping me today," Belinda replied stiffly.

"Really? I don't see them anywhere."

"Henry's outside putting a customer's purchase into her car, and Amy's in the storage room right now." Belinda didn't appreciate being treated like a child. As she listened to him go on about what he deemed important, she wanted to say what was really on her mind. *Monroe, never you mind. There's no need to worry about me. I'm fine and so is my family.*

"Well, if you ask me, someone should be up front here with you at all times," Monroe continued. "You never know when a person could come in and try to rob you of all the money."

Belinda bristled. Why was this man being so persistent and overbearing? Was he really that concerned about their well-being, or did Monroe enjoy being so controlling?

Monroe placed his hat back on his head and looked past Belinda when Amy approached. He fiddled with his suspenders a few seconds and gave them a tug. "It's good to see you finally have some help here again."

Belinda felt relieved when Amy joined her behind the counter.

"Hello, Mr. Esh." Amy offered him a smile, even though Belinda knew her daughter didn't care much for Monroe. "Are you here to buy some outdoor plants or maybe seeds for a vegetable garden?"

He gave a quick shake of his head. "Just dropped by to see how everyone was doing." He still looked only at Belinda.

She was reminded again of their courting days, and how Monroe could make her feel uneasy with his controlling mannerisms. *This may be far-fetched and wrong of me to think, but what if Monroe is the one behind the vandalism?* Belinda didn't know where that thought had come from. It was unlike her to think that way. She glanced at Monroe, with guilt mounting inside her head. *How ridiculous of me to think such a thought. What reason would Monroe have for vandalizing our place or trying to hurt my business? I'll need to pray about my unkind feelings toward him.*

"We're all fine, Monroe," Amy responded. "We are keeping plenty busy since the greenhouse reopened."

"That's good." He shifted nervously. "I just want to be sure your family stays safe."

"We'll be fine and appreciate your interest in our welfare." Belinda managed a smile.

About that time, Henry came through the

doorway and walked past Monroe without saying a word. Right behind him, two couples entered the building, so Belinda held her tongue. Later, when she could speak to her son alone, she would reprimand him for being impolite.

"Guess I'd best be on my way. I have a few other stops to make yet today." Monroe tipped his straw hat in Belinda's direction. "It was good seeing you. Please let me know if you need anything."

"Danki for stopping by." Belinda got off the stool and approached one of the couples who'd come in. "May I help you with anything?"

She glanced over her shoulder and saw Monroe head out the door. Hopefully he wouldn't be back anytime soon, unless it was to buy something. It wasn't in her nature to feel this way about someone, but Monroe's behavior got on her nerves.

Since Virginia's friend would be arriving today, she had spent the morning making sure the house was picked up and the guest room looked presentable. She figured Stella most likely wouldn't be here until close to suppertime, so there was time for her to rest awhile.

She took a seat in her recliner, hit the

lever, and lay back with her feet elevated. This position felt good and always made the pain in her leg subside.

Virginia picked up the remote and turned on the TV. Her favorite game show came on, and it didn't take long to become absorbed in the questions being asked of the contestants. Of course, Virginia tried to guess the answers along with them.

Fifteen minutes into the show, her eyes became heavy and her eyelids closed. A little power nap would feel good, and she'd be refreshed by the time Stella got here.

Virginia was on the verge of nodding off, when a knock sounded on the door.

*I hope it's not Amy needing to use my phone again.*

Virginia pulled the lever on her chair and when the footrest came down she got up and made her way to the door. When she opened it, she was surprised to see Stella on the front porch.

"Well, for goodness' sakes. I didn't expect you this soon." Virginia gave her friend a hug and invited her in.

"I got an earlier start yesterday than I'd planned, stopped early for the night, and left the hotel as soon as I woke up." Stella pulled her fingers through the ends of her short blond hair and yawned. "I'm pretty tired, but it's good to be here."

"I'm glad you made it okay." Virginia gestured to the sofa. "Should we sit awhile and visit, or did you want to get your luggage out of the car?"

"Let's sit first." Stella took a seat on one end of the couch.

"I'll go get us a cup of coffee. Unless you'd rather have something else."

"Coffee's fine. It'll keep me from falling asleep."

"Maybe you'd like to take a nap."

"No, I didn't come all this way to sleep in the middle of the day. I'd much rather get caught up with you."

Virginia smiled. "Same here. Make yourself comfortable. I'll be right back."

When Virginia returned to living room, she found her friend standing in front of the window facing the street.

"Here's your coffee." Virginia placed two mugs on the low table in front of the couch.

Stella turned to face her. "I was watching a horse and buggy coming down the street. It turned up the driveway by the sign for the greenhouse."

Virginia grunted. "Yeah, that's what I have to put up with all day." She wrinkled her nose. "*Clip-clop. Clip-clop.* The noise is so distracting."

"You think so?" Stella tipped her head. "I kinda like the sound. It's relaxing."

"You wouldn't say that if you had to hear it all day. When I sit out on the porch, it's even louder, not to mention the putrid smell of the droppings those horses leave in the middle of the road."

"You'll get used to it in time." Stella took a seat, picked up her mug, and took a drink. "Nice . . . This hits the spot."

Virginia joined her. "I have some store-bought cookies, if you'd like some."

"No thanks. I don't want to spoil my appetite for whatever you're planning for supper."

"I have a chicken cooking in the crockpot."

"Yum." Stella glanced toward the window. "I'd sure like to have a look at that greenhouse while I'm here. Could we take a walk over there?"

"You mean now?"

"Sure, why not?"

"Those people who run it are different. I'm sure you wouldn't like them."

"I'm not prejudiced, Virginia."

"Maybe we can go over there tomorrow. My leg's been acting up today, and I don't feel like goin' anywhere right now."

"I guess tomorrow might be better." Stella drank more coffee. "We'll both be rested up in the morning."

Virginia nodded. By tomorrow, she would make up some other excuse. The last thing she wanted to do was to take her friend over to that greenhouse and expose her to those strange people.

When Henry guided the horse and buggy up to the rail, Sylvia saw Dennis waiting on the porch for them in the same place he'd been when they'd met him here last week.

She stepped out of the carriage, and held her horse until Henry got down. Once he took over, she headed for the house and joined Dennis on the porch.

"Good evening, Sylvia. It's nice to see you again." Dennis's smile seemed so genuine — nothing like the fake-looking ones Monroe offered Mom and the rest of the family.

"Good evening." Sylvia took the key from her handbag and opened the front door. "The house has been thoroughly cleaned and everything is out of it that I won't need. If you'd like to walk around and inspect each of the rooms before you sign the rental contract, it's fine with me."

He shook his head. "No need for me to look around. I'm sure the rooms are okay."

Sylvia went in first, and Dennis followed. She led the way to the kitchen, and placed the written agreement on the table, along with a pen. "There's a carbon paper under the first page," she explained. "That way, we'll both have a copy."

"Makes sense to me." Dennis took a seat at the table and read the agreement. "Everything looks good. I have no problem with any of it and will gladly sign the papers." He reached for his wallet and handed her the first month's rent. "Since your address is on the invoice I'll know where to send the check each month. And if it's okay, I may drop by some time to check out the greenhouse."

"I may not be there when you come over, but either my mother or sister can show you around and offer any help you may need if you decide to purchase anything."

He gave a nod. "Do you and your brother have plans to do more birding anytime soon?"

Sylvia shrugged. "I don't know. We haven't talked about it."

"Let me know if you do. If it works into my schedule, maybe I can join you."

"Umm . . . maybe. We'll have to see how it goes."

Although the idea appealed to Sylvia, she

wasn't sure going bird-watching with Dennis was a good idea. She didn't want to start any gossip or speculation going around that either of them might have some interest in each other, for that was certainly not the case — at least not on her part. Furthermore, Dennis had given no indication that he might be interested in her. With him being new to the area, he was probably looking for companionship and someone to share his interest in birds. Since Dennis was older and more mature than Henry, he could also be a good role model for her brother. If Sylvia went along, it would only be if Henry wanted her to join them. It would also depend on whether either Mom or Amy was free to watch Rachel and Allen.

After Dennis signed the rental agreement, he asked a few questions, and she agreed to his requests regarding the use of the property. When he handed Sylvia the papers, she put her copy in her purse, along with Dennis's check and left his copy on the table. "My brother and I should get going, but don't hesitate to call if you have any questions about anything here in the house or other parts of the property."

"I appreciate that." Dennis shook her hand. "Danki for your willingness to rent this place to me. I'll do my best to keep everything nice and in good working order."

Sylvia said goodbye and returned to her horse and buggy, where Henry waited.

When they pulled out of the yard, a strange feeling came over her. Getting the first month's rent and giving Dennis a key to the home she used to share with Toby made his death seem so final — like coming to the end of a novel. Only, Sylvia didn't feel the satisfaction that came from reaching the end of a book. Her heart ached more than ever.

# CHAPTER 15

Dennis awakened the following morning, feeling a bit disoriented. The mattress he'd slept upon was not the unyielding cot he'd used at James's place. This bed was comfortable, making it hard to come fully awake.

He rubbed his eyes and sat up. Looking around the cozy room, Dennis appreciated that, unlike the drab accommodations he'd had before, this room looked freshly painted in a warm tan. It also came furnished with an oak dresser, bedframe, coat rack, and cedar-lined storage chest at the foot of the bed. The room, along with the others in the house, had oak-trimmed mopboards and window and door frames. Even the floors were finished in oak throughout most of the rooms, except the bathroom and kitchen. Dennis liked the place so far. It was more than adequate for his needs and quite comfortable.

He sat up and put his feet on the soft area

rug next to the bed. *This is what I envisioned for myself — a nice house with homey comforts.* Dennis smiled. *I wonder if Sylvia would mind if I got a* hund *and brought it into the house at night.*

He shook his head. *Guess that's not the best idea, since I'll be working most days and don't really have time to care for a dog. She may be opposed to having an animal in the house too.*

As Dennis made his way to the window and lifted the shade, he felt a sense of exhilaration. Last evening, after he'd signed the rental agreement, Sylvia had given him permission to mow down the field and create a track where he could train horses to pull a carriage. He would get started on that as soon as he'd eaten breakfast.

His stomach growled at the thought of food, but then he remembered there was nothing in the refrigerator yet. He would need to eat breakfast at one of the local restaurants and do some grocery shopping this morning.

Dennis looked for his wallet on the dresser but realized it wasn't there. *I seem to have misplaced it. I'd better keep looking.*

Dennis hurried to get dressed and went out to the kitchen for a glass of water. As he sipped it, he noticed his wallet sitting near the coffee pot on the counter. He groaned. *I remember now — I set it there last night to remind myself to buy some coffee.* He grabbed the wallet and put it in his pocket. It was nice that Sylvia had left plenty of dishes, as well as pots and pans in the cupboards for his use. He sure hadn't expected her to leave him coffee or other food staples.

Dennis had thought he would make out a grocery list but figured there was no use in doing that. He needed pretty much everything to start out with, so he'd just wander through the store and put whatever items he wanted into the cart as he went along.

*Guess I'd better comb my hair and brush my teeth before hitching my horse to the buggy and heading for town.* He pushed his chair back and stood. *Think I might pick up some birdseed today too. May as well see if I can lure some interesting birds into the yard. Then I can record them in my birding journal, along with the others I've seen while out bird-watching.*

Dennis hoped Sylvia had no regrets about renting her place to him, because he had a good feeling about living here. Sylvia had said she had no plans of moving back here, so someday, if things worked out, maybe she would agree to sell him the house and property. In the meantime, Dennis would make the most out of living here.

For the first time since moving to Lancaster County, Virginia found herself feeling less anxious and able to relax. She figured it was because Stella was here and her loneliness, if only for a short time, had gone away. Virginia wished her friend could live in Pennsylvania too. They could do many things together, like they did when she and Earl lived in Chicago. Now she and Stella only had a short time to squeeze in some fun and make a few memories.

*Sure wish I could convince her to move here, but since Stella's husband has a good job in Chicago, it probably won't happen.*

"Would you like more toast or another boiled egg?" Virginia offered as she and Stella lingered at the table over a cup of coffee. Earl had left for work half an hour ago. She reached for the creamer, added some to her coffee, and gave it a gentle stir. *My husband has been getting along well with our guest. He seemed to enjoy chatting with Stella last evening.*

"No more toast for me. I'm plenty full from what I already ate." Stella lifted her mug and took a drink. "As soon as we fin-

184

ish our coffee, let's put our dishes in the dishwasher and head across the street to your neighbor's greenhouse."

Virginia groaned inwardly. She'd hoped her friend would have forgotten about the silly notion of seeing the greenhouse and meeting the Amish family who ran it. *Stella acts like a full-blown tourist, wanting to see the Plain people. I hope she doesn't expect me to drive her all over the place in order to see more of them.*

"Virginia, did you hear what I said?"

Virginia blinked. "Umm . . . yeah, I heard you. Just not sure going over there's a good idea."

"Why not?"

"I told you yesterday — those people are strange. I have nothing in common with them, and neither will you."

"You never know. We might hit it off famously and discover we have some things in common." Stella winked.

Virginia lifted her gaze to the ceiling. "Right."

"So can we go?"

"Why don't you head over there while I take care of the dishes? The place is open now. I can tell by all the horse and buggy traffic."

Stella shook her head. "No way. I want

185

you to introduce me to your neighbors."

"Can't you make your own introductions? I mean, you're not a shy person."

"True, but I'd rather you went along."

Virginia wasn't sure what else she could say to dissuade her friend from going over there. *If I said I have a headache, would that help? No, Stella would probably see right through the fib. I could tell her my leg hurts this morning and I don't want to do much walking. Yeah, that's the best approach.*

Virginia finished the last of her coffee and reached down to rub her knee. "I'm in quite a bit of pain this morning. Don't think my leg can handle walking that far."

"Not a problem. We can drive over there in my car." Stella finished her coffee and pushed back her chair. "You sit there and relax while I put the dishes in the dishwasher. Then we'll be on our way."

*This is getting me nowhere. Stella is determined to follow through on this silly endeavor, and now I feel like I have no choice.* Virginia's shoulders curled forward as she cringed internally. She figured short of passing out cold, there was no way she could get out of going.

When Virginia entered the greenhouse with Stella, her palms became sweaty. Several

Amish people wandered up and down the aisles, and she caught sight of Belinda talking to one of them. This was definitely not Virginia's favorite place to be.

"Aren't you gonna introduce me to the young lady behind the counter?" Stella whispered close to Virginia's ear.

"Uh . . . yeah . . . sure." Virginia approached the counter, with Stella at her side. "This is my friend, Stella," she said, barely looking at Amy.

Amy stretched out her arm to shake hands with Stella. "It's nice to meet you. I'm Amy."

Stella smiled. "This is a really nice place you have here. I've always been fascinated with greenhouses."

*Seriously?* Virginia pursed her lips in an attempt to maintain a neutral expression. This was news to her. In all the time she'd known Stella, she'd never once heard her mention going to a greenhouse, much less having a fascination with them.

"I'm glad you like it." Amy smiled. "But the greenhouse isn't mine. It belongs to my mother. I just work here, along with my younger brother. Sometimes, in a pinch, our older sister helps out too."

"So it's a family affair?"

Amy nodded just before a customer approached the counter with a wagonload of plants.

"We'd better get going." Virginia nudged her friend's arm. "Things are getting busy here, and we don't want to get in the way."

Stella's gaze flicked upward. "I'm not ready to go yet. We just got here. I'd like to have a look around." She touched Virginia's arm. "If your leg's bothering you too much to walk with me, why don't you go out and wait in the car?"

Virginia's toes curled inside her sneakers. If she sat in the car, Stella would probably take longer to look around. But if she walked with her, Stella might hurry things along. "I'll be fine. I'm not waiting in the car," she responded.

"Okay then, we can walk slowly, so it doesn't put so much pressure on your leg," Stella slowed her pace.

*Oh great. At this rate we'll be here all day.*

By the time they'd made their rounds and seen all of the greenhouse, Stella had picked out several packets of seeds, plus some gardening utensils. She mentioned the idea of buying a few plants but decided not to since she wouldn't be going back to Chicago for a few more days, and was worried that they might not survive the trip home.

When they went to the counter to check

out, Amy and Belinda were both there. Amy introduced Stella to her mother, and the two women shook hands.

"It's nice to see you again, Virginia." Belinda offered her a pleasant smile.

Virginia managed to smile in return, while mumbling, "Uh, same here."

Several more minutes went by as Stella conversed with the Amish women. Virginia was relieved when her friend gathered up her purchases and moved toward the door with a cheerful, "Goodbye." Of course, Virginia felt forced to say goodbye to Amy and Belinda, before following Stella out the door.

Virginia wasn't sure what hurt the most — her pounding head or the throbbing in her leg.

As they drove the short distance back to her house, Stella chattered on about the lovely greenhouse.

When Stella pulled her vehicle onto the driveway and set the brake, she turned to face Virginia. "I can't understand why you don't like those people. Both women seemed very nice to me."

"Yeah, well, that's easy enough for you to say. You don't live across from them, and you're not being forced to hear the traffic noise brought on by all those people visiting that greenhouse nearly every day." Virginia got out of the car and limped her way onto the porch.

"I'm glad we went there," Stella said, upon entering the house.

"How's your family doing?" Virginia asked, needing to change the subject.

"Everyone's fine. Jim's wife got a new job last month, but I must have already told you about it."

Virginia shook her head. "I'm sure I'd remember if you did. What about your daughter? How's she getting along since her divorce?"

"It's been difficult, but she's adjusting to the change. Judy comes by and visits us quite often."

*Lucky you.* Virginia took a seat on the couch and motioned for Stella to do the same. *How nice it would be to have a family who would come and visit me and Earl.*

After Sylvia put the children down for their afternoon naps, she went outside to check the clothes on the line. With the gentle warm breeze that had been blowing for the last few hours, all or most of the clothes were bound to be dry by now.

When Sylvia stepped outside, the sight of clean sheets flapping in the breeze brought back childhood memories. Ever since she was a girl, Sylvia had enjoyed helping her mother hang the laundry. The fresh scent that followed her into the house when the clothes were dry was something she'd always looked forward to. It was strange how she viewed as special what some would see as a mundane chore.

Two sparrows splashing in the birdbath nearby caught Sylvia's attention. She paused from her job of removing the sheets to watch as the birds took drinks then flew in and out of their nests in the trees.

*No wonder Henry enjoys watching the birds so much. If I had more time I'd take a seat on the porch and just watch and listen.*

A bird on a branch overhead let loose with its mesmerizing song as it imitated other birds in the yard.

"That mockingbird is really something, isn't it?" Henry asked as he joined Sylvia by the clothesline.

She nodded. "I can't tell if it's trying to entertain or mock us."

"It's hard to say." Henry stared into the tree. "Did you know that young males often sing at night?"

Sylvia shook her head. "I don't know much about any kind of bird, but I'd like to learn."

"I bet Dennis could tell us more than I know. He seems to have a lot of knowledge about birds found here in this state."

"You could be right, Henry, but if you keep studying birds and learning all you can about them, it won't be long before you'll know as much as Dennis."

Henry's eyes brightened. "You think so?"

"I do." Sylvia took a sheet down from the line and placed it in her wicker basket. "You know, when Dennis met us at the house to get the key, he said that if either of us would like to go bird-watching again, to let him know, and he'd be glad to go along."

"I'd like that. Do you have his phone number? Can we give him a call?"

"He gave me his cell number, but I think it might be too soon to pester him about going bird-watching with us. He just moved into my house last night and will need time to get settled in. He'll also have to advertise and get his business of horse training going. If you want to go birding again soon, you can either go by yourself when you're not working, or wait till I'm free to go with you."

"I'd rather wait for you. Bird-watching is more fun when you do it with someone else."

Sylvia smiled. She was pleased that her brother had not only found a new hobby to enjoy but also wanted to include her. Hopefully, they'd be able to take some time to go birding soon.

enior but also wanted to include her Hopefully, they'd be able to take some time to go
hiking soon.

# CHAPTER 16

Belinda stood in front of the bathroom mirror, staring at her reflection. She still needed
to put on her headscarf before leaving for
work. She turned her head from side to side,
checking to be sure no hairs had come loose
from her bun. After fixing a few stray ones,
she tied the black scarf in place.

Belinda sighed. Today was her fifty-first
birthday and the depression she felt made
her feel like she was a hundred years old.
But it wasn't turning a year older that put a
lump in her throat. Today was the anniversary of her husband, son, and son-in-
law's deaths. Just when she thought she was
doing a little better, she was hit once again
with the reality that the three of them were
gone and wouldn't be coming back.

*Poor Sylvia. I'm sure she must be hurting
real bad too. This day must also be hard for
my other children as they think about the family members they lost.*

Tears welled in Belinda's eyes. *I hope the children haven't planned anything special for my birthday this evening. I need to keep my mind off what day it is, so I'll focus on my work in the greenhouse. This evening, it'll be a quiet meal with the family, and then off to bed. No fuss — no bother — just another regular day.*

Belinda dried her eyes and blew her nose on a tissue. Then she splashed cold water on her face. *I'll feel better once today is over.*

Amy scurried about the kitchen, hoping to get breakfast on before her mother got up. It was bad enough that Mom had to work on her birthday. She shouldn't have to cook for everyone too.

The children padded into the kitchen in their bare feet, and Allen asked his auntie what was for breakfast.

"I'm fixing pancakes," Amy replied. "If you and your sister will go out to the living room and play, I'll call you when breakfast is ready."

Allen grinned, grabbed Rachel's hand, and trotted out of the kitchen.

Amy smiled as she went back to preparing the meal. She hoped the day would go well for her mother and that she would have a pleasant birthday.

As a surprise, Amy and Sylvia had made

plans to hire a driver and take their mother out for supper at Shady Maple this evening. They hadn't told Henry yet, but Amy felt sure he'd enjoy going to the big buffet restaurant in East Earl. With so many options to choose from, diners found it nearly impossible not to find something they wanted to eat. Because today was also the one-year anniversary of their loved ones' deaths, it would be better to go out to celebrate Mom's birthday than to celebrate at home where the memory of that fateful day still lingered in each of their minds. She hoped by being in a public place with lots of food and action, Mom, as well as the rest of the family, would have an easier time. *Who knows,* she thought. *We might all relax and enjoy ourselves, even though we'll wish Dad, Abe, and Toby could be with us.*

Amy thought about Jared and how brokenhearted she'd be if something happened to him. Just pondering the idea was enough to put a lump in her throat. She couldn't fathom how Mom and Sylvia must feel, having lost their husbands.

When Sylvia entered the kitchen, she saw that Amy had already set the table and was now busy mixing pancake batter. Three banana peels lay next to the bowl, signaling that Amy was stirring together Mom's favorite — banana pancakes.

"I'm sorry for leaving you with all the work," Sylvia apologized. "When I woke up this morning and the reality of what day it was set in, I had to remain in my room awhile to get control of my emotions."

"It's fine. I understand."

*Do you really?* Sylvia wanted to ask, but she kept it to herself. There was no way Amy could understand, so nothing would be gained by posing such a question.

"Is Mom up yet?" Sylvia questioned instead.

Amy shrugged her slender shoulders. "She hasn't come in here, but she might be in her bedroom or the bathroom, getting ready to face the day."

"When should we tell her about our plans for this evening?"

"Not till the greenhouse closes for the day and we come up to the house. She'll no doubt say something about needing to get supper started, and that's when we can tell her our plans."

"So it'll be a surprise until then." Sylvia got out a cube of butter and the maple syrup bottle, along with a jar of honey, which she actually preferred on her pancakes.

Amy nodded. "I think eating supper at Shady Maple will be good for all of us."

"I hope so." Sylvia released a heavy sigh, looking toward the doorway. "Do you think it'll be a mistake to take Allen and Rachel along?" she whispered. "We could drop them off at Mary Ruth's. I'm sure she and Lenore wouldn't mind watching them while we're gone. I could go out to the phone shed and leave a message for them right now, which should give plenty of time for their response."

"It's up to you, Sister, but I'm fairly certain that Mom will want the whole family at her birthday supper."

"True, but our whole family won't be there. Ezekiel, Michelle, and their kinner will not be with us."

Amy turned to face Sylvia, with her chin tilted down. "I still wish our bruder would have moved back to Strasburg after Dad, Abe, and Toby died. We could certainly use his help in the greenhouse, not to mention the emotional support and spiritual guidance he would offer."

Sylvia didn't care about receiving spiritual guidance from her brother or anyone else, but it would have been nice if he'd decided to move back here and help in the greenhouse. It would take some of the load off

Mom, Amy, and even Henry. It would also mean Sylvia would never have to work in the greenhouse again. She couldn't help thinking that things might be better for all of them if Ezekiel and Michelle lived closer.

By the time their mother entered the kitchen, breakfast was done and ready to be put on the table. Coming into the room, she sniffed. "Something smells wunderbaar in here."

"Happy birthday, Mom," Amy and Sylvia said in unison.

"Danki." Mom's gaze went to the table. "For goodness' sake, you girls have outdone yourself this morning." She put both hands against her cheeks as she looked at the stack of pancakes piled high on a plate in the center of the table. "And it appears that you've fixed my favorite banana pannekuche."

"We sure did." Amy's lips pressed together. "Now if Henry would just get here, we could all eat."

"Where is our bruder?" Sylvia asked. "Shouldn't he be in from choring by now?"

Mom bobbed her head. "You're right, he should. Would one of you mind going out to the barn to see if he's still in there?"

"I'll go," Sylvia volunteered. "The kinner

are still playing in the living room and will come to breakfast when you call them." She pointed to the table. "There's no point in letting those delicious-looking pancakes get cold, so Mom and Amy, why don't you go ahead and start eating? I'll be back soon with Henry."

Mom called out to the children and tilted her head, as if weighing her choices. "Okay, if you insist, but when you see your brother, please ask him to hurry. If he's late eating breakfast, he'll be late coming to the greenhouse today."

"I'll give him your message." Sylvia seated the kids before she left the kitchen and then went out the back door. It didn't take long to see why Henry hadn't come into the house. She spotted him on the far side of the yard, looking up at a tree with his binoculars.

She hurried over to stand beside him. "What are you doing, Brother? Mom, Amy, and my kinner have already started eating breakfast, and Mom said you need to hurry so you're not late to work."

"I'm lookin' at a red-winged blackbird." He pointed, and then handed Sylvia the binoculars. "See it up there?"

She held them up and peered through the lenses. Sure enough, there sat the pretty bird that had begun warbling a pretty song. Sylvia watched it several seconds, then handed the binoculars back to Henry. "As nice as it is to watch the *voggel,* today is Mom's birthday, and the least we can do is sit with her at the table and enjoy the nice breakfast Amy made."

Henry continued to watch the bird. "I realize it's Mom's *gebottsdaag,* but I can't forget that it's also been a year since Dad, Abe, and Toby were killed in that horrible accident in front of our house." He sniffed a couple of times then cleared his throat. "I don't feel much like celebrating today, and I bet Mom doesn't either."

"None of us do, Henry, but sitting around all day feeling sorry for ourselves won't change our circumstances, will it?"

He gave a slow shake of his head.

"Mom doesn't know it yet, but we're all going out for supper this evening at the Shady Maple buffet." She touched his arm. "So please be careful you don't let it slip."

"I won't say a word, but I bet goin' out to supper won't keep Mom from thinkin' about what happened to our family members."

"Probably not, but it might cheer her up a bit."

"What about you, Sylvia?" Henry looked

at her pointedly. "Will a trip to Shady Maple take the pain of losing your husband, father, and brother away?"

"No," she admitted, "but after a year of mourning, I've come to the conclusion that it's time to put my black clothes away and at least try to start living again and looking for things to smile about. My kinner deserve a mudder who isn't always sad and moody."

"Guess you're right." Henry took hold of Sylvia's arm and started walking toward the house. "You wanna know something?"

"What's that?"

"I'm still mad at God for takin' three important men in my life away."

*Me too, Henry, and I'm not sure my faith will ever be restored again.* Sylvia gave her brother's arm a little squeeze, but she kept her thoughts to herself.

*Clymer*

"Are you all packed, Michelle?" Ezekiel called when he entered the house at nine-thirty that morning. He'd returned from his shop where he'd made sure he had plenty of work laid out for his employees, Joseph and Andy, to do during the four days he and his family would be in Strasburg. There was no point in traveling such a distance unless they could stay at least that long.

With their nine-month-old son in her arms, Michelle stepped into the living room, where Ezekiel waited. "Almost ready. Angela Mary's looking for one of her shoes, and I was trying to help her find it when you called out to me."

"Here, let me have this little guy while you assist our daughter." Ezekiel held out his arms and smiled when Vernon went to him willingly.

"You're looking forward to going to see your family as much as I am, aren't you?"

He nodded. "I'm glad we decided not to tell them we're coming. It'll be a fun surprise birthday gift from us when we show up unexpectedly."

"I hope they're home when we get there. But in case they're out somewhere, you might want to take your key to their house."

"I doubt they'll be gone, but don't worry. I have a spare on my key ring."

"Good. I'd like to be prepared in the event that they may have made plans to go out somewhere for supper to celebrate your mamm's birthday."

Ezekiel shook his head. "I can't remember a time in the past when we celebrated her or my daed's birthday anyplace but at home. They always said home was the happiest place they could be with their family."

Michelle leaned forward and encompassed Ezekiel and the baby in a hug. "I feel that way about my little family too. I have to admit, though, it is nice to eat out at a restaurant once in a while."

"Same here, but I assure you, when we get to Strasburg around five this evening, everyone will be home, and soon after we get there it'll be time for supper." Ezekiel gave a wide grin. "I can hardly wait to see the look on Mom's face when we show up."

# CHAPTER 17

*Strasburg*

Virginia set her crossword puzzle aside and made her way to the kitchen for a cup of coffee. It would be several hours yet before Earl came home from work, and she would need to come up with something for supper.

She scratched her head. *I'm drawing a blank on what to fix. Something different would be nice for a change.*

Her gaze came to rest on the new cookbook sitting there, full of Amish recipes. Unbeknownst to her, Stella had bought them both a copy, and she'd surprised Virginia with it on the last day of her visit.

She exhaled noisily. *Stella's my only true friend, and I miss her company.* Virginia lifted the cookbook and thumbed through the pages. *I wonder if she's tried any of these recipes.*

If Virginia had her way, she and Earl

would go out to eat every night, but that was unrealistic. He made enough selling cars to pay for their basic expenses, but he'd been trying to put some money into their savings account and had stated several times that there should be no unnecessary spending. He'd made it clear to Virginia that going out to a restaurant once or twice a month was all they could afford. Even then, he almost always chose less expensive restaurants.

*At least my husband isn't a cheapskate when it comes to buying new appliances when they quit working and cost too much to be repaired,* Virginia reminded herself. *Guess I should be grateful for that. And, he's never insisted that I get a job to help with our expenses.*

She filled her mug with coffee and took a seat at the table. *Stella and I had some good chats while she was here a few weeks ago. Sure wish I had a friend like her who lived close by.*

Virginia blew on her coffee. *I can't make friends with any of the Amish women who live nearby. We have nothing in common.* She tapped her fingers on the table. *What would we have to talk about — how many bales of hay they need to feed their horses? Or maybe*

206

*we could discuss how to wash dishes by hand or sew a plain dress.* She wrinkled her nose. *I don't think so. If I'm going to find a new friend, I'll have to look elsewhere, because sitting home by myself five days a week has left me in a depressed state.*

Belinda felt thankful that they'd been busy in the greenhouse all day, because it had kept her mind occupied and free of negative thoughts. Amy tried to be cheerful too, which helped a lot. Henry, on the other hand, hadn't said much to either of them, other than his quick, "Happy birthday," to Belinda this morning before they opened for business.

She still looked forward to a quiet supper with her family this evening and figured if it didn't rain, as predicted, they might get out the barbecue and grill some burgers. She hoped her daughters hadn't made any plans to fix an elaborate meal, because all she wanted was something simple. After supper and the dishes had been done, Belinda planned to sit in one of the recliners with her feet up and listen to the chatter of her grandchildren as they played with their toys.

The greenhouse door opened, and she shifted on her stool to see who'd come in. She was surprised to see Monroe enter the building, carrying a yellow gift bag.

"Happy birthday, Belinda." He handed her the gift. "I hope you like what I got for you."

Belinda wasn't sure how to respond. His appearance with a gift had taken her by surprise. She'd never expected Monroe to remember that today was her birthday, even though he'd attended a few of her birthday gatherings when they were teenagers.

"Umm . . . well, danki, Monroe. It was thoughtful of you to remember me today," she said earnestly.

"I think of you most every day, Belinda." He leaned close to the counter. "Go ahead — open it."

Belinda pulled the card from the bag first and read it silently. *To someone special, on her birthday. Your good friend, Monroe.*

She smiled and gave him a nod, then reached into the bag and took out a box of pretty stationery with yellow daisies and a matching kitchen towel. "These are lovely. Thank you, Monroe."

"Glad you like 'em." A relaxed smile crossed his face as he puffed out his chest a bit. "So are you doing anything special this evening to celebrate your birthday?"

"No, not really. It'll be a nice quiet evening at home with my family."

"I see."

Belinda held her breath, wondering if Monroe would drop any hints about joining them for supper, but to her relief he said nothing in that regard.

"Well, that's all I came here for — to give you the gift and wish you a happy birthday. So I guess I'll be on my way." Monroe started for the door.

"Thank you for coming," Belinda called to his retreating form. When the door clicked shut behind him, she breathed a sigh of relief. With Monroe being so nice and giving her a gift, it was difficult not to give in and invite him to join them for supper. But she'd made the decision not to encourage him in any way, and she needed to stick with it.

"You'd better hurry and change your clothes," Amy instructed her mother. "Our driver will be here soon to pick us all up."

Mom crooked an eyebrow. "What driver? Where are we going?"

"It's a surprise." Amy grinned. "Come on now, you need to get changed. Sylvia's getting the kinner ready, and as far as I know, Henry's dressed in clean clothes and ready to go too."

"Is Jared coming with us?" Mom asked.

209

"Jah, he should be here any minute." While Jared wasn't a family member, he would be soon, and as far as Amy was concerned, he should be at all family functions.

*It's too bad Ezekiel and his family can't join us tonight,* she thought with regret. He'd sent a birthday card for Mom, which had been in yesterday's mail, but there was no phone message from him today, which Amy thought was a bit strange. *If my brother was too busy, I would think Michelle would have reminded him to call our mother on her special day.*

Amy wondered if Mom's birthday and the anniversary of Dad, Abe, and Toby's death could have slipped her brother's mind. If so, then he had too many other, less important things, to think about.

Amy turned to her mother and said one final time, "Please, Mom, hurry now and change into a different dress."

"All right, I'm going." Mom glanced around, as if looking for some answers before hurrying from the room.

*East Earl, Pennsylvania*
"I wish you'd tell me where we are going," Mom said from the back seat of their driver Helen's van. "And I don't see why I have to

wear a scarf over my eyes."

Sylvia tapped her mother's shoulder. "You'll know soon enough."

"We're covering your eyes so you don't guess where we're going," Amy added from the front seat.

"I bet she knows anyhow, even with the blindfold," Henry chimed in. He sat beside Mom on the first seat in the back, with Sylvia and the children behind them.

"No, I don't." Mom shook her head. "But it's taking us a while to get there, so I'm sure it's not some restaurant close to home."

"You are right, Belinda," Helen interjected. "And we're almost there."

When they pulled into the parking lot in front of Shady Maple, Sylvia leaned forward and untied the scarf around her mother's eyes. "We're here — at your favorite place to eat."

"Mine too — especially when I'm really *hungerich,*" Henry put in.

Mom looked around and giggled like a schoolgirl. "Oh my — it's Shady Maple!"

Sylvia smiled. She hadn't seen her mother this happy since the last time Ezekiel and his family came to visit.

After Helen parked the van, they all got out and headed for the restaurant. Although Sylvia's mood wasn't the best it could be, it was good to see Mom so happy. And she certainly deserved to be.

*Strasburg*

"We're here!" Michelle exclaimed when their driver pulled into her mother-in-law's home. "After a seven-hour drive, it's nice that we can finally relax and stretch our legs."

Ezekiel gave a nod. "Why don't you take the kinner on up to the house, while I get our luggage out of the van and talk to our driver about the day and time we'll need to return home? Tell Mom and the rest of the family that I'll be in soon."

Michelle got out, helped Angela Mary down, and took Vernon out of his car seat. Then she told her daughter to walk beside her as they made their way onto the front porch.

"Knock on the door, Angela Mary," Michelle instructed.

The little girl did as she was told, but when no one answered, she turned and looked up at Michelle with a frown. "How come nobody's lettin' us in?"

"Maybe you didn't knock loud enough. Try it again, a little harder this time."

Angela clenched her small fist and pounded on the door.

Michelle bit back a chuckle. If someone inside didn't hear that and answer the door, they must need a hearing aid.

Michelle was about to try the door, when Ezekiel stepped onto the porch with two of their suitcases. "What's going on?" he asked. "Didn't you knock?"

"Our daughter did — the second time really hard — but nobody answered." She looked at her husband, then back at the door. "Do you think it's possible that no one's home?"

"Anything's possible, but it's doubtful. I can't remember Mom ever being anywhere but home on her birthday." Ezekiel rapped on the door. When there was no answer, he turned the knob, but the door didn't open. "Oh boy — it's locked. Now what are we gonna do?"

"Don't you have a key?"

"Oh, yeah, that's right, I do." Ezekiel fumbled in his pocket and withdrew a key. He put it in the lock, turned the key, and the door opened. "Anybody here?" he called.

There was no response, and the house was dark. His family had obviously gone somewhere.

"Let's turn on one of the overhead gas lamps and look around to see if they left us

213

a note," Michelle suggested.

"There'd be no reason for them to have left a note, because they didn't know we were coming, remember? Our being here for Mom's birthday was supposed to be a surprise."

"I guess we're the ones who are surprised." Michelle placed the baby in his carrier on the living room floor. "What are we going to do now, Ezekiel? We're all hungry."

"I suppose we could make some sandwiches. I'll go to the kitchen and see what's in the refrigerator while you take the kids' outer garments off." Ezekiel walked away before Michelle could respond. A few minutes later he was back with a desktop calendar. "I know where they've gone. It's written right here. Good thing I thought to open the roll-top desk and look around." He grinned at Michelle. "I really wasn't sure what to look for, but something told me to open the desk before checking for food in the refrigerator."

"So where'd they go?" Michelle asked. "I'm anxious to know."

"Shady Maple — Mom's favorite place to eat." He did an about-face. "I haven't taken all our things from the van yet, which means we still have a driver. Get the kinner ready, Michelle. We're goin' to Shady Maple!"

■ ■ ■ ■

*East Earl*

Belinda looked at her plate full of food and shook her head. This was more than she ate during an entire day, and she'd no doubt pay the price for it tonight when she tried to sleep. But it was ever so kind of her children to plan this surprise for her birthday, and she planned to enjoy every bite of the delicious food.

Belinda watched Amy and Jared from across the table. The love they felt for each other caused their eyes to glow and faces to smile whenever they looked at each other.

*My dear Vernon used to look at me like that,* Belinda mused. *And I hung on his every word.*

But those days were long past, and now she had to look to the future and be open to whatever plans God had for her. She felt sure, however, that they didn't include remarriage, and most assuredly not to Monroe.

"Well, well . . . So this is where you've chosen to spend your evening, is it?"

Belinda's head came up at the sound of a familiar voice. Her eyes widened as Ezekiel and Michelle stood beside their table, each holding one of their children. "What are you

215

doing here, and how'd you know where we would be?"

"We decided a few weeks ago to come down from New York to surprise you on your birthday, but we're the ones who got the big surprise when we arrived at your house and discovered you weren't at home." Ezekiel shook his finger at Amy and then Sylvia. "Why didn't one of you tell me you had plans to bring our mamm here?"

"We didn't tell you because we had no idea you were coming to see us." Amy shook a finger right back at him. "You should have called and let us know about your plans."

"And take the chance that Mom might find out? Never!"

"How'd ya know we were here?" The question came from Henry.

"When we discovered nobody was home, I used my key to open the door. Then, while Michelle and the kinner waited in the living room, I went to the kitchen to see if there was anything we could use for sandwiches. It was while I was there that I happened to look in the desk." Ezekiel paused a few seconds before he continued. "The words, 'Shady Maple,' were written on the calendar inside the desk, so I figured that must be where you'd all gone."

Tears welled in Belinda's eyes, nearly

obstructing her vision. She left her seat and gave her New York family a hug, with extra kisses for the children. "If you and Michelle would like to go fill your plates and Angela Mary's, we'll keep an eye on the children here at the table. Then when you get back, we can finish our meal and catch up with each other's lives."

"Good idea." Ezekiel situated Angela Mary on a chair, and placed little Vernon on Amy's lap. "We'll be back soon."

Belinda closed her eyes. *Thank You, Lord, for giving me such a loving family.* Although her birthday was somewhat bittersweet, because she missed their departed loved ones and wished they could be here to celebrate with them, Belinda was aware of God's many blessings.

# CHAPTER 18

*Strasburg*

After Virginia saw Earl off to work the following day, she sat on the front porch with a cup of coffee and her crossword puzzle book. It was a beautiful spring morning, with birds chirping from every tree in the yard, as well as those across the road. Her Amish neighbors across the street had a feeder hanging off a branch of a maple tree. It was nice entertainment to use her binoculars and watch the feeding frenzy going on. Sometimes the teenage boy in his straw hat would stand off gazing at the winged action. It seemed intriguing that Amy's young brother was interested in birds. Virginia figured he'd be off running around with other teenagers.

Virginia could see herself bird-watching as a hobby. It would be fun to be able to identify the species of birds in the area. *Maybe I'll buy a bird identification book the next time I'm out shopping.*

She blew on her hot coffee and tried to relax. Her leg had been hurting this morning, so she wouldn't do too much today. Instead, Virginia would sit here awhile, but once the horse-and-buggy traffic started, she'd have to go back inside if she wanted any peace and quiet.

She noticed Belinda King's teenage boy outside. She couldn't tell for sure from this distance, but it looked like he held a pair of binoculars in his hands. When he tipped his head back, as though looking into one of the trees in the yard, a bearded man came out of the house and joined Henry on the lawn. No doubt, the King family had overnight guests. What other reason would they be coming out of the house so early in the morning?

A short time later, a little Amish girl came out of the house, and the bearded man picked her up, then pointed to the tree.

Virginia left her chair and stood at the porch railing, hoping for a better look. *Maybe I should go inside and get my binoculars. I might be able to see what they're looking at.*

Virginia stepped inside, but by the time she came back out, Henry and the visitors were no longer in her line of vision. They'd either gone back to the house or moved somewhere else in the yard.

She thought of Stella and how she'd enjoyed sitting out here, soaking up the country air. One morning, they'd sat on the lounge chairs for over an hour, drinking coffee and chatting. Every now and then, her friend would jump up to watch an Amish carriage go up the road or turn onto the Kings' driveway. Stella had commented, "Don't you just love the quaintness of those Plain people and their old-fashioned mode of transportation?" Virginia would smile, not wanting to ruin Stella's enthusiasm over the very thing that left unsightly messes and brought in more flies.

She snapped her fingers. "Guess I may as well go back inside. So much for spying on the neighbors. Maybe I'll see more the next time."

When a horse and buggy pulled into the yard, Sylvia looked up from her job of pulling weeds in the flowerbed by the house. She was surprised to see Dennis get out of the carriage.

*"Guder mariye,"* he called after he secured his horse to the rail.

"Good morning." Sylvia rose to her feet and headed in his direction.

He met her halfway and offered a pleasant smile. "I'm sorry for the interruption, but I came by to ask a few questions I forgot when we met at your place and you gave me the key."

Sylvia wondered why Dennis hadn't called and left a message with his questions, but she supposed he preferred to ask in person. "What did you need to know?"

"There are some tools in the shed, and I wondered if you plan to take them, or would it be possible for me to buy them from you?"

Sylvia removed her gardening gloves and swiped one hand across her sweaty forehead. The tools had belonged to Toby, and she'd almost forgotten they were in the shed. "I'm not sure I want to sell them at this time, but you're welcome to use any of the tools while you are renting my house."

His chin tilted down as he broke eye contact with her for a few seconds, but then he smiled and said, "Okay, that's fine. I just didn't want to touch 'em till I'd spoken to you."

"I appreciate your consideration."

"I have another question."

"Oh? What's that?"

"I'm interested in getting a dog. Would you have a problem with that, if I kept it outside during the day and only brought it into the house in the evenings?"

Sylvia fingered her apron band as she mulled over his request. Her husband hadn't been a dog person. He'd said having a dog would be one more thing to worry about when they were away from home.

"Would you be leaving it inside when you're not at home?"

Dennis shook his head. "He'd be an outside dog during the day, and I'll even build him a pen to stay in when I'm away from the house." He offered Sylvia a boyish grin. "I've been thinking it would be nice to have a companion around to keep me company — especially in the evenings. Besides, it never hurts to have an extra pair of eyes and ears to let me know when a visitor comes by."

Sylvia smiled. How could she say no to his honest request? "Jah, it's fine. I don't see a problem with you getting a dog."

"Danki." He lifted his straw hat and pulled his fingers through the back of his thick hair. "Thought I'd take a ride Sunday afternoon to enjoy the nice weather and look for some unusual birds. Would you and your brother want to join me?"

A part of her wanted to instantly agree to his offer, but another part of Sylvia — the sensible one — remembered they had company.

"It would be fun to join you, and I'm sure Henry would enjoy it too, but my older brother and his family are here from New York right now. They came to help us celebrate my mamm's birthday, which was yesterday."

"Oh, I see. And I guess they'll still be with you on Sunday?"

"Jah. In fact, my brother Ezekiel, who is a minister, will most likely preach one of the sermons."

"So you'll be expected to spend the day with your family?"

"Not expected," she corrected. "We don't get to see Ezekiel and his family very often, so I want to be with them."

Dennis gave a nod. "I understand. Some families are very tightknit."

Sylvia was on the verge of asking if he and his family were close, when Ezekiel came out of the barn with Henry.

"That's my older brother." She gestured to them, then invited Ezekiel and Henry to come over.

"Hey, Mr. Weaver, it's good to see you." Henry gave Dennis an eager grin when he and Ezekiel joined them.

Sylvia made the introductions, and while

Dennis and Ezekiel shook hands, she told Henry why Dennis had dropped by.

"It wasn't just about the tools either," Dennis said. "I wanted to invite you and your sister to go for a ride with me tomorrow afternoon to look for birds."

"Oh, jah, that'd be great. Count me in." Henry gave a wide grin.

Sylvia placed her hand on his arm. "Henry, I told Mr. Weaver we couldn't go because we have company and will be spending the day with them."

"No problem," Ezekiel was quick to say. "I doubt you'll be gone more than a few hours, and you'll be with us the rest of the day."

Henry's head moved up and down. "See Sylvia . . . Ezekiel said it's okay."

Sylvia felt like she was a fly caught in a sticky trap. If she agreed to go birding with Dennis, what would the rest of her family say? Could they be as agreeable as Ezekiel, or might they think she ought to be with them the whole day?

Dennis waited for Sylvia's response, wondering if he'd made a mistake by asking her to join him Sunday afternoon. He didn't want to appear pushy, but Sylvia had been on his mind ever since their first meeting.

Seeing her wearing a dark green dress today let him know her year of mourning and black clothes had been set aside. However, it didn't mean she no longer mourned the death of her loved ones. That took time — possibly years. Dennis knew that firsthand. Even now, whenever he thought about his father's death, depression could set in. He was glad he'd let his guard down and shared the incident with Sylvia and her brother. Just talking about it had relieved some of his emotional pain.

"I would enjoy looking for birds with you." Sylvia's comment pulled Dennis's thoughts aside. "But would you mind very much if I went out to the greenhouse right now and talked to my mamm about it? I need to see if she's willing to —"

"I don't mind at all. In fact, I'd like to walk out there with you and meet her. It would also be nice to have a look around. I'd like to see what all you have available."

"Sure, that'd be fine." Sylvia led the way, and when they entered the building, she suggested that Dennis look around, while she spoke to her mother, who was currently with a customer.

"No problem." He smiled. "I would like to meet her before I leave, though."

"That's fine. I'm sure there will be time

for it when she's between customers."

"Okay then, I'm off to wander around."

With raised brows, Ezekiel looked at Henry. "Is there something going on between Sylvia and that man?"

Henry squinted. "What do ya mean?"

"Is he lookin' to court her?"

Henry thumped Ezekiel's arm. " 'Course not. What a dumm question."

"It's not dumb at all. I have a hunch from the way that fellow eyeballed our sister that he has more than looking for birds on his mind."

Henry grunted. "Are you kidding me? He barely even knows our sister. Besides, Sylvia's not looking to be courted by anyone. She still loves Toby. I've heard her say so many times."

Ezekiel glanced toward the greenhouse. "That may be, but the bird-dog expression on his face made me think about the way I felt when I first met Michelle." He thumped Henry's back. "There's an interest, all right, but it may only be wishful thinking on his part, because you're right — Sylvia's love for Toby went deep."

"Well, if you feel that way, then why'd you say it was okay for us to go birding with him tomorrow afternoon?"

"Because, little brother, Sylvia has been too serious since Toby, Dad, and Abe were killed. She deserves to have some fun, and so do you."

Henry kicked at a clump of grass with the toe of his boot. "I have fun when I'm with my friend Seth."

"Jah, well from what I've heard, Seth is not a good influence on you."

Henry crossed his arms and gave a huff. "Is that so? Who told you that?"

"Never mind. The point is, you shouldn't hang around with a fellow who might try to steer you in the wrong direction."

"None of my friends have control over me. I'll have you know I can think for myself."

Ezekiel held up his hands. "Now don't go getting your feathers ruffled. I just felt the need to give you a word of caution. I know what it's like to be sixteen, and even when I got older, there was a time when I caused Mom and Dad all kinds of heartache."

"Ya mean when you bought a truck and thought you might not wanna join the church?"

Ezekiel nodded. "But God got a hold of my life and showed me otherwise, and I'm sure glad He did."

"What's God really done for you, Brother?" Henry's tone had an edge to it.

"He let Dad, Abe, and Toby die, and He could have stopped the accident from happening."

Ezekiel put both hands on his brother's shoulders. "God gives everyone a free will, and if you'll remember, all three men wanted to get ice cream for Mom's birthday, even though she didn't want them to go."

Henry stared at the ground. "I remember."

"When they made that decision, they had no idea what their fate would be, but it was their choice, and perhaps even their time to leave this earth."

Henry slowly shook his head and walked off toward the greenhouse.

Ezekiel bowed his head. *Heavenly Father, please open my brother's eyes to the truth and help him come to terms with what happened. Blaming You for something that was an accident is not helping him recover from the anger he feels. Please help me to set a good example for him, and grant Henry peace of mind and the desire to serve You.*

Dennis stopped to look at primroses and a few other early spring flowers. Then he moved on to check out some of the outdoor items, such as birdbaths and solar lighting.

*A birdbath might be a nice touch to my yard,* he decided. Even though Sylvia's house didn't belong to Dennis, he still thought of it as home. Giving the birds that came into the yard a nice place to drink and bathe seemed like a good idea. He also planned to hang several bird feeders and houses. These would increase his chances of seeing a good variety of birds.

Dennis had made the complete tour of the greenhouse when Sylvia came up to him and said her mother was fine with her and Henry going with him Sunday afternoon. "She would like to meet you, though," Sylvia added. "And so would my sister, Amy."

"I'd enjoy meeting them too."

Dennis followed Sylvia to the front of the building, where a middle-age lady and a younger woman who looked close to Sylvia's age stood behind the checkout counter.

When Sylvia introduced Dennis to her mother and sister, he shook their hands. "This is a nice place you have here. There's a good variety of items for sale. And speaking of which . . . I want to buy one of your birdbaths today." He looked at Sylvia. "I'd like to put it in the front yard, near the big maple tree."

"That'd be nice." She smiled, although it seemed a bit forced.

"Are you sure you don't mind?"

She shook her head. "As long as you're

living there, feel free to put whatever you like in the yard and also the house."

"Danki, I appreciate that." Dennis walked back to where the birdbaths were located and brought the one he liked up front to pay for it. He then visited with the three women until two more customers came in. "I'd better get going. It was nice to meet you, Belinda and Amy."

"We enjoyed meeting you as well," Amy said.

Belinda nodded and moved down the aisle behind the people who had come in.

When Dennis walked out with the birdbath, Sylvia accompanied him.

"Hey, what have ya got there?" Henry asked, stepping around the side of the building.

Dennis chuckled. "You mean you work here and have never seen a birdbath?"

Henry snickered. " 'Course I've seen 'em. Just wasn't expecting to see you carrying one out of the greenhouse."

"I'm gonna put it in my front yard, and hopefully it'll lure in more birds." He started walking toward his horse and buggy and was pleased when Sylvia went with him.

Since the birdbath was in two pieces, he placed them both on the floor in the back of his buggy. "Is three o'clock a good time for me to pick you and Henry up tomorrow?" he asked.

"That should be fine."

"Okay, great. I'll see you then."

When Dennis pulled his rig out of the yard a few minutes later, he found himself whistling — not a tune to any song he knew — but the whistle of a young male mockingbird's song. He could hardly wait until tomorrow afternoon.

# CHAPTER 19

"What are you looking at, Virginia? You're not spying on the neighbors, I hope."

She whirled around to face her husband, nearly dropping the binoculars she held. "For heaven's sake, Earl, don't sneak up on me like that. You nearly scared me to death."

He rolled his eyes and moved closer to where she stood at the living room window. "What were you looking at?"

"Just watching the King family and their guests. There's a group of them, and they climbed into two buggies and headed out down the road. I'm surprised you didn't hear the horses clomping their hooves on the pavement."

He shook his head. "I was in the bathroom, and the only thing I heard was the water running while I showered."

She glanced out the window again. "There's more horse and buggies coming down the road now, so tell me you can't

232

hear those."

"Oh, I hear 'em all right." Earl peered out the window. "Looks like a whole procession."

"I wonder where they're all going."

"Probably church. From what I understand, the Amish worship in one another's homes every other Sunday."

Virginia lifted the binoculars for a better look. "Now that I think about it, there has been a string of Amish buggies going down the road on Sundays about this time of day, twice monthly." She lowered the binoculars and turned to look at Earl. "I wonder why they hold their worship service in people's homes instead of a church building. That seems strange, doesn't it?"

"It does to us, but I'm sure to them it's normal." Earl moved away from the window and motioned for her to do the same. "Come on, Virginia, that's enough spying for now."

She frowned. "What else do I have to do that's exciting?"

"Why don't you put on a sweater and we'll take a Sunday drive?"

"Where to?"

"I picked up a map the other day of covered bridges in the area. We could check those out."

"Okay, I'll get my sweater and meet you in the car." Virginia wasn't the least bit interested in looking at covered bridges, but it would be better than sitting home all day, listening to Earl snore up a storm when he fell asleep watching television.

Holding her children's hands, Sylvia entered the barn on Mary Ruth Lapp's property, where church was being held. She took a seat on a backless wooden bench, between Amy and their mother. They would both help keep the children quiet during the three-hour service.

Sylvia glanced at the men's side of the room, and noticed that Dennis wasn't there. Then she remembered that because he now occupied her old house, which was in another church district, today would be his off-Sunday. When Sylvia saw Dennis later today, if she didn't forget, she would mention that he'd be welcome to visit this church on his in-between Sundays.

She reached up and adjusted her head covering ties. *Listen to me — all worried about Dennis. I barely know him, so why should I be concerned about where he attends church?*

Sylvia thought about how she and Toby used to visit her parents' church whenever possible on their off-Sundays. Afterward they would go to Mom and Dad's house to visit and share a meal. Those were such happy times, although Sylvia had taken them for granted. She had believed that she and Toby would grow old together, raising their children, and someday becoming grandparents.

Thinking about all she'd lost caused Sylvia to choke up as she held Rachel firmly on her lap. Tears pricked the backs of her eyes when she saw Allen holding his grandma's hand. How sad that her son was missing out on the joy of being with his Grandpa King and didn't see Grandpa and Grandma Beiler nearly enough due to them living in another part of the state.

*At least my kinner have a grandma, an aunt, and one uncle who all live close by and will have a positive influence on them.*

Sylvia glanced at Henry sitting beside his friend, Seth. *I hope my younger brother will put aside his curiosity with worldly things and set a good example for Allen and Rachel. I'd hate to think otherwise.*

Sylvia's thoughts were pulled aside when the first song from the Ausbund was announced. She swallowed past the thickening in her throat and forced herself to sing along.

■ ■ ■ ■

Ezekiel rubbed a sweaty palm down his pant leg. As a guest minister, he'd been asked to deliver a sermon this morning, and he couldn't help feeling a bit nervous. *I hope what I plan to say will be beneficial to someone here today.*

Ezekiel had grown up in this church district and known many of the people for most of his life. It seemed strange to be put in a position where he'd be preaching to folks who'd known him during his running-around days. *I know people who go astray can return to the faith and be a good example to others.* Ezekiel hoped once again that he could prove this in the way he had cleaned up his own life and settled down.

He lifted his hand and rubbed the back of his neck, also wet with perspiration. *Can this congregation see me as a minister now, or to them will I always be the unsettled young man who'd once been dissatisfied with the Plain ways? Will they take me seriously and listen to what God has laid on my heart?*

Ezekiel would be preaching from the Book of Habakkuk on the topic of faith and trust in God during difficult times of unimaginable loss. The verses had helped him during unsettling times, and he hoped someone in the congregation would be helped by them today as well.

As he stood to deliver his sermon, Ezekiel gave a quick glance at the women's section. Michelle offered him a reassuring nod, as did his mother.

*Lord,* he prayed, *let the words that come from my mouth be Your words, not mine.*

As Ezekiel delivered his sermon, tears welled in Belinda's eyes. *If Vernon was here right now, he would be so pleased to hear his once-wayward son preaching God's Word.*

She glanced across the way to see if Henry's attention was where it should be. He sat with both elbows resting on his knees, and his chin cupped in the palms of his hands. Belinda couldn't tell what her teenage son was thinking, but she had a feeling he was bored and would probably tune Ezekiel's sermon out. Henry's thoughts might be on the time he and Sylvia would spend with Dennis Weaver this afternoon. He'd certainly mentioned it enough times since the plans had been made. Even Sylvia had brought up the topic this morning. Belinda felt a bit concerned by Sylvia and Henry's fascination with a near stranger.

Turning her attention back to Ezekiel, Belinda struggled to keep her tears at bay as he read several verses of scripture. One in particular, Habakkuk 3:18, spoke to her heart. "Yet I will rejoice in the Lord, I will joy in the God of my salvation."

"The prophet Habakkuk predicted that difficult times were on the way," Ezekiel declared. "Things sometimes get worse before they get better." He paused, as if to collect his thoughts. "How do we deal with unexpected financial problems, serious health issues, or the death of a loved one? Habakkuk stated that we need confident faith and trust in God, who is the source of our strength and salvation. In the end, we who trust Him will not be disappointed. When we go through difficult circumstances, God not only meets our needs, but He teaches us to encourage others when they are faced with a crisis."

When Ezekiel ended his sermon and returned to his seat, it was all Belinda could do to control her swirling emotions. Her husband, a son, and a son-in-law had been taken from them a year ago, and they had faced uncertain times concerning the greenhouse and whether their earnings would provide for them ever since. Vandalism and a threatening phone message had occurred, but nothing serious had happened, and no one had been hurt. Belinda had much to be thankful for, and like Habakkuk she could rejoice in the knowledge that during the past year, God had been with them and met all of their needs. Her only hope was that the rest of the family could see that and rejoice in the Lord too.

A sense of anticipation welled in Dennis's chest as his horse and buggy approached the Kings' place. Today had been his church district's off-Sunday, so he'd slept in this morning and spent the rest of the morning reading a recent issue of *Birds and Blooms* magazine. Tomorrow, Dennis would begin training a new horse his friend James had bought at an auction recently. Thanks to James's referrals, Dennis had two more people's horses he would begin working with soon. Dennis had already determined that he liked it here in Lancaster County, and unless something unforeseen came up, he planned to stay and make this area his permanent home. Whether he would continue renting from Sylvia or eventually buy her place remained to be seen.

*Who knows,* Dennis thought as he turned up the Kings' driveway. *If Sylvia doesn't want to sell her place, I might end up buying some other home with enough property for all my needs.*

When Dennis pulled his horse up to the hitching rail, he spotted two young children — a girl and a boy — on the front porch. They appeared to be fairly close in age. Dennis figured the children belonged to Sylvia's brother, Ezekiel, and his wife. He wondered if they had any other children besides these two.

Dennis had no more than gotten out of the buggy when Henry came running toward him. Sylvia followed, only at a slower pace. They both carried binoculars in their hands.

After greeting him, Henry got in the back of the buggy, and Sylvia rode up front. Then Dennis backed the horse away from the rail and headed off down the driveway.

Dennis gave Sylvia a sidelong glance and noticed that she sat stiffly in the passenger's seat, looking straight ahead. He cleared his throat. "I've been on the lookout for a hund, but so far I've come up empty-handed."

Sylvia remained quiet, but Henry spoke up. "You're tryin' to find a dog? Why not a puppy?"

Dennis jiggled the reins. "When I was a boy, I helped my daed raise some German shepherd pups, and it was a lot of work, which I don't have time for right now. If I could locate a fully grown German shepherd locally, that would be great."

"Maybe you oughta put an ad in *The Budget* or check at the animal shelter in Lancaster," Henry suggested.

"Jah, that might work."

Seconds ticked by before Dennis looked Sylvia's way again. *Why so quiet? She'd been talkative the last time I saw her. What could she be thinking about? I hope I didn't say anything to offend her.*

The silence between them felt awkward and seemed to be growing the farther they rode. *Why am I so tongue-tied right now? I deal with people all the time and always have something to say.*

Struggling to find a good topic, Dennis was about to ask Sylvia about one of the items he'd seen in her mother's greenhouse, when Henry tapped him on the shoulder and piped up with a question of his own.

"Have you seen any mockingbirds since you moved to Strasburg?"

"No, I can't say as I have. I am acquainted with the species though, because I saw some where I used to live in Dauphin County."

"Sylvia saw one the other day — or at least she thinks it was a mockingbird."

"Is that right?" Dennis glanced in her

241

direction. "What'd it look like, Sylvia?"

She turned her head to look at him, then looked back at the road ahead when a car whizzed by. "The bird was in one of the trees in our yard, and I saw it while looking out a window in the house. It was hard to tell for sure, but it appeared to have a gray body and head."

*Good. She's talking now.* "Was the tail mostly black with white outer feathers?" he questioned.

"I think so, but I can't be sure."

"A male mockingbird has a silvery gray head and back, with light gray chest and belly. It also has white wing patches, and a mostly black tail with white outer tail feathers. Oh, and its bill is black," he added.

"You seem to know a lot about birds," Sylvia said.

"That's because I've been studying them for several years. Of course, that doesn't make me an expert by any means."

"Well, you know more than we do," Henry interjected. "I bet if we get together and go birding with you from time to time, we'll learn a lot more."

"You're right, Henry, but it'll be the birds that'll teach us, not me."

Sylvia couldn't remember the last time

she'd enjoyed herself so much. Certainly not since Toby had died. Standing among trees and shrubs, listening to the call of various birds as she peered at them through the binoculars she'd brought along had transported Sylvia to a different world.

The rising whistle of *bob-white . . . bob-white,* caught her attention, and she pointed in the direction of the mostly brown stocky bird with a short gray tail. Upon closer examination through the field glasses, Sylvia realized the bobwhite had a prominent white eye stripe and white chin. She saw clearly that its sides and belly were reddish brown with black lines and dots.

She turned to look at Dennis and mouthed, "Isn't it beautiful?"

He grinned at her and gave a nod.

Henry was all-smiles as he watched the bird searching for insects on the ground.

"If I'd had any idea bird-watching would be so much fun, I would have taken up the hobby sooner," Sylvia whispered to Dennis.

"I agree with you. It's not only an educational hobby, but relaxing and entertaining too." Dennis moved closer to Sylvia. "Can we do this again next Sunday?"

"I'd like that. I'll need to check with my mamm first, but I'm pretty sure she'll be fine with Henry and me going birding with you again. By next Sunday, Ezekiel and his family will be gone, so maybe before or after we go bird-watching, you'd like to share a meal with us."

"That'd be great." There was no hesitation in Dennis's response.

Sylvia looked forward to next week and spending more time with this nice man who knew so much about birds. She hoped either Mom or Amy would be willing to watch Rachel and Allen so she wouldn't have to cancel her plans.

# CHAPTER 20

A lump formed in Belinda's throat as she stood on the porch Monday morning, waving goodbye as Ezekiel and his family gathered their things to put into the driver's van. Even though she'd done this more than once, it never got easier. She craved to have the whole family together, and all this did was fuel the flames. Wonderful as it was to have them visit, it always took her a few days to readjust when they left. However, having her children and grandchildren together in one place made the sting of not having Vernon, Abe, and Toby with them seem a little less severe.

*It's in my son's best interest to live where he does,* Belinda reminded herself. Each time Ezekiel and his family returned to Clymer, the need to keep Sylvia and the children nearby held her more tightly in its grip. Belinda wasn't certain, but it might be because she felt insecure without a man in her life. She had grown used to Vernon being there by her side and making the heavy decisions around the house. It made things simpler to trust his judgment, sit back, and relax. There were times when they would disagree on some topics, but the waters usually calmed quickly.

*Why can't things be easier for me now? I work hard and try to be considerate of others.* Belinda rolled her shoulders a couple of times. *If only my husband could give me his sound opinion on things. He allowed more time in figuring out how to work through everyone's problems. I want answers now.* She leaned against the railing, her fingers drumming the wooden surface.

"Are you all right, Mom?" Amy slipped her arm around Belinda's waist. No doubt she sensed her mother's anxiety.

Belinda stopped tapping. "I'm fine, or at least I will be once we go to the greenhouse and get busy."

"Jah. The quicker we get to work, the sooner our minds will be on other things." Amy looked at Henry, along with Sylvia and the children, who had come out to tell Ezekiel and his family goodbye.

Soon they were waving to each other as the van started down the driveway. They all stood watching the vehicle head away from

246

the house and onto the road.

"We'll miss them." Belinda's voice wavered.

Sylvia patted her arm. "Maybe someday we can all go to Clymer to visit them, Mom. Perhaps we could do it on a long weekend."

"I'd like that 'cause I've never been to the state of New York," Henry spoke up.

"That would be a fun trip," Amy agreed.

"I'd consider the plan, but it would have to be when the greenhouse is closed during the winter months. Of course, we'd need to ask someone to pick up our mail, take care of the animals, and check the house." Belinda looked at Amy. "We'll need to put the idea of the trip on hold until after your wedding, so if we go to Clymer, it'll have to be sometime after the first of the year."

Amy nodded. "I hope Jared and I will be able to join you."

Belinda patted her daughter's arm. "I hope so too."

They all remained on the porch for a while, looking out into the yard. The birds seemed to be enjoying the freshly filled containers Henry had taken care of earlier that morning.

Sylvia leaned against the railing by Amy and Belinda. Allen and Rachel came up to their mother, watching a barn cat give herself a bath near the porch. Things seemed somber for a time, as Belinda soaked up the quiet with her family. She looked toward the greenhouse before turning to face her children. "It's getting close to opening time, and even though our spirits are low, we need to get to work."

"You're right, Mom." Amy nudged Henry's arm. "Oh and you'd better get some honey. We're low on what we have available in the greenhouse to sell."

He sneered at her. "Don't be tellin' me what to do. You ain't my boss, you know."

Belinda stepped between them and spoke before Amy could respond to her brother. "Your sister is right — we do need more jars of honey. Would you please take care of that for me, Son?"

"Jah, okay." Henry stepped off the porch and headed for the outside entrance of their cellar, where they kept the raw honey from their bees in glass jars, along with other home-canned goods.

Belinda turned to Sylvia. "Amy and I will be heading to work now. We'll either take turns coming up to the house for lunch, or if we're too busy, one of us may run up and get sandwiches to take out to the greenhouse, which we'll eat whenever we can."

"Okay, Mom, but before you go, I need to

ask you a question."

Belinda looked over at Amy. "Would you mind opening up this morning while I talk to Sylvia? I'll be there as soon as I can."

"Sure, Mom. No problem." Amy stepped down from the porch and hurried off in the direction of the greenhouse.

Belinda turned toward Sylvia again. "What did you want to say?"

"Umm . . . just a minute, please." Sylvia opened the door and ushered her children into the house. Belinda heard her instruct them to play quietly in the living room. Then she returned. "Could we take a seat while I talk to you about something?"

"Of course."

After they were seated, Belinda cleared her throat. "What's on your mind, Daughter?"

"Dennis asked Henry and me to go bird-watching with him again this Sunday, and I wondered if you'd be willing to watch the kinner while we're gone."

"Certainly. I always enjoy spending time with my grandchildren." Belinda wasn't thrilled about Sylvia spending time with this stranger they knew so little about, but she couldn't say no to her request. It was good to see that her eldest daughter had found something to get her out of the house. This new hobby was something she and Henry had in common. For the past year, Sylvia had rarely smiled or gotten excited about anything. A fascination with birds and a desire to learn more about them had given her something to look forward to.

"There's one more thing." Sylvia placed her hand on Belinda's arm. "Would it be okay if Dennis joined us for supper Sunday evening, after we get back from birding? I probably shouldn't have, without asking first, but I sort of invited him to join us for the meal."

Belinda's muscles tightened, and she had to consciously force them to relax. Had Sylvia become interested in Dennis Weaver, or he in her? If she saw him regularly, might they end up courting? Although a year had passed since Toby's death, Belinda couldn't accept the idea of her daughter being courted — especially by a near stranger. *I'd like to say what's on my mind right now, but I don't want to undo the progress she's starting to make.*

Belinda had to give Sylvia an answer, and she didn't want to create a problem, so she forced herself to smile and say, "Jah, that would be fine."

Sylvia smiled and gave her a hug. "Danki, Mom. I'll give Dennis a call on his cell phone and let him know about Sunday."

"Cell phone?" Belinda clutched her apron. "Why does he have one of those? There's still a phone shed on your property, right?"

"There is, but the phone's been disconnected since the kinner and I moved out."

"He could have it reconnected and get a new number."

Sylvia nodded. "And he probably will, but he needs the cell phone for business purposes."

"Puh!" Belinda flapped her hand. "We've run a business here for several years, and never needed a cell phone. As I recall, the church district you used to belong to didn't allow their members to own a cell phone."

"Maybe they've changed the rule."

"Or maybe the church leaders aren't aware that Dennis has one." *I'd hate to think so, but this young man we barely know could be a bad influence on my son and daughter.*

The sound and sight of a horse and buggy coming up the driveway put an end to their conversation. "I need to go." Belinda stood. "I'll see you at lunchtime."

Sylvia entered the house and was greeted with the shrill scream of her daughter. With her heart beating a staccato, she raced to the living room to see what had happened.

Rachel sat in the middle of the room, tears coursing down her flushed cheeks, as her brother galloped a plastic horse in circles on the floor. Rachel's tiny baby doll had been draped over the horse's back. No wonder the poor thing was so upset.

Sylvia knelt on the floor, rescued the doll, and handed it to Rachel, who immediately stopped crying. Allen, however, pouted. "The horse has no rider," he said in Pennsylvania Dutch.

"He probably likes not having the dolly on his back." Sylvia reached for her son's hand. "Why don't you come with me to the kitchen? We'll bake some peanut butter *kichlin.*"

Allen's eyes widened, and he didn't have to be asked twice. He took off on a full run, and Sylvia found him sitting at the kitchen table when she entered the room. Her son loved cookies and would often ask to taste some of the batter. Truth was, Sylvia liked to test the cookie dough too.

She got out all the ingredients and let Allen help stir the batter. Then she showed him how to drop spoons of dough onto the greased cookie sheet. While the tasty treats baked, Allen colored a picture Sylvia had drawn of a bird. It was supposed to look like the mockingbird she'd seen in the yard, but her son colored it brown instead of gray.

Sylvia smiled. *It doesn't matter what color Allen chose for the bird. At least it's keeping him occupied while his sister plays quietly with her doll by herself.*

Sylvia remembered how, when she was a child, she and her siblings had sometimes quarreled over certain toys. Their mother, in all her wisdom, always came to the rescue by giving each of the children something different to do. Sometimes it turned out to be an unpleasant chore, while other times Mom gave them something fun to do, like helping bake a cake, pie, or cookies.

Back then, Sylvia had no choice but to do whatever her mother said, and now she was a grown woman, with two children of her own to care for.

Sylvia sucked in her bottom lip. *I don't understand why Mom still thinks it's her job to tell me what to do.* She opened the oven door and removed a batch of cookies, placing them on the cooling rack. *Since Mom said it was okay, I need to let Dennis know that he'll be welcome to join us for Sunday supper.*

The first hour after opening the greenhouse they'd been busy, but now things had slacked off. Amy was about to go to the storage room to look for a few items they needed to replenish, when Mom called her up to the front counter.

"What is it, Mom? Did you need me to get something from the storage room?" Amy questioned.

Mom shook her head. "No, I wanted to tell you about the conversation I had with your sister before joining you here after the greenhouse opened."

"Is everything all right with Sylvia?"

"She's not sick or anything, but I am feeling a bit *bekimmere* about her."

"I don't understand. Sylvia seems to be doing a little better lately emotionally, so in what way are you concerned?"

"She and Henry have plans to go birding again this Sunday with that man, Dennis Weaver."

Amy smiled. "I'm not at all surprised. My brother and sister both seem to have found a hobby they really enjoy."

Mom put both hands against her hips. "It's not their new hobby I'm worried about. It's the man they're going bird-watching with. Why, did you know that Dennis owns a cell phone?"

"No, I did not, but I don't see why his having a cell phone would cause you to worry about Sylvia."

"I think he might be worldly and maybe

even deceitful, since it's doubtful that he got permission from the leaders in his church district to have any kind of phone other than one that would be in a phone shed."

Amy was on the verge of telling her mother that whatever Dennis did had nothing to do with Sylvia, when Maude, the lady who lived in a nearby shack, came in.

Mom left her stool and went to speak with the unkempt woman. Before Maude left, she would probably be carrying a bag of groceries and whatever else Mom decided to share with her.

Amy pursed her lips. *Doesn't my mother even care that this elderly, eccentric lady has stolen from us?*

Since there was no one else in the building at the moment and Mom was busy talking to Maude, Amy hurried off to the storage room. When she stepped out several minutes later, she heard Maude criticizing the way Mom ran the greenhouse, saying that her prices were too high and the plants and flowers for sale needed to be rearranged.

Amy's finger curled into the palms of her hands. *Who does that woman think she is, talking to my mother that way?* Amy felt sorry for the elderly woman, but it was not good for business to have her here complaining about high prices and saying negative things about the greenhouse. If anyone else had come into the building while Amy was in the storage room, they might have heard Maude's grumblings and decided to take their business elsewhere.

Amy drew in a breath and blew it out with such force, the ties on her head covering swished across her face. *And that would certainly not be good. We need all the business we can get right now.*

# CHAPTER 21

"Things are sure slow this afternoon," Amy commented as she and her mother sat behind the counter, eating ham-and-cheese sandwiches. "If we'd known things would taper off like this, we could have taken turns eating lunch in the house."

Mom took a drink from her bottle of water. "I don't understand it. Usually in the spring we're so busy we can barely keep up." Her neck bent forward as she released a heavy sigh. "Maybe the things Maude said to me earlier today are true. We might be losing customers to the other greenhouse."

"As many kind things as you've done for Maude, she had no right to upset you." Amy's elbows pressed against her sides. "We can't afford to lose any business, Mom. Maybe we need to advertise more."

"Running an ad in the newspaper means more money out of pocket," Mom replied. "Word of mouth has always been our best

257

form of advertising, but if people aren't happy with our prices or the items we sell, they'll tell others not to shop here."

"Let's try not to worry about this." Amy tried to sound optimistic. "Today may just have been slow, and we can't put too much stock in what Maude has to say about things."

"I suppose you're right. Just the same, we do need to come up with some reasonable ways to bring in more business."

"I agree, and speaking of which . . . one of us needs to check with Sara's flower shop and see if there are some flowers her assistant might need. Since Sara's still at home with her new baby, Misty is most likely in charge of things in her absence."

"Why don't you go now, Amy? Since we're not busy and Henry's here to help, I'm certain the two of us can manage while you're gone."

"But Henry's not here, Mom. He went up to the house to eat lunch and hasn't come back yet."

"I'm sure he'll be here soon." Mom gave Amy's shoulder a tap. "Go ahead into town. A stop at the flower shop shouldn't take you long."

"Okay, I'll go get my horse and buggy ready." Amy stepped off the stool and went out the door.

On the way to the barn, she saw Henry coming out of the house with a pair of binoculars. "There's no time for bird-watching now, Henry. I'm going into town for a bit, and Mom will need your help in the greenhouse while I'm gone."

Henry kicked at a clump of tall grass, a reminder to Amy that it was in need of being mowed. "But we're not that busy today. Can't Mom get along without me for half an hour or so?"

"You'll have to take that up with her. Right now I need to get my horse so I can head for town."

Belinda had started a list of ways they might advertise reasonably, when Henry came in with a scowl on his face.

"How come Amy gets to go to town and I have to be in here when there ain't even any customers?" He leaned on the counter where Belinda sat.

She pointed a finger at him. "You know how I feel about that word *ain't.* I am sure you were never taught to say it in school."

"I ain't — I mean, I'm not in school anymore, Mom. Besides, all the fellows I hang around say *ain't.*"

"What your friends say or do is none of

259

my concern." She pointed at him again. "You, on the other hand, are still living at home and under my care, so you must do what I say as long as you're living here. Understood?"

Henry's features tightened as he gave a brief nod. "So since there are no customers right now, what do you need me to do?"

Belinda was about to respond when the front door of the greenhouse opened and Monroe stepped in. *Oh dear, I wonder what he wants. I hope he's not here to put pressure on me about seeing him socially. I thought we had that settled.*

"*Gut nammidaag,* Belinda." Monroe stepped up to the counter, almost bumping shoulders with Henry.

"Good afternoon," she responded. "Is there something I can help you with?"

"Not really. I came in to tell you that as I was going by your place, I noticed your sign by the front of the driveway is missing. Just wondered if you knew this and whether you may have taken the sign down for some reason."

Belinda's facial muscles slacked as her mouth dropped open. "The-the sign is gone?"

"That's what I said. I looked around in the tall grass but didn't see it anywhere."

"It was there last night when Seth dropped me off," Henry spoke up.

Belinda's face heated. "What were you doing with Seth? You said you were going out for a walk to look for unusual birds you could write about in your journal." She stared at Henry. "At no time did you mention that you'd be seeing Seth."

"I wasn't planning to see him, Mom. He just drove by as I was walking home and asked if he could give me a ride."

Belinda's mouth felt unexpectedly dry, so she took a sip from her water bottle. "Could Seth have taken the sign after he dropped you off?"

Henry shook his head. "Why would he do that?"

"He's still going through *rumschpringe,* right?" Monroe looked at Henry with wrinkled brows.

"Well, jah, but what's that got to do with anything?"

"Some young people going through their running-around time think it's funny when they pull a few pranks on someone — even a friend."

Henry sighed. "Think I'd better go have a talk with him."

Belinda held up her hand as she shook her head. "Not right now, Son. You have work to do here. Talking to Seth can wait."

"But what about the sign? If it's not hanging at the end of our driveway, how are folks gonna know we're here?"

Belinda massaged her forehead, hoping to stave off the headache she felt coming on. "I'll ask Sylvia to make up a cardboard sign that we can put out there temporarily until the old one is found."

"What if it's never found?" The question came from Monroe. "Maybe whoever has done some vandalism here in the past took the sign." His voice deepened as his brows drew together. "Someone wants to see your business fail, and I'm worried about you."

"There's no need for you to worry," Belinda assured him. "No harm has come to me or any of my family." She continued to rub her forehead. "It is obvious, however, that someone wants us to close the greenhouse permanently."

"I'm sorry this happened, Belinda. If you need anything let me know." Monroe reached across the counter and placed his hand on her shoulder, giving it several gentle taps. "I'll drop by again and check on you tomorrow."

Belinda was on the verge of telling Monroe that it wasn't necessary for him to come by, when one of their steady customers, Dianna

Zook, entered the greenhouse.

"Did you know your sign is missing out front by the road?" Dianna questioned.

Belinda nodded, feeling her head throb with every movement. She wished she could go up to the house and take a long nap. Sometimes, sleeping was the only thing that would shake off a tension headache such as this. But with the possibility of more customers coming in, Belinda needed to stay here until Amy got home.

"Did you take the old sign down to repair it or something?" Dianna asked.

"No," Henry spoke up, "but we'll be putting up one in its place real soon."

Belinda managed a weak smile. "Jah, that's right." She slipped out from behind the counter and stood next to Dianna. "If you'll tell me what you came for, I'll be happy to show you where it can be found."

Before Dianna could respond, Belinda glanced over at Monroe and said, "Danki for stopping by, Monroe. I hope the rest of your day goes well." She hurried away with Dianna without waiting for the man's response.

When Amy pulled her horse and buggy up to the hitching rail, not far from the flower shop, she spotted the girl Abe used to date,

Sue Ellen Wagler. She was walking down the street with a young Amish man Amy didn't recognize. No doubt he was from another church district. What caught Amy's attention the most, though, was that they were holding hands. Sue Ellen had no doubt found another boyfriend.

Amy felt a pang of regret. If Abe were still alive, he and Sue Ellen would be married by now. She couldn't really fault Sue Ellen for moving on with her life. Abe wasn't coming back, and she had every right to be courted by someone else.

*I wonder if my sister will ever meet another man, fall in love, and get married. After all, Sylvia is still young, and her children need a father to help raise them.*

Toby and Sylvia had been so happy together that it was hard to picture her with someone else.

Amy thought about her own wedding that would take place this fall. Sometimes she felt selfish for being so happy with Jared, especially when Sylvia had no one and still grieved her loss.

Amy loved Jared more than words could say, and she would be devastated if anything ever happened to him. He was all she'd ever wanted in a husband, and Amy felt grateful they'd been able to get their courtship back on track.

Her focus changed as the flower shop came into view. Two women came out of the building as Amy approached, and she stood off to one side, waiting for them to clear the door.

Once inside, she found Sara's helper Misty behind the front counter.

"Good afternoon," Amy said. "I came by to see if there are any flowers Sara wants you to order from our greenhouse this week."

Misty blinked rapidly and gave a sharp intake of breath. "Oh dear . . . hasn't Sara given you the news?"

Amy moved closer to the counter. "What news?"

"I'm in the process of buying her shop."

"We knew that might be a possibility, but I didn't realize it would be soon."

"So Sara hasn't said anything to you or your mother?"

Amy shook her head.

"I'm sure she hasn't kept the information from you intentionally." Misty tapped her pen against the invoice book lying on the counter. "With the adjustment of becoming a mother, Sara's probably been so busy she hasn't gotten around to contacting everyone yet."

265

"That's understandable." Amy smiled. "Congratulations on becoming the new owner of this business. We'll enjoy working with you the same as we did Sara."

Misty cleared her throat a couple of times as she pushed a wayward hair behind her left ear. "Umm . . . the thing is . . . I've already been approached by the other greenhouse in the area." She paused and swiped her tongue across her lower lip. "Since they are much closer to my shop here, and their prices are reasonable, I've agreed to purchase all my flowers from them."

Tilting her chin, Amy broke eye contact with Misty. "Oh, I see."

"I'm sorry, but I have to do what I think is best for my new business. I hope you understand."

*No, I don't understand at all.* Amy kept her thoughts to herself as she nodded. "Thank you for telling me. I'll pass the word along to my mother."

Amy's throat felt so swollen, she couldn't say another word. In order to keep her emotions under control, she turned and hurried out the door. *Oh boy . . . I dread telling Mom this bit of bad news. No sales to the flower shop will surely affect our finances.*

Amy wandered up the street a ways, feeling stunned. *Why do things have to change like this?* She was glad she'd had lunch before all this went down, because now her stomach was knotted up.

As she continued to absorb the news, she felt a light tap on the back of her shoulder. Amy turned.

Jared stood with his brows furrowed as he looked at her. "Is something wrong? You look umgerrent."

"I am upset," she admitted.

"Want to talk about it?"

"Jah." Amy explained about Sara selling the flower shop. "And I can't understand why she didn't let us know about it."

"But you knew it was a possibility, right?"

Amy nodded. "Never dreamed she'd go through with it and not tell us, though."

"I'm sorry, Amy." Jared stood close to her. "I wish there was something I could do for you. I'm sure your family appreciated having that account."

"Mom surely did. But there's not much we can do about it."

Jared's tone was gentle as he looked into her eyes with a tender expression. "Have you eaten yet?"

"Yes, and I don't think I could eat anything else." Amy placed both hands against her stomach. "I dread telling Mom this news."

"I was about to grab a bite to eat before heading back to work on the roof of a house nearby. Why don't you come along and keep me company?"

"Okay."

As they headed to the nearest restaurant, Amy released a lingering sigh. She wished she could stay here with Jared for the rest of the day, because she dreaded having to go home and share the bad news.

# CHAPTER 22

"Will this work as a temporary sign?" Sylvia asked Belinda the following morning. She lifted a wooden sign for the greenhouse that she'd painted the night before and placed it on the table.

Belinda smiled and gave an affirmative nod. "You did a good job, Daughter. In fact, since you painted the front and back of the sign with clear lacquer, it should be good enough to use as a permanent sign."

"You think so?"

"Definitely. I wouldn't have said so if it weren't true."

"But the letters I painted in green aren't nearly as nice as the original one we had professionally done."

"Doesn't matter. You made the letters clear and large enough to be seen from the road, so that's all I care about."

Belinda looked at Henry, who'd come into the kitchen, via the back door. "Your sister made a new sign for us. Would you please go out and hang it right now? I'll have breakfast on by the time you get back."

"There are a couple of spots that seem a bit tacky yet, so you'll need to be careful putting it up," Sylvia told him "As long as it has a chance to dry all the way, it should last us a long time."

Henry frowned. "I'll be careful, but can't it wait till after we eat? I'm real hungerich this morning."

Belinda handed him a sticky bun. "This should tide you over till you get back. By then, I'll be ready to serve breakfast."

"Okay, I'll take care of it now." Henry grabbed the sticky bun in one hand and the new sign in the other. When Belinda opened the door for him, he went out with a spring in his step.

She looked over at Sylvia and shook her head. "That brother of yours has more energy in his little finger than I do in my whole body. Think I must be getting old."

"You're not old, Mom." Sylvia gave her a hug.

"I feel like it sometimes."

"That's because you work so hard," Amy said when she joined them in the kitchen.

A flush of heat erupted on Belinda's cheeks. "You heard what I said?"

"Jah. And I'm right, Mom. You do work hard — in the greenhouse, in the garden, and here in our home."

"I do what needs to be done."

"But once in a while you ought to take a little break." Amy looked at Sylvia. "Don't you agree that our mamm should take it easy whenever she can?"

Sylvia replied with a quick nod.

"So fix yourself a cup of kaffi and take it to the table." Amy gestured to the chair their mother normally sat in. "Sylvia and I will fix breakfast this morning." She looked at Belinda with a smug expression. "We're perfectly capable, you know."

"I am well aware, but it's good for me to keep busy. Helps me not to focus on our current situation."

"You mean, Sara selling her shop and the new owner deciding not to order from us anymore?" Amy asked.

"Jah."

"And don't forget the greenhouse sign that someone took down yesterday," Sylvia interjected. "I hope they don't do the same to the one I made last night."

"Sure wish we knew who took the missing sign." Belinda drank some of her coffee.

"Too bad one of us isn't a detective. Then

271

we might find out who is behind this mystery."

"We need to pray it won't happen again and that God will bring us all the business we need." Belinda clasped her hands together, placing them against her chest. She wouldn't say it to her daughters, but if things didn't get better, and fewer customers came in, by this time next year they could be out of business.

Dennis took a seat at the kitchen table and bowed his head for silent prayer. This was something he'd been taught to do at an early age, so it became a habit. The only problem was, he'd never been sure if his prayers made it to heaven. His mother and dad believed in the Bible, but for a long time after his dad passed away, the scriptures seemed like a fairy tale to Dennis — something someone had made up for the benefit of people who needed something to believe in that would give them a hope for the future.

Dennis had determined that his focus should be on hard work and a determination to make something of himself. He'd remained Amish because it was the only way he'd ever known, and he liked living plain. He went to church every other Sunday, but sometimes his mind was focused on other things.

Dennis wanted something better from life than merely working hard at a job he disliked. That's what his father had done, and it had taken him nowhere.

*Who am I kidding?* Dennis asked himself as he peeled a hard-boiled egg. *My daed was satisfied, even though farming might not have been his first choice.*

Dennis's stomach clenched as he relived the day his father had been killed. He still hadn't forgiven Uncle Ben for ending his dad's life and wasn't sure if he ever could.

Nausea replaced the pang of hunger he'd felt when he'd woken up this morning. He pushed his plate aside and stood. *If I take one bite of that egg, it may not stay down.*

After tossing the paper plate and its contents into the garbage can, Dennis grabbed his Thermos full of coffee and went out the back door. Looking around the yard, he thought once more about how nice it would be to have a dog.

Dennis had checked *The Budget* earlier, but there was nothing except some puppies being advertised. When he had some free time, he would make a trip to the local animal shelter and take a look at the potentials waiting for a good home. If he found nothing there, he'd check the newspaper again in a few weeks.

Walking across the yard, Dennis smelled the odor of coffee and looked down. *Oh great! The Thermos is leaking on my trousers. Guess I'd better fix the lid before more of it seeps out.*

As Dennis paused to tighten the lid, he heard the horses whinnying and nickering from the barn. There was always some excitement when he added a new horse to the group. His friend's new mare was in the barn, waiting for her first day of training. For the next few hours, Dennis would think of nothing else except teaching the horse how to pull a buggy by first getting her used to a jogging cart.

After Mom, Amy, and Henry went out to the greenhouse, Sylvia fed her children, did the dishes, and cleaned up the kitchen. She hoped to get some potholders made today that could be sold in the greenhouse. The material she planned to use had birds on it, which reminded Sylvia of the hobby Henry had introduced to her.

Sylvia looked forward to going birding with Dennis again this Sunday and sharing a meal with him and the family afterward. It would give them a chance to get better acquainted in a relaxed atmosphere. She hoped he would also share some stories about unusual birds he'd seen when living in Dauphin County.

Right now, though, she wanted to take a look at the sign she'd made and make sure it looked okay.

When Henry came in for a drink of water, Sylvia asked him to stay with the children while she went outside.

"Okay," he responded. "There ain't much happening in the greenhouse right now anyway, so I probably won't even be missed."

Sylvia resisted the urge to correct his English. She left the house and trotted down the driveway until she reached the sign.

*It looks good, even if I do say so myself.* She hoped this new sign, which she'd painted with a brighter color than the old one, would bring in some new customers.

Sylvia was about to leave, when she noticed Maude across the road, loitering near the neighbors' place. She wondered if the strange little woman would come by soon for more goodies from Mom, or if some other item might vanish from their property again.

Sylvia heard some birds overhead, squawking to each other. A few black crows, like the one Henry had taken an interest in last year, sounded off, which she found to be annoying. She started to turn back toward the house when Maude approached.

"I reckon you're open for business again?"

Sylvia's brows knit together. "Excuse me?"

"Your sign was gone yesterday, so I thought you may have closed down the greenhouse."

"No, we're still open, and we don't know what happened to the sign. But as you can see, a new one is up now."

The old woman snickered behind her weathered-looking hand. "I wonder how long till the new sign disappears."

Before Sylvia could comment, Maude hurried ahead to the greenhouse. She couldn't tell if the elderly woman was kidding or not, but Sylvia chose not to let it bother her long, because she spotted a pair of cardinals on one of their hanging feeders. They were gorgeous in their red attire, as one chirped a pleasant song.

Sylvia planted her feet and watched intently as the pair took turns eating from the feeder. *I wish Dennis could see this with me. What a pretty sight.*

She remained fixated on the cardinals for several more minutes, until the birds flew away. Sylvia couldn't help smiling. Watching the cardinals reminded her of the fun she'd had on Sunday with Dennis.

*He appears to be such a kind man, and he's quite nice looking. It seems odd that Dennis isn't married,* Sylvia mused as she returned to the house to relieve Henry of his duty. *Maybe Dennis hasn't found the right woman yet. Or, he could be so focused on trying to get his new business going that he has no time for love and romance.*

Sylvia paused on the porch and tapped her chin. *I don't know why I'm thinking about this. It's none of my business what Dennis does or why he's not married. My concentration needs to be on raising my children and trying to help Mom come up with new ways to keep people coming to the greenhouse and buying the items she has for sale. Hopefully the money I'm now earning because of renting out my home will help compensate for any loss of business.*

About an hour after Earl left for work, Virginia got dressed, climbed in her car, and went shopping. Her friend Stella had worn some nice outfits during her visit, and Virginia had been inspired to buy something. *I hope there's enough room on the credit card I'll be using today. Earl says we need to budget our finances, so I'll try not to get carried away.*

Virginia found a dress shop a few doors down from Miller's Smorgasbord and parked her car. It had been too long since she'd bought herself new clothes, and she was determined not to go home empty-handed. She'd finally cleaned out her closet of several outdated outfits and donated them to a thrift store.

Virginia spent the next hour trying on outfits and jewelry. So far everything either didn't fit, wasn't in a color she liked, or cost too much money. She scrutinized the sale rack and found a pair of black knit leggings, as well as a floral print tunic. Seeing that the size and price were right, she carried the clothes to the dressing room. After trying them on, and turning different ways in front of the fitting room mirror, Virginia convinced herself that the tunic and leggings were made for her. She put her old clothes on and took the new ones up to the register, where she discovered a velvet-beaded double-strand necklace highlighted with crystals and gold links on display. It was the most unusual necklace she'd ever seen. The piece of jewelry cost almost as much as the tunic and leggings, but Virginia knew she couldn't leave the store without it.

*It's not like I'm spending a king's ransom in here.* Virginia watched the sales gal finish with the lady ahead of her. *I bet when Earl sees me in this new outfit, he'll think I look so nice he will want to take me out for supper this evening. And if he asks which restaurant I would like to eat at, I'll say, "Miller's Smorgy."*

After a clerk came to wait on Virginia, she plunked down a credit card. "You sure have some nice stuff in here. The next time my husband gets paid, think I'll come back and look around."

The middle-age woman gave Virginia a wide smile. "You'd be welcomed."

When Virginia left the store, she chose to ignore the pain in her leg as she headed for her car. She clung tightly to the fancy gift bag the clerk had put her purchases in. *Wow, if I'd known I was gonna feel this good about myself, I'd have bought some new clothes a lot sooner. Too bad my one true friend isn't here to go shopping with me.*

Virginia got in her car and looked at herself in the rearview mirror. *If I had a friend here with me right now, I'd find some place to change into my new clothes and invite her to go out to lunch.*

Her shoulders slumped. *But I guess makin'*

*a new friend is never gonna happen. Even if I did meet someone, who'd want to hang out with a woman who has a gimpy leg and doesn't have anything interesting to talk about?*

# CHAPTER 23

"You look real nice this evening, hon." Earl grinned at Virginia when he stepped in the door. "Did you go shopping today?"

"I sure did, and I found these clothes on a sales rack." Making no mention of the necklace she'd bought at full price, Virginia turned all the way around so he could see the front and back of her new outfit.

"You real did well." Earl stepped forward and gave her a kiss. "I'm glad you tried them on for me, but you might want to change clothes before you start cooking supper."

Virginia put on her best smile. "I was hoping we could go out for supper tonight."

Earl tipped his head from side to side, as though weighing his choices. "Well now . . . let me think . . ."

She puckered her lips. "Come on, Earl, pretty please."

"Didn't you have something already

planned for supper?"

She shook her head.

He jiggled his brows then pulled Virginia into his arms for a hug. "Okay, sweetie, it's a date. Just give me a few minutes to clean up and change my clothes. Then we can go to the restaurant of my choice."

"Your choice, huh?" She poked his stomach.

"Well, sure. Since it was your idea to go out to eat, don't you think it's only fair that I should get to choose which restaurant we go to?"

"I suppose." Virginia smiled. *What a thoughtful husband I have. I can't believe I was lucky enough to find him. I still have to wonder what Earl ever saw in someone like me.*

"Where are you and Jared going for supper this evening?" Sylvia asked her sister.

Amy turned away from the living room window, where she'd been standing for the last five minutes. "I'm not sure yet. Maybe Diener's in Ronks, or we might eat someplace here in Strasburg. When Jared stopped by the greenhouse today and invited me to go with him this evening, I said he could choose the restaurant."

"That was gracious of you. I hope it's a

282

place you like."

Amy smiled. "I'm sure it will be. There aren't many restaurants in our area that don't serve good food."

"You're right. Toby's and my favorite place to eat was the Bird-in-Hand Family Restaurant." A pang of regret shot through Sylvia as she thought of her dear husband, remembering more of the good times they'd spent together. She couldn't help feeling a bit envious of her sister. At the same time, Sylvia was happy for Amy. She deserved the chance to build a life with the man she loved. Someday Amy and Jared would have children and Mom would have more grandchildren to love and dote over.

Sylvia sighed inwardly. *Sure wish I could give Mom another grandchild or two, but I guess it's not meant to be. If Toby hadn't died, we'd surely have had more kinner.*

### Ronks

"What made you choose this restaurant, Earl?" Virginia asked after they were seated at a table at Diener's Country Restaurant.

"I heard they have good food. In fact, I was told that it's a favorite of the Amish in the area."

"I can tell." She looked around the room where several Amish people sat at tables and rolled her eyes. "Don't we get enough Amish exposure at home? I mean, almost every time I look out the window, a horse and buggy is going by or turning up the Kings' driveway."

"We're living in Amish country, so we're bound to see Amish people." Earl leaned closer to Virginia. "And please keep your voice down. Someone might hear what you're saying and think you're prejudiced."

She shrugged her shoulders. "So what if I am?"

Earl had no chance to respond, because a middle-aged waitress came and asked what they would like to drink.

"I'll have a glass of water and a cup of coffee," Virginia replied.

"Make that two," Earl chimed in.

The waitress smiled. "Is this your first time visiting our restaurant?"

"Yes, it is. I heard about this place from my coworkers," Earl spoke up.

"That's good. I hope you both enjoy your meal."

He gave a nod. "I'm sure we will."

Virginia looked around and overheard a man at a nearby table say, "This restaurant is a bit of a landmark."

Virginia took in the minimal decor, as well as all the homey-looking wooden tables and chairs. The place grew busier, with more and more people being seated. The room soon became abuzz with constant conversations all happening at once.

Their friendly waitress went over the way things worked with where the different food counters were located as she held out menus. "Would you like to order off the menu or choose the items you want from the buffet?"

"I'll go with the buffet." Earl looked at Virginia. "How about you, dear?"

"Guess I will too."

"Feel free to help yourself whenever you're ready. I'll get your beverages and be back with them soon." The woman turned and walked away.

Earl pushed his chair aside and stood. "Okay, Virginia, let's go after some food."

As they joined a few others in line at the buffet bar, Virginia noticed an Amish couple at one of the tables across the room. *Oh great. It's Amy King and Jared, the roofer. I hope they don't see us.*

Once their plates were full, Virginia followed Earl back to their table.

"Say, isn't that the guy who did our garage roof?" Earl gestured in that direction. "And I think he's with one of the young Amish women who lives across the road from us."

"I believe you're right." Virginia picked up the chicken leg she'd placed on top of her buttered noodles, because her plate was so full.

"Oh, look, they must have seen us, 'cause they're coming this way."

Virginia put the chicken down and held her elbows tightly against her sides, wishing there was someplace she could hide. The last thing she needed was feeling forced to carry on a conversation with someone she didn't care about.

"It's nice to see you folks," Jared said as he and Amy stood beside Earl and Virginia's table. "Is this your first time eating here?"

"Yes, it is, and I've heard they have good food."

"We like it." Amy looked at Virginia and smiled. "I'm sure you will too."

"Maybe, if our food doesn't get cold before we have a chance to eat it," Virginia mumbled, barely glancing at Amy.

Amy nudged Jared's arm. "We need to get our dessert from the buffet and let my neighbors eat their meal in peace."

"You're right, Amy." Jared clasped Earl's shoulder. "Sorry for the intrusion."

"Not a problem." Earl reached out and shook Jared's hand. "Your stopping by has

286

given me a chance to tell you once more what a good job you and your crew did when you replaced my garage roof. I've been telling some of the fellows I work with about you. So don't be surprised if you get a few phone calls from some of the people I told about you."

"Thanks, I appreciate that." Jared's cheeks turned a light shade of pink.

Amy gave Jared's shirtsleeve a little tug. "Let's get some dessert before it's all gone."

"Okay, okay." He looked at Amy and chuckled, then turned back to face Earl and Virginia. "I think my future wife is eager to satisfy her sweet tooth."

"Future wife?" Virginia repeated. "I didn't know you and Amy were engaged to be married. When's the big day?"

"The first Thursday of October." Jared spoke before Amy could form any words.

"Yes, and there's still much to be done before the wedding," she interjected.

"Thursday seems like an odd day to get married. Why not a Saturday?" Virginia asked.

"We Amish always choose a weekday for our weddings because the following day we need to clean up after the event," Jared explained. "A Saturday wedding would mean cleanup on Sunday, and since we don't work on Sundays . . ."

Virginia held up her hand. "Okay, I get it."

"Maybe you should save yourself the time and energy of all the fuss and preparations, and just elope." Earl snickered.

Jared shook his head. "Young couples who've joined the Amish church would never elope."

Amy nodded in agreement. "It's just not done."

"Perhaps you folks would like to come to the wedding service, or at least join us for one of the meals that will be served throughout the day."

"You serve more than one post-wedding meal?" Virginia thought this was a strange custom too.

"Yes," Jared replied. "We don't normally have enough room to accommodate everyone in the building where the wedding takes place, and having more than one meal afterward allows people who didn't come to the wedding to join the bride and groom, as well as their witnesses, in a meal. Of course," he added, "those who do attend the wedding are usually served directly after the service. Then later in the day, many people who did not attend the wedding come to the second meal."

Earl nodded, but Virginia merely looked down at her plate piled high with food. Amy figured her neighbor wasn't that interested in what had been said.

"So we'll make sure you receive an invitation in the mail — if not for the wedding itself, then for one of the meals." Jared looked at Earl, who bobbed his head once more.

Seeing her future husband's eager expression caused Amy to cringe internally. *What is he thinking? I'm not sure about Earl, but I seriously doubt that Virginia's interested in being a friendly neighbor, much less attending our wedding. I bet Jared was only being polite by bringing up the topic.*

"I hope you two will enjoy your meal." Amy inched her way farther from the table.

"Thanks, I'm sure we will." Earl picked up his knife and fork and cut into his piece of chicken breast.

Amy managed a smile before she and Jared walked away. "I don't think Virginia likes me," she whispered at the dessert bar as she took a piece of cherry pie with whipped cream on top.

"What makes you think that?"

"Really, Jared, couldn't you tell how disinterested she was when the topic of our wedding came up?"

He shook his head. "You might be a little overly sensitive when it comes to your English neighbor."

"I don't think so. Ever since our first meeting, Virginia has been standoffish."

"She might be one of those people who needs a little time to get acquainted with someone."

"Jah, especially someone like me and my family who live a completely different lifestyle than her."

"Just give her the chance to get to know you better." Jared put a large scoop of bread pudding on his plate and covered it with warm maple sauce. "Ready to go back to our table now?"

"Sure." Amy followed him across the room. She would need to check with her mother and see how many people they planned to invite to her wedding. Maybe the list would be too long and there wouldn't be enough room to include Virginia and her husband.

Virginia watched the young couple get some dessert and head back to their table. She looked at her plate and tried the noodles, followed by a bite of chicken. "Yum . . . this isn't bad at all. In fact the food here's pretty tasty."

Earl nodded as he shoveled in a mouthful of potatoes with gravy.

"You must like the food here too, 'cause you're taking big bites like there's no tomorrow." She snickered. "You'd better take it easy, Earl. There's still plenty up there for you to have seconds."

He thumped his belly. "Yep, and I'm gonna take advantage of that very thing."

Virginia took a drink of water. "This place would have been fun to bring Stella during the time she was here. What a bummer she couldn't be with us right now. Sure wish there was a way to lure my friend back here for another visit."

"She did seem to be taken in by the Plain people in the area. And there's plenty of 'em here in this restaurant this evening." He picked up his roll and buttered it. "Stella asked me some questions about the Amish, but I don't know them that well, so I had no concrete answers for her."

"Same here. I don't know much except what I've seen of our Amish neighbors." Virginia picked up her fork again. "But I did see Stella purchase a book about the Amish from one of the shops we stopped at during the time she was here."

"Maybe being in Lancaster County whet your friend's appetite enough that she'll come back for another visit." Earl looked toward the buffet counter, where another long line of people had formed.

*But who knows when that will happen? Stella may not be able to fit it into her schedule to come here anytime soon.*

An idea popped into Virginia's head, and she gave Earl's arm a tap. "Hey!"

"Hey, what?"

She waited for him to face her. "If we should get an invitation to Jared and Amy's wedding, and I share the news with Stella, I'm sure she'd want to come along."

Her husband chuckled. "Woman, your mind is always at work, isn't it? But you're right, an invitation to an Amish wedding would probably prompt your best friend to come for another stay."

Virginia nodded. *Maybe I'll need to be a bit friendlier to our neighbors. Oh bother, this is sure not what I'd like to do, but I desperately want Stella to come here again.*

"I'm going back up for seconds." Earl pushed away from the table. "Would you care to join me?"

"Guess I could eat another piece of that chicken, and maybe some more noodles with gravy."

They left their used plates behind and headed for the counter for new dishes. Earl went ahead of her as he loaded up his plate again. The grin he wore reassured Virginia that they'd be back here another evening in the future.

She picked out some pickled beets to go along with the chicken and noodles. *I'm glad the pants I'm wearing are stretchy and my tunic will hide my expanding belly.*

Virginia peeked at Amy and Jared, before scooting over to join Earl in front of the desserts.

"If I've got any room after all this, I might get some of that chocolate cake with frosting." He pointed to it.

"Same here." Virginia followed Earl to their table.

A few minutes later, a large group of Amish came in and were seated at a long table near them. It looked like three generations of folks getting settled in their chairs. Earl chuckled and mentioned something about how big their bill would be.

Virginia tried to watch them without staring. *I wonder if I'll ever understand the Plain people. This wouldn't even be an issue if we were still living in Chicago.*

# CHAPTER 24

Saturday morning when Amy went out to get the mail, she saw Virginia standing at her own mailbox.

"Good morning." Amy smiled.

"Morning." Virginia's response could barely be heard, and she avoided Amy's glance.

"Did you and your husband enjoy your meal at Diener's the other evening?"

"Yeah, it was good." Virginia grabbed her mail and was about to cross the road, but she stopped suddenly and turned to face Amy. "I noticed you have a new sign out front." She spoke louder and pointed in that direction. "What happened to your old one?"

"Apparently someone took it, so my sister made a new one."

"Bet I know who stole it." Virginia's lips pressed into a thin, flat line.

Amy moved closer. "Who do you believe it was?"

Virginia fiddled with one of her dangly earrings. "I think it was that scruffy-looking old woman who walks by here nearly every day." She looked directly at Amy. "I've seen her meandering up and down your driveway a few times too. She seems creepy to me, although I've never talked to her. Don't even know the woman's name or where she lives."

"You must be referring to Maude. She doesn't speak much, and we don't know a lot about her, other than that she lives most of the year in an old shack up the road."

"I see. Well, the other morning, around six o'clock, I saw her walking back and forth in front of your driveway. Her head was down, and she appeared to be looking for something. Then I noticed that it looked like she was holding an object behind her back."

"Could you tell what it was?"

"Nope, but I wouldn't be surprised if she's the guilty one who snatched your sign." Virginia shook her head slowly. "You need to keep an eye on that woman if she comes around again. A person like her can't be trusted. In fact, I'm gonna keep a watch out for her too. If she could lift your sign, then who knows what else might disappear from your place, or maybe ours next."

Amy thought about the things Maude had done previously, like taking some produce from their garden. Then there was the time she snatched some cookies they had setting out on the counter in the greenhouse. *Virginia might have a point. It's possible that Maude may have taken the sign out front and possibly the watering can that went missing last year.*

"Think I'd better get back to the house now and start a load of laundry." Virginia's comment broke into Amy's disconcerting thoughts.

"Okay, I need to take care of this mail." Amy tapped the envelopes against her other hand.

"See you around." Virginia smiled, looked both ways, and limped to the other side of the road.

Clasping the mail in her hands, Amy headed back up the driveway and turned toward the greenhouse. *If Maude did take our sign, what would she have wanted with it?*

Belinda had put the Open sign on the door and was about to check all the plants to see if any needed water, when Amy came in.

"I just talked with our neighbor across the

296

road, and she thinks Maude may have taken our sign." Amy breathed heavily.

"The new one Sylvia made?"

"No. It was the old sign that went missing."

"What makes Virginia think it was Maude? Did she see her take the sign?"

Amy shook her head. "No, but she saw her walking back and forth in front of our driveway that morning, and then Maude bent down like she was searching for something. Oh, and Virginia said it looked like the elderly woman had something behind her back."

Belinda flapped her hand. "For goodness' sake, Amy, that's no proof that Maude took the sign. She could have dropped something that belonged to her."

"I suppose, but you know how strange Maude acts at times. And don't forget — we have caught her taking things before."

"We certainly can't accuse her unless we have some proof."

"True, but —"

"Is that the mail you have in your hands?" Belinda decided it was time for a topic change.

"Jah." Amy handed the letters to her.

"Danki. Now, would you mind checking

the plants for water while I go through the mail?"

"I don't mind, but where's Henry? Shouldn't he be checking the plants?"

"I assume he's still in the barn, which is where he said he was going after we finished breakfast."

"Should I go get him?"

"It's not necessary. I'm sure he will come here when he's done. In the meantime . . ."

"No problem, Mom. I'll check on the plants." Amy turned and headed down the first row, while Belinda took a seat behind the counter.

*I'm glad Amy had a pleasant time with Jared last night. He's a nice young man, and they get along so well — just like Vernon and I did.*

Belinda sighed as she picked up a piece of mail. The first envelope she opened was a bill and there were two more after that. She clicked her tongue against the roof of her mouth. It seemed lately there were more bills than money coming in.

Belinda finished looking at the last piece of mail — an advertisement — when Monroe entered the greenhouse. *I wonder what he wants this time.*

"Morning, Belinda. I was on my way back from the doughnut shop and thought I'd drop some off for you." He set a sweet-smelling box on the counter and grinned at her. "I got busy at work and couldn't make it back here until today, but I wanted to come by and make sure no more vandalism has been done."

"Everything's fine. No more problems at all." Belinda lifted the lid and inhaled the delightful aroma of maple bars and chocolate-glazed doughnuts. "Danki, Monroe. It was thoughtful of you to think of us with these treats. I'll be sure to share the doughnuts with the rest of my family."

His smile widened. "I'll bring you more the next time I stop at the doughnut shop. Whenever I go there, I get the freshest baked pastries."

She held up both hands. "Oh, there's no need for that. If I ate treats like this too often, I'd surely get fat."

"No way!" He shook his head. "You still have the trim figure of an eighteen-year-old girl."

Belinda's face warmed. No man but Vernon had ever talked to her in such a personal way. It made her feel peculiar. If she wasn't careful, Monroe could end up worming his way in, making it harder to convince the determined man that she had no interest in a romantic relationship with him.

"Go on with you now." She waved her

hand. "I look nothing like I did when I was a teenager."

"You look good to me."

Belinda's face grew hotter, and to her relief an English couple came in and asked if she would help them with something.

"Yes, I'll be right with you."

Before Belinda could step down from the stool, Monroe lowered his voice and said: "By the way . . . I went by that new greenhouse and checked it out the other day."

"You did?"

"Jah. It's big, and they carry a lot of different things, but not personal like your business. I was not impressed with it at all."

"Danki for sharing your thoughts. Now if you'll excuse me . . ."

"Oh, sure. Guess I'd best be going anyway." He leaned closer to Belinda. "Feel free to let me know if you have any more problems."

"I'm sure we'll be fine." She slipped out from behind the counter and gave the customers her full attention as Monroe went out the door.

Sylvia mouthed the words to one of her favorite hymns, then began to hum the tune. The house was full of sunshine, and the kitchen smelled of fresh-brewed coffee. She felt light-hearted and could almost sense God's presence. *Maybe it's because of the song that popped into my head,* she thought. *Or maybe I'm beginning to heal. Some of the scriptures Mom read during our family time of devotions have made sense to me, and my anger toward God and the man responsible for the accident that killed our loved ones seems to have dissipated some. Maybe in time I'll feel whole again spiritually.*

"Whatcha doin', Mama?" Allen asked when he darted into the kitchen where Sylvia stood, mixing the batter to make sugar cookies.

"I was humming while getting ready to bake some kichlin. Would you like to help?"

Allen bobbed his head.

Sylvia pulled a stool over to the counter and helped him climb up. Then she showed him how to dip the bottom of a cup in a bowl of sugar and flatten each blob of dough she'd placed on the cookie sheet. Sylvia did it a couple more times, and then guided Allen's hands through the process.

He caught on quickly, so Sylvia sat back and took a drink from her cup of coffee. The kitchen was so warm and cozy, as she relaxed, watching Allen at work.

Things went well at first, and her son seemed to be having a good time until his sister came into the room and started to fuss. Allen turned to look at her, and in so doing, his elbow hit the canister, sending it flying off the counter and landing on its side. Sugar went everywhere — including Rachel's hair. The sobbing child dashed out of the room, leaving a trail of sugar as she shook her head.

Allen remained on the stool with his mouth gaping open, and Sylvia didn't know whether to laugh or cry. She set the cookie sheet aside, helped Allen off the stool, and followed the trail of sugar in search of her daughter.

Sylvia found Rachel in the hallway, outside the bathroom door, no longer crying, as she sat with her legs crossed. Looking up at Sylvia, the child slid a finger across the top of her head and then stuck it in her mouth. *"Zucker."*

"Yes, little one. You have sugar in your hair." Sylvia couldn't hold back the laughter bubbling in her throat. She had a mess to clean, but it could have been worse, and it felt so good to laugh about something. She needed to look at the humorous side of things more and not be so serious all the time.

Sylvia picked Rachel up and carried her to the back porch. The first chore was getting the sugar out of her daughter's hair, and then she would return to the kitchen to get the cookies baked. Hopefully they would turn out well and she could serve them when Dennis came over tomorrow to do more bird-watching and join them for supper.

When Dennis entered the house shortly after noon, he went to the bathroom and wet a washcloth. After wiping his sweaty forehead with it, and then scrubbing his hands with plenty of soap and water, he headed for the kitchen.

Once he'd fixed a peanut butter and jelly sandwich, Dennis poured himself a glass of milk and took a seat at the table. Since no one was here to see him, he didn't bother to offer a prayer, even though he did have much to be thankful for.

Dennis had spent the better part of the morning working with his friend's horse, and as soon as he finished eating lunch he had another person's gelding to work with. He'd hung several flyers around the area, advertising his business, and had run an ad in the local newspaper. Dennis hoped he'd soon have more business than he could handle.

He picked up one of his sandwich halves

and took a bite. *Who knows, maybe I'll eventually be able to hire someone to help around the barn — cleaning the stalls, along with feeding and watering the horses. A helper could also brush down the horses after their training sessions.*

This morning, before Dennis had gone out to the barn, he'd called the bird-watcher's hotline and was pleased to hear a few people talk about some sightings in this area. One person from Gap had seen several turkey vultures, as well as a Cooper's hawk and a blue jay. Another person, from a different area, stated that they'd spotted a blue-winged teal and some black terns. Dennis planned to take Sylvia and her brother to that area tomorrow afternoon. With any luck, they would find some interesting birds too.

Dennis eyed his stack of reading material on the counter. *I should look up those birds in one of my books. That way, if we do catch sight of any of the species talked about on the hotline, I'll be more informed about what I'm hoping to see.*

He was eager to see Henry and Sylvia again. He'd enjoyed their last birding adventure and been pleased to see Sylvia smile and hear her laugh a few times. She'd seemed more relaxed than she had previously, and Dennis looked forward to joining her family for a meal when they got back from birding. It would be nice to get better acquainted with Sylvia's mother and sister. He was curious to see how well Sylvia got along with her family. The sit-down supper should help him see this.

Home-cooked meals weren't the norm for Dennis these days. It was a nice treat for him to be invited to eat with the King family. He was sure there would be some kind of a dessert to follow the meal — something else to anticipate.

Dennis bit into his sandwich and drank some milk. His world seemed to be filled with more happiness as he'd gotten better acquainted with Henry and especially Sylvia. He didn't understand why, but he was drawn to her — had been from the moment they'd met.

*Maybe it's because I saw the hurt in her eyes and heard it in her tone of voice.* Dennis knew all the signs of emotional pain, because he'd felt them too, ever since his father died. Truth was, he wasn't sure he would ever fully come to grips with Dad's death, but keeping busy seemed to help some. And of course, his hobby of bird-watching was a pleasant distraction, so maybe it would be for Sylvia too.

# CHAPTER 25

*Clymer*

Michelle's heart swelled with joy as she sat in church, listening to her husband preach from Psalm 127:3–5. "Lo, children are an heritage of the Lord: and the fruit of the womb is his reward. As arrows are in the hand of a mighty man; so are children of the youth. Happy is the man that hath his quiver full of them. . . ."

Michelle looked at her daughter sitting beside her, so well-behaved, and then at the little boy in her lap. What a blessing and a privilege it was to be these children's mother.

Although far from perfect, Michelle did her best to be a good mother. She wanted her children to feel loved and safe — not hopeless and fearful, the way she'd felt as a child.

Michelle was thankful she'd married a good man who spent quality time with his children and gave them all the love and proper training they needed.

*I wish my dad had been like Ezekiel. I'm sure I would have turned out differently if he'd been a loving Christian father.* She reached into her tote and pulled out a couple of snack-sized bags for the children.

Michelle didn't think of her parents as often as she used to when she and her brothers were first put in foster care, but sometimes, like now, a vision of her mother and father came to mind. She wondered if they'd ever gotten help for their problems, or if they sometimes thought about her, Ernie, and Jack. Had her folks ever come to realize what bad parents they'd been? Were they sorry for the abuse their children had suffered?

Looking back on it now, Michelle was glad that she and her brothers had been taken from their parents. They were better off without them.

Her thoughts went to Ernie and Jack and what a nice visit they'd all had the last time they had gotten together. Michelle looked forward to the next opportunity for either of her brothers to come for a visit.

*Strasburg*

"Dennis should be here anytime. Would you

307

two like to join us today for some bird-watching?" Sylvia looked at Amy and Jared, who sat on the porch swing. They'd all recently returned from visiting a neighboring church district.

"It's nice of you to ask," Amy replied, "but Jared and I have other plans. We've been invited to my friend Lydia's house to play some games and join a few other young people for a barbecue. We'll be leaving soon."

"So you won't be here for supper?"

"No," Jared spoke up. "Our get-together will probably last until late evening."

"Sounds about right. Guess I'd better let Mom know so she doesn't fix too much chicken."

"I already told her that Jared and I won't be here," Amy said.

"Oh, okay." *It's hard to believe that this fall we'll be adding another member to our family. Jared will be a nice addition.* Sylvia gazed out into the yard. *Although I'm feeling more alive these days, it would take a miracle for me to find the same kind of bond with another man that I had with Toby.*

"Dennis is here!" Wearing binoculars attached to a leather cord around his neck, Henry bounded off the porch and raced over to the hitching rail as Dennis's horse and buggy came up the driveway.

Sylvia opened the screen door and called: "Henry and I are leaving now!"

"Okay, I'll have supper waiting when you get back," Mom responded from the living room.

"I'll see you two later." Sylvia smiled at Amy and Jared, grabbed her binoculars and notebook from the wicker table, and hurried down the porch steps. It was hard to believe the thought of bird-watching could have her feeling so enthusiastic. *If I'm being honest, maybe there is more to it than just excitement over the birds we might see.*

"I can't believe we were fortunate enough to see a female northern harrier hawk today," Dennis said as they headed back to the Kings' place that evening.

"Think I've seen one before, but I thought it was an owl," Henry chimed in.

"Its face does have a distinctive owl-like look," Dennis admitted. "It's actually one of the easiest hawks to identify."

"Why is that?" Sylvia questioned.

"For one thing, harriers glide just above the ground while searching for food."

"What do they eat?" Henry asked.

"Snakes, insects, mice, and small birds. Another interesting fact about the harriers is that they used to be called marsh hawks because they hunted over marshy areas. The female harrier, like we saw today, has a dark brown back with a brown-streaked breast, large white patch on its backside, and narrow black bands across the tail. The tips of its wings are black, and it has yellow eyes."

Henry tapped Dennis on the shoulder, from where he sat in the back seat. "Do the males look like that too?"

"They have the same yellow eyes and black tips on their wings, but the male's body is silver gray and its belly is white."

"I can't get over how much you know about birds," Sylvia commented. "I bet you could write your own bird book."

Dennis laughed. "I've taken plenty of notes about the birds I've seen, but I don't have what it takes to put it all together in the form of a book." He snapped the reins to get his horse moving quicker. "And as much as I know about training a horse to pull a buggy, I wouldn't try to write a book about that either."

Sylvia smiled. "We all have different things we're good at, but it doesn't mean we could write a book about them."

"Very true." Dennis had to force himself to keep his focus on watching the road ahead and making sure his horse behaved.

All he really wanted to do was look at Sylvia. She was a beautiful woman. What a shame she'd lost her husband at such a young age.

*I wish there was something I could do to offer her comfort.* Dennis also wished he had the nerve to ask Sylvia to go out for supper with him one night this week. If her brother wasn't sitting behind them, no doubt listening to every word being said, Dennis would ask her right now. Maybe he would have the opportunity sometime before the evening was out.

When they pulled up to the hitching rail at the King home, Henry hopped out and secured Dennis's horse.

"I hope you like cold, fried *hinkel,* because that's what my mamm said she'd be serving for our supper this evening," Sylvia said as Dennis walked between her and Henry.

He grinned. "Definitely. I mean, who doesn't like fried chicken, warm or cold?" All week Dennis had looked forward to having some home cooking. The bland sandwiches he'd been eating for lunch, or the so-so canned soups for supper paled in comparison to this.

"My brother Abe didn't care for hinkel," Henry said. "Fact is, he wasn't a chicken

311

eater at all."

"Did he like eggs?" Dennis asked as they neared the porch.

"Yep. He liked 'em just fine." Henry's voice lowered. "I sure do miss my bruder."

"I'm sure you do." Dennis gave the boy's shoulder a squeeze. "It's never easy when you lose someone close to you." He glanced at Sylvia, wondering if she would say anything, but she was silent. No doubt she still missed her husband, brother, and father. A person never really got over a tragedy like that, although in time the pain became less raw and more bearable to deal with. Maybe a distraction from time to time could help them both to better cope with their losses.

Dennis looked up at the gutter on the front of the house and noticed the drain spout had come loose. He stepped under it and pointed. "Sometime tomorrow, with the aid of a *leeder,* I could put that back together."

"It's up there pretty high. Are you sure you want to do it?" Sylvia asked.

Before Dennis had time to answer, Henry jumped in. "I could help by holding the ladder for you, Dennis."

"That'd be great. I'd appreciate your help if you're available when I come over."

"I'll bring the matter up to Mom," Sylvia said.

"That's fine. It shouldn't take me long at all." Dennis moved toward the front door.

When they entered the house, Sylvia's mother came into the living room, and he shook her hand. "Danki for including me in your supper plans this evening."

"You're welcome." Belinda smiled, but it didn't quite reach her eyes. No doubt she still grieved for her deceased family members. Either that, or Dennis figured Sylvia's mother might not care much for him.

*But how can that be?* he wondered. *This is only the second time we've met.*

"If you'll excuse me, I need to get back to the kitchen and finish setting things out for our meal." Belinda hurried from the room.

Sylvia invited Dennis to take a seat on the couch, before excusing herself to help her mother. "We should have supper on the table soon, so just sit and relax with Henry. I'll call you both when the food's on the table."

"Okay, thanks." Dennis sat on the couch, and Henry seated himself in an overstuffed chair. *This is a nice house. It's bigger than the home I'm renting, but I don't need a place this big.*

"I sure had fun birding with you and Sylvia today." Henry looked over at Dennis and grinned.

"I enjoyed it too." *Henry's a good kid. I bet he could use a big brother in his life.*

"I'm always watchin' for different birds in our yard." Henry clasped his hands around one knee. "Birding's a lot more interesting than takin' care of *ieme.*"

"Are you a beekeeper?"

"Not by choice. It was my brother Ezekiel's job before he and his fraa moved to New York. After that, Abe took it over. When he died, I got stuck with the bees." The boy wrinkled his nose. "Can't tell ya how many times I've been stung."

"Don't you wear protective clothing?"

"Course I do, but sometimes those pesky insects find their way to my skin."

"It's a good thing you're not allergic to bees."

Henry bobbed his head. "That's for sure."

"Don't you also work in the greenhouse with your mother and sisters?" Dennis asked.

"Jah, only Sylvia doesn't work there 'cause she . . ."

Henry stopped talking when two young children darted into the room. The little girl hid behind the chair where Henry sat, but the young boy walked right up to Dennis and said in Pennsylvania Dutch: "Who are you?"

"My name is Dennis Weaver. *Was is dei naame?*"

The boy pointed to himself. "Allen." Then he pointed at the chair where the girl hid. "That's Rachel."

The child peeked out from behind the chair, her brown eyes growing large as she stared at Dennis. Then just as quickly, she ducked back again.

"Are these children your little brother and sister?" Dennis looked at Henry.

Henry shook his head. "No, they're . . ."

At that moment, Sylvia entered the room. When she approached the couch, the little girl came out from behind the chair and shouted, "Mammi!"

Dennis's jaw dropped. He had no idea the children were Sylvia's. She'd never mentioned anything about being a mother.

Sylvia bent down and picked Rachel up. Then she took hold of Allen's hand. "These are my kinner, Allen and Rachel."

"Your son greeted me already, but your little girl hid behind the chair until you came in."

"Rachel is shy around new people, so don't let it bother you." She kissed the girl's dimpled cheek.

Dennis reached around and rubbed the back of his neck. "I didn't realize you had children, but then since you were married, I guess it should be no surprise."

Sylvia smiled. "If you'll come with me to the dining room, supper is on the table."

Dennis stood, and both he and Henry followed Sylvia and her children out of the room.

Moments before they bowed their heads for silent prayer, Sylvia noticed Dennis looking at her children. Allen sat on a booster seat at the table, and Rachel had been seated in the wooden high chair Sylvia's father had made. She'd spoken to her mother about the loose downspout near the front porch, and Mom said she was fine with Dennis fixing it for them at his convenience.

After the prayer and while Mom passed the platter of chicken around, Sylvia watched her brother's face light up when Dennis spoke to him. She thought about how well Henry and Abe had gotten along in the past. No doubt Henry still missed him and needed a big brother who lived close by. *No wonder he seems so drawn to Dennis, since they share the same hobby.*

*If only Toby, Dad, and Abe could see how much the children have grown,* Sylvia thought before closing her eyes. Although her prayer was a short one, she managed to ask God to keep her family safe, and to be with Dennis as he settled into the community.

When Sylvia opened her eyes, she was surprised to see Dennis looking once more at Allen and Rachel. She wondered if little ones made him nervous, or perhaps he wished he was married and had children of his own.

As they ate their meal, Dennis and Henry struck up a conversation centered around birds. Sylvia wasn't surprised, since Dennis knew a lot about birding, and Henry wanted to know more. As a matter of fact, so did she. Studying birds and writing down specific things about them was a nice break from household chores, cooking, and taking care of her children. Not that Sylvia minded those things. It was just nice to do something out of the ordinary that she found fascinating.

Although Sylvia would never admit it out loud, she enjoyed being with Dennis. It was too soon to say whether she could develop strong feelings for him or if he felt anything for her, but if Dennis should invite her to go bird-watching with him again, Sylvia would definitely say yes.

# CHAPTER 26

Dennis paced, shuffling through the straw scattered across the floor in front of his horse's stall. It would be two weeks tomorrow since he'd had supper with Sylvia and her family. The food had tasted good, and he'd enjoyed spending time with Sylvia and her children, as well as Henry.

But her mother, who'd been less than friendly toward him, had excused herself and gone to her room soon after they'd finished eating, saying she'd developed a headache. He hoped she hadn't used it as an excuse.

A day later, Dennis and Henry fixed the downspout, and soon it was back together. The two of them talked more about birding. Henry was easy to talk to and full of curiosity.

Since that day, Dennis hadn't spoken with Sylvia or Henry. Between training three new horses and struggling with his fear of commitment, Dennis had decided it would be best for both him and Sylvia if he didn't see her socially anymore. That, of course, would mean no more outings to do bird-watching. With the decision made, it was probably for the best that he hadn't asked her to go out with him.

*Or maybe,* Dennis told himself as he made another pass by his horse's stall, *I should set my concerns aside, follow my heart instead of my head, and take a leap of faith.*

Virginia made a face at herself in the bathroom mirror. *What's up with my hair? It doesn't want to cooperate, and the graying roots are starting to show. I need to see a hairdresser, that's for sure.*

Virginia turned off the bathroom light and headed for the kitchen. *I could sure use a cup of coffee right now.* She was glad to see that there was still enough in the pot Earl had started for himself before he left for work, and he'd left it on warm for her.

She grabbed a mug, and in the process of pouring coffee into it, some spilled onto the counter. Virginia pulled a paper towel off the cardboard roll and wiped it up. "No wonder I spilled it," she muttered. "The traffic on the road out front has increased again, and it's made me edgy. Wish we'd never moved here. Don't know what Earl was thinking, buying a place in the country."

Virginia's cell phone rang. She tossed the damp paper towel in the garbage and picked up her phone. When her friend Stella's number showed in the caller ID, Virginia wasted no time answering. "Hey, Stella, how are you doing?"

"I'm fine. How are you?"

"Except for being bored out of my mind, I'm okay."

"Have you made friends with anyone in the area yet?"

"Nope. Not yet." Virginia picked up her mug and drank the rest of her coffee.

"I'm sorry to hear that. I'd hoped you would have made a friend or two by now."

Virginia heaved a sigh. "Even if I had any friends in the area, I wouldn't like living here."

"I enjoyed my time there when I came to visit. It was fun going over to the greenhouse across the street too."

Virginia's gaze flicked upward. *Fun for you maybe, but not for me.*

"Are you going to plant a vegetable garden this year?"

"I don't think so. We can get all the produce we want at the local farmers' market." Virginia moved over to the kitchen window and looked out at the backyard. "Earl's working part of the day, so while he's gone I may go outside and do a little work in the flowerbeds."

"That should make the time go quickly," Stella said. "Fresh air and a little exercise are good for a person too."

"Yeah, I suppose." Virginia shifted the phone to her other ear. "Say, Stella, not long ago, Earl and I ate supper at a restaurant in Ronks. While we were there we saw our neighbor, Amy King, and her fiancé, Jared. They spotted us and came over to our table. And you know what the best part was?"

"I haven't a clue."

"Jared invited us to their wedding, which will take place this fall."

"How nice. Are you planning to go?"

"Maybe so. Would you like to come along?"

"Are you kidding me?"

"Nope. I'm tellin' the truth." Virginia couldn't help but smile. This was one sure way to get Stella to come back for a visit.

"Wow! Once you know the exact date, let me know and I'll cancel anything I may have scheduled. I wouldn't miss going to an Amish wedding for anything. I'm so excited right now, you could knock me over with a feather."

"Glad to have made your day, my friend, and I already know the date. It's the first Thursday of October. I just need to wait for a formal invitation."

"That's great! Now what were we talking about earlier?"

"I seem to have forgotten, Stella."

"Oh. Now I remember. It was about you working in your flowerbeds. You should go over to the greenhouse and see what kind of plants they have. You might find something that would look nice in your yard."

Virginia's jaw clenched. Truth was, she'd prefer to do any shopping for plants at the new greenhouse across town. But she couldn't let on to Stella how she really felt, because if her friend knew the way she felt about the Amish family across the road, she'd probably say Virginia was prejudiced.

"Umm, Virginia, I'd better go. I have another call coming in."

"Oh, okay. I'll talk to you again soon, Stella. Bye for now."

When Virginia clicked off her phone, she went out to the utility porch and grabbed her gardening gloves, some hand-clippers, and a shovel. At least her friend would likely come to visit again in the fall, which made Virginia happy.

Now maybe a little time spent outdoors

would help her work off some of her stress.

"Would you look at these beautiful daffodils in bloom? I think they're prettier than ever this spring." Sylvia's mother gestured to the flowers adorning the flowerbed near the front porch.

Sylvia, deep in thought, hung a pair of Allen's trousers on the line and gave a brief nod.

"You seem distracted this morning," Mom said. "You haven't spoken more than a few words since we came outside with the laundry basket."

"Sorry, Mom. I've just been thinking, is all."

"About what?"

"Nothing in particular. Just thoughts about life in general." No way would Sylvia admit that she'd been thinking about Dennis and wondering why she hadn't heard from him since he'd come over to fix the downspout. They'd had a pleasant time when they'd gone birding and he'd joined them for supper — at least Sylvia had, and Dennis had mentioned going bird-watching again. It seemed strange that he wouldn't have at least called or come by. Could training horses be keeping him that busy?

"Daughter, did you hear what I said?"

Sylvia turned abruptly when Mom bumped her arm. "Uh . . . no, sorry, I did not. What was it, Mom?"

"I wondered if you'd have time to make up some hanging baskets for us to sell in the greenhouse. You made some lovely ones last year, and they sold quite well."

"Of course, I'd be happy to make more. I enjoyed using my creativity, and I've been thinking about some new ways I could arrange some flowering plants this year." Sylvia picked up a towel from the laundry basket and gave it a snap before hanging it on the line. "I'll get started on them as soon as all the laundry is hung."

"Danki. I look forward to seeing what you come up with." Mom turned her head in the direction of a horse and buggy coming up the driveway. "Looks like Mrs. Yoder, our first customer of the day is here. I'm sorry to run off and leave you with the rest of the clothes to hang, but I really should go to the greenhouse and help Amy."

"No problem. You go right ahead." Sylvia hurried to finish hanging the laundry, and then she carted the empty wicker basket back to the house. Seeing that the children were playing happily in the living room, she went to the kitchen and sat at the table with a notebook and pen. Since Mom wanted her to make up some hanging baskets, Sylvia thought it would be a good idea to start by making a list of all the plants she might want to include. At least she had something to keep her busy and take her mind off Dennis.

Sylvia had only been working on the list a few minutes when she heard Rachel crying from the living room. She pushed her chair aside and hurried to the other room, where she found her tearful daughter pointing at the open door.

Sylvia looked out and saw Allen sprinting toward the greenhouse. She picked Rachel up and hurried out the door. *Sure hope I get to him before he enters the greenhouse.*

Preparing to wait on a customer who'd entered the building a few minutes ago, Belinda felt a tug on her apron. She looked down and was surprised to see Allen looking up at her with a rubber ball in his hands. *"Gleichscht du balle schpiele?"*

"Jah, Allen, I like to play ball, but Grandma is busy working right now."

The boy's bottom lip protruded as he held the ball over his head.

Belinda glanced around hoping either Henry or Amy was nearby and could take Allen up to the house. Neither of them was in sight. She couldn't leave the greenhouse unattended, and hoped they were at least somewhere in the building.

Belinda bent down and scooped Allen into her arms, but it obviously was not what he wanted. Allen began to thrash around, and ended up knocking Belinda's reading glasses on the floor. The next thing she knew, the woman she'd been about to help stepped back and the glasses shattered.

Belinda gasped, and Allen started to howl. This was not a good way to begin the morning.

The woman apologized for ruining her glasses and offered to pay for new ones.

Belinda waved her hand. "They're an old pair, and I have another, so there's no need to worry about it."

The woman apologized again and headed down one of the aisles. By then, Allen had calmed down some. Belinda's only consolation was that she had another pair of reading glasses in the house. If she could only remember where she'd put them.

Sylvia entered the greenhouse in time to see Mom down on the floor, picking up the pieces of her broken glasses. Allen stood next to her, whimpering, which made Rachel's tears start up again.

"What happened here?" Sylvia questioned.

As Mom explained, Sylvia clasped her son's hand.

A few seconds later, Amy came around the corner. "Mom, what's going on?" She looked down at what was left of their mother's glasses.

While Sylvia tried to get her children calmed down, Mom repeated the story.

"Why don't you go up to the house and look for your other glasses?" Amy suggested. "Henry's in the storage room right now, but I'll get him. The two of us will wait on customers while you're gone, and make sure things go okay here."

"All right." Mom held onto the remnants of her glasses. "Oh, by the way . . . a lady came in a few minutes before Allen showed up, and I was going to see if she needed any help." She gestured to Aisle 2. "She went that way."

"No problem. I'll see if I can help her."

Mom disposed of the broken glasses, and then she left the greenhouse, along with Sylvia and the children.

They'd barely entered the house when Sylvia heard a horse and buggy come into the yard. She stepped out onto the porch to see if it was anyone they knew and felt pleasure, seeing that it was Dennis.

Sylvia remained on the porch until he secured his horse and joined her there.

"It's good to see you, Sylvia. How have you been?" he asked.

"Fairly well. How are things going for you?"

"Not bad at all. My business is picking up, so that's a good thing."

"I'm glad it's working out."

Dennis shuffled his feet and leaned against the porch railing.

*Is it my imagination, or could Dennis be nervous about something?*

He took a step toward her and cleared his throat. "This is kind of a last-minute invitation, but I wondered if you'd be free to go out for supper with me this evening."

Sylvia had mixed feelings about being alone with Dennis, but at the same time, the idea of having supper with him appealed.

"If you're not free this evening, then maybe some other time." Dennis shuffled his feet a few more times.

"It's not that," Sylvia was quick to say. "I'll just need to see if someone would be willing to watch Rachel and Allen for me."

"Wouldn't your mamm do that?"

"Probably." Sylvia smiled. "My kinner love spending time with her. Allen even snuck

328

out to the greenhouse a while ago, just to be with his grossmammi."

Dennis chuckled. "I bet that little guy keeps you busy."

"He certainly does. Jah, both kinner keep me plenty busy."

"So how about it, Sylvia? Are you willing to go out for supper with me?"

She gave a quick nod. A few months ago she wouldn't have believed she'd be spending the evening alone with a man, much less one she found to be both interesting and attractive. Even though she felt a bit nervous about going out with Dennis, Sylvia looked forward to this evening.

"Okay, good. I'll come by around six to pick you up." Dennis took a few steps back, and then stopped. "Oh, by the way . . . I thought you might want to know that when I was coming up your driveway, I noticed that the greenhouse sign was no longer hanging — it was lying on the ground."

Sylvia was at a loss for words. *Oh, no . . . Not another act of vandalism!*

# CHAPTER 27

After Dennis left, Sylvia went into the house, where she found her mother sitting on the sofa in the living room. Allen sat on one side of her, and Rachel was seated on Mom's lap.

"Did you find your glasses?" Sylvia asked.

Mom shook her head. "I haven't had a chance to look. Someone needed to watch the kinner while you were out there talking to that man."

"His name is Dennis, and I wasn't out there very long."

"What'd he want?" Mom set Rachel on the couch beside her brother and went over to the wicker basket by her rocking chair.

Sylvia felt the tension building in her mother's words. She'd been down this road once already, when Dennis came for supper and Mom acted so distant.

Rummaging through the basket, Mom spoke again. "Well, what did Dennis want?"

330

"One thing he mentioned was that he noticed our sign by the road was lying in the dirt when he came up the driveway."

Mom stood up straight, her eyebrows drawing together. "Was it intentionally cut down?"

Sylvia shrugged. "I don't know. Dennis just said it was down."

"I'll have Henry put it back in place. Maybe he didn't secure the sign you made tightly enough when he put it up."

Sylvia drew in her bottom lip. "I hope that's the case. It's upsetting to think that someone might be targeting the greenhouse by removing our sign."

"The worst part is, we don't know who or why." Mom sank into the rocking chair. "Nothing like this ever happened when your father was alive."

Sylvia nodded. "Everything was better for all of us before the accident."

"That's true, but God is still with us, and we must remember to depend on Him for all of our needs."

Sylvia gave no response. Even after a year of being a widow, her faith was still on shaky ground. There were still moments when she couldn't get past the anger she felt about Toby, Dad, and Abe having been taken away. She didn't see how any good could come from their absence. *I'd like to know the reason the Lord allowed their lives to be taken.* Sylvia pondered this a moment.

"I think I know where my other pair of glasses is." Mom stood up suddenly. "I believe I may have left them on the nightstand in my bedroom." She turned in the direction of the hallway.

"Umm . . . before you go, there's something I need to ask you."

Mom turned back to face Sylvia. "What is it?"

"Would you be willing to watch the kinner for me this evening?"

Mom blinked. "How come? Won't you be here to watch them?"

"Normally I would be, but Dennis asked me to go out for supper with him."

Mom's forehead wrinkled as she pinched the bridge of her nose. "Are you serious? You haven't known that man long enough to go anywhere alone with him."

"I may not have known Dennis long, but I think I'm a pretty good judge of character. And there's nothing to worry about, because Dennis and I are just friends. Besides, I thought you wanted me to get out more and do something fun."

"I do, but not with a man you barely know." Mom moved closer and placed her hand on Sylvia's arm. "There are other single men in our church district, you know. Please think about what I've said."

"I'm not interested in any of them, and none have shown interest in me." Sylvia shrugged her mother's hand away. "If you don't want to watch Rachel and Allen, that's fine. I'll see if Amy is free to do it."

"I did not say that. I'm always willing to spend time with my grandchildren, and if you are determined to go out with Dennis, then I will watch the kinner."

"Danki. Now I'd better get back to my flowering plant list, and I'm sure you want to find your missing pair of glasses before heading back to the greenhouse." Sylvia gave her mother a hug. She hoped there were no hard feelings.

When Belinda returned to the greenhouse, she found Henry putting fresh jars of honey on the shelf. She stepped up beside him and placed her hand on his shoulder. "Those amber-filled containers sell well, that's for sure. So many of our customers like to buy raw, unfiltered, local honey."

"Beekeeping's a lot of work, and sometimes I get stung, but like Dennis said, at least I'm not allergic to bee venom."

Belinda nodded. "When you're done with

that, would you please go out and rehang our sign by the road?"

His eyes widened. "The sign is down?"

"Jah. Dennis was here a while ago to see Sylvia, and he informed her that he'd seen the sign lying in the dirt. I'm sorry, Son, but you'll need to hang it back up again."

A flush of red erupted on Henry's cheeks. "I wonder how that happened. Sure hope it wasn't taken down on purpose."

"Maybe there's a simple explanation."

"Like what?"

"You might not have secured it tightly enough."

There was a visible tightness in Henry's jaw. "So now I'm to blame, huh?"

"I didn't say that. I just thought —"

"When I put the sign up I made sure it was secured."

Belinda held up one hand. "Okay, I believe you did your best. Now would you please go out and put the sign back in place? We can't afford to lose any customers for lack of a sign."

"Jah, okay. I'll go out to the tool shed and get what I need." Henry put the last two jars on the shelf and went out the back door.

Belinda heaved a sigh. *I didn't mean to imply that his work was inadequate, but I wanted to steer my son away from thinking it was vandalism.* Henry had been a little easier to deal with lately. She hoped he wasn't back to his old defensive ways.

Belinda straightened a few other items for sale and headed up front to the counter where Amy sat. Since there were no customers in the building at the moment, she said, "This day has not begun the way I'd hoped."

Amy tipped her head to one side. "What's wrong, Mom?"

"Well, for starters, our business sign out by the road is no longer hanging up. I just told Henry about it, and he's going to put it back in place."

"Do you think it was done intentionally? Could it have been the same person who took the other sign?" Amy leaned forward with both arms on the counter.

"I have no idea, but I hope not. With all the things that have been done over the past year, I'm a little skittish."

"Me too. If we knew who was responsible for the vandalism, maybe we could talk to them and find out what made them do those things."

Belinda readjusted her left apron strap. It was close to falling off her shoulder. "The sign being down isn't all that has me upset."

"What else is wrong?" Amy brushed some

dirt off the counter. "What's going on?"

"Dennis asked your sister to go out to supper with him this evening, and she wants me to take care of Rachel and Allen while she's gone."

A wide smile spread across Amy's face. "I think that's great. Sylvia needs to get out once in a while without the kinner."

"I agree, but it's too soon for Sylvia to be seeing a man socially, especially one we know so little about."

"What did you tell her about watching the children?"

"I agreed to it, but I'm not happy about the situation. As I said, we know little or nothing about Mr. Weaver, and I still feel your sister was hasty in letting him rent her house." Belinda pinched the skin at her throat. "I can't put my finger on it, but there is something suspicious about that man. I hope he doesn't worm his way into Sylvia's life. She's been through enough emotional pain. It would be horrible if Dennis did anything to hurt her."

"What in the world are you doing, woman?"

Virginia jumped, nearly dropping the pair of binoculars she held in her hands. "For goodness' sakes, Earl, you shouldn't sneak up on me like that. I could have dropped these expensive things."

"Right, Virginia, and they're intended to be used for looking at wild-life, not spying on the neighbors. That is what you were doing, correct?"

"Maybe I was bird-watching. You know, birding is a hobby, and you need binoculars to do that." She held them back up to her eyes.

He patted her shoulder. "What kind of birds are you observing out the front window?"

"Umm . . . Well, okay, you caught me."

"I thought so. Who are you watching this time?"

"Henry King. He's out by the road hanging up their greenhouse sign."

"Good grief, you've become a red-haired spy. I can see what he's doing from right here standing next to you. Anyways, I thought they already had a sign."

"They did, but I guess somebody took it down. When he picked it up, it had been lying in the dirt." Virginia tapped her foot. "I can't blame whoever did it either. I'm sure no one who lives on this road appreciates all the heavy traffic or piles of smelly road apples."

He quirked an eyebrow. "You're sure about that?"

"Yep. Only a person who's hard of hearing could deal with the steady *clip-clop,* not to mention all the cars that go up the Kings' driveway." She clenched her fingers tightly around the binoculars. "I've said this before, and I'll say it again. I wish we'd never moved here, Earl."

He slipped his arm around her waist. "Oh, come on now. It's not so bad."

"That's easy enough for you to say. Those people aren't right, with their backward mode of transportation and the way they have to dress so plain. You're at work most of the time, and I'm left here all alone, putting up with that." Virginia pointed out the window. "It's not fair."

"If you'd get out more and try to make some friends, I'm sure you'd adjust and find some fun things to do."

She set the binoculars on an end table near the couch and folded her arms. "I'm never gonna be happy here, and I will probably never make any new friends."

"With that kind of negative attitude, you probably won't."

"I'm gonna try and be more accepting of the Kings. I want Stella to come visit again, and the only way I can keep my friend on board with the idea is to get that wedding invite from Amy and Jared."

"So you're going to try to win over the Amish neighbors?"

"Yep." *If I can find the determination and courage to do it.*

"What is your plan?"

"For starters, I need some plants for the yard. So I'm gonna make myself go across the street and pick some out." Virginia pointed to the greenhouse.

He let out a hearty chuckle. "I won't believe it till you're walking in that direction and returning with a flat of pretty petunias or some other flowers."

"Are you getting a big bang out of this, Earl?"

"No, not really."

"I'm flat out miserable, or can't you tell? I have to go to a place I don't wanna go, just to ensure that we'll get invited to that wedding."

"Why don't you simply try to be yourself and get along with the neighbors, like I'm sure you're capable of, instead of acting like you want to be their friend?"

She put one hand against her hip. "You plainly don't understand me. Guess I'm just a complicated person with strange needs and wants."

"I didn't say that. Just go ahead and do what you like, but they'll probably see through your deception." Earl turned and walked out of the room.

Virginia picked up the field glasses again and looked out the window. The greenhouse sign was back in place now, and Henry was out of sight. *I wish those people would move someplace else. At least that would be one problem resolved.*

# CHAPTER 28

Sylvia felt a lightness in her chest as she waited on the porch for Dennis's arrival. She'd told Rachel and Allen goodbye before coming outside, as well as Mom and Amy.

Henry's friend Seth had come by in his car a short time ago to pick Henry up. They planned to go out for pizza. When Henry had told Seth about their greenhouse sign, Seth denied knowing anything about the one that went missing or the sign Sylvia had made that Dennis found on the ground.

Mom still wasn't happy about Henry's friendship with Seth, but Sylvia had heard her tell Amy that she didn't want to hold the reins too tightly on Henry, or he might rebel.

Sylvia figured Mom was probably right and had made the best decision letting Henry go with Seth. She hoped her brother would behave himself this evening.

Sylvia took a seat on the porch swing.

Glancing into the yard, she heard a bird calling from the maple tree. Sylvia wondered if it was that mockingbird again. Since the sun had begun to set, she couldn't make out what the bird looked like.

She'd just gotten the swing moving when a horse and buggy entered the yard. Sylvia knew right away it was Dennis because she recognized his well-groomed horse. Before he had a chance to pull up to the hitching rail, she stepped off the porch and approached his buggy.

"*Guder owed.* I wasn't expecting you to be waiting for me outside," Dennis said when Sylvia took her seat on the right side of the buggy.

"Good evening." She turned to him and smiled. "Figured I'd save you the trip of coming up to the house to get me."

"I wouldn't have minded." Dennis guided his horse down the driveway and out onto the road.

Normally, when Sylvia rode in anyone's buggy, her nerves were on edge. She'd been like this ever since the accident that took her husband's life. But this evening, seeing how self-confident Dennis seemed to be, she allowed herself to relax while riding in a carriage for the first time in over a year. As long as Dennis's horse didn't act up or a vehicle came up behind them going too fast, she might stay in her relaxed state of mind all the way to the restaurant.

"Have you decided where we're going to eat?" she asked.

Dennis shook his head. "Thought I'd leave that up to you. What's your favorite restaurant?"

"There are many good ones in our county, but I'm kind of partial to the family restaurant in Bird-in-Hand. Have you been there since you moved here?"

He shook his head. "Not yet, but I've heard good things about the food. So that's the direction we'll head."

Sylvia clasped her fingers loosely in her lap as she drew in a deep, satisfied breath. It was difficult to explain, even to herself, but when she was with Dennis she felt like a different person. Although Sylvia hadn't forgotten that she was the mother of two small children, as the horse's hooves clopped along the pavement, she felt like a teenager again, going on her first date.

"Did you get the kinner settled in bed?" Amy asked when Belinda entered the living room and seated herself in the rocking chair.

"Jah and now I can relax. It took a little prompting to get Allen to fall asleep this evening. He said he wanted to see his mom, and I had to remind him that he'd see her tomorrow morning." Belinda reached into the basket near her feet to get the dishcloth she'd been working on in her free time.

Amy plumped up one of the throw pillows on the couch where she sat. "Sylvia's kinner are adorable, and I love them both, but they can be a handful sometimes."

Belinda nodded. "But I wouldn't trade any of my *kinskinner* for all the world."

"I hope when Jared and I have children that I'll be as good a mother as Sylvia. She's so patient with Rachel and Allen and always seems to know what to say and how to handle any situation that arises with them."

Belinda got the rocking chair moving as her knitting needles clicked together. "You're right, she is a good mudder. I just wish she would use common sense where Dennis is concerned."

Amy tipped her head. "In what way?"

"She barely knows the fellow, yet she agreed to go out to supper with him." Belinda stopped rocking and leaned slightly forward.

"Going out to supper is a good way for Sylvia to get to know him better, don't you think?"

Belinda shrugged. "Maybe so, but they

could do that in mixed company, not alone. What if someone from our church district sees them together at the restaurant? Why, there could soon be a round of gossip and speculation about Toby's widow being involved with the *geheem fremmer* who came to our area."

Amy laughed. "Really Mom, Dennis is hardly a mysterious stranger. He seems like a nice man. Sylvia and Henry believe he is too. I've heard them both say so several times."

Belinda was going to say more, but a knock sounded on the front door.

"That must be Jared." Amy rose from the couch and went to let him in.

Belinda had forgotten Amy had mentioned earlier that her future husband would be coming by.

A few minutes later, Amy entered the room with Jared. Belinda couldn't help but notice the circle of red on both his and Amy's cheeks. She wondered if he and Amy had embraced and possibly kissed, when he'd entered the house, the way she and Vernon used to do when they were courting.

"Guder owen, Belinda." Jared came over to Belinda and extended his hand. "How did things go for you today?"

She shook his hand and smiled. "It went all right. At least there were no mishaps in the greenhouse, and we sold a fair amount of flowers."

"Good to hear." Jared took a seat on the couch beside Amy. They sat quietly looking at each other.

*These two probably want to be alone to discuss their plans for the future.* Belinda put her knitting aside and stood. "I'm kind of tired this evening. Think I'll head to my room and get ready for bed."

Amy didn't try to dissuade her. She merely smiled at Belinda and said, "*Gut nacht,* Mom."

"Good night, Daughter. Good night, Jared."

After Jared replied, Belinda left the room. *Oh, to be young and in love again,* she thought. *My dearest Vernon, I miss you ever so much, but I'll never forget the special bond of love we shared.*

"You were right about the food being good at the Bird-in-Hand Family Restaurant," Dennis said as they traveled back to the King home.

"I'm glad you enjoyed it."

*Not as much as I enjoyed being with you.* Dennis kept his thoughts to himself. It was too soon to tell Sylvia that he was beginning to have strong feelings for her. He'd never felt like this before, and no way did he want to scare her off.

Dennis couldn't believe he was setting his concerns aside about establishing a relationship with a woman that could possibly lead to a permanent relationship. Of course he was putting the buggy before the horse when it came to any future he might have with Sylvia. For all Dennis knew, she had no intention of falling in love or getting married again. The love she'd felt for her husband might be so deep that she could never love another man.

*I need to quit thinking about this,* Dennis chided himself. *I'll just take things slow and easy with Sylvia and see how it all goes.*

When Dennis pulled his horse and buggy onto the Kings' driveway, Sylvia surprised him by asking if he'd like to come in for coffee and dessert. "I made some whoopie pies earlier today," she added.

"That's tempting," he said, "but I'm too full from supper to eat anything else. Besides, it's getting late, and we both need to get up early for church tomorrow morning."

She turned in her seat to face him. "Didn't you say during our meal that tomorrow is your off-Sunday?"

"That's right, but I thought I'd visit your church district's service tomorrow. Would that be all right with you?"

"Of course. You are welcome any time." Sylvia gave Dennis the address of the place where church would be held in the morning.

Dennis cleared his throat. "There's something else I'd like to ask."

"Oh?"

"I was wondering if you would be free tomorrow after church to go birding with me again."

"That sounds wunderbaar, but I had planned to take my kinner on a picnic."

Dennis reached over and lightly touched her arm. "Would you mind if I tag along? Maybe we'll see some interesting birds while we're there."

"Of course, you're more than welcome to join us. If you'd like, you can come over here right after our church's noon meal."

"Think I'll go home and change clothes first. Then I'll be over to join you."

"Sounds good."

Dennis stepped down from the buggy, secured his horse, and came around to help Sylvia exit.

"I had a nice time this evening, Dennis.

Danki for inviting me to join you for supper."

"You're welcome." He had to restrain himself to keep from leaning down and giving her a kiss on the cheek. *What am I thinking? That might scare her off.*

He said a pleasant, "Good night," and watched as Sylvia made her way to the house, using the flashlight she'd brought along to guide the way.

As Dennis directed his horse and buggy back down the driveway, he smiled. *Sylvia must like me a little bit, or she wouldn't have invited me to go on a picnic with her and the kids tomorrow.* He pressed his lips together. *Of course, I did actually invite myself. Even so, she was agreeable, so I'll take that as a positive sign.*

When Sylvia entered the house, the scent of freshly made buttered popcorn filled the air. This only added to her pleasant mood, and she couldn't wait to spend more time with Dennis. *I'm looking forward to going on a picnic and getting out with the children. They'll enjoy it, and creating fun memories is an added bonus.* She found Amy and Jared in the living room, working on a jigsaw puzzle. A bowl of popcorn sat between them.

Amy looked up and smiled. "Did you have

a nice evening?"

"Jah. We ate at the family restaurant in Bird-in-Hand."

Jared looked at Sylvia and wiggled his brows. "Good choice. I enjoy their buffet."

"I ate a lot of my favorite foods there but got a little carried away, I'm afraid. Dennis must have liked it too, because when I invited him in for coffee and a whoopie pie, he declined, saying he was still full from supper."

Jared looked over at Amy and his chin dropped down slightly. "There are whoopie pies in the house and you never offered me any? Is that how you're gonna treat me once we're married?"

Amy giggled and tossed a piece of popcorn at him. "Sylvia made those whoopies to take on the picnic she and her kinner are going on tomorrow afternoon. If I'd offered you one, you'd probably have eaten so many there wouldn't be enough left."

"Not true." He shook his head. "If you'd have told me why Sylvia baked them, I'd have only taken one."

Sylvia got a kick out of watching her sister and Jared's playful banter. That was how it used to be with her and Toby. He often teased her, and she enjoyed it, because his teasing was always done in a fun, loving way.

Dennis seemed more serious-minded than Toby, but Sylvia enjoyed being with him, nonetheless.

*I can't believe I'm comparing my deceased husband to someone brand-new in my life.* She scratched an itch near the side of her nose. *I never expected to have so much fun. Maybe a little too much. It doesn't make sense that I feel so comfortable with him. It seems like we've been friends for a good many years.*

"Mom put the kids to bed some time ago, and she went to her room soon after." Amy's comment broke into Sylvia's musings.

"Oh, good. Did they behave themselves for you and Mom this evening?"

Amy bobbed her head. "There were no problems, other than that Mom had to work with Allen to get him to go to bed. He wanted his mommy to say goodnight. Otherwise, thing went as usual around here."

"I'm glad." Sylvia leaned over the card table and put a piece of puzzle in place. "Say, I have an idea. Why don't you and Jared join us on the picnic tomorrow? I'm sure Dennis would enjoy some male company."

Amy's eyebrows squished together. "I thought it was just you and the kinner going on a picnic. When did Dennis come into the picture?"

"Tonight, when he brought me home, I mentioned the picnic, and he sort of invited himself to join us." Sylvia's cheeks warmed. "Of course, I could hardly say no."

Amy gave Sylvia a knowing look. "No, I'm sure."

"What do you mean?"

Amy waved her hand. "Oh, nothing."

"Well, would you two like to go with us or not? I'm sure it will be fun, and being outdoors someplace different would be a welcome change."

"I'm in," Jared spoke up. "I'd like to get to know this Dennis fellow."

"You'll like him. He's a very nice man."

Amy shot Sylvia another look, but she chose to ignore it. "When I see Mom and Henry in the morning, I'll invite them too. It should be a fun day for all of us."

"Speaking of Henry . . . You'll be happy to know that he came home from his evening with Seth about thirty minutes ago."

"I'm glad to hear it." Sylvia turned toward the door leading to the stairs. "It's getting late, so I'm turning in now. Good night, Amy. Good night, Jared."

"Gut nacht," they said in unison.

Sylvia smiled as she left the room. *I'm glad my sister is with the man she loves.*

# CHAPTER 29

The sound of gunfire reverberated in Dennis's head, and he woke up with a start. Several seconds passed before he realized where he was. Thankfully, the gun going off had only been a dream — one he'd had too often.

Dennis tried to calm down. He had hoped these recurring episodes would fade away over time, but they had not. Some day he would like to look back and say he hadn't had that nightmare for a long, long time. *Just when I thought I was beginning to heal, my feelings of anger toward Uncle Ben have surfaced all over again.*

Dennis rolled out of bed and looked at the clock on his nightstand. It was nine o'clock. "Oh great, I've overslept." He thumped his head and groaned. "Must have forgot to set my alarm." Dennis picked up the clock and checked the back side. *I definitely did not set this alarm!* He set it back on his nightstand and squinted at the light breaching into the room through the partially open window shade.

He ambled over to the window and looked out. The sky looked blue, with only a few scattered puffy clouds. It should be a good day for a picnic. Unfortunately, Dennis would not have time to get dressed, eat breakfast, and make it on time to the home Sylvia told him would be hosting church in her district this morning. Since the service would have already started, he'd feel like a fool showing up so late. *I'll make it up to Sylvia and try to attend her church on my next off-Sunday.*

Dennis ambled over to the closet to pick out something to wear. He was low on clean clothes, and that meant doing laundry soon. Dennis didn't like washing clothes, but it had to be done. With the nicer weather, at least things would dry quickly. When he lived at home, Mom had taken care of his clothes, even mending tears or pressing wrinkles out of stubborn pieces.

*I wonder how she's doing.* It had been a while since Dennis had called home to check on things. He was surprised she hadn't called him. No doubt Mom and the rest of his family would be in church today. Dennis's family had been diligent about at-

tending church services during his childhood.

Dennis found a shirt he liked and slipped
it on. It would be better to forget about
church and just show up at the Kings' place
around two o'clock. He would have some
explaining to do, but at least he'd get to
spend the afternoon with Sylvia. At least, he
hoped she'd still want to see him. She might
be angry because he missed church.

Sylvia sat stoically on her bench, looking
straight ahead. It was difficult to focus on
the message being preached when all she
could think about was why Dennis hadn't
shown up for church. Had he gotten sick
between last night and this morning? Or
perhaps he couldn't find the place; although
she thought she'd given good directions.

Sylvia shifted on the bench when Rachel
began to squirm on her lap. Her mind went
from one thing to the next, as she worried
about why he hadn't come today. *Maybe
Dennis changed his mind and decided not to
come. If so, he probably won't show up for
the picnic this afternoon either. That sure
would be a disappointment. I've been thinking
warmly about this since we made plans for
the day.*

Sylvia's hands began to sweat as another

thought popped into her mind. *What if Dennis was involved in an accident this morning?*

"I thought you said Dennis would be attending our church service this morning," Amy commented as she drove the horse and buggy on their way home that afternoon. Since the home their service had been in this morning was only a mile away, Henry had decided to walk. Otherwise, they would have taken two buggies, and either Mom or Henry would have been in the driver's seat.

"That was my understanding too, but I guess something must have happened to detain him." Sylvia's fingers tightened around her purse straps. "I hope nothing bad has happened."

Mom glanced over her shoulder, from her seat at the front of the buggy beside Amy. "Maybe he forgot or changed his mind about coming. Some folks can be unpredictable, you know."

Sylvia clamped her lips shut to keep from saying anything she might later regret. *Is Mom trying to put doubts in my mind about Dennis's dependability? If so, she needn't bother. I've been questioning it myself. I can't wait to find out the reason for him not coming to church. Hopefully, nothing serious occurred.*

*I'd feel bad if something had.*

"Sylvia, did you hear what I said?"

"Yes, Mom, and when we get home I'll check the phone shed for messages. Maybe he left me one."

As they approached their driveway, Rachel began to fuss. No doubt it was time for a nap.

When they pulled up to the hitching rail, Henry came out of the house. He'd left soon after their noon meal following church, so it was understandable that he'd arrived home before them.

"I'll take care of the horse and put the buggy over by the barn for now. When Dennis gets here, and we're ready to go out for a picnic, I'll bring Dusty back and get him hitched to the buggy." Henry looked over at Amy. "Would you mind drivin' Mom's buggy so I can ride with Dennis?"

"It's fine if you want to ride in Dennis's rig," she responded, "but I'll be riding in Jared's buggy. "Did you forget that he was invited to our picnic?"

Before Henry could respond, Sylvia spoke up. "We're not even sure if Dennis is coming. He wasn't in church, even though he said he would be."

"No need to worry." Henry held up his hand. "Since I didn't see Dennis in church,

I stopped at the phone shed on my way into the yard to see if he might have left us a message."

"And did he?" Mom asked.

"Jah. Said he forgot to set his alarm and woke up too late, but he'll be over in time for our picnic. Dennis also said he'd try to make it to our church service on his next off-Sunday."

Mom made a little grunting sound in her throat. "Waking up late on a Sunday morning doesn't sound like someone's who very dependable. I've always managed to get up in time to go to church."

Sylvia felt relieved, knowing Dennis was all right and still planned to join them, and by this time, she had the children out of the buggy. So rather than comment on her mother's judgmental statement, she headed straight for the house with her little ones. Rachel needed a diaper change, and both she and Allen were going down for a nap. Otherwise, they'd be cranky the rest of the day. Besides, Sylvia was eager to get inside before her mother said anything more about Dennis. Hopefully while they were on their picnic, Mom would get to know him better and realize what a nice man he was.

"Hmm . . . So far still no German shepherds

being offered in *The Budget* or local newspaper." Dennis tapped his fingers against the table where he sat drinking a second cup of coffee. "I suppose I'll have to go to the animal shelter soon and have a look-see."

He glanced at the clock on the kitchen wall. It was about time to leave. Dennis pushed back his chair and went into the bathroom to see if his hair had been combed neatly enough.

*I hope Sylvia forgives me for goofing up and sleeping in this morning.*

Dennis moved away from the mirror and headed out the back door. When he entered the barn, he was greeted by friendly stomping and nickering of the geldings. Midnight looked in his direction, and the closer Dennis got to his stall, the more pawing his horse did.

"Okay, buddy, simmer down. You and I are going for a ride to the Kings' place." He led Midnight out of the paddock and got the animal geared up and hooked to the buggy.

"Sure hope Sylvia got my message." Dennis spoke out loud. Although his horse couldn't understand what he was talking about, the gelding's ears perked up.

Dennis chuckled. "You think I'm talking

to you, don't you, boy?"

Midnight whinnied and flipped his tail.

"You're a schmaert one, huh?" Dennis climbed into the buggy, backed the horse up, and flicked the reins.

All the way to the Kings' house, his thoughts were on Sylvia. Would she be pleased to see him or upset because he hadn't shown up in church? He hoped it wouldn't be the latter. He couldn't help wanting to be with Sylvia. He'd gone out with other Amish women before, but no one had interested him until now. It frightened Dennis a bit, but not enough to stay away. His fear of commitment was beginning to wane.

As they traveled along, Dennis thought about his business and how he'd gained more clients. If he could keep things moving along at this rate, he should be able to support a wife and children.

*Would I make a good father to Sylvia's kinner?* He let go of the reins with one hand and pinched the bridge of his nose. *I shouldn't be thinking this way. We're still in the early phase of a relationship, and it's not in my nature to rush ahead.*

When Dennis started up the Kings' driveway, he spotted Henry in the yard, playing fetch with his dog. The boy threw the stick and raced over to Dennis's horse as soon as he pulled up to the hitching rail.

"I'll tie him up for you," Henry called.

Dennis nodded, and once Midnight was secure, he climbed down from the buggy.

"Glad you could make it." Henry spoke rapidly as he moved toward Dennis. "Sorry you didn't come to church, but we got your message."

"Good to hear." Dennis looked toward the house. "Is Sylvia inside?"

"Jah, and so are the others. I'll go let 'em know you're here. Then we can all head out for our picnic." Henry rushed inside.

Figuring it would be best not to barge into the house uninvited, Dennis took a seat on the porch swing.

Several minutes went by, and then Dennis caught sight of a male mockingbird sitting on top of a shrub in the yard. He recognized the bird's silvery gray head and back, with a light gray chest and belly. It didn't take long before it began to sing.

Caught up in the moment, Dennis's head jerked to one side when the screen door slammed. He turned and saw Sylvia standing in front of the door with a wicker basket in her hands. "I'm glad you could make it."

He gave a nod. "So am I. Sorry about missing church this morning. I'll have to try again in two weeks."

"That'd be nice."

He rose from the swing and approached her. "Want me to take that basket and put it in my buggy?"

"Yes, please." Sylvia handed it to him.

"So where's everyone else?"

"They're coming." She gave Dennis another heart-melting smile.

He drew in a quick breath. *Why am I so affected by this woman?* The fact that Sylvia had children didn't bother him in the least, which surprised him most of all.

As Sylvia sat on a blanket near the pond located a few miles from her mother's home, she breathed deeply of the wildflowers growing nearby. Lily pads floated on the surface of the water, and a pair of mallard ducks swam nearby. A bird flapped its wings overhead as it took flight, and Dennis leaned closer to Sylvia and pointed. "Did you see that Horned Lark?"

"I saw a tannish-brown bird but didn't know what it was called."

"Horned Larks are birds of open ground," Henry interjected. "They're common in rural areas like this and are usually seen in large flocks."

Dennis nodded. "I'm impressed with your

knowledge, young man."

Henry grinned and grabbed another chocolate whoopie pie from the dessert basket. Although her brother had eaten more than his share of ham-and-cheese sandwiches, not to mention several peanut butter cookies, apparently he had room for more.

Sylvia glanced at her mother, sitting on a separate blanket with the children. They'd spread both blankets side-by-side, so they could all visit while enjoying the picnic lunch Sylvia, Amy, and Mom had prepared.

Sylvia couldn't help but notice how quiet Mom was today. When she did say something, it was directed to Amy and Jared, who sat close to her.

Sylvia felt a little guilty that her mother was stuck caring for Allen and Rachel, but she'd volunteered to oversee them while eating, so she must not mind.

Once everyone had finished eating, and the food had been put away, Dennis suggested that he and Sylvia take a walk.

"Just the two of us?"

"Jah. If no one else minds."

Sylvia looked in Amy and Jared's direction. Jared shrugged, and Amy smiled and said, "Go ahead. I'll stay here with Mom to keep an eye on the kinner."

Mom sat quietly, holding Rachel in her

lap. Since she made no objection, Sylvia picked up her binoculars and stood. She looked over at Henry and noticed his wrinkled brows but didn't feel it was her place to invite him on the walk.

Dennis led the way down a path that followed the circumference of the pond. When her family was no longer visible, he stopped walking and placed his hand on her arm. "I . . . uh . . . don't quite know how to say this, Sylvia, but I really enjoy your company. Would it be okay if I stop by to visit you one evening this week?"

She moistened her lips with her tongue and swallowed hard. Was Dennis asking if he could court her? Did she want him to?

# CHAPTER 30

Sylvia needed to answer Dennis's question, but she could barely find her voice as she stared at the ducks in the pond. *I'd like to see more of Dennis, and it's wonderful to know he enjoys my company.* The fact that Dennis wanted to see her again must mean he was interested in her. And if Sylvia were being completely honest with herself, she was interested in him too. She'd never imagined having feelings for anyone but Toby, but Sylvia felt drawn to Dennis.

She lifted her head and turned to face him. "I'd be pleased if you came over to see me. It would make me happy to spend more time with you."

A wide smile formed on his face. "What evening would work best for you?"

"How about Wednesday, and why don't you plan on joining us for supper?"

"That'd be great, if it won't be any trouble."

Sylvia shook her head. "Not a bit. Is there anything special you'd like me to cook?"

"Nope. Whatever you fix is fine. I'm not a picky eater."

"Neither am I, but my Allen sure is. I have to coax him to try new things."

Dennis chuckled and then pointed to another pair of ducks. "Look over there. In case you didn't know, those are called blue-wing teals."

"No, I didn't know. I've seen ducks like that before but never knew their name." Sylvia moved closer to the pond, watching as the male and female, both smaller than the mallards they'd seen previously, dipped their beaks in the water to catch a few bugs.

"The ducks' name comes from the fact that they have a blue wing patch, but it's usually only seen when they're in flight." Dennis squatted down in the grassy area. "These are some of the smallest ducks in North America. They are also one of the longest-distance migrating ducks."

"The female looks pretty plain," Sylvia commented. "The large, white crescent-shaped mark at the base of the mallard's bill certainly sets him apart."

Dennis nodded. "It does, as well as his black tail with a small white patch."

Sylvia knelt beside him. "I still can't get

over how much you know about the birds in this state. You must retain everything you learn."

Dennis shrugged. "Maybe so, but I mostly remember things I care about." He looked at Sylvia intently.

Her heart beat a little faster than normal. She remembered how Toby used to look at her like that.

"Hey, you two — didn't you hear us calling?"

Sylvia looked over her shoulder and saw Jared heading their way.

Dennis took hold of Sylvia's hand and helped her stand. It was a good thing too, because her legs felt like they were made of rubber. She wasn't sure if she could take a step forward.

"What were you calling about?" Dennis asked.

"Sylvia's kinner are getting fussy, and it'll be getting dark soon. Your mamm thinks we should be heading for home."

Dennis looked up at the darkening sky. "She's right, and from the looks of things, we might be in for a storm. Sure don't want to be caught out here if it starts raining heavily."

"Me neither," Sylvia agreed as they turned and headed back to the place where they'd had their picnic meal.

Virginia washed the last of the lunch dishes by hand, since there weren't enough to fill the dishwasher. "I'll be glad to get this done so I can relax."

"I thought you were going over to the greenhouse to buy some plants or flowers today," Earl said when he came in from outside, wiping perspiration from his forehead.

"I was, and I'm still planning to go there, so don't worry." Virginia had hoped he wouldn't notice the empty flowerbed along the side of the house. "It's not like I can go there today, anyway," she added. "Since it's Sunday, their business is closed."

"Then lucky you, it seems." He chuckled.

She finished up her work at the sink and shut off the running water.

He took a glass from the cupboard and filled it with orange juice from the refrigerator. "After I drink this, I'm heading back outside to finish painting that trim I sanded yesterday."

"Okay." Virginia took a seat at the table. *I'm glad he quit bugging me about those flowers. But I still need to go over to the greenhouse and play nicey-nice, or we'll never get a wedding invitation.*

Amy looked over at Jared and smiled. She felt fortunate to have him in her life, and it was hard to believe in just a few months she would become his bride. She couldn't imagine her life without him.

As the swaying of Jared's buggy threatened to lull her to sleep, Amy's thoughts turned to other things.

*I wonder if Mom is right about Dennis. Could he be interested in Sylvia as more than a friend?*

She looked toward a large home coming up on the right. *I'd like to have a place like that after Jared and I are married. But whatever size our home turns out to be, I plan on entertaining our family and friends.*

Switching gears, Amy recapped what her mother had said earlier. Soon after Dennis and Sylvia walked away together, Mom had begun talking about him and not in a good way. She'd mentioned one more time, with a look of disapproval, that she thought Dennis had set his cap for Sylvia. Amy saw nothing wrong with this, as long as he and Sylvia didn't rush into anything. They needed time to get to know each other well, and it would be good if Sylvia met Dennis's parents and siblings. Mom thought it was strange that he hadn't told Sylvia much about his family — only that they lived in Dauphin County.

To give Dennis the benefit of the doubt, Amy figured he probably wanted to get to know Sylvia's family first. *If he approves of us, then he'll surely want my sister to meet and get to know his parents too.*

Jared reached over and took Amy's hand. "You're awfully quiet. Are you feeling *mied* and anxious to get home?"

"I am a little tired," she admitted, "but I've mostly been thinking."

He stroked her hand with his thumb. "About us?"

"Jah, mostly." Amy thought it best not to mention her sister and Dennis — not with Mom in the back seat with the children. Although Rachel and Allen had fallen asleep, their grandmother was no doubt listening to Amy and Jared's conversation. If Amy brought up the topic of Dennis, Mom would want to add her two cents.

Amy leaned back against the seat and closed her eyes. She tried to visualize what it would be like on the day of her and Jared's wedding. All of their family and friends would be present. She hoped the fall weather would cooperate for their special day and everything would go as planned. *Oh, what a joyous occasion it will be.*

The entire way home, all Belinda could think about was how improper if had been for Dennis to ask Sylvia to go for a walk with him alone. *They should have had some supervision. When Vernon and I were courting, we followed the rules. We didn't step out of line and do things that might cause our parents to worry or fret over our actions.*
Her fingernails cut into her skin as she drew them tightly into her palms. *Why didn't Dennis ask my son to walk with them? He knows how much Henry enjoys bird-watching.* The longer Belinda reflected on the way things had gone, the more frustrated she became.
*On top of my daughter agreeing to walk with Dennis alone, she hardly paid any attention to her children while we were eating lunch. The responsibility of looking after Rachel and Allen fell on me and Amy, and it wasn't fair.* Belinda shifted on her unyielding seat as she sat between her precious grandchildren. *These two deserve their mother's full attention, and Sylvia should be riding back here with them, instead of in Dennis's buggy.*
Belinda craned her neck to look between

Jared and Amy. She saw Dennis's horse and buggy moving along at a pretty good clip ahead of them.

*At least he invited Henry to ride in his rig.* Belinda leaned her head against the seat-back. *But then, what other choice did he have? There wasn't room in Jared's carriage for more people.*

Belinda hoped Dennis wouldn't come around too often. It wasn't good for Sylvia to be so distracted. She had two young children to raise, and that should come first.

Sylvia glanced over her shoulder, wondering why her brother was so quiet. He hadn't said a word since they'd begun their journey home. Henry sat slouched in the back seat with his arms folded and lips pressed together. Was he tired, or could he be upset about something?

*Maybe he felt left out because Dennis and I took a walk by ourselves,* Sylvia reasoned. *I probably should have invited him to go along.* Sylvia fiddled with the ties on her head covering. *But since it was Dennis's idea to go for the walk, and he only asked me, it wasn't my place to invite my brother. Besides, I enjoyed the time Dennis and I had alone. It gave us another chance to get to know each other better.*

Sylvia thought about how things could change in the years to come. Jared and Amy would be married this year. She and Dennis could even end up that way sometime in the future. Also, Mom might eventually find someone if she chose to. Of course, Henry would, in due time, find a special woman to court and sooner or later get married. Sylvia felt a little overwhelmed at the prospect of what could be, with the addition of new family members.

Marriage to Dennis was a silly notion, given the fact that they were so newly acquainted, but Sylvia found herself wondering if she might possibly have a future with him.

*Would Toby approve if it did happen?* she wondered. *And how would the rest of my family feel about it? Would Dennis be a good stepfather, and could my children accept him as such?*

It wasn't like her to think such thoughts about another man, much less the prospect of having a future with him. She felt relieved when Dennis struck up a conversation about birds that included both her and Henry.

She glanced at Dennis, then looked quickly away. *I'm glad he can't get into my head and know my thoughts. That would be most embarrassing.*

As they drew closer to home, Sylvia caught sight of Maude ambling along the shoulder of the road. Keeping her head down, the elderly woman never even glanced their way. Surely she had to hear the horses plodding along.

*I wish we knew more about that poor lady.* Sylvia repressed a sigh. *Surely she must have some family somewhere.*

"Who is that woman?" Dennis asked. "Is she one of your neighbors?"

"Her name is Maude, and she lives down the road from us in a rundown shanty."

"That's sad." He slowed his horse before the turn. "Well, we're here. Glad we made it back before it got dark or decided to rain."

Dennis guided Midnight up the driveway. "What's that on the greenhouse?" He pointed. "It wasn't there when we left for the picnic."

As they approached the building, on the way up to the house, Sylvia's thoughts became fuzzy, and her ears began to ring. Every visible window on the side of the building had been splattered with black paint.

*Oh my! Who could have done this, and why? Was it the same person who did all the other acts of vandalism?*

# CHAPTER 31

Sylvia stood with Dennis, Jared, and her family, staring at the black-painted windows. This was yet another unnecessary act for her and the rest of them to deal with. It seemed as though they were being targeted, and it was getting old. It bothered Sylvia that Mom had refused to notify the sheriff, but she understood why her mother didn't want Ezekiel to know.

*This kind of thing gets me upset and makes it hard to trust the Lord,* she thought. "Why did such a beautiful day have to be ruined like this?" Sylvia drew in a few raspy breaths as she looked at her mother.

Mom shook her head slowly. "This is our family's business — the way we make our living. I can't understand how or why anyone could be so mean."

"Unfortunately there are some not-so-nice people who like to do destructive things." Jared frowned. "I hope you're going to call the sheriff's office."

"No, we're not." Mom spoke in a low-pitched voice.

"Why not?" Dennis asked. "Don't you want the person who did this to be punished?"

"First of all, we don't know who did it." Mom looked at each of them with a serious expression. "We need to pray harder for God's protection and that the person who did this will fall under conviction."

"I bet it was Seth," Henry spoke up.

"Why would you think it was Seth?" Amy questioned. "He's supposed to be your friend. Right, Henry?"

"Jah, but Seth invited me to go someplace with him this afternoon, and I turned him down 'cause I was goin' on the picnic with all of you." Henry's eyes narrowed as he folded his arms across his chest. "And a lot of good that did me. Spent most of the day lookin' for birds by myself." He glanced briefly at Sylvia, then back at the painted windows.

Sylvia's chin dipped slightly. Although she had enjoyed her time alone with Dennis, it was rude of them not to include Henry — especially since he enjoyed birding so much. *I sure wasn't thinking, and my brother has good reason to be upset.*

Mom gestured to one of the windows. "I don't think Seth would do something like this just because you had other plans today."

"He might though." Henry frowned. "He was pretty miffed when I said I couldn't go with him."

"Where did he want you to go?" The question came from Jared.

Henry shrugged. "Don't know for sure. Just hang around with him and some of his friends, I guess."

"I'm afraid Seth's friends are not good company, Son." Mom put her hand on Henry's shoulder. "There's no telling where they would go or what they might do. You were better off with your family today."

"I suppose."

"If this is the sort of thing Seth and his friends deem as fun, then I'm relieved you were not hanging around them today." Mom's gaze remained fixed on Henry. "Have they done something like this before, or said anything to you about doing this sort of thing to anyone else?"

"No. I haven't heard anything." He shook his head forcefully. "I'm just suspecting them, is all, but I aim to ask Seth about it. If he and his friends had anything to do with painting the windows black, I'm gonna tell their parents." Henry's shoulders slumped.

"Just makes me sick to think that my friend might have been involved in this."

Sylvia figured Henry felt betrayed by her for ignoring him at the pond, and also by his friend who was possibly responsible for blackening their windows. *My poor brother.*

When Sylvia heard Rachel fussing from the buggy, she realized the children were probably both awake. Since Jared's horse was secured well to the rail, Sylvia had thought it best to let them sleep while she and the others went to take a closer look at the greenhouse windows.

"Rachel's awake, and Allen probably is too." She looked at Dennis, who stood close to her side. "I'd better get those two out and take them up to the house." Sylvia glanced at the ugly windows again and frowned. *I hope what Mom is doing by not involving the sheriff isn't a mistake. I wonder how Dad would have handled this and all the other vandalism that's taken place.*

"I'll go with you," Dennis was quick to say. "I'll carry one of your kinner, and you can carry the other."

"Danki." Sylvia followed Dennis to the buggy. She appreciated his thoughtfulness so much. Once again, she couldn't help thinking about Toby and how Dennis reminded her of him in many ways.

"Let's take a walk around the rest of the greenhouse," Jared suggested, "Maybe not all the windows were painted."

"Good idea." Belinda led the way. To her relief, only the one side of the greenhouse windows had been painted black. All the others looked clear.

"Whew! That's a blessing." She reached out to Amy and clasped her arm. "This means we won't have quite so much work to do in the morning."

"You won't have to do it alone either," Jared said. "I'll be over bright and early to begin scraping."

"It's very much appreciated. Hopefully we can get the job done before any customers show up." Belinda's brows furrowed. "The last thing we need is for people to spread the word about the vandalism that's gone on here from time to time. If too many people know, Ezekiel's bound to find out. He still has some friends in this area, you know."

"Don't you think he has the right to know?" Henry grunted and folded his arms.

This was not the first time one of Belinda's children had asked this question.

She shook her head forcefully. "We've had this discussion before, Son, and my answer is always the same. If your brother knew what was happening here, he'd pack up and move back to Strasburg, no matter how much he'd be giving up by leaving his home there."

"I realize that, Mom."

Amy released a heavy sigh. "I can't believe anyone would do something like this in broad daylight."

"Maybe we should check with your closest neighbor and ask if they saw anything going on here while we were gone," Jared suggested. "Amy and I can go over there right now."

"That's a good idea," Henry said. "While you're doin' that, I'm gonna go check in the barn and the rest of our place to make sure nothing else is wrong."

*I hope nothing else is amiss around here. We'll have our hands full enough trying to remove all that black paint.* Belinda closed her eyes. *Please keep us from harm, Lord, and also, I pray that this would stop and the person responsible for the vandalism would fall under conviction.*

Amy remained close to Jared as they stood on her neighbor's front porch, waiting for someone to answer the door. She was glad he'd come with her, because something about Virginia made her feel uncomfortable. Although the woman had never said anything unkind to Amy, she always seemed a bit curt as if she couldn't wait to get away from her. Amy had a feeling the neighbor lady didn't much care for her and probably not the rest of the family either.

She held her breath a few seconds and released it slowly. *Maybe this is a mistake, coming over here. Virginia may not want to talk to us.*

After Jared's second knock, the front door opened, and Earl greeted them with a smile. "Well hello there, Jared. It's nice to see you." He glanced at Amy. "What brings you two by here this evening?"

Amy spoke first and quickly explained about the painted windows.

"We were wondering if you or your wife saw anybody hanging around the greenhouse this afternoon," Jared put in.

Earl shook his head. "I saw no one, although Virginia may have." He turned and called his wife's name.

A few seconds later, Virginia showed up. Her short red hair was in disarray — as though she'd just gotten out of bed. "What's up?"

"These people want to know if either of us saw anyone hanging around their green-house today."

Virginia pursed her lips. "From our house we can only see one side of the building."

"Did you see anyone in our yard at all?" Amy questioned.

"Nope. I've seen nothing out of the ordinary while we've been home. Course we weren't here all day. Earl and I went out for lunch this afternoon. When we got home, we took a nap — me in the bedroom and him in his easy chair while watching TV." Virginia picked at her thumbnail. "We were up late the night before, and so I ended up sleeping nearly two hours during my nap." She hesitated a moment. "I wouldn't be one bit surprised if that scruffy old woman — oh yeah, Maude — may have been hanging around your place. As I mentioned previously, I've seen her there before."

"Yes, I remember you saying that."

"Maude seems suspicious to me — the way she wanders up and down the road, like she's lookin' for something — or maybe ready to snatch something that doesn't belong to her." Virginia's bland expression changed to one of sympathy, and she spoke in a soothing tone. "Sure wish I could be of more help to you, and I hope you find out who's been messing around your place."

Amy gave a brief nod. "Thanks for your time." She and Jared said goodbye and stepped off the porch.

Amy walked along, holding tightly to Jared's hand. "Virginia seemed like a different person to me, especially toward the last of our conversation."

"What do you mean?" Jared asked.

"Like I mentioned before, she's usually not very talkative or friendly."

"People can change, right?"

"I hope so."

After they crossed the street, Jared stopped walking and looked directly at Amy. "Someone needs to convince your mamm to call the sheriff."

"That's a good thought, and I totally agree, but when my mother sets her mind on something, no one but my daed has ever been able to change it."

"Guess I'll have to start coming by here more often to check on things." Jared squeezed her fingers as they headed up the driveway. "It'll give me another good reason to see you."

Amy smiled. "How *glicklich* I am to have found a man like you."

"And I am lucky to have you, *mei lieb.*"

A ripple of joy shot through Amy's soul

whenever Jared referred to her as his love.

Virginia ambled into the living room and flopped onto the couch. "I'm having a tough time, Earl."

He looked at her with a curious expression. "What do you mean?"

"I need to speak kindly to those people, because if I'm nicer, they'll be more apt to invite us to their wedding. On the other hand, I wish they'd stop coming over here and bothering me. I mean, why would they think we knew anything about the vandalism?"

Earl looked at Virginia as if she'd lost her mind. "Because we live across the street."

A warm flush crept across Virginia's face. "Please don't look at me like that, Earl."

He took a seat in the recliner and picked up the remote. "Now can we stop talking? I'd like to watch one of my favorite TV shows."

"Sure, whatever!" Virginia got up and limped out of the room. She went out the back door and walked around the house, trying to imagine how it would look with more flowers. Even some hanging baskets on the porch would look nice.

She came toward the front of the house and shuffled across the driveway. Looking toward the greenhouse, she could see only one side of the building. So at least what she'd told Amy and Jared was the truth.

Virginia heard the blaring TV through the open living room window and cringed. "I'm sure Earl is napping in his recliner again, and he isn't even watching whatever program he has on."

As raindrops began to fall, she reached down and rubbed her leg, which hadn't hurt much earlier in the day. *I wish Stella was still here. At least then I'd have someone to talk to. Doesn't Earl even care how much I hate living here?*

# CHAPTER 32

Early the following morning, before breakfast had even been started, a knock sounded
on the back door. Sylvia hurried to see who
it was. When she opened the door, she was
surprised to see Dennis on the porch holding a scraper.

"I came to help scrape paint off the
windows. Has anyone started on it yet?" he
asked.

She shook her head. "We thought it would
be best to eat breakfast first, which I'm
about to start. Would you like to join us?"

"No, that's okay. I had a cup of coffee and
a doughnut before I left the house, so I'll
head on out to the greenhouse and get busy.
Once all the windows are cleaned off, I'll
need to get going. I got a call this morning
from a man who needs his horse trained to
pull a buggy, and he'll be bringing the horse
later this morning." Dennis gave Sylvia a
dimpled smile. "Am I still invited for sup-

per on Wednesday?"

"Of course. Are you sure there isn't something special you'd like me to fix?"

He shook his head. "Whatever you decide to cook is fine, and I look forward to seeing you." Dennis tipped his straw hat and stepped off the porch. "See you soon, Sylvia."

She watched as he sprinted across the yard and disappeared around the corner of the house. *What a thoughtful man.*

When Sylvia returned to the kitchen, Mom, Amy, and Henry were there.

"Who was at the door?" Mom asked. "I heard someone knocking as I came down the hall."

"It was Dennis. He came to help scrape paint off the windows, and he's headed out to the greenhouse now."

"That's so kind of him." Amy looked at their mother. "Don't you think so?"

Mom moved her head slowly up and down and turned to look at Sylvia. "Did you tell him we'd planned to eat breakfast before starting on the windows?"

"I did, and I even invited him to join us, but he said he wanted to get started on them now. He has a horse to train today, so he'll have to leave here as soon as the windows are done," Sylvia replied.

"We could have gotten by without him." Mom grabbed a bowl of boiled eggs from the refrigerator and placed them on the table. "After all, Jared said he'd help with it, plus Amy, Henry, and I will be scraping. I'm sure we can manage to get the job done before any customers show up."

Sylvia said nothing as she set the table. Mom obviously didn't feel Dennis's help was needed, but it made no sense. The more hands working, the sooner they'd get the job done. Her fingers clenched around the glass she held in her hand. *Why is my mother being like this toward Dennis? He's trying to fit in and is acting out of kindness toward our family. What could be wrong with that?*

Sylvia wished she could help too, but the children would be getting up soon, and she'd have to fix their breakfast. Besides, she couldn't leave Allen and Rachel alone in the house or let them run around the yard while she was busy scraping windows.

Another knock sounded on the door, and this time, Amy went to answer it. She returned with Jared at her side.

"Guder mariye, Jared." Mom smiled when he entered the kitchen.

"Good morning, all."

*If Mom can be so nice to Jared, why not be cordial to Dennis? Shouldn't they both be*

388

*treated kindly and with respect?* Sylvia greeted him, and Henry gave a nod in his direction.

"We're about to eat breakfast." Amy moved closer to Jared. "Would you like to join us?"

He shook his head. "I came here to work, not eat. Besides, I already had some breakfast."

"Dennis is here too," Sylvia spoke up. "He's out at the greenhouse, scraping windows."

"Is that so? Guess I'd better join him." Jared gave Amy a quick hug and headed out the door.

"How ya doin?" Dennis asked when Jared showed up.

"I'm fine. How about you?"

"Can't complain." Dennis gestured to the scraper Jared held. "Looks like you also came early to help clear off these windows."

"Jah. Amy and her family are getting ready to eat breakfast, but with the exception of Sylvia, they'll be out to help soon, I expect."

"No problem. We might have the project done by the time they show up."

They worked quietly for a while, and then Dennis pointed at the window he'd been working on and posed a question. "Has this kind of thing happened many times before?"

"More than it should have, unfortunately." Jared's forehead creased. "I think someone wants Belinda to shut down the greenhouse."

"How come?"

Jared shrugged. "Don't know. Maybe to be spiteful, or it could be someone who's just plain mean."

"Any ideas who may have done it?"

"Not really. But I have a hunch that it might be one of the owners of the new greenhouse on the other side of town."

Dennis stopped scraping and tipped his head. "You're kidding? Don't they believe in fair competition?"

"Maybe not. According to what Amy told me, the man who owns the other greenhouse came by here to check things out soon after his place opened for business." Jared pulled his scraper down the window in front of him. "The Kings' greenhouse has been around a good many years, and they have lots of steady customers. Also, with it being Amish-run, Amy has mentioned that the tourists seem to enjoy coming by and asking all sorts of curious questions."

Dennis pushed the brim of his hat upward. "May I ask what?"

"Oh things like, 'Why aren't you open on Sundays?' 'How come you use a horse and buggy instead of a car?' Sometimes they sneak pictures here." Jared's eyebrows rose.

Dennis shook his head "I know what that's like. I've had a few cameras pointed at me too."

"I wouldn't be surprised." As Jared scraped, the paint curled against his tool. "Anyways, the owners of the other greenhouse don't have that advantage. Even though their place is bigger and they sell a lot more things, they may not have gained a steady flow of customers yet."

"Hmm . . ." Dennis drew in a deep breath and released it slowly. "If it was the other greenhouse owner who did this, then he needs to be stopped. I think Belinda ought to notify the sheriff. Do you agree?"

"It doesn't matter what I think," Jared answered. "I'm not a member of this family yet."

"But you will be soon, right?"

"Jah, Amy and I will be getting married in early October." Jared glanced toward the house. "Here comes Belinda, Amy, and Henry, so we'd better drop this subject. Sure don't want to say anything that'll put me on the bad side of my future mother-in-law."

■ ■ ■ ■

Belinda was surprised to see how much Jared and Dennis had already accomplished. Only a few windows were left to scrape.

"If you ladies have something else you need to do, Dennis and I can finish the rest of the windows," Jared said.

"Actually, I do have a couple of things I need to do in the greenhouse before opening it to the public this morning." Belinda smiled. "So danki, Jared."

"No problem at all." He grinned at Amy. "Do you want to stay and help, or do you also have something to do in the greenhouse?"

"Nothing that can't wait." She looked at Belinda. "Right, Mom?"

"Right. You can stay out here and enjoy yourself, Daughter. You too, Son," Belinda added, pointing at Henry.

He rolled his eyes. "Okay, Mom. There's nothin' I'd rather do than scrape off the black paint."

She gave him a gentle poke before heading to the front door of the building.

Once inside, Belinda set to work watering all the plants, while the noise of windows being scraped by metal tools sounded in the

392

background. *I must say, more hands do make less work. At this rate, that job will be done in short order. My Vernon would be well pleased with the help we've received.*

By the time Belinda finished watering, Amy came inside. "The windows are all clean, and Jared and Dennis are getting ready to head out," she announced.

"What about Henry? What's he up to right now?"

"Said he had something to do in the barn."

Belinda's brows furrowed. "I thought he did all his chores before we had breakfast."

"Maybe he forgot something and decided to take care of it now."

"Or he could be in the yard looking at birds." Belinda shook her head. "I don't mind that he and Sylvia have a new hobby, but he sometimes gets so caught up in watching for birds that he forgets about the things I've asked him to do."

Amy laughed. "Mom, Henry did that even before he got into birding."

"True."

Belinda slipped behind the front counter just in time to greet their first customer of the day.

"Guder mariye, Belinda." Herschel Fisher

reached across the counter and shook her hand.

Belinda smiled. "Good morning, Herschel. What can we do for you today?"

"I came to buy a nice plant for my mamm. She's been down with a bad cold for the last week, and I thought it might cheer her up."

"Sorry to hear she's not feeling well." Belinda made a sweeping gesture. "Why don't you have a look around? I'm sure you can find something to your liking down one of the aisles."

"Okay, I'll take a look, but first, I was wondering . . ."

Another customer came in, and it was Jared's mother, Ava. She smiled and came over to the counter. "I saw my son leaving here as I was coming in on my scooter. He told me last evening that he'd be at your place first thing in the morning."

"Jah, we appreciated Jared's help."

"Dennis was here helping too," Amy hollered.

Ava looked at Herschel and smiled, and then she patted Belinda's hand. "Just think, it won't be long until the wedding."

"I'm looking forward to it." Belinda pushed her reading glasses in place. "We still have lots of planning and work ahead of us though."

Ava nodded. "We'll help in any way we can."

Herschel leaned on the counter. "Before I go searching for a plant to give my mamm that will brighten her day . . ."

"Is she under the weather?" Ava questioned.

"Jah, but she's some better this morning." He looked back at Belinda. "I wondered if you know of anyone in the area who might want to rent my house."

"Are you leaving Gordonville?"

"Oh no. I have no plans of moving. I meant the little house I own here in Strasburg. It's the one Jesse Smucker used to rent from me before he married Lenore."

Amy left her job of sweeping the floor and stepped up to him. "Jared and I might be interested in renting the house. We'll be getting married in October, and we haven't found a place to live yet. We've been looking, but most of the homes come with a lot of property. With his roofing business, Jared doesn't have time to keep up a big place."

"Sounds like my rental might be just right for you then." There seemed to be a gleam in Herschel's eyes as he looked at Amy. "Can we set up a time for me to show it to you and your future husband?"

"That would be great. If you'll give me your phone number, I'll ask Jared to call and set up an appointment." Amy gave Herschel a wide grin. "I'm looking forward to seeing it. Can you tell me how much the rent will be?"

"We can wait and talk about that after you've toured the house. If you don't like it, that's okay too. But if it pleases you, then maybe Jared could move in right away. The previous renter moved out two weeks ago, and I'd prefer not to leave it vacant much longer." Herschel reached into his pocket and handed her a small card. "This has my bulk food store's number on it. It's probably the best number to reach me, because I check messages in the shed outside the store regularly."

Ava grinned. "Sounds like it might be something my son would be interested in."

"Danki, Herschel." Amy handed Belinda the card. "Would you put this on the shelf under the counter for me? I'll get it when I go up to the house at the end of the day."

Belinda took the card, and Amy went back to sweeping the floor. Ava went off to look at the selection of plants.

Not long after, Belinda noticed their neighbor Virginia come in.

"Well, I'd better get busy and choose a

plant for my mamm," Herschel announced before hurrying down aisle 1.

Belinda stepped out from behind the counter and walked over to Virginia. "Hello. It's good to see you again. Is there something I can help you with today?"

Virginia nodded. "I popped in to see what kinds of flowers you have that I can plant along the side of my house."

"Most of the plants are in the first three aisles. Just take your time looking, and if you have any questions, I shouldn't be too hard to find. Amy is here too."

"All righty, then. Oh, by the way — did you find out who was on your property yesterday?"

Belinda shook her head.

"That's too bad. Well, hopefully you'll find out soon." Virginia lowered her voice. "I'm thinking that Maude lady might be responsible for what went on here."

"Oh?"

"Yeah, she seems suspicious enough to me. Maude wanders up and down the road quite often. In fact, I've been keeping an eye on her." Virginia caught her breath. "I bet she's the one who took your original sign that went missing."

Feeling the need for a change of subject, Belinda rested one hand on her hip and said, "One of these days, when things slow down a bit here, we'll have you and your husband over for a meal."

"That'd be real nice, Mrs. King." Virginia turned and headed toward the first row of flowering plants.

Belinda's thoughts turned to the offer Herschel had made to Amy, and her heart clenched. Although she was happy her daughter had found a wonderful man to marry, the thought of Amy moving out of the home she'd grown up in was difficult to accept. Ezekiel had already left the nest, and soon Amy would be gone too. *At least she won't be living in another state.* Belinda consoled herself with that thought. *But what will happen when she and Jared have a family of their own? She won't be able to help in the greenhouse anymore. And what about Sylvia? What if she ends up marrying Dennis, or some other Amish man?* Belinda's eyes teared up. *Someday Henry will be grown and ready to start a new life too. What then? Will I have to give up the greenhouse and live on this property all by myself?*

# CHAPTER 33

Dennis had spent the better part of the morning working with an uncooperative horse, and he was exhausted. He'd brushed the animal down in its stall and then gotten things ready for the next client's horse.

Tired and frustrated, Dennis came into the house to take a lunch break before going back out to continue with his schedule. He wouldn't let his fatigue, however, interfere with his plans to have supper at the Kings' house this evening. Dennis found himself thinking about Sylvia more and more, and he looked forward to spending time with her this evening. Hopefully he'd have an opportunity to be alone with her, even if only for a short time.

Dennis took his boots off by the back door and headed for the kitchen. He was in need of something cold to drink to help his parched throat. After filling a glass with water from the sink, he opened the refrigerator, took out two hard-boiled eggs and a slice of ham, then sat down at the table. Dennis required the extra protein to ramp up his energy. He would work until four, and then clean up and get ready to head to the Kings' place by five. Dennis had already laid out his clean clothes to wear after he showered and shaved at the end of his workday. He'd gone shopping the other day and purchased a couple of new shirts, including two white ones he would wear for church services.

While Dennis ate with one hand, he reached for his cell phone with the other. *Think I'll check the birding hotline. Maybe there'll be some interesting bird sighting I can tell Sylvia and Henry about this evening.*

Ever since she'd finished breakfast, Sylvia had been scurrying around the house, making sure everything was clean and orderly for Dennis's visit this evening. The kids' toys were still out in the living room, but she could wait to pick those up until closer to Dennis's arrival. Sylvia had made a new dress, which she would wear this evening. The color was a dark purple — one of her favorite shades.

"Is lunch ready?" Henry asked, bursting into the kitchen where Sylvia stood at the counter slicing a loaf of bread.

"It will be soon, but if you can't wait, grab a knife and make your own sandwich."

"No, I can wait. We're not that busy in the greenhouse right now, so I'm in no hurry to get back." Henry flopped into a chair at the table. "I'd rather be in the barn, looking out the hayloft window and watching for birds."

"You'll have time for that later, Henry." Sylvia frowned. "Don't you think you ought to wash your *hend* while you're waiting?"

He held up his hands. "Already done. I washed 'em at the sink in the greenhouse."

"Okay." Sylvia went to the refrigerator and took out the chicken-salad spread she'd mixed up earlier.

She thought of Dennis, and wondered what he was having for lunch. Being a bachelor, there was no telling what he'd make — probably something quick and easy to fix.

Sylvia blinked. *Why am I always thinking of him? Dennis is on my mind so much of the time.*

"Will Mom and Amy be coming up to the house to eat, or do they want you to take their lunch out to them?" she asked, needing to focus on something else.

"I'll take Mom's lunch out to her after I

401

eat, but Amy won't be here for the noon meal."

Sylvia turned to face him. "How come?"

"Jared came by a while ago to pick her up. They're meeting Herschel Fisher at the house he owns not far from here."

"Oh, that's right. I forgot about that. I didn't see his buggy pull in, but I've been busy with the kinner and getting some chores done." Sylvia pulled the cutting board with the sliced bread closer and put the sandwiches together. "I hope they like the place and it works out for them to rent it."

"Me too. If Amy lives close after they're married, she'll be able to keep workin' at the greenhouse and not so much will fall on me." Henry scrunched his face. "But I don't know what'll happen once Amy and Jared start havin' *bopplin*. If you would help out things might go better."

Her spine stiffened. "You know I'm needed here to take care of my kinner as well as cook, clean, and keep up with the laundry."

"You could hire someone to watch Rachel and Allen. I think you just don't wanna work in the greenhouse."

"That's right, I don't, but it's none of your concern." Sylvia hurried to finish Henry's sandwich and handed it to him. "You can eat it in here if you want, but let's not talk about me working in the greenhouse anymore."

Henry wrapped his sandwich in a napkin, stood up, and tromped across the room toward the back door. "I'll tell Mom she can come eat her lunch now."

"I thought you were going to take it out to her." She handed him a lunch basket with food for Mom.

Henry's face flushed. "Oh, yeah, that's right. See you later."

When her brother left, Sylvia blew out an exasperated breath. She felt guilty enough for not helping in the greenhouse without having a reminder from her brother of the fact. *I wish Mom could afford to hire another pair of hands to work in there. Especially with my sister soon to be married and eventually having children of her own. The pressure of me being next in line to work in the greenhouse is stifling.* Sylvia tapped her foot. *And then there would be the expense of getting someone to watch Rachel and Allen. If that should be expected of me, then why not Amy? When the time comes, she could get a sitter for her kinner too.*

"My children come first," she mumbled. "They're better off having me take care of them than they would be with a sitter."

Another thought popped in Sylvia's head. *If it doesn't work out for me or Amy to work in the greenhouse after she's married, then what will Mom do?*

Amy's skin prickled with excitement as Jared pulled his horse and buggy onto the driveway at the address Herschel had given them. From the outside, the small white house looked cozy and inviting. She could hardly wait to see the inside. This just made it more real to her. Here they were, about to look at a place in hopes of setting up their new lives together as the future Mr. and Mrs. Jared Riehl.

Herschel's horse had been secured at the hitching rail, and Jared pulled his horse alongside it and got out, while Amy held onto the reins. Once his horse was secured, she climbed down from the buggy, and the two of them headed for the house.

They'd no more than stepped onto the porch when Herschel came out the front door and greeted them. "Did ya have any trouble finding the place?"

Jared shook his head. "Not a bit. I've been by this house many times. Just never been invited to see the inside till now." He glanced at Amy and smiled. "We're excited to see it."

Herschel opened the door wide. "Come on in. As you can see, the front door leads right into the living room."

When they stepped inside, Amy tried to take it all in at once. A comfy-looking recliner sat near an upholstered sofa. Both appeared to be in fairly good condition. Built-in bookshelves graced either side of the fireplace, and two end tables were positioned on both sides of the couch, as well as another one alongside the recliner. A battery-operated lamp sat on each of them.

"Nothing fancy, but it should serve your needs," Herschel said. "Of course, you'd be free to buy furniture of your own if you don't care for what's here."

"It's adequate for me." Amy looked at Jared and was pleased when he nodded.

"Should we move on to the bedrooms and bathroom?" Herschel asked.

Amy and Jared both nodded and followed Herschel through a narrow hallway, where the two bedrooms and bathroom were located.

Each of the rooms was furnished with a wooden-framed bed, dresser to match, and a closet with a door. In one of the rooms there was also a small desk. No doubt that would be the room Amy and Jared would claim for themselves.

The bathroom had a tub-shower combination, as well as a toilet and sink, with a mirror above the vanity.

"Are you ready to see the kitchen?" Herschel asked.

"Jah." Amy was the first to respond, and Jared nodded.

Back down the hall they went, and they soon entered a spacious kitchen. It was nearly the size of the two bedrooms put together. The layout reminded Amy of Sylvia's kitchen. The cupboards were different and the color was lighter than her sister's place, but it gave off a comfortable feeling that she liked.

Amy smiled. She enjoyed cooking, and this kitchen with a propane-operated stove and refrigerator would be perfect for fixing meals. The table was quite large, so even though the house had no dining room, they could easily eat in the kitchen and serve several guests at one time.

Amy leaned close to Jared and whispered, "I like the house. Do you?"

He nodded. "We'd be pleased to rent this from you, Herschel, and I'd like to move in as soon as possible."

"Don't you want to know the price I'm asking for the rent?"

"You told me when we talked on the phone to set up this meeting."

Herschel's cheeks flushed pink above his beard. "So I did." He moved toward the back door. "Maybe you should take a look at the yard and also the washhouse for doing laundry. There's an older model ringer-washer in there, but it could be replaced with a newer one if you choose."

"We'll take a look, but I don't think we're going to change our mind about renting the place." Jared grinned at Amy. "Right?"

She bobbed her head.

As they stepped into the backyard, Amy spotted a wooden table with benches on either side, situated near a fire-pit. "Oh, this would be perfect to use year-round. What a nice place for entertaining our friends and family."

"I agree." Jared clasped her hand and gave her fingers a tender squeeze.

Amy's words felt rushed as she told Herschel how much she appreciated the chance to rent this cozy home. "We'll have you over for supper one night after Jared gets settled in."

He smiled but kept his gaze toward the ground. "That'd be real nice."

Amy wandered across the yard to a small garden patch. *Maybe I'll invite Mom to join us when we plan an evening to have Herschel for supper. He may be a little shy, but he's such a nice man. I believe they might enjoy each other's company. Of course, I won't say anything to Mom about it right now. It could even turn out to be a surprise.*

After returning from a relaxing evening at the Kings' house, Dennis was ready to call it a night. The meal had been good and he'd been able to spend a few minutes alone with Sylvia, so the evening couldn't have gone much better. He'd even enjoyed sitting on the floor, playing with Allen and Rachel for a while before the meal. Except for Belinda's cool tone whenever she spoke to him, Dennis had almost felt like part of the family.

*I don't think she cares much for me,* he thought as sat on a chair in the kitchen and removed his black dress shoes. *What I can't figure out is why. Could she be worried that I might ask for her daughter's hand in marriage some day?* He rubbed his chin. *Is that a possibility?*

Dennis continued to contemplate things until his cell phone rang. He recognized the number and figured he may as well answer it or she'd keep calling until he finally responded.

Dennis swiped his thumb across his phone. "Hi Mom, how are you?"

"More to the point, how are you and why haven't you answered any of my calls lately? Neither I nor any of your siblings have heard from you for several weeks." Her shrill voice made Dennis's pulse quicken. Mom hadn't been like this before Dad died. At least not with Dennis. Maybe the fact that he was the youngest of five children made her more possessive of him.

"Sorry for not responding to your messages," he said, struggling to keep his voice calm. "I've been super busy with my new business and some other things."

"Too busy to call your mamm?"

"I said I was sorry." His excuse for not returning her calls was weak, but listening to her carry on about him moving away from her and the rest of the family was hard to take. Especially when she had no understanding of his reasons for leaving Dauphin County.

Dennis shifted on his chair. *Don't I have the right to make a new start?*

"You broke Sarah Ann's heart when you moved, you know. She'll probably never recover from the hurt."

Mom's ridiculous statement caused the muscles in Dennis's face to tighten. "There

409

is no reason Sarah Ann's heart would be broken. She and I weren't even courting."

"But you were friends since childhood, and I'm sure she assumed —"

"Mom, is that why you called — to talk about a relationship that never developed into anything romantic?"

"Well, uh . . . no . . ." There was a pause. "Your brother has some business in Lancaster next week, and I'm planning to come with him. Does the house you're renting have room for the two of us to stay with you a few nights?"

*I know where this is leading, and boy, it doesn't leave me with a lot of time to get things ready for company.* He bit down on his bottom lip. *I'll need to get the beds ready and stock the cupboards and refrigerator with enough food.*

Dennis's face warmed, and he fanned himself with the back of his free hand. "Umm . . . yes, there are enough bedrooms, but —"

"Good. Gerald and I will see you next Monday, sometime before noon."

"Mom, I don't think —"

She said goodbye and hung up before Dennis could finish his sentence.

Dennis felt like his chest had caved in. The last thing he needed was company to interrupt his work schedule — not to mention all the unwanted advice he'd no doubt get from his mother.

*But I'll get through it,* he told himself. *After all, it'll only be for a few days.*

# CHAPTER 34

On Monday, when Dennis headed for the house to wash up and fix lunch, a black van pulled into the yard. It caught him off guard at first. Then he realized the vehicle belonged to his brother. Gerald had never joined their Amish church and attended a Mennonite church, so he'd owned a vehicle since he'd turned eighteen. Both of their parents had made an issue of it, but their eldest son had a mind of his own.

*Just like me,* Dennis thought as he moved toward the vehicle. *Only I chose to remain Amish and join the church.*

A few seconds later, Dennis's mother and his tall, gangly brother got out.

"It's so good to see you," Mom shouted as she hurried toward Dennis. The short, slender woman could certainly move fast for a woman in her early sixties.

Dennis met his mother halfway and gave her a hug. "It's good to see you too, Mom."

Tears welled in her blue eyes and she sniffed. "It's been far too long."

Dennis didn't bother to remind her that he hadn't been in Strasburg all that long. "Why don't you go on up to the porch and wait for me while I help Gerald with the luggage?"

"Okay." She reached in her handbag and pulled out a tissue, dabbing at her eyes, before heading toward the house.

Dennis greeted his brother with a hearty handshake. "It's good to see you."

Gerald grinned and gave his neatly trimmed beard a tug. "Same here."

"So what kind of business do you have here in Strasburg?" Dennis asked.

"It's not in Strasburg. It's in Lancaster, but I figured if I was gonna come this close to you I oughta bring Mom along." Gerald placed his hand on Dennis's shoulder. "She really misses you, and so do the rest of us, for that matter."

"I miss my family too, but I needed to start over — someplace where there was a lot of horses and people who needed them to be trained." *And where there weren't so many reminders of Dad.*

"I understand, but Mom thinks you left because of Dad's untimely death. She believes you might blame yourself, some-how."

Dennis's spine stiffened. "Why would I be to blame for him getting shot? That was Uncle Ben's fault, not mine."

"But you were out hunting with him that day. Have you ever wondered if you'd been paying close attention to what was happen-ing, things might have gone differently?"

"You're right, I was there, and of course, I've wondered how I might have made things turn out different somehow. But I had no idea when Dad invited me to go hunting with him and Uncle Ben that an accident would occur. If I'd known, I would have tried to prevent it from happening somehow, or at least talked Dad out of go-ing into the woods that day."

Gerald shook his head. "No one could stop our daed from doing anything he set his mind to. Dad liked to hunt, and he'd go out as often as he could to find his next trophy. Some folks in our community said he was the most adventuresome person they knew."

Dennis kicked at the gravel beneath his boots. "You're right about that. Dad loved to get out into nature, even when he wasn't hunting for deer. He enjoyed showing people his collection of antlers too. I used to like listening to his stories when I was a boy."

"Same here."

Dennis reached into the van and grabbed a small suitcase, along with a tote bag, which he recognized as his mother's. Glancing back at his brother, he asked, "So what kind of business dealings will you be having in Lancaster?"

Gerald took out his suitcase and they began walking toward the house, where their mother still waited on the porch. "I'll be talking with a Realtor about the possibility of buying a couple of vacation homes that have come on the market near Bird-in-Hand."

Dennis stopped walking and turned to face his brother. "Why would you want to buy vacation homes? If you, or any of the family, wants to vacation in Lancaster County, you'd be welcome to stay here."

"No, the homes aren't for us. It would be an investment, and I would give part of the proceeds to Mom, so she never has a need."

"What needs would she have that aren't already being met?" Dennis asked. "She's still living with Dorcas and her family, right?"

Gerald bobbed his head. "But it would be nice for our mother to have some money of

415

her own and not have to rely on others when she wants to buy something. Don't you agree?"

"Jah, I suppose." Dennis wasn't sure their mother would accept such a gift from Gerald, but what his brother chose to do was none of his business.

*Clymer*

"I talked to my sister today," Ezekiel said as he took a seat at the kitchen table to eat the lunch Michelle had prepared.

"Which one? You have two sisters you know." Michelle chuckled and poked Ezekiel's arm.

The children followed suit with giggles of their own. Angela Mary may have understood what was so funny, but surely not little Vernon.

Ezekiel tweaked the end of his daughter's nose. "The sister I spoke to was your aunt Amy."

"What did she have to say?" Michelle questioned.

"I'll tell you as soon as we've finished praying." Ezekiel bowed his head. *Dear Lord,* he prayed silently, *Please bless my family back home, as well as our family here. Help us to be receptive to Your will at all times. Thank You for this food, as well as the hands*

416

*that lovingly prepared it.*

Ezekiel opened his eyes and cleared his throat, at which point, Michelle also opened her eyes. The children's eyes were already open, and he wasn't sure if they'd ever closed them. He supposed it didn't matter that much, as long as they learned the importance of prayer and thanking God for His many blessings. As Angela Mary and Vernon grew older, they would understand more about traditions.

"So what did Amy have to say?" Michelle prompted as she handed Ezekiel a plate of cold chicken left over from last night's supper.

"She said that she and Jared met with Herschel Fisher last week and toured the home he has for rent."

"Oh, that's right. You did mention when you talked to your mother last week that she'd told you Herschel offered them the opportunity to rent the house he owns in Strasburg. It's the same one Jesse used to rent from him, right?"

Ezekiel nodded and put some macaroni salad on his plate.

"Did they like the house?"

"Jah, and Jared's already moved in."

"That's good news. I bet Amy's excited." Michelle forked some of the chilled salad

417

into her mouth.

He nodded. "That's an understatement. When I listened to the message Amy left, her voice was at least an octave higher than normal. My poor ear is still vibrating from the experience. Oh, and wanna know what else she told me?"

"Sure."

"She's going over to Jared's this evening to cook supper, and they've invited two guests who don't know the other one is coming. I think my sister is up to something."

Michelle tipped her head, looking at Ezekiel through half-closed eyelids. "Who are the guests?"

"My mamm and Herschel." He took a bite of chicken.

Michelle's eyes widened. "Why would they invite them both without telling the other?"

Ezekiel shrugged. "Can't say for sure, but Amy did say the meal is to thank Herschel for letting them rent the house for a reasonable price."

"And the reason for your mamm's invitation?"

Ezekiel leaned closer to his wife and whispered, "I believe my sister may have matchmaking on her mind."

418

"Between Herschel and your mother?"

"Jah. He's a kind person. You never know — Herschel Fisher might be just what my mamm needs."

Michelle put her hand up to her mouth. "Oh my."

*Strasburg*

"I still don't understand why you felt the need to invite me to supper this evening. Honestly, I'm going to feel like an extra wheel on the buggy being with you two," Mom said as she and Amy headed with Mom's horse and buggy toward the rental where Jared was staying.

"Please don't feel that way, Mom. We like having you around. Besides, I wanted you to see the homey place and maybe give some ideas on how we might make it even cozier."

"I'm sure you and Jared can figure that out on your own without my opinion."

"Bouncing ideas off you could help with some decisions I'm not sure about. Also, I thought you deserved a night off from helping cook supper and doing dishes." From the driver's seat, Amy glanced at her mother. She noticed a smile form on Mom's lips.

"That's nice of you, but don't expect me to sit idly and watch you cook the meal this evening and not offer to help."

"You can offer, but Jared and I will be doing the cooking."

Mom's eyebrows lifted slightly. "You are blessed if your future husband likes to cook. I could never get your daed to do any kind of cooking except when it came to using his outdoor grill."

"I do remember, but Dad had many other good qualities."

"How well I know." Mom released a lingering sigh. "I still miss him so much, Amy. Life has been different without your daed around. But with the Lord's strength and the help of my loving family, I've been able to keep going."

Amy held the reins with one hand and reached over to clasp her mother's hand. "Of course you do. The love you and Dad had was strong and true. A part of him will always be with you and with us too."

"Jah, that is for certain."

They rode quietly for a while, and then Amy asked a question. "Do you think if the right man came along that you would ever remarry?"

Mom didn't respond for several seconds, and then she said in a near whisper: "Perhaps, but it's doubtful. He'd have to love me deeply, and I, him."

"Do you think Monroe might be in love with you?"

"I believe so — or at least he thinks he is."

"How do you feel about him?"

She wrinkled her nose. "He's just a friend from the past. I have no strong feelings for him, but I suppose that could change down the road."

"I see." Amy decided it was best to move on to another topic. "It was good to see that business in the greenhouse picked up a bit today."

"Jah, and it helps to make the time at work move along faster when we keep busy. I am hoping as the summer progresses we'll see even more customers."

Amy relaxed her shoulders. "In spite of the new greenhouse moving into the area, it hasn't really hurt our business that much, thanks to the tourist trade."

"True. Even so, we need to come up with more things people would be interested in purchasing. Maybe we should run an ad in the local paper when we have our next sale. Since we can't count on business from the flower shop Sara used to own, we need to think of other ways to increase our business."

"And even though ads cost money, they

usually pay for themselves in sales," Amy said.

"Agreed."

Amy loosened her grip on the reins a bit. "Mom, there's something else I've been meaning to talk to you about."

"Oh, what's that?"

"Jared and I have been talking about whether I should work or not after we're married."

Mom sat very still, looking straight ahead. "What have you decided?"

"We agreed that I should continue working at the greenhouse until we're expecting our first child. After the boppli is born, my responsibility will be to take care of my family, and I can't do that and work in the greenhouse too."

"I understand, and when the time comes, we'll just have to make do." Mom's voice trembled a bit.

Amy couldn't help feeling guilty, but at the same time, her responsibility would soon be to Jared and any children they had. She was about to mention that perhaps her mother could hire someone outside the family to work in the greenhouse, but the rental house came into view.

As Amy turned the horse and buggy up the driveway, she spotted Herschel standing in the front yard, talking to Jared.

"I see Herschel is here," Mom commented. "Did you know he was coming?"

Amy nodded. "Jared invited him for supper to say thank you for allowing us to rent this place for a reasonable fee."

Mom's cheeks colored a bright pink. "I hope Herschel doesn't mind me being here. He's quite shy around women, you know."

Amy reached across the seat and patted her mother's hand. "I'm sure it'll be fine. Let me get the horse secured, and then we can go inside and I'll show you around."

# CHAPTER 35

Seeing Herschel's surprised expression when he looked her way, Belinda could only assume that he had no idea she'd been included in their supper plans. She noticed the dressy, aqua shirt he wore. It made his silver-gray hair and beard stand out more than usual. Belinda didn't mean to gawk, but this was the first time she'd realized what a handsome man he was.

Hoping he hadn't seen her staring, she looked in the direction of the house her daughter and future son-in-law would occupy once they were married. Feeling a bit unsure of herself, Belinda stepped up to Herschel. "Good evening. I hope you don't mind that I'm joining the three of you for supper. Amy extended the invitation, and I presume you didn't know."

"No, I did not, but it's nice that you're here." He offered her a timid smile as well as a warm handshake.

Belinda thought it was kind of cute how a grown man could have such a shy streak.

"Why don't the three of you go inside while I put your gaul away?" Jared gestured to Belinda's horse. "You're going to be here a while, and he'd become too restless if he remained at the hitching rail."

"I'll help you," Herschel was quick to say.

"Danki, I appreciate that."

When the men headed for Belinda's horse, she followed Amy into the house. She stopped in the living room and peeked out the front-room window, watching as Herschel and Jared began leading the horse to the barn.

"So here's the living room." Amy made a sweeping gesture with her hand. "It's nowhere near as big as our living room at home, but it should be adequate for Jared and me, don't you think?"

"Jah, I would say so." Belinda moved over to stand beside the fireplace. "You'll enjoy this during the winter months, I imagine."

Amy bobbed her head. "Oh, yes. I can picture a nice fire burning, and its heat warming up this area. Now let's go down the hall, and I'll show you the bedrooms. These rooms aren't large, but they'll certainly serve our needs."

"Sounds good." Belinda followed her

daughter out of the room.

By the time Amy showed her mother the rest of the house, Jared and Herschel had come inside. She found them sitting in the living room. Herschel kept his gaze toward the floor, and Jared looked at Amy with a wrinkled forehead as he bounced one leg over the other.

"Jared and I are going into the kitchen now to prepare supper." Amy looked at Mom. "You and Herschel can make yourselves comfortable and visit while we get the meal prepared."

Herschel nodded, but he didn't look up or even glance at Mom. Amy's mother, however, folded her arms and shook her head. "Jared, why don't you sit here and relax? I can help Amy with the meal."

"No way." Jared stood with his feet firmly planted. "Amy and I invited you and Herschel for supper, and we're going to do the cooking." As though the matter was settled, he marched out of the room. Amy hurried behind him.

It was quiet in the living room, with neither Herschel nor Mom saying anything. Amy listened from the kitchen, near the doorway, and it wasn't long before she heard her mother try to get the ball rolling.

"I've been by this place many times, Herschel, and never imagined that one day my youngest daughter might be living here. The house seems to be in good shape, and the layout is nice."

"Jah."

"I like the built-in shelves on either side of the fireplace. That's an extra feature you don't see in many newer homes."

"Uh-huh."

Amy grimaced and moved away from the door. "I hope we didn't make a mistake by leaving those two alone," she whispered to Jared. "So far, things don't seem to be going so well. Mom is doing most of the talking and Herschel's only said a few words."

Jared kissed Amy's cheek. "Just give it some time. I'm sure Herschel will open up and say more. He's kind of shy, you know."

Amy was hopeful as she moved over to the refrigerator to take out the chicken, while Jared heated the frying pan on the stove. Maybe once everyone began eating the meal, they would all relax and have a good time.

"This is a good meal." Dennis cut into another piece of succulent roast beef. "Danki for taking the time to fix it, Mom."

She looked across the table at him. "And

why wouldn't I want to feed my sons a nice meal?"

"You're my guests," Dennis replied. "I should be the one serving you."

Gerald rolled his eyes. "Since when did you learn how to cook?"

"I admit, I don't know my way around the kitchen very well, but we could have gone out to eat supper. There are some pretty good restaurants here in Lancaster County."

"I'm sure there are, but I enjoy cooking, so there's no reason for us to go out. Besides, you don't often get many leftovers when you eat at a restaurant." His mother sprinkled some pepper on her food. "How about the nice meatloaf sandwiches with the toasted rolls you like? I could make those for supper tomorrow."

Gerald nodded with a mouthful of potatoes Mom had mixed with sour cream.

"I'd like that." Dennis forked the piece of meatloaf into his mouth, and as he chewed, he mulled over the idea of whether he should say anything about Sylvia or not. He wanted to tell his mother about the feelings he'd begun to develop for Sylvia but wasn't sure of her reaction.

"So what have you been up to other than horse training since you moved to Strasburg?" Gerald asked.

Dennis placed his fork on the plate and wiped his lips with his napkin. "I'm still doing some birding when I have the time."

"Good to hear." Mom smiled. "Everyone needs an outlet that doesn't involve work."

Dennis fiddled with his knife handle a few seconds and took a drink of water. "The young widow who rented me this home is also a bird-watcher and so is her youngest brother."

"That's nice." Mom dished some scalloped potatoes onto her plate and took a bite.

"We've gone birding together and shared some meals at her mamm's place."

"Sounds like they're a hospitable family," Gerald commented.

"They are, and Sylvia has the cutest kinner. Rachel's kind of shy, but I think Allen's taken a liking to me." Dennis paused for a breath. "Oh, and I recently asked Sylvia if I could court her."

Mom's brows shot up. "You're courting a widowed woman with children?"

"Correct."

"Congratulations for taking such a big step!" Gerald reached over and gave Dennis's shoulder a squeeze. "By this time next year you could be a married man. That'd be

429

great news."

Dennis shrugged. "You never know, but I don't plan to rush it. Sylvia's been through a lot, losing her husband, father, and oldest brother all in one accident."

"Wow! Just goes to show we're not the only family dealing with a loss." Gerald's face sobered.

Mom looked around the cozy kitchen, where Sylvia's touches could be seen. "So this is the place she and her husband lived before his death?"

"Jah, but she and the kinner have been living with her mamm."

"I'm surprised she didn't sell it."

"I believe the thought occurred to her, Mom, but she decided to rent the place out instead."

"Is there any chance that we could meet her before we head back home before the end of the week?" Mom asked.

"Umm . . . I don't know . . . maybe. I'm not sure what her schedule is like." Dennis wasn't sure that his mother meeting Sylvia was such a good idea, but when Mom pressured him on it, he agreed to see if Sylvia would be free tomorrow evening. "I'll make the call when we're done with supper."

*Well, at least my family is interested in meeting the woman I'm courting. That's a step in the right direction and a positive sign.*

"I hope she's free," Gerald interjected, "because I'd like to meet the young lady who could end up being my sister-in-law."

Dennis lifted his gaze to the ceiling. "Let's not get ahead of ourselves. There's been no talk of marriage yet." He reached up and rubbed the back of his much-too-warm neck. *I hope if Mom and Gerald do get to meet Sylvia that neither of them says anything to embarrass me. They can both be pretty blunt at times.*

"Has anyone checked for phone messages today?" Sylvia asked as she sat in the living room with her mother and sister after they returned from having supper at Herschel's rental. The children were in bed, and so was Henry.

"I went to the phone shack this morning before the greenhouse opened," Amy said. "There was a message from Toby's folks, checking to see how things are going, and there was also one from Sara. She apologized for not telling us that she'd sold her business. Sara said her only excuse was how busy she's been taking care of the baby and trying to keep up with church-related functions. She also thought Misty would notify all of her customers."

Mom frowned. "I can understand her busyness, but I wish we hadn't heard the news second-hand. It would have been nice if she'd been the one to tell us."

"Were there any other messages besides the one from Sara?" Sylvia asked, quickly changing the subject. She'd been hoping she might hear something from Dennis today. The last time she'd seen him, he'd said something about wanting to get together with her this week.

Amy nodded. "They were all related to greenhouse business."

"Oh, I see." Sylvia couldn't hide her disappointment.

Sylvia saw a gleam in her sister's eyes as she turned in her chair to look at her. "Why don't you go out right now and see if there are any new messages? He may have called since I checked earlier today."

"He?" Mom tipped her head. "Are you referring to Dennis?"

"Jah. That is who you were hoping to hear from. Right, Sister?" Amy gave Sylvia's arm a gentle poke.

Sylvia's face heated. "Jah. Think I'll go check for messages."

Amy smiled, but Mom pressed her lips tightly together as she pushed her feet against the floor to get the rocking chair moving.

Sylvia stood. "I'm going to grab a flashlight and head out to the shed now." She ambled out of the room. *Mom still seems to have concerns about me and Dennis as a couple.*

Belinda fanned her face with her hand. "Does it feel hotter than normal in here to you?" She looked over at Amy, who appeared to be quite comfortable on the couch.

"Maybe a little. Should I open another window? If a breeze has come up, it would surely help cool this room."

"Jah, that might help." Belinda took the corner of her apron and blotted the perspiration from her forehead. *I wish my daughter hadn't agreed to let Dennis court her so soon. For all we know he could have a girlfriend up in Dauphin County.*

Amy got up and went to open the second window.

"If you ask me, your sister is too eager to see Dennis. She needs to keep her focus on the children. Don't you agree?"

"She's not neglecting them, Mom, if that's what you mean." Amy returned to her seat. "Sylvia's a good mother, but she deserves to have some happiness that doesn't involve the kinner."

"I thought she enjoyed her new hobby of bird-watching."

"She does, but she likes — maybe even loves — Dennis, and Sylvia has the right to develop a relationship with him."

Belinda's hands went limp in her lap. "If she knew him better, I might agree, but things are happening too fast for me."

"Dennis knows what Sylvia has been through, so I'm sure he will take it slow."

*Or maybe he'll lose interest in her and move on to someone else.*

Rather than dwell on this topic, Belinda let her mind focus on the nice evening she'd had with Amy, Jared, and Herschel. Things had been a bit awkward between her and Herschel at first, but Belinda had managed to think of several things to talk about, and he'd seemed to relax some too. After supper, Jared had gotten out a game of Rook and they played that while eating chocolate cake for dessert. Belinda hadn't admitted it to herself until now, but she had not enjoyed herself so much in a long while.

*Perhaps I need to get out and socialize more,* she told herself. *Maybe in the next week or two, I'll get together with one of my friends.*

■ ■ ■ ■

Dennis was relieved when his phone rang and he recognized the Kings' phone number on his screen. "Hello."

"Hi, Dennis, it's Sylvia."

"It's good to hear from you."

"Same here."

"I assume you got my message." Dennis moved over to his bedroom window to breathe the fresh air blowing in.

"Yes, I did, and I would be pleased to meet your mother and brother."

"Would it be okay if we came by tomorrow evening after supper?"

"That will be fine." Sylvia was tempted to invite them to join her family for a meal, but figured that might not go over too well with Mom. It stressed her out when they had last-minute guests, the way it had when Monroe used to come by close to suppertime.

"Would seven-thirty work for you?"

"That should be fine. I'll fix something special to serve for dessert."

"Don't go to any trouble on our account."

"It won't be any trouble," she said.

"Okay then. We'll see you tomorrow evening. Bye, Sylvia."

"Goodbye, Dennis."

Dennis couldn't help but smile. *She wants to see me tomorrow and meet some of my family. I see that as a good sign. Sure hope Mom and Gerald like Sylvia and her family. For that matter, I hope Sylvia likes my family too.*

He set his device on the counter and frowned. *I'm a bit worried though. Can't help but wonder how Mrs. King will respond to Mom and Gerald, since she tends to be so cold toward me.*

# CHAPTER 36

Last night Virginia had bumped her previously injured knee on the coffee table, and this morning, her leg hurt so bad that she needed to use her cane. She'd pulled a bag of frozen peas from the freezer and iced her knee while lying on the sofa. Virginia had whined to Earl about how much it hurt, but the cold soon made the soreness diminish. As long as the bag cooled her knee, Virginia felt pretty good. After a while, though, the pain returned. But she wouldn't let it keep her from making another trip to the greenhouse today to put on a friendly front.

*Think I'll get some jars of honey this time,* Virginia told herself as she cautiously crossed the road. One never knew when a horse and buggy or some motorized vehicle might approach.

On the other side, she made her way slowly and painfully up the driveway. Of course she had to dodge some horse droppings. *Why can't someone take a shovel and clean up these gross landmines? I feel like I'm wasting time here, limping around all these useless piles of yucky debris.*

It was a relief when she finally made it to the front door of the greenhouse. Stepping inside, she spotted Belinda seated behind the front counter, thumbing through some paperwork.

"Good morning, Mrs. King." Virginia spoke in what she hoped was a cheerful tone.

Belinda looked up and smiled. "It's nice to see you, Virginia. And please call me, Belinda."

"Okay, sure." Virginia leaned against the counter. "How are things going with your business?"

"Fairly well, all things considered. We manage to keep busy."

"I bet."

"Did you make a trip over here for something specific?" Belinda asked.

Virginia bobbed her head. "Came to get some more of that tasty honey — if you have any, that is."

"Yes, we have a few jars left. They're right over there." Belinda pointed to the shelves across the room. "Would you like me to get you a jar?"

"Actually, I'd hoped for two. My husband and I both enjoyed the honey you gave us previously, and it went real quick."

"I'm glad you liked it, and we can certainly spare two jars for you."

"Do you have a sturdy bag for me to carry them in? I am using a cane today and can only carry with one hand."

Belinda's brows furrowed. "Oh, I'm so sorry. Did you suffer an injury recently?"

"Well, sort of. I bumped my knee on our coffee table, and it aggravated an old wound I had from long ago."

"I can see if my son Henry is free to carry your purchase over to your home for you."

Virginia flapped her hand. "Naw, that's okay. I can manage." She turned and made her way over to the shelf where the jars of honey stood. Once she'd chosen two glass containers, she realized she couldn't carry them both in one hand and manage her cane in the other.

Belinda must have realized her predicament, because she stepped out from behind the counter and came right over. "Here, let me carry them for you."

Back at the counter, where Belinda had set the jars, Virginia pulled a twenty dollar bill from her jeans pocket. "I believe the sign above the bigger jars of honey stated that they are ten dollars per jar."

"That's correct." Belinda took the money and put it inside the cash register drawer.

While she wrapped the jars with bubble wrap and placed them in a brown paper sack with handles, Virginia contemplated what her next move should be.

She cleared her throat and plunged ahead. "Say, I heard that Amy and Jared will be getting married this fall."

Belinda gave a nod. "Yes, that is correct. The wedding will take place the first Thursday of October."

"How nice." Virginia managed a fake smile. "I've never been to an Amish wedding. I imagine they are quite different from an English one."

"Yes, our weddings are similar to one of our regular church services, with the addition of sermons being preached specifically for the benefit of the bride and groom. And of course, there's a time for the wedding couple to say their vows as they answer certain questions presented to them by the bishop."

"Sounds interesting." Virginia was on the verge of telling Belinda that Jared had mentioned they might get an invitation, when a tour bus pulled into the parking lot, and several enthusiastic-looking people rushed into the building.

"Things are going to get kind of hectic right now," Belinda said, "but we'll talk some other time."

"Umm . . . yeah, okay." Virginia picked up the sack and headed out the door. *I'll come back some other time,* she told herself. *Maybe I'll ask when the wedding invitations will be sent out. At least then I would have some idea when to watch for ours to come.*

Sylvia stood with one arm holding the other at the elbow as she looked at the clock. She and the family had eaten supper, and the dishes were done. Now all she had to do was wait for Dennis and his family to arrive. It was hard not to be nervous. Sylvia had never been comfortable around strangers — even more so since Toby died. But oddly enough, she hadn't been nervous around Dennis, not even the day they'd first met.

*I hope his mother and brother approve of me.* Continuing to stare at the clock, she tapped her foot. *And I hope I like them. If they're anything like Dennis, then things should be fine. We'll sit around and get to know each other while we eat the dessert I prepared for this evening.*

"Sister, are you fretting?" Amy bumped

Sylvia's arm, causing her to jump. "Oh, sorry if I frightened you. Thought you knew I was still here in the kitchen."

Sylvia turned to face Amy. "A part of me is eager to meet some of Dennis's family, but another part is a nervous wreck. If they don't like me, Dennis might decide to pull away."

Amy slipped an arm around Sylvia's waist. "I'm sure they'll like you, and even if for some reason they don't, Dennis will not pull away."

"How can you be so sure?"

"I've seen the way he looks at you. That man is smitten."

"How does he look at me?"

"With shining eyes and a silly grin that hardly leaves his face. I realize you two haven't known each other very long, but I recognize two people in love when I see them looking at each other with rapt attention." Amy moved her hand from Sylvia's waist to the small of her back and gave it a few pats. "Jared sees it too. In fact, he told me the other day that he believes Dennis is head over heels in love with you."

Sylvia's face heated. "I don't know about that, but I do think he cares for me. And the truth is, I have strong feelings for him too."

"Then stop thinking negative thoughts, try to relax, and enjoy being with him this evening. Keep your focus on Dennis and quit worrying about what his family may or may not think of you."

Sylvia gave her a sister a hug. "Danki, Amy. You're always full of good advice."

*I must have lost my mind to agree to this,* Dennis thought as he headed for the Kings' with his mother and brother. Gerald sat up front with Dennis, and Mom was seated in the back of the buggy. Midnight seemed well-behaved as he trotted along at an easy pace. Gerald had said he would drive them there in his van, but Mom insisted they go by horse and buggy.

The rest of the day had gone well. Dennis's brother had come out to watch him train a horse for a while, and then Dennis talked Gerald into driving him to the animal shelter in search of a German shepherd. While there, Gerald had pointed out a few different breeds, but Dennis kept looking until he found the right dog.

After the arrangements were made, and the black and tan shepherd had been loaded into the van, they went to buy dog food and some other needed supplies. Dennis was glad he'd finally found the right dog and felt it had been worth the wait.

Dennis's thoughts brought him back to the present, and the closer they got to the Kings' place, the more nervous he became. To get his mind off that, he brought up the topic of his new dog.

"I'm gonna need some help putting a pen together for my hund." He glanced at his brother. "I don't want him getting out and possibly being hit by a car when I'm not with him."

Gerald groaned. "I know where this going. I'll help you while I'm here, so don't worry."

"That would be much appreciated."

"Does the mutt have a name?" Mom tapped Dennis on the shoulder. "Or will you have to come up with one?"

"No, I'll need to name the dog."

"How 'bout Goliath? He's certainly big enough to be considered a giant." Gerald chuckled.

Dennis shook his head at his brother's suggestion. "I'll figure it out soon. Maybe after we get back from the Kings', and I let the hund out of the barn."

The closer they got to Sylvia and her family, the more stress Dennis felt. *What if Mom says something to Sylvia that embarrasses me? I don't understand why she was so desperate to meet the young woman. It's not like we're planning to get married or anything.*

A trickle of sweat rolled down his forehead as the Kings' place came into view. All Dennis could do was hope and pray that things went well here this evening, because there was no turning back now.

After the introductions had been made, Sylvia invited everyone except the children, who were already in bed, to take seats around the dining room table. Once they were all seated, she excused herself to get the dessert.

Dennis was quickly on his feet. "I'll go with you. I'm sure you'll need help bringing everything in."

Sylvia smiled. "Danki."

When they entered the kitchen, she got out her Cherry Melt-Away bars as well as a plate with two kinds of cookies on it.

"Looks like you've been busy today." Dennis stepped up to her. "I hope you didn't go to all this trouble on account of me bringing my mamm and bruder over to meet you and your family."

A pink flush crept across her cheeks. "Well I'll admit I did hope the desserts would help, in case they didn't care for me as a person."

445

"Are you kidding?" It was all he could do to keep from taking her into his arms. "You're the kindest, sweetest woman I've ever met, and I'm sure it's obvious to others too."

Sylvia lowered her gaze. "I'm not always kind or sweet. For the first several months after Toby, my daed, and my bruder died, I was quite difficult to live with."

"It's understandable. After my dad was accidentally shot, I felt full of rage. Some of my family avoided me because they never knew when I would say something unkind." He placed his hand on her arm. "We've all been through difficult times, and when someone we love dies, there are several stages of grief we must go through."

"I know." Her chin trembled, followed by tears in her eyes, and it was almost his undoing.

Unable to control his own swirling emotions, Dennis put his arms around Sylvia's waist and pulled her into an embrace. It seemed right for him to hold Sylvia like this. At this moment, Dennis felt that God had brought her into his life for a reason, and they were meant to be together. He was on the verge of kissing away her tears, when someone entered the room. Dennis let go of Sylvia and turned around.

"What's goin' on in here? Mom sent me to see if —" Henry stopped talking and stared at Sylvia. "Have you been cryin' Sister?"

She nodded.

Henry pointed at Dennis. "Did you say something to make her cry?"

"I suppose I did," Dennis replied. "But it wasn't intentional. We were talking about grief, and how hard it is to deal with the loss of a loved one."

Henry pressed a fist against his chest. "Ya don't have to tell me about it."

Dennis rested his hand on the boy's shoulder. "You still miss your daed and bruder, don't you?"

"Jah."

"It's okay to grieve for them, Henry, but your dad and brother would want you to move on with your life." Dennis's skin tingled. This was the first time he'd realized that he was actually beginning to move on with his life. *Guess I really have forgiven my uncle and accepted the fact that the accident wasn't his fault. Now maybe I can somehow help Henry to work through his pain.*

Henry looked up at Dennis. "I'm glad God brought you into our lives 'cause I really like you."

Dennis gave Henry's shoulder a squeeze.

"I like you too."

Sylvia sniffed and reached for a tissue to blow her nose. "Guess we'd best get the desserts taken out before someone else comes looking for us."

"My son tells me you're also a bird-watcher." Dennis's mother, Amanda, looked across the table at Sylvia.

"Yes, that's right. It's a fairly new hobby for me. My brother Henry is also into birding. In fact he got into it before I did."

"That's right," Henry interjected. "Sylvia and I were out looking at birds the day we met Dennis."

"It's nice you three have that in common. Don't you think so, Belinda?" Amanda turned to look at Sylvia's mother.

Sylvia held her breath, waiting to hear Mom's response.

Mom nodded slowly. "Yes, I am happy that my son and daughter found a hobby they can both enjoy."

Since there was no mention of Amanda's son, Sylvia felt the need to say something on his behalf. "Dennis has taught Henry and me a lot about the various species of birds in our area. I think we have learned more from him then from the bird book Henry has."

Amanda smiled as she looked at Dennis with a gleam in her eyes. "My son's interest in birds began when he was a young boy, and he's learned a lot over the years."

"My mamm's right," Gerald spoke up. "Whenever my bruder went missing, we always knew he was off looking at birds somewhere on the farm."

Dennis held up his hand. "Okay, that's enough talk about me. Let's move on to some other topic, shall we?"

"We could talk about the wonderful way you have with horses," his mother said. She looked at Sylvia's mom. "He's had that ability since he was a boy as well."

"Yes, Sylvia's told me that Dennis trains horses." Mom's smile didn't quite reach her eyes. Sylvia figured she was only being polite.

Abruptly, Mom changed the subject. "My daughter Amy is planning to be married this fall. It's too bad her fiancé couldn't be with us tonight."

"Jared's a roofer, and he had an out-of-town job so he wouldn't have gotten back in time to be here," Amy explained. "Perhaps some other time when you come to visit Dennis, you can meet Jared."

Amanda smiled. "I'll look forward to that."

As the conversation around the table

changed to talk about the weather, Sylvia's thoughts turned inward. *What do Dennis's mother and brother think of me and my family? Are they okay with their son courting me?*

She glanced at her mother, sitting straight in her chair. *Will Mom ever accept the idea of me seeing Dennis and making him a part of my life? Sometimes I wish I'd never moved back into her house and had toughed it on my own after Toby died. Then she wouldn't know so much of my personal business and might be more accepting of my new friend.*

# CHAPTER 37

Today, Dennis had brought out his new dog from the pen he and Gerald had put together. The shepherd seemed timid around the horses, but Dennis kept him nearby while working. He hoped in due time the dog he'd named Brutus would be fine around Midnight and any other horse.

It had been a week since Dennis's mother and brother left, and she'd called him nearly every day since. Gerald had called once, just to tell Dennis that the deal had fallen through on the vacation home he'd wanted to buy. He'd also mentioned that their mother had seemed kind of out-of-sorts since they came home and kept asking him what he'd thought of Sylvia.

Dennis's mother could get curious at times about certain topics. And when it came to her boys getting involved with a potential mate, her antenna went up in a hurry. He couldn't believe how interested she was, so sometimes he'd go off the topic and talk about his dog, or some of the things going on with his work.

Mom said she had more questions about Sylvia and his intentions toward her. Dennis didn't say much, other than that he was taking it one day at a time and would let her know if anything serious developed.

Dennis grunted as he combed Midnight's mane. "How am I supposed to respond to my mamm's questions about my relationship with Sylvia when I don't have any answers myself?"

The horse's ears perked up, and he let out a noisy nicker.

"Yeah, I know, boy. You don't have any answers for me either." Dennis patted Midnight's flanks and looked over at the dog. "What do you think, Brutus?"

The dog tilted his head and watched.

"I feel like I've got a little family of my own right here." Dennis paused to clean out the comb he'd used on the horse.

"I can't even consider marriage until my business is making enough money to support a real family." Dennis continued his one-way conversation with both the horse and his black and tan dog. "After all, it wouldn't just be me and Sylvia to worry about — she has two children."

452

Midnight stomped his hooves impatiently when Dennis kept combing the same section of his mane. Dennis couldn't help it — Sylvia, Allen, and Rachel were forefront on his mind. He wanted to be a good provider for them. His biggest concern was how long it would take before that chapter in his life began.

"Well boy, I can't stay here all day — I've got work to do." Dennis put the curry comb away. "And tonight I'm taking my best girl and her kinner on a picnic supper at the park." He reached down and patted Brutus's head. "Maybe I'll take you along. The kids might enjoy being introduced to you."

After a busy day in the greenhouse, Amy had decided a warm shower would be a perfect way to wind down. Now as she sat at the kitchen table, working on her guest list for the wedding, her long, damp hair hung down her back. "Who, besides family, do you think we should invite to the wedding?" she asked her mother.

Mom looked up from the two-page letter she'd been writing. "Well, our close friends, of course, like Mary Ruth, as well as Lenore, Jesse, and their little family. We'll also include the families in our church district. I think you'll have a good amount of members present for your service and also for the afternoon and evening meals."

Amy picked up a tube of lotion she'd placed on the table and squirted some into her hand as she thought about their neighbors across the street. While she wasn't particularly fond of Virginia, Jared had extended them a verbal invitation, so they should probably be included. After rubbing the lotion in well, she wrote Virginia and Earl's names on the evening meal list.

"What about Herschel?" Amy asked.

"He's not in our district."

"I realize that, but he's a friend, and if it weren't for him, Jared and I wouldn't have a place to live after we're married."

"I'm sure you would have found something else." Mom tapped her pen against the writing tablet. "I hope I haven't left anything out."

Amy inhaled the lavender-mint scent of her lotion, lingering on her skin. "That's a good-sized letter you're working on. Who are you writing to?"

"Ezekiel and Michelle. I'm filling them in on our local news, here and in our community." Mom set her pen aside. "I wouldn't mind using some of that lotion too. It sure smells nice."

"Help yourself." Amy passed it to her. "So

how come you don't just call them and leave a message?"

"It's easier to write it all down." Mom placed a dollop of the moisturizer on her hands and rubbed it in. "Besides, we don't do enough letter writing these days."

"True." Amy glanced at her list. "So what do you think — is it okay if I invite Herschel?"

Mom shrugged her shoulders and grabbed her pen. "It's your wedding, so it's up to you. It would be a nice gesture, I suppose."

"Okay, I'm going to add him to the list." When Amy finished writing Herschel's name, she looked back at her mother. "Can I ask you something else?"

"Of course."

"Did you enjoy the time we spent with Dennis and his family last week?"

Mom put her pen down and looked directly at Amy. "They seem nice enough, and I don't think Dennis is a bad person, but I believe he's pushed your sister into a relationship too soon."

"It's not too soon for Sylvia to be in a relationship, Mom. She's been widowed over a year, and I don't think she would have agreed to let Dennis court her if she didn't feel ready to begin again."

"I've been without my mate the same time

as her, and I'm not ready to be courted by anyone." Mom shifted on her chair. "Monroe would like me to be, but I'm not in love with him."

Amy bobbed her head. "I agree. No one should begin a serious relationship with someone unless there is love — or at least the beginning of those feelings."

"You're right, and I have a feeling Sylvia still loves Toby. She may only be looking for a father for her kinner, which is ridiculous since Dennis has never had any children."

"He does well when he's around Rachel and Allen, and I believe they — especially Allen — are drawn to him," Amy argued.

"That doesn't mean —"

Mom stopped talking when Henry entered the room. "Seth just pulled up in his car, and I wanna go talk to him. I've been trying to connect ever since the greenhouse windows were painted black, and he hasn't answered any of my messages."

"You can go out and talk to him," Mom replied, "but please do not get into his *fuhrwaerick.*"

Henry shook his head. "Don't worry — I'm not gonna get in Seth's vehicle. I just want to ask if he's the one who did that to our windows."

"Okay, go ahead, but don't stay too long.

We'll be starting supper soon."

Henry glanced around. "Where's Sylvia? Figured she'd have supper started by now."

"She and the kinner went out with Dennis this evening, remember? And we met his new dog, Brutus, right before they left. Where's your head, Son? Are you sure it's on straight today?"

"Of course it is. My mind's just pre-occupied with getting some answers out of Seth." Henry turned and raced out the back door.

Amy scrunched her face. "Poor guy. He's definitely upset over this."

"Do you think one of us should go with him?" Mom asked. "Maybe he'll need some help convincing Seth to tell the truth."

Amy shook her head. "Seth is a closed-mouth kid. He's not likely to admit anything to either of us."

"Guess you're right." Mom heaved a sigh. "Let's just hope if Seth is the one responsible for the vandalism that he owns up to it and promises not to do anything like that again."

Sylvia was glad Dennis had decided that they should go on a picnic, rather than eating in a restaurant. Rachel got fussy if she was made to sit very long, and here at the park, both children could run and play after they ate. Of course, they would still need some supervision.

Allen and Rachel seemed to take a liking to Brutus right away. He was a big hit and kept the children well entertained. Sylvia watched Allen running around with the dog, while Rachel stood on the sidelines clapping her hands.

"Brutus is a friendly, nice-looking hund." She looked over at Dennis.

"I agree. He's a beautiful dog and a keeper. His personality around the horses is still somewhat timid, but I think he will eventually toughen up," he responded.

"At least he isn't the other way — aggressive around anyone or anything."

Dennis shook his head. "I couldn't afford to have a dog that would be unsafe — especially when I'm running a business with people coming and going."

Sylvia felt contented as she soaked up the nice view here at the park. The children laughed at Brutus chewing on a stick he'd found. It was a warm evening, and the birds seemed to be everywhere.

Dennis pointed to a couple of doves. "It's interesting that they're related to pigeons."

"I never thought about that, but they do look similar."

"I hope it was okay to come here and have a picnic."

Sylvia nodded, and then looked over at the children again. Between all the activity her son and daughter experienced here this evening, as well as the hearty picnic fare they would eat soon, she felt sure they'd both sleep well tonight. Dennis had furnished the picnic food from a local deli and included peanut butter and jelly sandwiches that the children would enjoy.

*If only my mother could understand my needs and how Dennis makes me feel.* Sylvia let her thoughts wander as she sat back until she could rest comfortably against the bench where she and Dennis sat. *She thinks my only priority should be raising my kinner, and I'm doing that. Doesn't Mom see that being with Dennis brings me joy? I don't see anything wrong with it. Maybe I'll be like my sister in the near future, planning for a wedding. I wonder what my mamm would say about that.*

"I enjoyed meeting your mother and brother last week," Sylvia said as they watched the children run around. Brutus ran with them, playfully barking and wagging his tail.

Dennis looked over at Sylvia and smiled. "Mom and Gerald were pleased to have met you and your family. Every time my mamm's called me this past week, she's asked about you."

"That's nice to know." Sylvia sat quietly for a few minutes and gathered up her courage to say something that had been on her mind since she and Dennis had begun courting. "I want to apologize for my mother's curtness toward you."

Dennis shifted on the bench so they were directly facing each other. "I had noticed it, and I think I know why."

"Oh?"

"Your mamm probably thinks our relationship is moving too fast."

"That is part of the reason," Sylvia admitted. "But I believe there's more to it."

"Such as?"

"Mom's afraid I might end up getting married someday, and then it would be just her and Henry to run the greenhouse."

"Married to me?"

Sylvia's cheeks warmed. "Well, she might think that, I suppose."

Dennis reached for her hand. "And she might be right. I've thought about it a lot, in fact."

"You . . . you have?" Sylvia's skin tingled beneath his gentle touch.

"Jah." Dennis stroked the top of her hand

with this thumb. "Even though our relationship is still fairly new, I feel like I've known you all of my life."

"I feel the same way about you."

"The thing is, I can't really think about marriage until I'm making more money. I need to build up my business, so it's successful. But in the meantime, I'd like to continue our relationship, making it stronger."

Sylvia licked her lips, feeling cautious hope. "I'd like that."

Belinda had finished mixing the ingredients for the macaroni and cheese she'd planned for supper, when Henry burst into the room. "I talked to Seth, and now our *freindschaft* is over. *Sis nau futsch.*"

She turned to face him. "In what way is your friendship ruined now?"

"Seth said he's not the guilty one, and he's mad at me for thinkin' he would do something like paint the greenhouse windows black." Henry sank into a chair at the table and groaned. "I apologized to him for making the accusation, yet he refused to forgive me. There's no doubt about it — I've lost my good friend." He held his fist against his chest. "Something right here told me he wasn't the one who did it, but I had to ask,

461

just the same."

"Don't be so dramatic," Amy said from across the room, where she stood making a tossed green salad. "If Seth was ever a friend, he won't hold it against you because you asked if he had anything to do with the vandalism."

"Your sister is right." Belinda put the casserole dish into the oven. "And if he does break your friendship off, then maybe it's because he was in fact guilty and refused to admit it. Some people are like that, you know. When they're caught doing something they shouldn't have, they try to lie their way out of it and can even go so far as to put the blame on someone else."

Henry shook head. "Seth didn't blame anyone else, Mom. He just said he didn't do it. Now I don't have my friend to hang around with anymore." His shoulders slumped.

"You really weren't spending much time with Seth anyway, Son," Mom said.

"That's 'cause I'm workin' so much around here and in the greenhouse."

"Well, the fact that he got angry with you tells me there's something amiss. Maybe I should speak to Seth's mother about this matter."

Henry rubbed his sweaty forehead. "Please

462

don't do that, Mom. It would make Seth even more umgerrent with me."

"If he's innocent, then he has no reason to be upset." Amy put the finished salad in the refrigerator then she came over to the table and put her hand on Henry's shoulder. "If Seth's not guilty of anything, then give him a little space. I bet by this time next week, he'll come around and resume his friendship with you."

Henry shrugged his shoulders. "We'll see, but I'm not holding my breath. Seth was pretty upset, and he basically told me to leave him alone."

Belinda's heart went out to her son. She watched him as he shuffled up the stairs. *I have a feeling Henry will go up to his room and mope around over this now.* He did what he thought was right by talking to Seth about the blackened windows, and now he has to worry about losing his friend.

Belinda sighed. *I hope for Henry's sake that he is right and his friend is innocent, because it's not easy to watch my boy suffer. But if Seth was responsible for the damage, then my son is better off without him.*

# CHAPTER 38

Sylvia went blissfully through the summer months as she and Dennis saw each other more frequently. They went to church together, spent time with the children, and continued birding — most times together and sometimes by themselves or with Henry. These adventures brought them even closer, as they compared notes, sightings, and messages they'd heard on the bird-watcher's hotline — like the buff-breasted sandpiper someone had seen near the end of August.

Sylvia felt certain that Dennis was the right man for her, and she thought if Toby could look down from heaven, he would approve of the special relationship she'd found herself in. Sylvia looked forward to the day Dennis would feel ready to propose marriage and knew her answer would be yes.

Her mother still hadn't fully accepted Dennis, but Sylvia continued to hope that would change once Mom realized what a good husband and father he'd make.

Today was the first Monday in September, and Amy's wedding was only a month away. Sylvia looked forward to the occasion and especially to being one of her sister's witnesses, along with Amy's friend Lydia. She felt honored to have been asked.

Jared's best friend was Gabe Fisher, whom he'd known since he was a boy, so he had asked him to be one of his witnesses, as well as Jared's younger brother Daniel.

This morning, Sylvia had gotten up early to do some baking while the kitchen was cooler than it would be later in the day, and with the children still in bed, there would be no interruptions.

Sylvia heard a bird creating a racket outside the window. She opened it wide and peered out. There sat that silly old mockingbird chirping out a song.

"Hush now. It's too early to be making a nuisance of yourself."

*Chirp . . . chirp . . . chirp . . .*

Sylvia put a hand on her hip. "Are you mocking me?"

The bird flitted to another tree and continued to warble.

Sylvia couldn't be sure what a mockingbird really sounded like, because according to what she'd read in Henry's bird book, these birds often took on the tone of other birds in the yard. *I sure enjoy being able to identify the species around our yard. I couldn't do such a thing a few months ago. Thank you, Henry and Dennis, for your encouragement.*

"What are you doing?"

Sylvia jerked at the sound of her brother's voice. "*Ach,* you scared me, Henry. I didn't think anybody else was up."

"Just me, as far as I can tell. I thought I was the only person up till I came in here and found you." Henry went to the cupboard and took out a glass. "How come you got out of bed so early?"

"I wanted to get some baking done before the kitchen gets too hot and everyone is up and about."

He sniffed and looked around. "Don't see or smell anything yummy."

She poked his arm playfully. "That's because I haven't started anything yet, silly."

"Well hurry up. I'm hungerich." Henry opened the refrigerator and took out a jug of apple cider Jesse Smucker had given them recently. It had been frozen when he'd brought it over, and he'd said it was the last of the previous fall's squeezing that he'd put in the deep freezer he rented. With autumn around the corner, it wouldn't be long before Jesse would get out the cider press, and there'd be plenty of apple cider to share with others.

"What's your reason for being up so early?" Sylvia asked as her brother poured cider into his glass.

"Wanted to check all the feeders. They're probably getting low. I need to keep our feathered friends happy and coming back to visit." He grinned. "I'll probably spend some time just lookin' at birds after I'm done with the chore."

"Here in the yard, I hope. Mom wouldn't like it if she found out you went somewhere without asking."

He crossed his arms and frowned. "I don't think our mamm trusts me. Truth be told, she probably still thinks I'm the one responsible for all the vandalism that's been done here since Dad, Abe, and Toby died."

"Don't be silly Henry. It's been a long time since Mom's suspected you, and since you weren't at home when some of the things were done, she has no reason to believe it was you."

He pulled out a chair and sat down. "Guess you're right. As soon as I drink my cider, I'm going out in the yard to look for birds — or maybe I'll climb up into the loft like I've done before. I prefer goin' up there, 'cause it's got a nice soft place with loose hay to sit and lean into." Henry gulped some cider and licked his lips clean. "The vantage point is nice because I can see into the big tree in our yard. There can be a lot of bird action goin' on in that old maple."

"That explains why you like to go up there more than not." Sylvia opened the pantry door and took out the ingredients needed to make cornmeal muffins. *If we could get to the bottom of who's responsible for the vandalism, no one would be a suspect anymore.*

Virginia pulled open the door to her mailbox. After retrieving the mail, she stood thumbing through each piece. She couldn't help glancing up her neighbors' driveway to take a look around. Her thought was to catch someone outside to chat with about the upcoming wedding. Hopefully it might lead to a verbal invitation.

Virginia saw no one in sight. The place appeared quiet and still. *Think I've done a decent job of playing nice to these Amish neighbors, and I really want Stella to come for another visit.*

Her forehead wrinkled. Still no invitation in the mail from the Kings, and that wedding was just a month away. Virginia had gone over to the greenhouse a few weeks ago, and dropped a couple more hints about the wedding, asking when they'd be mailing out invitations. Belinda had been really busy that day and hurriedly said, "About a month before the wedding."

Virginia slammed the flap shut, and after looking both ways, she limped back across the street. *I wonder if they forgot about us. This really stresses me out.*

Virginia drew in a couple of deep breaths and tried to calm herself. *Of course, maybe one of them might come over and deliver the invitation in person.* "At least I can console myself with that," she mumbled as she made her way up to the house.

A robin flew past and landed on the garage roof. Virginia watched it preen itself for a minute. She thought the Kings' yard and the feeders they had hanging brought a lot of bird activity.

*I should buy myself a few of those bird hoppers to draw more birds into our yard, but Earl might think it's silly and too expensive.*

Once inside, she tossed the mail on the coffee table. She'd hoped she might catch one of the King family members outside, but that hadn't panned out.

Virginia's fingers trembled as she pulled them through the ends of her hair. *I've got to calm my nerves. Maybe some coffee would help, but I know something else that would take the edge off.*

Virginia went to the hall closet and took out a metal box where she'd hid a carton of cigarettes. If Earl knew she had started smoking again, he'd have a conniption.

She took one cigarette out and put the rest back, then walked out to the kitchen and looked at the clock. "I've got plenty of time to ease my stress before starting supper." She stepped over to her mug, filled it with creamer from the refrigerator, and then topped it off with coffee.

After grabbing a book of matches, Virginia went out the back door and took a seat at the picnic table. Once her cigarette had been lit, she took a puff and inhaled deeply before blowing out the smoke. "Ah, that's better. Now I feel more relaxed."

Virginia propped her bum leg on a nearby chair. As the sunshine warmed her up, she admired the pretty flowerbed that held an abundant array of flowers. The hanging baskets she'd put up also added a splash of color up under the eaves of the house. She'd bought all the plants from the greenhouse across the street. So far they looked happy, slowly putting on more buds. "At least these plants should do well, since I didn't add any of that dumb horse manure to the soil.

My poor tomato plants — now that was sure a waste last year." Virginia took another puff from her cigarette.

Virginia had quit smoking nearly a year ago, but since moving to a place she didn't like, she'd started up again whenever she felt testy. Virginia kept the evidence well-hidden and always smoked outside and made sure her clothes were aired out or washed before Earl came home from work. She used mouthwash and toothpaste to freshen her breath and either washed her hair or applied a lot of hairspray and perfume to mask the smoky odor. So far Earl hadn't caught on, and she aimed to keep it that way.

*After I finish my cigarette, think I'll get out the binoculars and watch whatever birds come into the yard. If that gets boring, I may sit on the front porch and spy on the neighbors.*

*Clymer*

"Look what came in the mail today," Ezekiel said when he entered the kitchen, where Michelle had breakfast waiting for him. He held an envelope out to her and grinned.

She looked at the return address. "It's from Amy, right?"

He nodded. "Go ahead and open it."

She opened the flap carefully and removed

471

a card. "It's our invitation to her and Jared's wedding." Michelle put her arms around Ezekiel and gave him a hug. "I can hardly wait to witness their marriage and see all the rest of our family and friends in Strasburg."

"Same here. It's been five months since we last saw them, and by the time we arrive for the wedding, it'll be six."

"Will we get to go a few days early so we can help out? As you well know, there's a lot to be done those last few days before the big event."

"You're right, and we will definitely want to be there for that."

Excitement bubbled in Michelle's soul. *How wonderful it will be to see not only Ezekiel's family but Mary Ruth, Lenore, and maybe even Sara as well.* Until then, Michelle would count off each one of the days. The first Thursday of October couldn't come soon enough.

*Strasburg*
Virginia remained at the picnic table, drinking more coffee, while working on a crossword puzzle. This one was harder than most in the book she'd purchased last week, but she was determined to finish the puzzle,

even if she had to get out the dictionary for help.

As she sat trying to decide what a word meant for "someone who complains a lot," something rubbed against her leg.

Virginia looked down, and her eyes widened when she saw a gray-and-white cat with its furry tail flipping back and forth across her leg.

"Now where'd you come from?" She leaned over and pet the critter's soft head. Virginia had never seen the cat before and wondered if it was a stray.

"You lookin' for food?" She continued to stroke the cat. "I'm sorry, but I have nothing for you except maybe a bowl of milk or a can of tuna."

She pulled her hand back and thumped the side of her head. "What am I thinking? If I feed the stray, he's bound to keep coming around. Nope, not a good idea. I need to use some common sense."

"Common sense about what?"

Virginia whirled around. "Earl, what are you doing home so early?" She glanced at her cell phone. "It's only two o'clock."

"I've been fighting a headache all day, so the boss said I could go home." He gestured to the metal-framed hammock he'd bought earlier this summer and set up on the patio.

"I thought maybe a cold beer and a nap in that might help."

"It's too hot to sleep out here. Why don't you go inside and lie on the bed?"

"Because I want to take my nap outside."

*Meow!*

Earl looked toward Virginia's feet, and his brows shot up. "Where'd that mangy cat come from?"

"It's not mangy, and it just showed up here a few minutes ago. I have no idea where it came from."

"Well it's not staying." Earl clapped his hands as he took a few steps toward Virginia.

The poor cat took off like it had been shot out of a cannon.

Virginia scowled at him. "Now look what you've done. I bet that poor animal will never come back."

"Exactly." Earl put his nose in the air and sniffed. "What's that putrid odor?"

She shrugged. "I don't smell anything."

"Smells like cigarette smoke." He sniffed again. "Virginia, have you started smoking again?"

"No, Earl."

He leaned close to her head and took in some air. "Phew! Your hair reeks of cigarette smoke. I'd recognize that aroma anywhere."

With rushed speech, Virginia made up a

story about having gone shopping this morning. "And when I came out of the store, there was this guy smoking like a diesel. That man blew smoke curls everywhere. Guess the odor must have stayed with me."

Earl rolled his neck from side-to-side then massaged his forehead. "You'd better be telling the truth. Need I remind you that when you quit smoking, you said it was for good?"

"I don't need any reminders." Virginia gathered up her empty mug and puzzle book. "I'm going to the house to get more coffee. Want me to get you some?"

"No thanks. I'm just gonna lie in the hammock. If I'm not up by suppertime, give me a holler." His forehead wrinkled. "On second thought, don't holler. Better give me a gentle shake instead."

"Okay, Earl. Have a good nap."

Virginia went inside and closed the back door. *Whew, that was a close one. I wasn't expecting Earl to come home early or I'd have taken my shower sooner. I'll need to be more careful next time I decide to have a cigarette.*

# CHAPTER 39

"Well, if that doesn't beat all." Virginia stood in front of the living room window, shaking her head. She turned to face her husband.

"What's wrong?" Earl asked from where he sat putting on his work shoes.

"You should see all the horses and buggies, as well as some cars, pulling into the Kings' driveway."

"More greenhouse traffic, huh?"

She shook her head. "Today is Jared and Amy's wedding, don't ya know? And of course, we didn't get an invite to it, which is why Stella didn't come."

"It's not the end of the world, Virginia. We barely know those people, and we're not Amish, so they might not want outsiders at the occasion."

"I realize that, but if you'll recall, Jared said we would be invited." She tapped her foot, as anger flooded her soul. "I have half a notion to go on over there and crash that wedding. I wonder how that would go over."

"Not very well, I imagine. So just get the idea right out of your head." Earl stood. "And for crying out loud, get away from the window. It's doing you no good to spy on those folks."

"If we can't go, then I may as well see what I can from here." Virginia moved over to the coffee table and picked up the binoculars. *I wonder if there's a way to get a better look over there. If I could find a spot to see into their property well, maybe then I'd be satisfied.*

Earl moved toward her. "Listen, I don't think . . ."

She waved him away. "You'd better get going, or you're gonna be late for work."

"Yeah, okay. But promise me you'll be good today and find something constructive to do."

She gave him a salute. "Will do."

Virginia waited until she heard Earl's vehicle pull out before she went back to watching the goings-on across the road.

Amy paced the living room floor, every once in a while stopping to draw a quick breath. This was the most exciting, but nerve-racking day of her life. It felt like she'd been waiting for this special event to take place forever — certainly since she'd fallen in love with Jared.

*I wonder if he's feeling as nervous as I am right now. Oh, I hope the love of my life has no regrets.*

"You need to stop pacing, or you'll wear a hole in the floor."

Amy stopped walking and turned to face her oldest brother. "I can't help it, Ezekiel. I'm a nervous wreck."

"Of course you are. All brides and grooms are *naerfich* on their wedding day. I sure was, and if you ask Michelle, she'll admit to having been nervous too."

"How did you get through it without falling apart?"

"I prayed for peaceful thoughts and did a lot of deep breathing."

Amy gave him a hug. "Danki, big brother. I'll try to do both throughout the wedding service." She turned toward the hallway as the rest of their family entered the living room.

"You look pretty." Michelle came over and gave Amy a hug. "I'm so glad we could be here to help celebrate your marriage."

Amy smiled. "It wouldn't be the same without all of my family." Her smile faded and tears welled in her eyes. "Oh how I wish Dad, Abe, and Toby could be here. I never expected to be getting married without their presence."

Mom got teary-eyed and so did Sylvia. The three of them gathered in a group hug.

"We need to get control of our emotions," Mom said. "There are a lot of people waiting outside the barn, and they'll soon be seated. Are you ready to head out now, Daughter?"

"Jah." Amy gave a nod.

Mom took Allen and Rachel's hands and led them out the door. They would sit with her during the service. Ezekiel, Michelle, and their two children went next, followed by Henry.

Sylvia came alongside Amy and clasped her hand. "I am honored to be a part of your special day."

"And I'm happy you are one of my witnesses." Amy paused and said a quick, silent prayer. It was hard to believe, but in the next few hours she would become Mrs. Jared Riehl.

Sylvia sat up straight in her chair as she listened to the message being preached on the topic of husbands and wives. She remembered her own wedding with Toby and how excited yet nervous she felt sitting across from her groom as they waited to say

479

their vows. She also recalled how all of her family and friends had been there to offer their blessings and approval. The thought that she might lose her husband in a few years was the furthest thing from Sylvia's mind. As a young bride, she'd been full of hope for the future and felt certain that she and Toby would be together for a long time.

A lump formed in Sylvia's throat. She would never forget what she and Toby had together, but she couldn't bring him back, and she had no regrets about her decision to move on with her life. *Toby would not have wanted me to mourn for him indefinitely. He'd want me and the children to be happy and cared for.*

Sylvia glanced at Dennis sitting in the men's section of the barn. She felt more convinced than ever that he was the right man for her.

As Jared and Amy stood before the bishop to say their vows, Dennis watched Sylvia. He wouldn't say anything today, of course, but he wondered if it was too soon to ask her to marry him. His business had grown throughout the summer months, and he had some money saved up. He would wait until he had the approval of Sylvia's mother, however, before asking Sylvia to become his wife.

*My mamm would be excited if Sylvia and I got married, although probably disappointed because we'll stay here in Strasburg. No doubt she would like me to move back to Dauphin County, but she'll have to accept the fact that I've established a new home here.*

Dennis snapped back to attention when the bride and groom returned to their seats. He'd missed hearing the rest of their verbal commitment to each other. He glanced at Sylvia again, and saw her wiping tears on her cheeks. *Are they tears of joy for her sister, or could Sylvia be thinking about her deceased husband and the years they spent together? Is she ready to commit to me, or am I fooling myself to believe she's truly in love with me?*

His fingers curled into his palms. *I have to know, and it needs to be soon.*

Belinda could hardly control her emotions as Amy and Jared said their vows. She was happy her daughter had found happiness with the man she loved, but she would miss Amy so much when she moved into Herschel's rental with Jared.

*I'm glad Jared doesn't have a problem with Amy working at the greenhouse until she becomes pregnant with their first child.* Belinda patted Rachel's back as the little girl leaned against her chest and slept. *I am concerned, little one, as to what will transpire if your mammi should marry Dennis. Will she move you and your brother back to her old place, or could Dennis decide to pack up and move back to Dauphin County where his family lives? It's hard enough having Ezekiel living in New York. It would really be difficult if Sylvia and the children moved away too.*

*Try not to think about it,* she told herself. *No one but God knows what the future holds.*

Sitting beside her groom at the *Eck,* or the corner table, Amy felt like pinching herself. It was hard to believe she had finally become Jared's wife. What a joyous occasion. Everything had gone just as planned. Now as she and Jared ate a delicious wedding meal with their guests, Amy tried to absorb it all. Since there would be no pictures taken, Amy wanted to instill everything about this wonderful day into her memory so she would never forget it.

"Are you enjoying the meal?" Jared leaned close to Amy, brushing his lips against her ear.

"Oh jah, very much."

"Me too." He looked out at all the people sitting at the long tables beneath the tent.

"Too bad your neighbors couldn't have made it today."

"Which neighbors?"

"Earl and Virginia. Remember the night we met them at Diener's, and I said they would probably get an invitation to the wedding or at least one of the meals afterward? Did you include them?"

Amy blinked. "I'm sure I put them on the invitation list for the second meal. Maybe they were unable to come." *Or maybe, they weren't interested in attending the event.*

Virginia walked out to get her mail, limping all the way. She'd brought the binoculars, but in her hurry, she had forgotten to bring her cane along and now regretted it. As she approached the box, she heard the sounds of laughter and people talking from the Kings' yard. Before getting the mail, Virginia decided to walk up the driveway a bit, curious to see what was going on. Earlier, she'd heard singing and figured it must be part of the wedding service. Now with the laughter and chattering, she felt sure the wedding must be over.

Virginia moved slowly toward the event and pulled the binoculars up to her eyes. She still didn't have a good spot to do any viewing. *I'll walk closer until I can see some-*

483

*thing. It's unfair that I'm reduced to this, slinking about to get a glance at what I should have been able to attend. At the very least, I'd like to have something to tell Stella about.*

Halfway up the driveway she spotted a couple of large white tents set up near the barn. This was an area of their yard she couldn't see from her house. Open flaps on the canvas gave her a clear view of some of the guests, but she couldn't see any sign of the bride and groom. Behind Virginia, she heard someone humming and the sound grew closer. Her first instinct was to hide, so she ducked behind some shrubs and peeked out. Not long after, she saw that odd, gray-haired woman wearing shabby clothes and ambling up the driveway. Virginia watched Maude walk toward the greenhouse. *I wonder what she's up to. Hmm . . . she definitely isn't going to the wedding looking like that.*

In a crouched position, Virginia continued to watch Maude. A few minutes went by, and she saw Mrs. King come out of the tent and hand the old woman a plate full of food. Virginia couldn't believe her eyes as Maude took a seat on a wooden bench and gobbled up the fare.

"Now that certainly takes the cake. They're eating a meal, and now Maude's getting in on it too." Virginia spoke quietly through clenched teeth. *A meal that I should be sitting down eating right now — along with Stella and Earl.*

Virginia smelled the food from where she hid, but her knees were beginning to go numb and might buckle if she didn't stand up soon. *I need to get out of here before someone sees me.*

As Virginia tried to stand, she lost her balance and fell backward into some kind of bush with vines, and her arm got tangled up in it. *Oh great. Now what should I do?*

After a few failed attempts at trying to get up, she was finally on her feet. However, as her left foot came down, it landed in something strange. *Oh boy. What did I just step in?* Virginia looked down at her sandal, enveloped in a pile of fresh dung. *Oh sugar . . . this can't be happening to me. I shouldn't have even bothered coming over here.*

Virginia shook her foot, trying get rid of the stuff, and even tried wiping it in the grass. Worried that someone would see her, she limped toward home. *I've got to either clean this well or throw the sandals away. I can't let Earl know I've been out spying on the neighbors and on their property, no less.*

She looked over her shoulder. No one seemed to have taken notice of her. She made her way to the mailbox and grabbed the contents. Now her hip hurt as well as her bum leg.

Once she was in her own backyard, Virginia placed the mail on the picnic table and grabbed the hose to wash off the mess on her sandal. Most of it came off, but now it looked stained. *I'm gonna have to throw them both out. This really bums me out. Those shoes are my favorite because they're so comfy.* With a groan, Virginia walked over to the garbage can and tossed them in.

Once inside the house, she put the mail on the counter and suddenly realized the binoculars hadn't made it back home with her. She figured she must have dropped them in the weeds when she fell. *When can I go back over there and get them?*

She stepped up to the front window and saw Maude moseying down the driveway like she didn't have a care in the world. No doubt she was quite satisfied after that meal she'd eaten.

*Guess I could try to go back over there and fetch them now, but I'd be taking a chance of that wedding gathering being over soon, and then people getting into their rigs would surely see me.*

Virginia thought about Stella again. She still felt bad having to tell her best friend that they hadn't received an invitation to Amy and Jared's wedding, but she had asked Stella to come visit anyway. "We can sit on the front porch and listen to the festivities," she'd told her friend. But Stella had declined, saying she'd made other plans for this week.

"Other plans my foot," Virginia muttered. "I bet the only reason she backed out of coming is because we wouldn't be going to an Amish wedding."

She kicked at a stone beneath her feet and groaned as a searing pain shot up her leg. "A lot of good it did me to try and be friendly with those Plain people. Think I'm gonna have a cigarette to help me calm down."

# CHAPTER 40

"I wish we didn't have to go back home so soon," Michelle complained to Ezekiel as they put the children to bed that evening. "The wedding was wonderful, and we got to visit with several people, but I didn't get to spend enough time talking to Mary Ruth or Lenore, and I was sort of hoping we could stop by to see Sara, Brad, and the baby since they couldn't make it to the wedding."

"We can stay through tomorrow, but we'll need to head back to Clymer Thursday morning as planned. If there's time tomorrow evening, maybe we can see if our driver would be free to take us over to see the Fullers." Ezekiel patted their son's back before putting him in the portable crib they'd brought on this trip.

Michelle tucked Angela Mary in and bent to kiss the little girl's forehead, and then she and Ezekiel tiptoed out of the room.

Standing in the hall outside the guest room, her voice lowered to a whisper. "Isn't it hard for you to come here for special occasions and then have to leave, knowing it might be several months before we see any of your family again?"

"Jah, but I'm happy living in Clymer." Ezekiel looked at her pointedly. "I thought you were too."

"I am for the most part, but it's always hard to say goodbye to our loved ones here."

"Just think about how the pioneers must have felt when they left their families and homes to travel to lands unknown in the West. Some of them never saw any of their relatives back home again. At least we only live one state away and get to see our family several times a year."

"You've made a good point, and I'll try not to get so emotional when we say goodbye this time." After their last visit, Michelle had shed tears most of the way home.

"Let's go back to the living room and visit with the others for a while before it's time for bed," Ezekiel suggested.

"Okay." Michelle breathed a heavy sigh and started down the hall toward the living room, where the rest of the family had gathered. Amy and Jared had left to spend their first night as a married couple in their rental. They would be back in the morning to help with the clean-up and putting things away that had been set up for the wedding. In a few weeks or so, they planned to take a trip out West by train. Michelle had never been to the West Coast, but hoped someday after Angela Mary and Vernon were older she and Ezekiel could make such a trip. If it was off-season for the greenhouse, perhaps Ezekiel's mother would be willing to watch the children.

"Virginia, what is this?" Earl marched into the living room, where she sat on the couch reading a magazine about birds in the state of Pennsylvania.

She put the magazine down, and when she looked up at him, her eyes widened. "Where'd you get that?"

"Found it in the hall closet, inside a box." He held up a carton of cigarettes. "So you haven't started smoking again, huh?"

"Well, umm . . ." Virginia squirmed on the couch.

"How long has this been going on, and how come you lied about it?"

Earl's stern tone caused Virginia to cringe. She feared he might become violent and hit her. Although he'd never done anything like that in the past, this was something Virginia feared could happen if Earl became angry enough.

"I started smoking again because I'm a nervous wreck, and I didn't admit it to you, because I knew you'd be disappointed in me." Virginia's lips quivered and tears sprang to her eyes as she lowered her head. "Guess I'm nothing but a big failure, and you probably regret having married me."

"Not true, Virginia." Earl came over and sat down beside her. "I am disappointed that you're smoking again, but I don't regret marrying you."

Virginia sniffed and leaned her head on Earl's shoulder. "I don't know what I did to deserve a wonderful man like you." She gestured to the carton of cigarettes. "I'll try really hard to quit smoking, but I can't promise. As long as we're living among the Amish here in Strasburg, my nerves will be on edge." She nodded her head toward the living room window. "Those people over there can't be trusted."

"Are you still fretting about not getting an invite to that wedding?"

"Uh-huh. I can't help it, Earl. It was my ace in the hole to get Stella back here for a visit." Virginia wiped her tears away. "Now I'm stuck here with no friends at all."

He put his arm around her. "Not true,

Wife. I'm here with you, and I thought we were friends."

"We are, Earl, but I need someone I can hang out with when you're not at home." She sniffed. "Even a dog or a cat would be nice."

"Well, if it means that much to you, then we can go looking for a dog at the animal shelter on Saturday."

"How about a cat? That gray-and-white one that rubbed my leg would make a nice pet if it shows up here again."

"I'm sure that cat belongs to someone. What you need is a pet that doesn't already have a home."

"Yeah, maybe." Virginia was pleased that Earl cared enough to get her a pet — especially when he wasn't that fond of cats or dogs. Still a critter couldn't take the place of a human friend — at least not for her.

What continued to weigh heavily on Virginia's mind, though, were the binoculars she'd dropped in the weeds across the street. She needed to fetch them before Earl realized they were missing, so she wouldn't have to explain the whole stupid story of her spying on the Kings. Earl would be ready for his after-supper nap pretty quick. He already had his favorite TV show on, and it wouldn't be long till he was out like a light.

Virginia limped to the kitchen and poured herself some coffee. She had previously cleaned up everything from their meal. Despite the gnawing pain in her leg, she felt determined to sneak back over to the neighbors as soon as possible.

Virginia returned to the living room with the coffee in hand and took a seat again on the couch. Sure enough, like clockwork Earl reclined in his chair, engrossed in his show. *Wild horses couldn't rouse him out of that chair right now.* She covered her mouth to keep from snickering.

Earl glanced in her direction briefly but didn't say anything. He turned his head back to his favorite program, while Virginia waited for his nap to start.

As she looked through her magazine, her mind got to thinking that it was getting later and darker outside. She'd probably need a flashlight in order to see. Virginia hoped no one would catch her shining the beam of light around their driveway. *I just need to be careful, is all, and make sure I'm not seen.*

It didn't seem that long before Earl was slouched in his chair and snoring. He had mentioned during supper that he'd been busier than normal at work today and felt more tired than usual.

Now was Virginia's chance to take care of the task. She grabbed a flashlight, put on an old pair of shoes, and crept out the back door. It was dark, and she needed both hands to carry things, so again, she left her cane behind. *I'll get those binoculars quickly and will be back in no time.*

Virginia paused to wait for a passing car, then headed across the road. She shined a beam of light in front of her, and halfway up the Kings' driveway, she headed for the side she'd last had the field glasses.

"Okay, it was about here that I was crouched," Virginia whispered as she kept the light pointed directly at the ground. "Ah, that must be it." She caught sight of something shiny on the ground, but it turned out to be an aluminum can, so she gave it a kick. *Ouch! That was dumb.*

As Virginia kept searching, her leg started hurting again. *Come on — where are those binoculars? I'm pretty sure this is where I was before.* She continued to search, but was interrupted when a couple of horse and buggies pulled in. Virginia ducked behind a tree and waited until they passed.

*What's the deal? Are they having more people coming to this event? Oh, yeah, I bet it's the second meal Jared and Amy had told us about.*

Others followed in both cars and Amish rigs. Her nerves were about shot from hiding and waiting for the guests to quit flowing in. *Why did I decide to do this? If Earl wakes up and I'm not there, he'll come looking for me.*

When the coast was clear, Virginia did more hunting. After a few minutes, she bumped something hard with the toe of her shoe. At last she'd found the binoculars, so she leaned down and grabbed them up. Now the goal was to head back home quickly, but her leg throbbed even worse, making walking more difficult.

Virginia was almost to the mouth of the driveway, when another buggy came down the road. She moved into the shadows, out of sight, but managed to slip and fall. Her knee took the brunt of it, and when the rig went past, she clambered to her feet and, despite the pain, made a beeline straight for her house and in through the back door.

Breathing a sigh of relief, she put away the flashlight and carried the binoculars into the living room.

Earl sat up in his chair and looked at her. "What are you up to, woman?"

"What do you mean?" Virginia's heart pounded so hard she worried Earl might hear it from across the room.

"You're holding those field glasses. Are you spying on someone again?"

"I could be." She sat down on the couch.

He pointed at her knee. "What's that on your pant leg? It looks like dirt and grass stains."

"Um, well . . . maybe." She tried to brush it away.

"You red-headed spy. Were you outside in the dark, trying to see what our neighbors are doing?" He shook his head. "Woman, we need to find you a better hobby."

"I was bored, Earl, that's all."

"That is an understatement." He sat back and grabbed the TV remote.

Virginia was glad her husband didn't know any of the details about what had really happened. She still couldn't help feeling cheated by those Amish people. How could they have forgotten to send her an invite?

She crossed her arms and frowned. *I can't help being mad over the whole thing. I wish we lived somewhere else right now.*

Sylvia tried to relax and enjoy the evening, but she was tired from the long day and felt a headache coming on. She'd put Allen and Rachel to bed half an hour ago and wished she could join them, but didn't want to be impolite. After all, it wasn't every day they got to visit with Ezekiel and Michelle. Since they would be returning home the day after tomorrow, she wanted to spend as much time with them as possible.

"Would anyone like more cake or coffee?" she asked.

Mom yawned as she shook her head. "I'm too full and tired to eat anything more. How about the rest of you?"

"No thank you. I'm full too," Michelle said.

"Same here." Ezekiel looked at Henry. "I bet you've got room for some more cake. Am I right, *bissel* bruder?"

Henry blew out his breath in a noisy huff. "I ain't your little brother. I'm almost a man, and I work full time in the greenhouse and other places around here, so in my book, that makes me a man."

Mom lifted her hand toward Henry from across the room, where she sat in her rocker. "You're right, Son. You do the work of a man, and it's much appreciated."

Henry shrugged in response, then got up out of his chair. "Think I'll go on up to my room." He hurried off before anyone could say goodnight.

Sylvia felt sorry for her brother. He had a

lot on his young shoulders and had been cheated out of being able to fully enjoy his teenage years. She was thankful Dennis had come into their lives, because he'd filled a void in both her and Henry's lives.

She leaned back in her chair and closed her eyes, remembering how handsome Dennis had looked today. She'd invited him to stay awhile after everyone else went home, but he said he'd better go and tend to his dog and the horses. Dennis did promise to return in the morning to help clean up and put everything back together.

Her lips formed a smile. *What a kind and thoughtful person he is.*

"What are you grinning about, Sylvia?"

Her eyes snapped open at the sound of Ezekiel's question. "Oh, nothing much — just reflecting on what a nice day we all had." She wasn't about to admit that her focus had mostly been on Dennis. Quite likely her brother would start in with some teasing, which Sylvia didn't feel like dealing with right now.

"It was a good day, wasn't it?" Mom spoke up.

Michelle bobbed her head. "Yes, it was great. Amy and Jared make such a nice couple. Their faces glowed with the happiness they shared on their wedding day." She looked over at Ezekiel and smiled. "And I know exactly how it feels."

He grinned back at her. "Same here, Fraa. Being married to you has made me so happy."

"Michelle, you have been a welcome addition to our family," Mom said. "We all love and appreciate you."

Patches of pink erupted on Michelle's pretty face. "Danki, Belinda. I love and appreciate all of you too."

Sylvia's thoughts turned to Dennis. *Why can't Mom be as accepting toward him as she is with Michelle? Of course,* Sylvia reasoned, *it wasn't always that way. In the beginning of Ezekiel and Michelle's relationship, Mom made no bones about how absolutely she opposed their courtship. My sister-in-law had to prove herself before Mom would let her in. Hopefully Dennis will eventually do or say something that will cause my mamm to see him in a positive light.*

Around midnight, after Belinda and the others finally retired for the night, she lay in bed, unable to sleep. Too much excitement from the day might be part of the reason, but mostly Belinda couldn't turn off the thoughts swirling through her head concerning her family and the situations each of them was in. Her oldest son seemed content living in Clymer, New York, while she sensed his wife would rather they still lived in Strasburg. But Michelle had agreed to be content living away from the friends she'd made here and seemed supportive of her husband and his business aspirations.

Amy was now a married woman and would settle into a routine as Jared's wife. No doubt children would come in the next few years.

Henry still struggled with the turmoil of losing his father and brother. Even when he smiled and things seemed to be going along okay, Belinda sensed a battle raging inside her son.

Then there was Sylvia, who had made progress in accepting her husband's death, and now appeared to be looking to the future with another man.

Belinda reached back and clutched the edges of her pillow. *I just wish things weren't moving so fast between Sylvia and Dennis. I still don't think she knows enough about him to make a permanent commitment, and I hope Dennis doesn't push her into a marriage she's not ready for.*

A fiery orange shone through Belinda's bedroom window, putting an end to her musings. *Could the sun be coming up al-*

*ready? Could I have fallen asleep and not re-alized it?*

She pushed her covers aside and crawled out of bed, then padded over to the window and lifted the shade. She froze, rooted to the spot, before she let out an ear-piecing scream and ran from the room. "Fire! Our barn is ablaze!"

ready? Could I have fallen asleep and not realized?

She peeped her covers aside and crawled
out of bed, then padded over to the window.
As she lifted the shade. She froze, rooted to
the spot, before she let out an ear-piercing
scream and ... "Oh, no ... Fire! Our
barn is on fire!"

# CHAPTER 41

Belinda stood with tears rolling down her
cheeks, staring at what was left of their barn.
She still couldn't believe it was gone. *Oh
Vernon, you sure liked that old building, and
so did I.*

She plucked a tissue from her sweater
sleeve. In the light of day it looked worse
than it had in the blackness of night.

After she'd seen the fire and called out to
her family, they'd all rushed outside, and
Henry dashed to the phone shed to call for
help. In the meantime, Belinda, along with
Ezekiel, Michelle, and Sylvia made every effort to put out the fire with the hose and
buckets of water. By the time the fire trucks
arrived, nearly half the barn was gone.
Ezekiel and Henry had managed to get the
horses out in time, and Henry's dog, as well
as the barn cats had all escaped danger.

Belinda had left a message on Amy and
Jared's voice mail, but she couldn't be sure

when they might check it and learn the sad news. *Maybe they won't know until they get here.* Belinda gripped her face on both sides. *Oh my . . . what a shock it will be.*

Sylvia stepped up to Belinda and reached for her hand. "How could this have happened, Mom? Was the fire set on purpose, or could a gas lamp have gotten knocked over?"

Belinda shook her head. "The only evidence the firemen found was an empty pack of cigarettes outside the barn."

"Who do you know that smokes and might have been in our barn? Could it have been someone who attended the wedding yesterday?" Michelle asked. She'd been in and out of the house several times, checking on the baby, who lay sleeping in the living room in his playpen. The other children played outside by the house, where it was safe, while the adults stood around the site of the damage.

"I know of nobody specifically," Belinda responded, "but I suppose the empty package could have been from one of our guests." She crossed her arms as she looked at her youngest son, who appeared to be fidgeting. *What's going on with my boy?* Henry wasn't looking at her much, which seemed odd to her.

"Seth smokes," Henry finally spoke up.

"What was that, Son?" Belinda blinked.

"I said, 'Seth smokes.' Of course he wasn't at the wedding." His brows furrowed. "Seth has been in the barn before, and maybe he came here late last night after everyone else had gone home."

"Why would he show up that late and drop a pack of cigarettes outside the barn?" Ezekiel looked at Henry.

"He's mad at me right now."

"Oh? How come?" Ezekiel tilted his head.

Henry explained Seth's reasons, and Belinda quickly spoke up. "I don't believe Henry's friend would deliberately set our barn on fire. It was probably some kind of an accident that started the blaze." Belinda turned her head as Jared's horse and buggy entered the yard. He brought it to a halt at the hitching rail, then both he and Amy jumped out of the carriage.

"What in the world?" Amy's ashen face reflected her shock. "Did this fire happen during the night?" She pointed to what was left of the barn.

Belinda nodded. "We discovered it shortly after midnight."

"I wish you had notified us," Jared interjected. "We would have come over right away."

"I left a message on your voice mail but not until the fire had been put out," Belinda explained.

Jared pulled his fingers through the back of his hair. "Amy and I slept longer than we expected, and I forgot to check for messages before coming here."

Amy's cheeks colored a bit as she nodded. "Yesterday was a long, busy day, and we were pretty tired."

"And it turned out to be a long night." Ezekiel gazed down with his hands clasped behind his back.

"I hope this was not another act of —"

Belinda looked at Amy and put a finger to her lips. No way did she want Ezekiel or Michelle to know about any of the damage that had been done on the property.

"We'll need to have a work party to clean this mess up." Jared gestured to the debris. "And also build a new barn."

"We'll stay long enough to help clean things up and also come back to help with the reconstruction."

"There's no need for that," Belinda was quick to say. "I'm sure we'll have more than enough help when it's time to have a barn raising."

"Maybe so, but I wouldn't feel right about not being here for that, so I'll try to make sure it will happen." Ezekiel gave Belinda a hug. "You know, Mom, I'm still willing to move back here if you want me to."

She shook her head determinedly. "Not a chance! I won't ask you give up the life you have created for your family there in New York. Is that understood?"

He bobbed his head.

Belinda drew in a sharp breath. She hoped no one else would bring up any of the things that had previously been done to their property.

When Dennis showed up a short time later, Sylvia felt like running to him and throwing herself into his arms to release her pent-up emotions. But she held herself in check when he joined them in front of the devastation and stared with incredulity.

Sylvia noticed her mother's quick look of disapproval toward Dennis. Did she think he shouldn't have come to help out?

"What happened here?" He looked at Sylvia and placed his hand on her arm. "I came this morning to help clean up after the wedding but never expected to see something like this."

Sylvia didn't trust her voice to respond to his question, but she was saved from having to answer when Mom spoke up. "During

506

the night, someone or something started the fire in the barn."

"Oh my!" His mouth opened slightly.

"We did our best to put the fire out," Ezekiel interjected, "but on our own we couldn't do much until the fire trucks arrived. Even then, they couldn't save much of the barn."

"I'm so sorry." Dennis's words were spoken in a kind, soothing tone.

Sylvia felt better with him being there, and it gave her heart pleasure, despite the charred remains that lay in front of them.

"We'll be having a clean-up frolic and later a new barn will be raised," Jared said. "I'll get the fellows who work for me to help put on the new roof when the structure's ready."

"I will help in any way I can." Dennis slipped his arm around Sylvia's waist. "Are you okay? Was anyone hurt?"

"I'm fine, and so is everyone else. Thank the Lord for that."

"Yes, indeed."

Sylvia felt comforted by Dennis's presence, and his arm around her waist made her feel protected and loved. *I'm certain that he loves me,* she thought. *I love him too. I hope as Mom sees how much Dennis cares about all of us that she'll change her mind about him.*

Sylvia looked up when that crazy mocking-bird began to carry on. "Go away, you silly bird." Once again, she thought it seemed as if the feathered fowl had been mocking them.

Virginia stood at the living room window with her binoculars. She tried to see, but it was hard with the amount of trees and bushes covering part of their neighbors' property. She looked up their driveway intently. *Sure wish I could see into their yard better. I know where there's a good place to see things, but I'd have to go back to the spot where I was yesterday.*

"Are ya lookin' at the devastation caused from the fire across the road?"

She whirled around. "Earl Martin, do not sneak up on me like that."

"I wasn't sneaking. Just wandered into the room to get my empty mug from last night. And big surprise, I found you here snooping again."

"I wasn't snooping. Just wanted to get a better look at what we couldn't see last night when those blaring sirens woke us out of a sound sleep."

"I'm not sure how sound it was. You were rolling around in that bed like a mouse was crawling up your leg." Earl took the binocu-

508

lars from her and set them on the end table by the couch. "If you can tear yourself away from the window long enough, I'd appreciate some breakfast before I leave for work."

Virginia's toes curled inside her slippers. "No problem, Earl. I'll get your breakfast going right now."

Once in the kitchen, she heated up the skillet. "Are you fine with some hash browns and eggs?" she called.

"Yeah, that sounds good. Do we have any ketchup for the potatoes?"

Virginia opened the refrigerator and grabbed the bottle, along with a carton of eggs. "Yep, there's plenty of ketchup," she hollered back.

"Good deal!"

While Earl showered and got dressed for work, Virginia made their breakfast and had it warming in the oven. She then returned to the living room with a hot cup of coffee, to which she'd added her fancy creamer.

As she waited for her husband to come down the hall, her thoughts took her down a negative path. *If we'd only gotten an invite to that wedding, Stella would be here with me. She and I would be doing something fun today, like going out to lunch and shopping for clothes.*

When Virginia heard Earl coming, she

headed back to the kitchen and pulled the food from the oven.

"Breakfast smells good, and I can't wait to eat." Earl poured some coffee and took a seat at the table.

She set the skillet and the small casserole dish on potholders. "We'd better get started while the food is hot."

"I'm ready to eat. I'll go ahead and dish up."

Virginia waited for him before helping herself. "Guess I'll do some bird-watching today."

Earl chuckled. "I'm sure you will, except I should remind you that birds don't wear bonnets or straw hats. If you really want to know what happened, go on over there and ask. I'd go myself if I didn't have to head for work in a few minutes."

"Very funny. You don't have to believe me, but I'm gonna look for birds today." Virginia spooned some eggs and hash browns on her plate.

As Earl ate his food, Virginia nibbled on the hash browns and stared out the window. After her husband left, she'd be bored and lonely. It was too bad they had a fire last night, but she couldn't help feeling jilted by those Amish folks.

*Maybe they think they're better than me.*

She grimaced. *I can't believe I fell for Jared's promise of an invite to their wedding when we met at Diener's.*

"What's got your smile turned upside-down? You're not still upset about not going to that wedding, are you?"

"Of course I am. Everything would've been perfect if we'd received an invitation and gone across the street for Jared and Amy's big day. Stella would have loved it. That much I know." Virginia took a drink of coffee.

"They have a teenage boy over there, you know. I'm sure there'll be a wedding for him sometime in the future. Maybe we'll get invited to that." Earl stood and carried his dishes to the sink.

Virginia wasn't impressed with that bit of news. Mrs. King's son might wait years to get hitched, and there was no guarantee that they'd get an invitation to his wedding either.

*I should feel bad about those people's barn burning, but they don't care a hoot about me, so why should I care about them?*

Amy and Jared walked together around the rubble. Her heart sank while looking at the remains of the old barn that once stood large and tall on her parents' property.

511

Some recognizable things lay among the blackened remains, but none of it looked usable. Amy felt the burden of it all. If she'd been here at the house last night, she could have helped out.

"I'm sorry about what happened to your family's barn," Jared said.

"So am I, but I can't help feeling bad that I wasn't here instead of —"

"Instead of where? Being with me at our new place?" Jared's tone had an edge to it.

"Oh, come on now, Jared. That's not what I meant."

"It sounded like it to me." He took off his hat and fanned his face with the brim. "Do you really think you could've done something to prevent this from happening or made it better somehow?"

"I could have tried to do something." Amy's hand went to her hip.

He frowned. "It still would have turned out like this."

They stood silently for a few moments. The sunshine felt nice as it shone down upon them. Amy's family had headed off in the direction of the large tents that needed to be dismantled and ready to be returned to the place where they'd rented them.

Amy's arm fell to her side as she turned to face Jared. "I just feel bad for not being here to help out is all — not because I was with you." She looked up at him. "I love you, Jared."

"I love you too." He grinned and let out a chuckle.

"What's so funny?"

"I do believe we've just had our first tiff."

Amy smiled and laughed too. "Jah, I guess we did."

"We'd better go help the others now, don't you agree?"

"Most certainly." Amy walked alongside Jared. *I'm sure there will be more misunderstandings in our marriage, but we'll talk them through, just like we did now. How thankful I am for such a loving husband. I surely hope my sister finds that kind of happiness with the man she loves.*

# CHAPTER 42

Holding her binoculars in front of her face, Virginia stood poised at the living room window. She shook her head in disgust as the steady *clippity-clop, clippity-clop* pounded the pavement in front of her house. Every single one of those horses and buggies turned up the Kings' driveway. Earl had said he'd talked to Belinda's teenage son yesterday and learned they'd be having a new barn built today. He'd also stated that many from their community would be at the event, so the constant flow of buggy traffic was no surprise. That didn't make it any easier to deal with.

Virginia's nerves were on edge, and she couldn't wait for Earl to leave for work so she could light up a cigarette. Although she'd promised to give up smoking, Virginia couldn't seem to help herself. Her habit was a strong crutch, and she wasn't sure she could quit. Her life now was easy compared to how it used to be during her first marriage, but since coming to Amish country, she'd been uptight most of the time. Earl had told her once that her aversion to living here made no sense, yet his statement had done nothing to change the way Virginia felt. If she'd known what it would be like before moving here, she never would have agreed to leave Chicago. At least there, she had Stella to talk to. Now all she had was Goldie, the fluffy orange cat she'd brought home from the animal shelter a week ago.

Virginia continued to watch the activity across the road. *I would love to see what's happening even better over there. It's too bad the fire didn't burn some of those trees down, so I could see into their whole yard.*

"Ah-hem." Earl cleared his throat. "Since I don't detect any pleasant aromas coming from the kitchen, I can only assume that breakfast has not been started."

She lowered the binoculars and turned to face him. "It's still early. Figured I had plenty of time to start breakfast."

"Well, you don't. I told you last night that the boss called a special meeting at work this morning, and I need to go soon."

"Sorry. I must've forgot. I'll get something going now. Maybe I've got enough pancake mix to make some flapjacks."

He shook his head. "Don't bother. I'll pick up a doughnut and coffee on the way to Lancaster." Earl gestured toward the window. "I hope you can find something meaningful to do with your time and don't spend the whole day staring out the front window. Gazing through those field glasses is not going to change the fact that our neighbors are Amish and they still live across the road."

She scrunched up her face. "That's not funny, Earl."

"It may not be funny, but it's a fact." He stepped up to Virginia and kissed her cheek. "Have a nice day, dear, and don't forget to feed the cat."

"Yeah, you have a good day too." She reached down and petted Goldie's head. *Well, at least I'm not alone anymore.*

As soon as Virginia heard the back door open and shut, she picked up the binoculars and resumed her snooping. *If I keep watching long enough, I might see something that will pique my interest.*

Belinda stood on the front porch of her home, watching and listening to the work going on in the yard. The soon-to-be structure was currently just a concrete-block foundation, but it wouldn't be long before a new barn stood tall. Men had gathered into small groups, and after a few minutes, those who'd come to work broke up and everybody found a job to do. Soon, the air was filled with the pounding of hammers, along with the hum of saws cutting wood.

Belinda was awed by the large number of people from their community who had come to help out. Monroe Esh was among them. Herschel Fisher came even though he was from outside their church district. Jared arrived with his crew of roofers. Dennis was also among the men who were already working up a sweat. Belinda noticed that he would glance back at the house from time to time — no doubt hoping to catch a glimpse of Sylvia. Both of Belinda's daughters would be inside most of the day, getting a noon meal ready for the workers. Other women from their community had also come here today to help cook and serve the men.

Belinda looked toward the road and heaved a sigh. Too bad Ezekiel couldn't be here. Michelle had come down with a nasty flu bug, and even though one of his wife's friends had offered to help out, he didn't want to leave her when she wasn't feeling well. Belinda had assured her son that they would have plenty of help today and reminded him that his place was with his family. He'd sounded relieved when she'd assured him that she'd let him know how things went once the new barn was done.

"Sure is a good turnout today, jah?" Jared grinned at Dennis as they worked alongside each other.

Dennis nodded. *Sylvia's mamm is still giving me the cold shoulder, though. I said, "Hello, Mrs. King" to her this morning, and she barely responded to my greeting.* He let out a huff. *Sure wish I knew how to break the ice with her so we could become friends. Even with Sylvia's reassurances that eventually her mother will come to like me, I have my doubts.*

"You've been awfully quiet this morning. Is everything okay?"

"Let's just say they're not the way I'd like them to be." Dennis's breaths came faster as he continued to hammer.

"Hey, slow down. There's no need to rush." Jared put his hand on Dennis's shoulder. "If there's something bothering you, it might help if you get it off your chest."

Dennis glanced at the men working nearby. "I'd rather not talk about it right now."

"Then let's take a break. We've been working hard, and sitting for a few minutes with some cold water to drink will help." Jared pointed to the table that had been set up in the yard with cups and glasses for water and coffee.

"Okay, sure." Dennis set his tools aside and joined Jared at the table. After they'd poured water into their paper cups, they walked around to the side of the house and took a seat on a wooden bench.

"So what's on your mind?" Jared asked.

Dennis swiped a hand across his sweaty forehead. "I think it would be better if I wasn't courting Sylvia anymore."

Jared's eyes widened. "How come?"

"Her mudder doesn't like me, and I don't want to come between Belinda and Sylvia." Dennis paused and took a drink. "And then there's my mamm. She keeps saying that she wants me to get married, but I need to make sure Sylvia's the right woman and that I shouldn't rush into things."

"What are you going to do?"

Dennis shrugged. "I don't know. My head tells me the right thing to do is break things off with Sylvia, and . . ." His voice trailed off. There was no point in talking about this, because he couldn't make Belinda like him, no matter how hard he tried. He gulped down the last of his water and stood. "Guess we need to get back to work."

Jared nodded. "If you need to talk about this again, I'll listen and offer my advice if needed. I'll also be praying for your situation. I'm sure this can't be easy, but take heart — the Lord can work out problems, no matter how big they seem."

"Danki." Dennis tossed his paper cup in the trash and hurried back to the construction site. Putting his tool pouch back on, he looked around at the other busy men. *I shouldn't have opened my big mouth and spilled some of my personal business to Jared. And then he goes and brings up the Lord. I've felt sometimes like the heavenly Father has forgotten about me since I've refused to forgive my uncle for accidently shooting my daed. Thought all I needed was a happy life with the woman I love. I'm beginning to realize I can never find true happiness until I've learned to forgive.* He closed his eyes briefly. *Lord, please help me to do that and give me a sense of peace. I'm sorry for holding a grudge against Uncle Ben. Please forgive me for that. I'll give my uncle a call as soon as I can and make things right with him.*

Sylvia's hand felt tired from cutting so many sliced cucumbers, carrots, and celery sticks to go with the ranch dip one of the ladies had brought this morning. Hearing voices outside the house, she dried her hands and stepped up near the open doorway, where she caught sight of Jared and Dennis engaged in conversation.

Her ears perked up when she heard her name mentioned and listened to what else was said. Sylvia stood frozen, with her hands clenched at her sides. She had lost interest in going outside to see if more water and coffee was needed. Dennis was going to break up with her, and there was nothing she could do about it.

*It's Mom's fault,* she fumed inwardly. *If she'd only accept the fact that I'm in love with Dennis and welcomed him as she did Jared, he would not be having second thoughts about us.*

The more Sylvia thought about it, the more frustrated she became. *I need to talk to Mom about this when there's no one else around and make her see how miserable I'd be if Dennis broke things off with me. She wouldn't have liked it if her mother had tried to come between her and Dad when they were courting. Surely she must remember what it was like to fall in love and look forward to a promise of marriage. As much as she loved Dad, she couldn't have forgotten it by now.*

Fighting tears that threatened to spill over, Sylvia turned and went to the living room to check on Allen and Rachel. She found Allen playing with some toys by himself.

"Where's your sister?" Sylvia asked in Pennsylvania Dutch.

Allen shook his head. "Don't know."

Thinking her daughter may have gone to her room, Sylvia headed up the stairs. The door to Rachel's bedroom was open, and when Sylvia walked in, she found the room empty. *That's strange. I wonder where the little rascal could be.*

Sylvia went quickly to each room on the upper level and checked all of them thoroughly, calling her daughter's name. At the end of her search on the second floor, it was apparent that her daughter wasn't there.

She went back downstairs and searched every room in the house, calling Rachel's name. When she entered the kitchen and asked her mother if she'd seen Rachel, Mom shook her head. "I thought she was playing with Allen in the other room."

"No, she's not, and I can't find her anywhere in the house."

"We'd better check outside." Mom dried her hands on a towel, told the other women she'd be back soon, and followed Sylvia out the back door.

They both ran around the yard calling Rachel's name. It was hard to hear if she'd answered them or not, because of the amount of noise coming from the workers. They also checked the greenhouse to see if she might have found an open door and gone inside. But there was no sign of the little girl there either.

"I'm really worried." Sylvia clutched the hem of her apron. "What if we can't find her? What if she left the yard and is walking down the road somewhere all alone?"

Mom caught hold of Sylvia's hand. "Let's go up to the worksite and see if any of the men have seen Rachel."

"Jah. That's what we should do all right."

When they approached the new barn that was taking shape, Sylvia asked every person she met if they'd seen her daughter.

One of the English men, whom Sylvia didn't recognize, said he'd seen a young girl who fit Rachel's description talking with a ragged-looking English woman.

"Where are they now?" Sylvia questioned.

The man shrugged, then pointed toward the driveway entrance. "They walked out of the yard about an hour ago. The woman she was with had gray hair, walked stooped over, and wore tattered-looking, baggy clothes."

"Why, that sounds like Maude." Mom's brows drew together. "Oh my! Do you think she kidnapped Rachel?"

Sylvia covered her mouth, trying to gain control of her swirling emotions. *No, no, no . . . this can't be happening! That woman has taken other things from our yard. Could she possibly have stolen my precious little girl?*

# CHAPTER 43

"What's going on?" Amy asked, rushing up to Sylvia and their mother. "I heard you calling for Rachel."

Sylvia's voice cracked. "She's missing, and a man over there said he saw her heading out of the yard with Maude." She shivered. "At least we think it was her. I'm so afraid for my daughter. I just want her back in my arms."

Sylvia's mother stepped right over and put an arm around her. "It'll be okay. We'll get her back. You'll see."

Amy's mouth opened wide. "Oh dear. Do you think Maude may have taken Rachel to that old shack she lives in?"

"I don't know, but I aim to find out. I'm going there right now."

"Someone should go with you," Mom put in.

"I'll go."

Sylvia turned and saw Dennis and Jared

walking toward them at a fast pace.

"Amy and I can go one way down the road, while you and Dennis go the other way."

"Maybe we should call the sheriff." Mom's chin quivered as she released her embrace of Sylvia.

Sylvia shook her head firmly. "Not until we see if we can find her first."

"Sylvia's right." Dennis looked at Mom and spoke softly. "Give us an hour, and if we aren't back with Rachel by then, I'll call the sheriff myself." He reached into his pocket and pulled out his cell phone.

Mom nodded. "I'll be praying."

"Same here." Sylvia prayed silently, *Lord, please let my little girl be safe. Allow us to bring Rachel safely home, and forgive me for the lack of faith I've had in You. I trust You, Lord, and I believe You will take care of my daughter.*

Dennis and Sylvia hurried out of the yard and turned right at the end of the driveway, while Jared and Amy went left. About halfway to Maude's place, Sylvia paused to catch her breath.

"I don't know what I'd do if something happened to my precious little girl. Rachel and Allen mean the world to me, and I can't imagine my life without either of them."

"We'll find her." Dennis's tone was reassuring. "I promise, we won't return without Rachel."

Sylvia didn't see how he could be so sure, but she'd prayed for her daughter's safety and needed to trust God to answer that prayer.

They started walking fast again, and a short time later, Sylvia spotted a rundown shack, not much bigger than some people's chicken coops. "There it is." She pointed with an unsteady hand at the dilapidated shanty. "That's where Maude lives."

Dennis's forehead wrinkled as he squinted at the wooden hovel. "Seriously?"

She nodded as her pace kept up with his until they reached the border of Maude's overgrown yard. Dennis led the way on a worn path. Sylvia didn't like the eerie feeling this place gave her. It was so neglected, and it didn't seem possible that anyone could actually live here.

"How does she survive the winters in there?"

"I believe Maude goes someplace else during the colder months. We've never seen her during the wintertime."

They approached the small building cautiously, and Sylvia reached out with a trembling hand to knock on the door. When no one answered, Dennis pushed the squeaky door open. There sat Maude and Rachel at a small table with wobbly legs, eating cookies.

In addition to the table and two folding chairs, the sparsely-furnished cabin had only an old cot with a faded, torn quilt; an antiquated woodstove; a dry-sink; and two unpainted boards used for shelving. A beat-up looking suitcase sat at the foot of the cot. Sylvia also noticed a pile of things on the floor that Maude had no doubt stolen from people in their neighborhood, including a watering can like the one that went missing last year outside the greenhouse.

Before Sylvia had a chance to say anything, Dennis bent down and lifted Rachel from the chair. She looked up at him with wide eyes, called him, *"Daadi,"* and then turned her head in Sylvia's direction. *"Kichlin* is gut."

"Jah, I'm sure the cookies are good, but it's time for us to go home." Sylvia glanced in Maude's direction. "It's wrong to take things or people that don't belong to you, Maude. We were worried about my little girl." Sylvia spoke quietly, in a gentle tone. She wasn't sure what Maude might be capable of doing and didn't want to rile the woman.

Maude mumbled something Sylvia didn't understand, and then the old woman spoke again, more clearly. "Rachel's a pretty girl. We were havin' a tea party but without the tea."

Sylvia tried to hold it together as she talked more with Maude, and a feeling of compassion filled her soul. "From now on if you want to spend time with Rachel, you will need to ask me first. Maybe sometime we can all have a tea party with cookies at the picnic table in my mother's yard. Would you like that, Maude?"

The elderly woman nodded her head and bid them goodbye.

As Sylvia and Dennis walked back to the house, with Rachel clinging to Dennis's neck, Sylvia blurted out a question that was heavy on her mind. "I heard you talking earlier with Jared. Are you planning to break things off with me?"

He stopped walking and turned to face her. "I have been thinking about it because your mamm doesn't approve of me. But I don't think we should talk about this right now, do you?" He reached up and touched Rachel's arm, still held firmly around his neck.

"You're right. I don't know what I was thinking. I need to take my daughter home and get her cleaned up. Her face and hands are smeared with chocolate from the iced cookies she and Maude were eating." Sylvia wondered if the cookies had been stolen from someone's home or perhaps a store in Strasburg. She kept that thought to herself, however. Sylvia had already said too much in front of her young daughter. Even though Rachel was still quite young, there was no telling how much she understood — especially when they spoke in Pennsylvania Dutch, as they had since leaving Maude's shack.

When they arrived home, Sylvia's mother ran out to greet them. "Ach, I'm so relieved that you found her. Where was our precious Rachel?"

"She was with Maude in her little shack, but I'll explain later. I don't think Rachel was frightened by her, but she clung tightly to Dennis the whole way home. Even called him Daadi when we found her."

Mom reached out and stroked Rachel's back. "I'm so glad to see that she's okay." She looked at Dennis with a sincere expression. "Danki for helping Sylvia find her daughter."

"You're welcome. When I heard that she

was missing, all I could think about was getting her back. Rachel is a special child, and I love her and Allen as if they were my own."

Amy came out of the house and clapped her hands when she saw Rachel. "I'm so glad you found her. Jared and I looked and called, and when we saw no sign of her, we came back here to wait for you, hoping you'd had success." She hugged Sylvia. "Where did you find her?"

"In Maude's shanty."

Amy blinked rapidly. "What was she doing there?"

Sylvia explained the details, including what she'd said to Maude before they came home.

"We're going to have to watch that woman more closely," Mom said. "Stealing cookies and produce from our garden is one thing, but taking a child is another matter — one that could have involved the sheriff."

"We could still call him," Amy asserted. "It's possible that Maude's the one responsible for the vandalism here and maybe even the fire. I personally think she should be investigated."

"No way! We are not going to involve the sheriff in that matter." Mom shook her head vigorously.

Sylvia put her finger to her lips. "Can we

talk about this later? Rachel needs to get cleaned up and fed a nourishing lunch." She looked at Dennis. "Maybe when I come back out, we can finish our talk."

"I can take her inside and see to her needs," Amy offered.

"Okay, thank you."

When Amy reached for Rachel, the child went willingly into her arms. Sylvia watched with gratitude as her sister carried Rachel into the house. She closed her eyes briefly. *Thank You, Lord, for helping me and Dennis find my daughter, and Thank You for my kind, loving family.*

"It won't be long before we'll need to feed our helpers who are working so hard on the new barn. I should get back to my kitchen duties and helping the other women soon," Mom said. "But before I go, there's something I'd like to say to Dennis." She looked directly at him. "I am sorry for being so cold to you all these months. I . . . I didn't think you were the right man for Sylvia, but I can see now that I was wrong." She paused and swiped at the tears trickling down her flushed cheeks. "My daughter loves you, and I can see that her daughter does too. I give you my full blessing to court Sylvia, and if the two of you decide someday to get married, you'll have my blessing for that too."

Dennis's face broke into a wide smile. "Thank you, Belinda. What you have said means a lot to me." He looked at Sylvia's shining eyes, then back at her mother. "I love your daughter very much, and if she'll have me, after an appropriate time and once I'm sure I can support her and the children, I will make a formal proposal of marriage."

"And my answer will be yes." Sylvia smiled as she reached for Dennis's hand, not caring in the least who might be witnessing her act of love.

A bird twittered from a nearby tree branch, and Sylvia looked up and smiled. *Go ahead, little mockingbird, sing your song.* She no longer felt as if the bird mocked her. Instead, Sylvia simply enjoyed the bird's melodic song as she and Dennis held hands. She didn't know what might lie ahead, but if they held tight to their faith and trusted in God, she felt confident that He would see them through anything they had to face in the days ahead.

Sylvia thought of Psalm 30:5, the Bible verse she'd read last night: "Weeping may endure for a night, but joy cometh in the morning." *Thank You, Lord, for restoring my faith and filling my heart with joy again.*

# RECIPE FOR SYLVIA'S CHERRY MELT-AWAY BARS

Ingredients:
2 cups flour
2 eggs, separated
1 1/2 cups sugar, divided
1 cup margarine or butter
2 (21 ounce) cans or 1 quart cherry pie filling
Dash of cream of tartar
1 teaspoon vanilla
1/2 cup chopped walnuts

Preheat oven to 350 degrees. Cream together flour, egg yolks, 1 cup sugar, and margarine. Press into 9x13-inch pan. Spread pie filling on crust. Beat egg whites with cream of tartar until very stiff. Gradually beat in ½ cup sugar and vanilla. Spread over pie filling. Sprinkle with nuts. Bake for 30 to 35 minutes. Cut into bars once sufficiently cooled.

# DISCUSSION QUESTIONS

1. Sylvia became afraid to drive a horse and buggy after the accident that killed her husband, father, and brother. She also didn't go out or socialize much during the first year after their deaths. Do you think that was a normal reaction? Would you react in a similar way and not drive again because of an accident that happened to a family member or close friend?

2. Sylvia and her younger brother, Henry, were angry at God for the accident, and even after a year, it had affected their faith. Why were their reactions so different from their mother's and other siblings? Some went to God for comfort, while others turned their backs on Him. Which would you do?

3. Sylvia rented her house to Dennis Weaver, a man she didn't know and who gave her

no references. Do you think that was wise? Would you rent your home to a total stranger?

4. Belinda started trying to control her children's lives — especially Sylvia's. Why do you think she did this?

5. The Kings' neighbor, Virginia, didn't want to connect with the Amish family. She thought they were strange and that she had nothing in common with them. Have you ever felt reluctant to reach out to someone who is different from you? What were your reasons?

6. Belinda couldn't seem to say anything nice about Dennis. Why do you think she was negative toward him? Could she have been jealous of Sylvia or simply overly protective? Should she have been happy that her daughter found a new friend and was getting out of the house more?

7. Dennis struggled with commitment and with forgiveness toward the person responsible for his father's death. What do you think caused his lack of commitment and his inability to forgive?

8. Virginia was stressed over not getting an invitation to Amy and Jared's wedding, so much that she started smoking again. Why was going to the wedding so important to her?

9. Sylvia and Dennis's relationship grew quickly. Do you think she should have waited longer to get involved with a man who could possibly become her husband?

10. With all the trouble at the greenhouse and then the barn fire, do you think Belinda should have called the sheriff? Why do you think she didn't?

11. Was it right for Belinda to hide their problems from her oldest son, Ezekiel? Was her reason for doing it justified?

12. Amish weddings are not the same as English weddings. Based on what you read in this story, how are they different? Have you ever attended an Amish wedding? If so, what were your thoughts?

13. When Sylvia's youngest daughter disappeared, do you think the elderly woman, Maude, thought she was doing something wrong? Did you agree with the way Sylvia

handled it? Do you know someone like Maude? How would you reach out to her?

14. Were there any scriptures or spiritual insights in this book that spoke to your heart or helped you in some way?

15. Like Sylvia and her family, every person is faced at one time or another with difficult situations. What are some things we can do to strengthen our faith when it becomes weak due to a hardship or loss we have faced? How can we help someone who has suffered a loss and seems to have lost their faith?

# ABOUT THE AUTHOR

*New York Times* bestselling and award-winning author **Wanda E. Brunstetter** is one of the founders of the Amish fiction genre. She has written more than 100 books translated in four languages. With over 11 million copies sold, Wanda's stories consistently earn spots on the nation's most prestigious bestseller lists and have received numerous awards.

Wanda's ancestors were part of the Anabaptist faith, and her novels are based on personal research intended to accurately portray the Amish way of life. Her books are well-read and trusted by many Amish, who credit her for giving readers a deeper understanding of the people and their customs.

When Wanda visits her Amish friends, she finds herself drawn to their peaceful lifestyle, sincerity, and close family ties. Wanda enjoys photography, ventriloquism, gardening, bird-watching, beachcombing, and spending time with her family. She and her husband, Richard, have been blessed with two grown children, six grandchildren, and two great-grandchildren.

To learn more about Wanda, visit her website at www.wandabrunstetter.com.